GONE SOUTH

Books by Robert McCammon

Baal
Bethany's Sin
Blue World
Boy's Life
Gone South
Mine
Mystery Walk
The Night Boat
The Queen of Bedlam
Speaks the Nightbird
Stinger
Swan Song
They Thirst
Usher's Passing
The Wolf's Hour

Published by POCKET BOOKS

GONE SOUTH

ROBERT McCAMMON

POCKET BOOKS
New York London Toronto Sydney

Pocket Books
A Division of Simon & Schuster, Inc.
1230 Avenue of the Americas
New York, NY 10020

This book is a work of fiction. Names, characters, places, and incidents either are products of the author's imagination or are used fictitiously. Any resemblance to actual events or locales or persons, living or dead, is entirely coincidental.

This Pocket Books trade paperback edition October 2008

POCKET and colophon are registered trademarks of Simon & Schuster, Inc.

For information about special discounts for bulk purchases, please contact Simon & Schuster Special Sales at 1-800-456-6798 or business@simonandschuster.com.

Designed by Claudia Martinez

10 9 8 7 6 5 4 3 2 1

ISBN-13: 978-1-4165-7779-9

For my family

Foreword

Why I Wrote *Gone South*

This book was my followup to *Boy's Life,* and was written basically from a dark place of despair.

I've had difficulty writing this commentary, because it takes me back to a point in time that was not very happy. In fact, it was just before I started writing *Speaks the Nightbird,* and when I knew I had to do something drastic to keep my career going. So: unfortunately, no sunshine or smiley faces to be found in here. But since I've been asked to do this—and *paid* to do it, as well—I am fulfilling an obligation.

Bear in mind that I had thought *Boy's Life* was the best book I'd written up to that point, and I was pretty much dashed down upon the hard rocks when I realized *Boy's Life* was not going to get much—if any—promotion. *Gone South* was the second book in a two-book contract following *Boy's Life.* It was really tough for me to get myself together and write it, thinking that a great opportunity for success had been mishandled.

Now, I hate to get back into all this, because some will say I ought to be glad I was ever published at all, and I certainly am. But let me assure you that the road leading to *Gone South* is littered with a lot of pain and disappointment, and it is impossible to say anything about why I wrote this book without dredging up some of it.

Let me go back to the beginning of my career. I came into the business with the book *Baal,* published as a paperback original by Avon Books in 1978. At that time, Stephen King had just started to take off, the supernatural was "hot," and publishers were looking for writers to get on the bandwagon. I was stuck in a dead-end job writing headlines at a local newspaper here in Birmingham, but I'd always enjoyed reading supernatural or "horror" fiction, and writing short stories in that particular genre, so I thought I'd try to write a book. Looking back, I don't think *Baal* was a very good book, but it was the best I could do at the time.

Baal was my first effort. I had no other "trunk novels," as many writers do. So I basically learned how to write in public, for better or for worse.

I went through the early eighties as a horror writer, with most of my books being published as paperback originals. I was paid very well for these and I was on the track of doing a book every year. But in the late eighties I began to want more. I thought my writing was getting better, I was building a fan base, and I wanted to move away from doing strictly "horror" because I simply had other ideas I wanted to try. I also wanted my books to be published in hardback because I wanted them to remain on the shelves and get more attention than the average paperback receives.

But I started running into resistance. I was told repeatedly that my fans expected a certain type of book from me, and that was the bottom line. I suggested that I might try writing under a pseudonym, but I was told that wouldn't work because then my fans "couldn't find me."

The point being, I was beginning to understand that I had a particular place in the publishing world—that place was "horror" and I ought to be satisfied with where I was. At the same time, I drew the wrath of hardcore horror readers who thought I wasn't bloody enough, or that I was at best a Stephen King imitator, and I drew the scorn of other writers (and booksellers) in my hometown because I wasn't writing Southern fiction. Please understand that I'm not bashing "horror," because I loved doing it and I reserve the right to go in that direction again if I want to. I'm bashing the idea that once you do a particular kind of writing, you're expected to do that over and over until you die or—I guess—give up and stagger away.

I was in a book featuring Southern writers a few years ago. The chapter that profiles me has the heading of "Frustration."

Now I'm getting to *Gone South*.

First, though, I want to put into your mind and imagination the myth of Sisyphus, who was decreed by the gods to push a giant rock up a steep hill, but could never quite reach the top before the rock broke loose from his grasp and rolled back to the bottom, where he had to start all over again and again and again and again and again. Forever.

Much has been made of my retirement from publishing for ten years or so. I tried to step out of the "horror" box, first with *Speaks the Nightbird* and then with a World War II novel called *The Village*. The latter novel got not a single offer. It was only by sheer luck and happenstance that *Speaks the Nightbird* was published by an Alabama publisher and in time I found my way back to the bright lights of New York.

The really *weird* thing about my career is that I sometimes feel everything would be okay if I went back to writing on the level of *Baal,* and if in some fractured insane universe I could be *happy* not wanting to grow or challenge myself or try to do anything that hasn't already been done. For a writer—or anyone in the arts, really—not doing something that involves risk is a path to a slow death. Here, of course, is the classic confrontation between business and the arts: one seeks to minimize risk, the other revels in it. It's been true throughout history and is particularly true today, in this time of corporate mergers, falling stocks, and all the entertainments that are readily available to people who would rather not take the time or effort to read, or who see a book as a chore instead of a door.

Sisyphus. The giant rock. Again and again and again.

Gone South is a scream. It begins in fire and desolation and follows the plight of a Vietnam veteran named Dan Lambert, whose bad luck turns downright tragic when he gets in a fight with a bank's loan manager, a gun goes off, and he finds himself on the run with a bounty on his head. On his trail are two bounty hunters, one a seasoned veteran with three arms and the second an addled Elvis Presley imitator.

Yes, there's humor in the book. Sometimes you have to laugh while you're screaming.

See, this *means* something to me.

I am not and have never been a writer just for money. I can't be. An agent looked at me in anger one time and said, "Rick, just do the goddamned work!" But I can't, if I don't believe in it.

This means something to me. I am not a sell-out. I am not a self-promoter or a celebrity wannabe. I am a writer, by God.

Yes, by God. Because I was born to do this. I care about two things in this world: my family and my creations. I was born to do this, and though I might have had to pull back for ten years to figure out what I had to do next to keep creating, I am still here.

Still pushing that rock, again and again and again.

Gone South is a journey from Hell back to the Garden of Eden. Back to a fresh start.

Back to being new again.

I told that once to a tableful of publishing executives. Blank stares followed.

But even if no one gets what I'm trying to do, or no one cares, this means something to me.

It means purity and hope, and struggle when you think you can't go on another step, and laughing with bloody teeth in the fucking face of failure, and lighting a candle against the dark, and standing as firm as a human can against a howling wind, and going deep into yourself to find out what makes you tick, and what your limit of mental anguish is, and how long you can go without sleep.

All to create a world and people who did not exist before I gave them life and purpose. All to speak in my own voice about the world we live in and the people we are, and I hope you get the fact that my voice may be quiet under the voices of my people, but in no way am I silent about the things I think are meaningful, important, and valuable.

It does mean something to me. Almost everything.

It means enough to me to continue pushing that rock, again and again, with hopes that this time—*this* time—I may reach the top.

Or not.

But it's who I am, and it's what I do. Sometimes I wouldn't wish it on my worst enemy, but there you go. The good with the bad.

As you struggle along with Dan Lambert into the Louisiana swamp, with bounty hunters coming up behind you and your life in shambles, with no friends to call for help and nowhere to go but the deeper darkness that lies before you . . . fear not.

I have already been there.

And I came through just fine.

Robert McCammon
July 2, 2008
Just after midnight

1

The Good Son

I T WAS HELL'S SEASON, and the air smelled of burning children.

This smell was what had destroyed Dan Lambert's taste for barbecued pork sandwiches. Before August of 1969, the year he'd turned twenty, his favorite food had been barbecue crispy at the edges and drenched with sloppy red sauce. After the eleventh day of that month, the smell of it was enough to make him sick to death.

He was driving east through Shreveport on 70th Street, into the glare of the morning sun. It glanced off the hood of his gray pickup truck and stabbed his eyes, inflaming the slow ache in his skull. He knew this pain, and its vagaries. Sometimes it came upon him like a brute with a hammer, sometimes like a surgeon with a precise scalpel. During the worst times it hit and ran like a Mack truck and all he could do was chew on his rage and lie there until his body came back to him.

It was a hard thing, dying was.

In this August of 1991, a summer that had been one of the hottest in Louisiana's long history of hellish seasons, Dan was forty-two years old. He looked ten years older, his rawboned, heavily lined face a testament to his ceaseless combat with pain. It was a fight he knew he couldn't win. If he knew for certain he would live three more years, he wasn't sure if he'd be happy about it. Right now it was day-to-day. Some days were all right, some weren't worth a bucket of warm spit. But it wasn't in his nature to give up, no matter how tough things got. His father, the quitter, had not raised a quitter. In this, at least, Dan could find strength. He drove on along the arrow-straight line of 70th Street, past strip malls and car lots and fast-food joints. He drove on into the merciless sun and the smell of murdered innocents.

Lining the commercial carnival of 70th Street was a score of barbecue restaurants, and it was from their kitchen chimneys that this odor of burned flesh rose into the scalded sky. It was just after nine, and already the temperature sign in front of the Friendship Bank of Louisiana read eighty-six degrees. The sky was cloudless, but was more white than blue, as if all the color had been bleached from it. The sun was a burnished ball of pewter, a promise of another day of misery across the Gulf states. Yesterday the temperature had hit a hundred and two, and Dan figured that today it was going to be hot enough to fry pigeons on the wing. Afternoon showers passed through every few days, but it was just enough to steam the streets. The Red River flowed its muddy course through Shreveport to the bayou country and the air shimmered over the larger buildings that stood iron-gray against the horizon.

Dan had to stop for a red light. The pickup's brakes squealed a little, in need of new pads. A job replacing rotten lumber on a patio deck last week had made him enough to pay the month's rent and utilities, and he'd had a few dollars left over for groceries. Still, some things had to slide. He'd missed two payments on the pickup, and he needed to go in and see Mr. Jarrett to work something out. Mr. Jarrett, the loan manager at the First Commercial Bank, understood that Dan had fallen on hard times, and cut him some slack.

The pain was back behind his eyes. It lived there, like a hermit crab. Dan reached beside himself on the seat, picked up the white bottle of Excedrin, and popped it open. He shook two tablets onto his tongue and chewed them. The light turned green and he drove on, toward Death Valley.

Dan wore a rust-colored short-sleeve shirt and blue jeans with patches on the knees. Under a faded blue baseball cap, his thinning brown hair was combed back from his forehead and spilled over his shoulders; haircuts were not high on his list of priorities. He had light brown eyes and a close-cropped beard that was almost all gray. On his left wrist was a Timex and on his feet was a sturdy pair of brown, much-scuffed workboots. On his right forearm was the bluish-green ghost of a snake tattoo, a reminder of a burly kid who'd had one too many cheap and potent zombies with his buddies on a night of leave in Saigon. That kid was long gone, and Dan was left with the tattoo. The Snake Handlers, that's what they'd been. Not afraid to stick their hands in the jungle's holes and pull out whatever horror might be coiled up and waiting in there. They had not known, then, that the entire world was a snake hole, and that the snakes just kept getting bigger and meaner. They had not known, in their raucous rush toward the future, that the snakes were lying in wait not only in the holes but in the mowed green grass of the American Dream. They got your legs first, wound around your ankles, and slowed you down. They slithered into your guts and made you sick and afraid, and then you were easy to kill.

In the years since that Day-Glo memory of a night in Saigon, Dan Lambert had shrunken. At his chest-thumping, Charlie-whomping best he'd stood six-two and carried two hundred and twelve pounds of Parris Island–trained muscle. Back then, he'd felt as if he could swallow bullets and shit iron. He weighed about a hundred and seventy pounds now, and he didn't think he was much over six feet. There was a gauntness in his face that made him think of some of the old Vietnamese people who'd huddled in their hootches with eyes as terrified as those of mongrel dogs expecting a boot. His cheekbones jutted, his chin was as sharp as a can opener under the beard. It was the fact that he rarely ate three meals a day, and of course a lot of his shrinkage was due to the sickness, too.

Gravity and time were the giant killers, he thought as he drove along the sun-washed highway with the back of his sweat-wet shirt stuck to the seat. Gravity shrank you and time pulled you into the grave, and not even the Snake Handlers could beat such fearsome enemies as those.

He drove through pale smoke that had drifted from the chimney of Hungry Bob's Barbecue Shack, the cook getting all that meat good and black for the lunch crowd. A tire hit a pothole, and in the truck's bed his box of tools jangled. They were the hammers, nails, levels, and saws of a carpenter.

At the next intersection he turned right and drove south into an area of warehouses. It was a world of chain-link fences, loading docks, and brick walls. Between the buildings the heat lay trapped and vengeful. Up ahead a half-dozen pickup trucks and a few cars were parked in an empty lot. Dan could see some of the men standing around talking. Another man was sitting in a folding chair reading a newspaper, his CAT hat throwing a slice of shade across his face. Standing near one of the cars was a man who had a sign hanging around his neck, and on that sign was hand-lettered WILL WORK FOR FOOD.

This was Death Valley.

Dan pulled his truck into the lot and cut the engine. He unpeeled his damp shirt from the backrest, slipped the bottle of aspirin into his pocket, and got out. "There's Dan the man!" Steve Lynam called from where he stood talking with Darryl Glennon and Curtis Nowell, and Dan raised a hand in greeting.

"Mornin', Dan," Joe Yates said, laying his newspaper in his lap. "How's it hangin'?"

"It's still there," Dan answered. "I think."

"Got iced tea." A plastic jug and a bag of Dixie cups sat on the ground next to Joe's folding chair. "Come on over."

Dan joined him. He drew iced tea into a cup and eased himself down beside Joe's shadow. "Terry got a ticket," Joe said as he offered Dan some of the newspaper. "Fella came by 'bout ten minutes ago, lookin' for a man to set some Sheetrock. Picked Terry and off they went."

"That's good." Terry Palmeter had a wife and two kids to feed. "Fella say he might be needin' some more help later on?"

"Just the one Sheetrock man." Joe squinted up toward the sun. He was a lean, hard-faced man with a nose that had been broken and flattened by a vicious fist somewhere down the line. He'd been coming here to Death Valley for over a year, about as long as Dan had been. On most days Joe was an amiable gent, but on others he sat brooding and dark-spirited and was not to be approached. Like the other men who came to Death Valley, Joe had never revealed much about himself, though Dan had learned the man had been married and divorced the same as he had. Most of the men were from towns other than Shreveport. They were wanderers, following the promise of work, and for them the roads on the map led not so much from city to city as from hot-tarred roofs to mortared walls to the raw frameworks of new houses with pinewood so fresh the timbers wept yellow tears. "God, it's gonna be a cooker today," Joe said, and he lowered his head and returned to his reading and waiting.

Dan drank the iced tea and felt sweat prickling the back of his neck. He didn't want to stare, but his eyes kept returning to the man who wore the desperate hand-lettered sign. The man had sandy-blond hair, was probably in his late twenties, and wore a checked shirt and stained overalls. His face was still boyish, though it was starting to take on the tautness of true hunger. It reminded Dan of someone he'd known a long time ago. A name came to him: *Farrow*. He let it go, and the memory drifted away like the acrid barbecue smoke.

"Looky here, Dan." Joe thumped an article in the paper. "President's economics honcho says the recession's over and everybody ought to be in fine shape by Christmas. Says new construction's already up thirty percent."

"Do tell," Dan said.

"Got all sorts of graphs in here to show how happy we oughta be." He showed them to Dan, who glanced at the meaningless bars and arrows and then watched the man with the sign again. "Yeah, things are sure gettin' better all over, ain't they?" Joe nodded, answering his own cynical question. "Yessir. Too bad they forgot to tell the workman."

"Joe, who's that fella over there?" Dan asked. "The guy with the sign."

"I don't know." He didn't lift his gaze from the paper. "He was there when I got here. Young fella, looks to be. Hell, every man jack of us would work for food if it came to that, but we don't wear signs advertisin' it, do we?"

"Maybe we're not hungry enough yet."

"Maybe not," Joe agreed, and then he said nothing else.

More men were arriving in their pickups and cars, some with wives who let them out and drove off. Dan recognized others he knew, like Andy Slane and Jim Neilds. They were a community of sorts, scholars in the college of hard knocks. Fourteen months ago Dan had been working on the payroll of the A&A Construction Company. Their motto had been We Build the Best for Less. Even so, the company hadn't been strong enough to survive the bottom falling out of the building business. Dan had lost his job of five years and quickly found that nobody was hiring carpenters full-time. The first thing to go had been his house, in favor of a cheaper apartment. His savings had dwindled amazingly—and frighteningly—fast. Since his divorce in 1984 he'd been paying child support to Susan, so his bank account had never been well padded. But he'd never been a man who needed or expected luxuries, anyway. The nicest thing in his possession was his Chevy pickup—"metallic mist" was the correct name of its color, according to the salesman—which he'd bought three months prior to the crash of A&A Construction. Being behind the two payments bothered him; Mr. Jarrett was a fair man, and Dan was not one to take advantage of fairness. He was going to have to find a way to scrape some cash together.

He didn't like looking at the man who wore the hand-lettered sign, but he couldn't help it. He knew what trying to find a steady job was like. With all the layoffs and businesses going under, the help-wanted ads had dried up to nothing. Skilled laborers like Dan and the others who came to Death Valley were the first to feel the hurt. He didn't like looking at the man with the desperate sign because he feared he might be seeing his own future.

Death Valley was where men who wanted to work came to wait for a "ticket." Getting a ticket meant being picked for a job by anyone who needed labor. The contractors who were still in business knew about Death Valley, and would go there to find help when a regular crewman was sick or they needed extra hands for a day or two. Regular homeowners sometimes drove by as well, to hire somebody to do such jobs as patching a roof or building a fence. The citizens of Death Valley worked cheap.

And the hell of it, Dan had learned by talking to the others, was that places like Death Valley existed in every city. It had become clear to him that thousands of men and women lived clinging to the edge of poverty through no fault of their own but because of the times and the luck of the draw. The recession had been a beast with a cold eye, and it had wrenched families young and old from their homes and shattered their lives with equal dispassion.

"Hey, Dan! How many'd ya kill?"

Two shadows had fallen across him. He looked up and made out Steve Lynam and Curtis Nowell standing beside him with the sun at their backs. "What?" he asked.

"How many'd ya kill?" Curtis had posed the question. He was in his early thirties, had curly dark brown hair, and wore a yellow T-shirt with NUKE THE WHALES stenciled on it. "How many chinks? More than twenty or less than twenty?"

"Chinks?" Dan repeated, not quite grasping the point.

"Yeah." Curtis dug a pack of Winstons and a lighter from his jeans pocket. "Charlies. Gooks. Whatever you dudes called 'em back then. You kill more than twenty of 'em?"

Joe pushed the brim of his cap up. "You fellas don't have anythin' better to do than invade a man's privacy?"

"No," Curtis said as he lit up. "We ain't hurtin' anythin' by askin', are we, Dan? I mean, you're proud to be a vet, ain't you?"

"Yes, I am." Dan sipped his tea again. Most of the Death Valley regulars knew about his tour of duty, not because he particularly cared to crow about it but because Curtis had asked him where he'd gotten the tattoo. Curtis had a big mouth and he was on the dumb side: a bad combination. "I'm proud I served my country," Dan said.

"Yeah, you didn't run to Canada like them draft-dodgin' fuckers did, huh?" Steve asked. He was a few years older than Curtis, had keen blue eyes and a chest as big as a beer keg.

"No," Dan answered, "I did what I was told."

"So how many?" Curtis urged. "More than twenty?"

Dan released a long, weary breath. The sun was beating down on his skull, even through the baseball cap. "Does it really matter?"

"We want to know," Curtis said, the cigarette clenched between his teeth and his mouth leaking smoke. "You kept a body count, didn't you?"

Dan stared straight ahead. He was looking at a chain-link fence. Beyond it was a wall of brown bricks. Sun and shadow lay worlds apart on that wall. In the air Dan could smell the burning.

"Talked to this vet once in Mobile," Curtis plowed on. "Fella was one-legged. He said he kept a body count. Said he knew how many chinks he'd killed right to the man."

"Jesus Christ!" Joe said. "Why don't you two go on and pester the shit outta somebody else? Can't you see Dan don't want to talk about it?"

"He's got a voice," Steve replied. "He can say if he wants to talk about it or not."

Dan could sense Joe was about to stand up from his chair. When Joe stood up, it was either to go after a ticket or knock the ugly out of somebody. "I didn't keep a body count," Dan said before Joe could leave the folding chair. "I just did my job."

"But you can kinda figure out how many, right?" Curtis wasn't about to give up until he'd gnawed all the meat off this particular bone. "Like more or less than twenty?"

A slow pinwheel of memories had begun to turn in Dan's mind. These memories were never far from him, even on the best of days. In that slow pinwheel were fragments of scenes and events: mortar shells blasting dirt showers in a jungle where the sunlight was cut to a murky gloom; rice paddies shimmering in the noonday heat; helicopters circling overhead while soldiers screamed for help over their radios and sniper bullets ripped the air; the false neon joy of Saigon's streets and bars; dark shapes unseen yet felt, and human excrement lying within the perimeter wire to mark the contempt the Cong had for Uncle Sam's young men; rockets scrawling white and red across the twilight sky; Ann-Margret in thigh-high boots and pink hot pants, dancing the frug at a USO show; the body of a Cong soldier, a boy maybe fifteen years old, who had stepped on a mine and been blown apart and flies forming a black mask on his bloody face; a firefight in a muddy clearing, and a terrified voice yelling *motherfucker motherfucker motherfucker* like a strange mantra; the silver rain, drenching the trees and vines and grass, the hair and skin and eyes and not one drop of it clean; and the village.

Oh, yes. The village.

Dan's mouth was very dry. He took another swallow of tea. The ice was almost gone. He could feel the men waiting for him to speak, and he knew they wouldn't leave him alone until he did. "More than twenty."

"Hot damn, I knew it!" Grinning, Curtis elbowed Steve in the ribs and held out his palm. "Cough it up, friend!"

"Okay, okay." Steve brought out a battered wallet, opened it, and slapped a five-dollar bill into Curtis Nowell's hand. "I'll get it back sooner or later."

"You boys ain't got trouble enough, you gotta gamble your money away?" Joe sneered.

Dan set his cup down. A hot pulse had begun beating at his temples. "You laid a bet," he said as he lifted a wintry gaze to the two men, "on how many corpses I left in 'Nam?"

"Yeah, I bet it'd be more than twenty," Curtis said, "and Steve bet it'd be—"

"I get the drift." Dan stood up. It was a slow, easy movement though it hurt his knees. "You used me and what I did to win you some cash, Curtis?"

"Sure did." It was said proudly. Curtis started to push the fiver into his pocket.

"Let me see the money."

Still grinning. Curtis held the bill out.

Dan didn't smile. His hand whipped forward, took the money, and had it in his grip before Curtis's grin could drop. "Whoa!" Curtis said. "Give it here, man!"

"You used me and what I did? What I *lived* through? I think I deserve half of this, don't you?" Without hesitation, Dan tore the bill in two.

"Hey, man! It's against the fuckin' law to tear up money!"

"Sue me. Here's your half."

Curtis's face had reddened. "I oughta bust your fuckin' head is what I oughta do!"

"Maybe you ought to. Try, at least."

Sensing trouble, a few of the other men had started edging closer. Curtis's grin returned, only this time it was mean. "I could take you with one hand, you skinny old bastard."

"You might be right about that." Dan watched the younger man's eyes, knowing that in them he would see the punch coming before Curtis's arm was cocked for the strike. "Might be. But before you try, I want you to know that I haven't raised my hand in anger to a man since I left 'Nam. I wasn't the best soldier, but I did my job and nobody could ever say I'd gone south." Dan saw a nerve in Curtis's left eyelid begin to tick. Curtis was close to swinging. "If you swing on me," Dan said calmly, "you'll have to kill me to put me down. I won't be used or made a fool of, and I won't have you winnin' a bet on how many bodies I left in my footprints. Do you understand that, Curtis?"

"I think you're full of shit," Curtis said, but his grin had weakened. Blisters of sweat glistened on his cheeks and forehead. He glanced to the right and left, taking in the half-dozen or so onlookers, then back to Dan. "You think you're somethin' *special* 'cause you're a vet?"

"Nothin' special about me," Dan answered. "I just want you to know that I learned how to kill over there. I got better at it than I wanted to be. I didn't kill all those Cong with a gun or a knife. Some of 'em I had to use my hands. Curtis, I love peace more than any man alive, but I won't take disrespect. So go on and swing if you want to, I'm not goin' anywhere."

"Man, I could break your damn neck with one punch," Curtis said, but the way he said it told Dan he was trying to decide whether to push this thing any further.

Dan waited. The decision was not his to make.

A few seconds ticked past. Dan and Curtis stared at each other.

"Awful hot to be fightin'," Joe said. "Grown men, I swear!"

"Hell, it's only five dollars," Steve added.

Curtis took a deep drag on his cigarette and exhaled smoke through his nostrils. Dan kept watching him, his gaze steady and his face placid though the pain in his skull had racheted up a notch.

"Shit," Curtis said at last. He spat out a shred of tobacco. "Give it here, then." He took the half that Dan offered. "Keep you from tapin' it back together and spendin' it, at least."

"There ya go. Ya'll kiss and make up," Joe suggested.

Curtis laughed, and Dan allowed a smile. The men who'd thronged around began moving away. Dan knew that Curtis wasn't a bad fellow; Curtis just had a bad attitude sometimes and needed a little sense knocked into him. But on this day, with the sun burning down and no breeze stirring the weeds of Death Valley, Dan was very glad push had not come to shove.

"Sorry," Steve told him. "Guess we didn't think it'd bother you. The bet, I mean."

"Now you know. Let's forget it, all right?"

Curtis and Steve moved off. Dan took the Excedrin bottle from his pocket and popped another aspirin. His palms were damp, not from fear of Curtis, but from fear of what he might have done had that particular demon been loosed.

"You okay?" Joe was watching him carefully.

"Yeah. Headache."

"You get a lot of those, don't you?"

"A few."

"You seen a doctor?"

"Yeah." Dan put the bottle away. "Says it's migraine."

"Is that so?"

"Uh-huh." He knows I'm lyin', Dan thought. There was no need to tell any of the men here about his sickness. He crunched the aspirin between his teeth and washed it down with the last of his iced tea.

"Curtis is gonna get his clock cleaned one fine day," Joe said. "Fella don't have no sense."

"He hasn't lived enough, that's his problem."

"Right. Not like us old relics, huh?" Joe looked up at the sky, measuring the journey of the sun. "Did you see some hell over there, Dan?"

Dan settled himself back down beside his friend's chair. He let the question hang for a moment, and then he said, "I did. We all did."

"I just missed gettin' drafted. I supported you fellas all the way, though. I didn't march in the streets or nothin'."

"Might've been better if you had. We were over there way too long."

"We could've won it," Joe said. "Yessir. We could've swept the floor with them bastards if we'd just—"

"That's what I used to think," Dan interrupted quietly. "I used to think if it wasn't for the protesters, we could've turned that damn country into a big asphalt parkin' lot." He drew his knees up to his chest. The aspirin was kicking in now, dulling the pain. "Then I went up to Washington, and I walked along that wall. You know, where the names are. Lots of names up there. Fellas I knew. Young boys, eighteen and nineteen, and what was left of 'em wouldn't fill a bucket. I've thought and thought about it, but I can't figure out what we would've had if we'd won. If we'd killed every Charlie to a man, if we'd marched right into Hanoi and torched it to the ground, if we'd come home the heroes like the Desert Storm boys did . . . what would we have won?"

"Respect, I guess," Joe said.

"No, not even that. It was past time to get out. I knew it when I saw all those names on that black wall. When I saw mothers and fathers tracin' their dead sons' names on paper to take home with 'em because that's all they had left, I knew the protesters were right. We never could've won it. Never."

"Gone south," Joe said.

"What?"

"Gone south. You told Curtis nobody could ever say you'd gone south. What's that mean?"

Dan realized he'd used the term, but hearing it from the mouth of another man had taken him by surprise. "Somethin' we said in 'Nam," he explained. "Somebody screwed up—or cracked up—we said he'd gone south."

"And you never screwed up?"

"Not enough to get myself or anybody else killed. That was all we wanted: to get out alive."

Joe grunted. "Some life you came back to, huh?"

"Yeah," Dan said, "some life."

Joe lapsed into silence, and Dan offered nothing else. Vietnam was not a subject Dan willingly talked about. If anyone wanted to know and they pressed it, he might tell them hesitantly about the Snake Handlers and their exploits, the childlike bar girls of Saigon and the jungle snipers he'd been trained to hunt and kill, but never could he utter a word about two things: the village and the dirty silver rain.

The sun rose higher and the morning grew old. It was a slow day for tickets. Near ten-thirty a man in a white panel truck stopped at Death Valley and the call went up for two men who had experience in house-painting. Jimmy Staggs and Curtis Nowell got a ticket, and after they left in the panel truck everybody else settled down to waiting again.

Dan felt the brutal heat sapping him. He had to go sit in his truck for a while to get out of the sun. A couple of the younger bucks had brought baseball gloves and a ball, and they peeled off their wet shirts and pitched some as Dan and the older men watched. The guy with the hand-lettered sign around his neck was sitting on the curb, looking expectantly in the direction from which the ticket givers would be coming like God's emissaries. Dan wanted to go over and tell him to take that sign off, that he shouldn't beg, but he decided against it. You did what you had to do to get by.

Again the young man reminded Dan of someone else. Farrow was the name. It was the color of the hair and the boyish face, Dan thought. Farrow, the kid from Boston. Well, they'd all been kids back in those days, hadn't they? But thinking about Farrow stirred up old, deep pain, and Dan shunted the haunting images aside.

Dan had been born in Shreveport on the fifth of May in 1950. His father, who had been a sergeant in the Marine Corps but who liked to be called "Major" by his fellow workers at the Pepsi bottling plant, had departed this life in 1973 by route of a revolver bullet to the roof of the mouth. Dan's mother, never in the best of health, had gone to south Florida to live with an older sister. Dan understood she had part interest in a flower shop and was doing all right. His sister, Kathy, older than he by three years, lived in Taos, New Mexico, where she made copper-and-turquoise jewelry. Of the two of them, Kathy had been the rebel against the major's rigid love-it-or-leave-it patriotism. She'd escaped just past her seventeenth birthday, jumping into a van with a band of folksingers—"scum of the earth," the major had called them—and hitting the road to the golden West. Dan, the good son, had finished high school, kept his hair cut short, had become a carpenter's apprentice, and had been driven by his father to the Marine recruiting center to do his duty as a "good American."

And now Dan was waiting, in the city of his birth, for a ticket in the hot stillness of Death Valley.

Around eleven-thirty another panel truck pulled up. Dan was always amazed at how quickly everybody could move when the day was passing and tickets were in short supply. Like hungry animals the men jostled for position around the panel truck. Dan was among them. This time the call was for four laborers to patch and tar a warehouse's roof. Joe Yates got a ticket, but Dan was left behind when the panel truck drove away.

As twelve noon passed, some of the men began leaving. Experience taught that if you hadn't gotten a ticket by noon, you'd struck out. There was always tomorrow. Rain or shine, Death Valley and its citizens would be here. As one o'clock approached, Dan got into his pickup, started the engine, and drove through the charred-meat smoke for home.

He lived in a small apartment complex about six miles from Death Valley, but on the same side of town. Near his apartment stood a combination gas station and grocery store, and Dan stopped to go inside and check the store's bulletin board. On it he'd placed an ad that said "Carpenter Needs Work, Reasonable Rates" with his telephone number duplicated on little tags to be torn off by potential customers. He wanted to make sure all the tags weren't gone; they were not. He spent a few minutes talking to Leon, the store's clerk, and asked again if Mr. Khasab, the Saudi-Arabian man who owned the store, needed any help. As usual, Leon said Mr. Khasab had Dan's application on file.

The apartment building was made of tawny-colored bricks, and on these blistering days the little rooms held heat like closed fists. Dan got out of his truck, his back sopping wet, and opened his mailbox with his key. He was running an ad in the Jobs Wanted section of the classifieds this week, with his phone number and address, and he was hoping for any response. Inside the mailbox were two envelopes. The first, addressed to "Occupant," was from a city councilman running for reelection. The second had his full name on it—Mr. Daniel Lewis Lambert—and its return address was the First Commercial Bank of Shreveport.

"Confidential Information" was typed across the envelope in the lower left corner. Dan didn't like the looks of that. He tore open the envelope, unfolded the crisp white sheet of paper within, and read it.

It was from the bank's loan department. He'd already assumed as much, though this stiff formality was not Mr. Jarrett's style. It took him only a few seconds to read the paragraph under the *Dear Mr. Lambert,* and when he'd finished he felt as if he'd just taken a punch to the heart.

. . . valued loan customer, however . . . action as we see proper at this time . . . due to your past erratic record of payment and current delinquency . . . surrender the keys, registration, and appropriate papers . . . 1990 Chevrolet pickup truck, color metallic mist, engine serial number . . .

"Oh my God," Dan whispered.

. . . immediate repossession . . .

Dan blinked, dazed in the white glare of the scorching sun. They were taking his truck away from him.

2

Ticking

W HEN HE PUSHED THROUGH the revolving door into the
First Commercial Bank at ten minutes before two, Dan
was wearing his best clothes: a short-sleeve white shirt, a tie with
pale blue stripes, and dark gray slacks. He'd removed his baseball
cap and combed his hair, and on his feet were black shoes instead
of the workman's boots. He'd expected the usual cold jolt of full-
blast air-conditioning, but the bank's interior wasn't much cooler
than the street. The air-conditioning had conked out, the tellers
sweating in their booths. Dan walked to the elevator, his fresh
shirt already soaked. In his right hand was the envelope, and in
the envelope was the letter of repossession.

He was terrified.

The loan department was on the second floor. Before he went
through the solemn oak door, Dan stopped at a water fountain to
take another aspirin. His hands had started trembling. The time
of reckoning had arrived.

The signature on the letter was not that of Robert "Bud"
Jarrett. A man named Emory Blanchard had signed it. Beneath
Blanchard's signature was a title: *Manager*. Two months ago Bud

Jarrett had been the loan department's manager. As much as he could, Dan steeled himself for whatever lay ahead, and he opened the door and walked through.

In the reception area was a sofa, a grouping of chairs, and a magazine rack. The secretary, whose name was Mrs. Faye Duvall, was on the telephone at her desk, a computer's screen glowing blue before her. She was forty-nine, gray-haired, fit, and tanned, and Dan had talked to her enough to know she played tennis every Saturday at Lakeside Park. She had taken off the jacket of her peach-hued suit and draped it over the back of her chair, and a fan aimed directly at her whirred atop a filing cabinet.

Dan saw that the closed door behind her no longer had Mr. Jarrett's name on it. On the door was embossed MR. E. BLANCHARD. "One minute," Mrs. Duvall said to Dan, and returned to her phone conversation. It was something to do with refinancing. Dan waited, standing before her desk. The window's blinds had been closed to seal out the sun, but the heat was stifling even with the fan in motion. At last Mrs. Duvall said good-bye and hung up the phone, and she smiled at Dan but he could see the edginess in it. She knew, of course; she'd typed the letter.

" 'Afternoon," she said. "Hot enough for you?"

"I've known worse."

"We need a good rain, is what we need. Rain would take the sufferin' out of that sky."

"Mr. Jarrett," Dan said. "What happened to him?"

She leaned back in her chair and frowned, the corners of her mouth crinkling. "Well, it was sudden, that's for sure. They called him upstairs a week ago Monday, he cleaned out his desk on Tuesday, and he was gone. They brought in this new fella, a real hard charger." She angled her head toward Blanchard's door. "I just couldn't believe it myself. Bud was here eight years; I figured he'd stay till he retired."

"Why'd they let him go?"

"I can't say." The inflection of her voice, however, told Dan she was well aware of the reasons. "What I hear is, Mr. Blanchard was a real fireball at a bank in Baton Rouge. Turned their loan department around in a year." She shrugged. "Bud was the nicest fella you'd ever hope to meet. But maybe he was too nice."

"He sure helped me out a lot." Dan held up the letter. "I got this today."

"Oh. Yes." Her eyes became a little flinty, and she sat up straighter. The time for personal conversation was over. "Did you follow the instructions?"

"I'd like to see Mr. Blanchard," Dan said. "Maybe I can work somethin' out."

"Well, he's not here right now." She glanced at a small clock on her desk. "I don't expect him back for another hour."

"I'll wait."

"Go ahead and sit down, then. We're not exactly crowded at the minute." Dan took a seat, and Mrs. Duvall returned to her task on the computer screen. After a few moments, during which Dan was lost in his thoughts about how he was going to plead his case, Mrs. Duvall cleared her throat and said, "I'm sorry about this. Do you have enough money to make one payment?"

"No." He'd gone through his apartment like a whirlwind in search of cash, but all he'd been able to come up with was thirty-eight dollars and sixty-two cents.

"Any friends you could borrow it from?"

He shook his head. This was his problem, and he wasn't going to drag anybody else into it.

"Don't you have a steady job yet?"

"No. Not that, either."

Mrs. Duvall was silent, working on the keyboard. Dan put the letter in his pocket, laced his fingers together, and waited. He didn't have to be told that he was up Shit Creek without a paddle and that his boat had just sprung a leak. The heat weighed on him. Mrs. Duvall got up from her chair and angled the fan a little so some of the breeze came Dan's way. She asked if he wanted a cold drink from the machine down the hall, but he said he was fine.

"I tell you, this damn heat in here is somethin' awful!" she said as she backed the cursor up to correct a mistake. "Air-conditionin' busted first thing this mornin', can you believe it?"

"It's bad, all right."

"Listen, Mr. Lambert." She looked at him, and he winced inside because he could see pity in her expression. "I've gotta tell you that Mr. Blanchard doesn't go for hard-luck stories. If you could make up for one payment, that might help a whole lot."

"I can't," Dan said. "No work's been comin' in. But if I lose my truck, there's no way I can get to a job if somebody calls me. That truck . . . it's the only thing I've got left."

"Do you know anythin' about guns?"

"Pardon?"

"Guns," she repeated. "Mr. Blanchard loves to go huntin', and he collects guns. If you know anythin' about guns, you might get him talkin' about 'em before you make your pitch."

Dan smiled faintly. The last gun he'd had anything to do with was an M16. "Thank you," he said. "I'll remember that."

An hour crept past. Dan paged through all the magazines, looking up whenever the door to the hallway opened, but it was only to admit other loan customers who came and went. He was aware of the clock on Mrs. Duvall's desk ticking. His nerves were beginning to fray. At three-fifteen he stood up to go get a drink of water from the fountain, and that was when the door opened and two men entered the office.

"Hello, Mr. Blanchard!" Mrs. Duvall said cheerfully, cueing Dan that the boss had arrived.

"Faye, get me Perry Griffin on the phone, please." Emory Blanchard carried the jacket of his light blue seersucker suit over his right arm. He wore a white shirt and a yellow tie with little blue dots on it. There were sweat stains at his armpits. He was a heavyset, fleshy man, his face ruddy and gleaming with moisture. Dan figured he was in his mid-thirties, at least ten years younger than Bud Jarrett. Blanchard had close-cropped brown hair that was receding in front, and his square and chunky face coupled with powerful shoulders made Dan think the man might've played college football before the beers had overtaken his belly. He wore silver-wire-rimmed glasses and he was chewing gum. The second man had likewise stripped off the coat of his tan-colored suit, and he had curly blond hair going gray on the sides. "Step on in here, Jerome," Blanchard said as he headed for his office, "and let's do us a li'l bidness."

"Uh . . . Mr. Blanchard?" Mrs. Duvall had the telephone to her ear. She glanced at Dan and then back to Blanchard, who had paused with one hand on the doorknob. "Mr. Lambert's been waitin' to see you."

"Who?"

Dan stepped forward. "Dan Lambert. I need to talk to you, please."

The force of Blanchard's full gaze was a sturdy thing. His eyes were steely blue, and they provided the first chill Dan had felt all day. In three seconds Blanchard had taken Dan in from shoetips to the crown of his head. "I'm sorry?" His eyebrows rose.

"Repossession," Mrs. Duvall explained. "Chevrolet pickup truck."

"Right!" Blanchard snapped his fingers. "Got it now. Your letter went out yesterday, I recall."

"Yes sir, I've got it here with me. That's what I need to talk to you about."

Blanchard frowned, as if his teeth had found a fly in his chewing gum. "I believe the instructions in that letter were clear, weren't they?"

"They were, yeah. But can I just have two minutes of your time?"

"Mr. Griffin's on the line," the secretary announced.

"Two minutes," Dan said. *Don't beg,* he thought. But he couldn't help it; the truck was his freedom, and if it was taken from him, he'd have nothing. "Then I'll be gone, I swear."

"I'm a busy man."

"Yes sir, I know you are. But could you just please hear me out?"

The chilly blue eyes remained impassive, and Dan feared it was all over. But then Blanchard sighed and said resignedly, "All right, sit down and I'll get to you. Faye, pipe ol' Perry into my office, will you?"

"Yes sir."

Dan settled into his chair again as Blanchard and the other man went into the inner office. When the door had firmly closed, Mrs. Duvall said quietly, "He's in a good mood. You might be able to get somewhere with him."

"We'll see." His heart felt like a bagful of twisting worms. He took a long, deep breath. There was pain in his skull, but he could tough it out. After a few minutes had passed, Dan heard Blanchard laugh behind the door; it was a hearty, gut-felt laugh, the kind of laugh a man makes when he's got money in his pockets and a steak in his belly. Dan waited, his hands gripped together and sweat leaking from his pores.

It was half an hour later when the door opened again. Jerome emerged. He looked happy, and Dan figured their business had been successful. He closed the door behind him. "See ya later on, Faye," he told Mrs. Duvall, and she said, "You take care, now." Jerome left, and Dan continued to wait with tension gnawing his nerves.

A buzzer went off on Mrs. Duvall's desk, and Dan almost jumped out of his chair. She pressed a button. "Yes sir?"

"Send Mr. Lambert in," the voice said through the intercom.

"Good luck," Mrs. Duvall told Dan as he approached the door, and he nodded.

Emory Blanchard's office was at a corner of the building, and had two high windows. The blinds were drawn but shards of sunlight arrowed white and fierce between the slats. Blanchard was sitting behind his desk like a lion in his den, imperial and remote. "Shut the door and have a seat," he said. Dan did, sitting in one of two black leather chairs that faced the desk. Blanchard removed his glasses and wiped the round lenses with a handkerchief. He was still chewing gum. The sweat stains at his armpits had grown; moisture glistened on his cheeks and forehead. "Summertime." He spoke the word like a grunt. "Sure not my favorite season."

"It's been a hot one, all right." Dan glanced around the office, noting how this man had altered it from Bud Jarrett's homey simplicity. The carpet was a red-and-gold Oriental, and behind Blanchard on oak shelves that still smelled of the sawmill were thick leather-bound books, meticulously arranged tomes that were for display more than for reading. A stag's head with a four-point rack of antlers was mounted on a wall, and beneath it a brass plaque read THE BUCK STOPS HERE. Prints of fox hunts were hung on either side of the stopped buck. On the wide, smooth expanse of Blanchard's desk were framed photographs of an attractive but heavily made-up blond woman and two children, a girl of seven or eight and a boy who looked to be ten. The boy had his father's cool blue eyes and his regal bearing; the girl was all bows and white lace.

"My kids," Blanchard said.

"Nice-lookin' family."

Blanchard returned the glasses to his face. He picked up the boy's picture and regarded it with admiration. "Yance made all-American on his team last year. Got an arm like Joe Montana. He sure raised a holler when we left Baton Rouge, but he'll do fine."

"I've got a son," Dan said.

"Yessir." Blanchard put the photograph back in its place next to a small Lucite cube that had a little plastic American flag mounted inside it. Written on the cube in red, white, and blue were the words I Supported Desert Storm. "You wait about nine more years, you'll see Yance Blanchard breakin' some passin' records at LSU, I guarandamntee it." He swiveled his chair around to where a computer screen, a telephone, and the intercom were set up. He switched the computer on, pressed a few keys, and black lines of information appeared. "Okay, there's your file," he said. "You a Cajun, Mr. Lambert?"

"No."

"Just wonderin'. Sometimes you can't tell who's a Cajun and who's not. Allllrighty, let's see what we've got here. Carpenter, are you? Employed at A&A Construc—oh, you *were* employed at A&A Construction until November of last year."

"The company went bankrupt." He'd told Mr. Jarrett about it, of course, and it had gone into his file.

"Construction bidness hit the rocks, that's for sure. You free-lancin' now, is that it?"

"Yes sir."

"I see Jarrett was lettin' you slide some months. Delinquent two payments. See, that's not a good thing. We can let you get by sometimes if you're one payment behind, but two payments is a whole different story."

"Yes sir, I know that, but I . . . kind of had an understandin' with Mr. Jarrett."

Even as he said it, Dan knew it was the wrong thing to say. Blanchard's big shoulders hunched up almost imperceptibly, and he slowly swiveled his chair around from the computer screen to face Dan. Blanchard wore a tight, strained smile. "See, there's a problem," he said. "There is no Mr. Jarrett at this bank anymore. So any understandin' you might've had with him isn't valid as far as I'm concerned."

Dan's cheeks were stinging. "I didn't mean to be—"

"Your record speaks for itself," the other man interrupted. "Can you make at least one payment today?"

"No sir, I can't. But that's what I wanted to talk to you about. If I could . . . maybe . . . pay you fifteen dollars a week until a job comes along. Then I could start makin' the regular payments again. I've never been so long between jobs before. But I figure things'll pick up again when the weather cools off."

"Uh-huh," Blanchard said. "Mr. Lambert, when you lost your job did you look for any other kind of work?"

"I looked for other jobs, yeah. But I'm a carpenter. That's what I've always done."

"You subscribe to the paper?"

"No." His subscription had been one of the first items to be cut.

"They run classified ads in there every day. Page after page of 'em. All kinds of jobs, just beggin'."

"Not for carpenters. I've looked, plenty of times." He saw Blanchard's gaze fix on his snake tattoo for a few seconds, then veer away with obvious distaste.

"When the goin' gets tough," Blanchard said, "the tough get goin'. Ever hear that sayin'? If more people lived by it, we wouldn't be headin' for a welfare state."

"I've never been on welfare." The pain flared, like an engine being started, deep in Dan's skull. "Not one day in my life."

Blanchard swiveled to face the computer's screen again. He gave a grunt. "Vietnam vet, huh? Well, that's one point in your favor. I wish you fellas had cleaned house like the boys did over in Iraq."

"It was a different kind of war." Dan swallowed thickly. He thought he could taste ashes. "A different time."

"Hell, fightin's fightin'. Jungle or desert, what's the difference?"

The pain was getting bad now. Dan's guts were clenched up. "A lot," he said. "In the desert you can see who's shootin' at you." His gaze ticked to the Lucite cube that held the plastic flag. Something small was stamped on its lower left corner. Three words. He leaned forward to read them. *Made in China.*

"Health problem," Blanchard said.

"What?"

"Health problem. Says so right here. What's your health problem, Mr. Lambert?"

Dan remained silent.

Blanchard turned around. "You sick, or not?"

Dan put one hand up against his forehead. Oh, Jesus, he thought. To have to bare himself before a stranger this way was almost too much for him.

"You aren't on drugs, are you?" Blanchard's voice had taken on a cutting edge. "We could've cleaned house over there if so many of you fellas hadn't been on drugs."

Dan looked into Blanchard's sweating, heat-puffed face. A jolt of true rage twisted him inside, but he jammed it back down again, where it had been drowsing so long. He realized in that moment that Blanchard was the kind of man who enjoyed kicking a body when it was beaten. He leaned toward Blanchard's desk, and slowly he pulled himself out of the black leather chair. "No, sir," he said tersely, "I'm not on drugs. But yeah, I *am* sick. If you really want to know, I'll tell you."

"I'm listenin'."

"I've got leukemia," Dan said. "It's a slow kind, and some days I feel just fine. Other days I can hardly get out of bed. I've got a tumor the size of a walnut right about here." He tapped the left side of his forehead. "The doctor says he can operate, but because of where the tumor lies I might lose the feelin' on my right side. Now, what kind of carpenter would I be if I couldn't use my right hand or leg?"

"I'm sorry to hear that, but—"

"I'm not finished," Dan said, and Blanchard was quiet. "You wanted to know what was wrong with me, you oughta have the manners to hear the whole story." Blanchard chose that moment to glance at the gold Rolex watch on his wrist, and Dan came very close to reaching across the desk and grabbing him by his yellow necktie. "I want to tell you about a soldier." Dan's voice was roughened by the sandpaper of raw emotion. "He was a kid, really. The kind of kid who always did what he was told. He drew duty in a sector of jungle that hid an enemy supply route. And it was always rainin' on that jungle. It was always drippin' wet, and the ground stayed muddy. It was a silver rain. Sometimes it fell right out of a clear blue sky, and afterward the jungle smelled like flowers gone over to rot. The silver rain fell in torrents, and this young soldier got drenched by it day after day. It was slick and oily, like grease off the bottom of a fryin' pan. There was no way to get it off the skin, and the heat and the steam just cooked it in deeper." Dan drew up a tight, terrible smile. "He asked his platoon leader about it. His platoon leader said it was harmless, unless you were a tree or a vine. Said you could bathe in it and you'd be all right, but if you dipped a blade of sawgrass in it, that sawgrass would blotch up brown and crispy as quick as you please. Said it was to clear the jungle so we could find the supply route. And this young soldier . . . you know what he did?"

"No," Blanchard said.

"He went back out in that jungle again. Back out in that dirty rain, whenever they told him to. He could see the jungle dyin'. All of it was shrivelin' away, bein' burned up without fire. He didn't feel right about it because he knew a chemical as strong as that had to be bad for skin and bones. He knew it. But he was a good soldier, and he was proud to fight for his country. Do you see?"

"I think so. Agent Orange?"

"It could kill a jungle in a week," Dan said. "What it could do to a man didn't show up until a long time later. That's what bein' a good soldier did to me, Mr. Blanchard. I came home full of poison, and nobody blew a trumpet or held a parade. I don't like bein' out of work. I don't like feelin' I'm not worth a damn sometimes. But that's what my life is right now."

Blanchard nodded. He wouldn't meet Dan's eyes. "I really, truly, am sorry. I swear I am. I know things are tough out there."

"Yes sir, they are. That's why I have to ask you to give me one more week before you take my truck. Without my truck, I don't have any way to get to a job if one comes open. Can you please help me out?"

Blanchard rested his elbows on his desk and laced his fingers together. He wore a big LSU ring on his right hand. His brows knitted, and he gave a long, heavy sigh. "I feel for you, Mr. Lambert. God knows I do. But I just can't give you an extension."

Dan's heart had started pounding. He knew he was facing disaster of the darkest shade.

"Look at my position." Blanchard's chewing gum was going ninety miles a minute. "My superiors kicked Bud Jarrett out of here because of the bad loans he made. They hired me because I don't make bad loans, and part of my job is to fix the mess Jarrett left behind. One week or one month: I don't think it would really matter very much, do you?"

"I need my truck," Dan rasped.

"You need a social worker, not a loan officer. You could get yourself checked into the VA hospital."

"I've been there. I'm not ready to roll over and die yet."

"I'm sorry, but there's nothin' I can do for you. It's bidness, you see? You can bring the keys and the paperwork tomorrow mornin'. I'll be in the office by ten." He swiveled around and switched the computer's screen off, telling Dan that their conversation was over.

"I won't do it," Dan said. "I can't."

"You will, Mr. Lambert, or you'll find yourself in some serious trouble."

"Jesus Christ, man! Don't you think I'm already in serious trouble? I don't even have enough money to buy decent groceries! How am I gonna get around without my truck?"

"We're finished, I think. I'd like you to leave now."

Maybe it was the pain building in Dan's skull; maybe it was this final, flat command from the man who was squeezing the last of the dignity from his life. Whatever it was, it shoved Dan over the edge.

He knew he should not. Knew it. But suddenly he was reaching out toward the photographs and the Made in China American flag, and as he gritted his teeth the rage flew from him like a dark bird and he swept everything off the top of Blanchard's desk in a swelling crash and clatter.

"Hey! Hey!" Blanchard shouted. "What're you doin'?"

"Serious trouble," Dan said. "You want to see some serious trouble, mister?" He hefted the chair he'd been sitting on and slammed it against the wall. The sign that said The Buck Stops Here fell to the floor, and books jittered on the perfect shelves. Dan picked up the wastebasket, tears of frustration and shame stinging his eyes, and he threw its contents over Blanchard, then flung the wastebasket against the stag's head. A small voice inside

Dan screamed at him to stop, that this was childish and stupid and would earn him nothing, but his body was moving on the power of single-minded fury. If this man was going to take his freedom from him, he would tear the office apart.

Blanchard had picked up the telephone. "Security!" he yelled. "Quick!"

Dan grabbed the phone and jerked it away from him, and it too went flying into the shelves. As Dan attacked the fox-hunt pictures, he was aware in a cold, distant place that this was not only about the truck. It was about the cancer in his bones and the growth in his brain, the brutal heart of Death Valley, the jostling for tickets, the dirty silver rain, the major, the village, his failed marriage, the son who had been infected with his father's poison. It was all those things and more, and Dan tore the pictures off the walls, his face contorted, as Blanchard kept shouting for him to stop. *A good soldier,* Dan thought as he began pulling the books off the shelves and flinging them wildly around the office. *A good soldier good soldier I've always been a good—*

Someone grabbed him from behind.

"Get him out!" Blanchard hollered. "He's gone crazy!"

A pair of husky arms had clamped around Dan's chest, pinning his own arms at his sides. Dan thrashed to break free, but the security guard was strong. The grip tightened, forcing the air from Dan's lungs. "Get him outta here!" Blanchard had wedged himself into a corner, his face mottled with red. "Faye, call the police!"

"Yes, sir!" She'd been standing in the open door, and she hurried to the phone on her desk.

Dan kept fighting. He couldn't stand to be confined, the pressure on his chest driving him to further heights of frenzy. "Hold still, damn it!" the guard said, and he began dragging Dan to the door. "Come on, you're goin' with—"

Panic made Dan snap his head backward, and the guard's nose popped as bone met cartilage. The man gave a wounded grunt, and suddenly Dan was free. As Dan turned toward him, he saw the guard—a man as big as a football linebacker, wearing a gray uniform—sitting on his knees on the carpet. His cap had spun away, his black hair cropped in a severe crew cut, his hands cupped over his nose with blood leaking between the sausage-thick fingers. "You busted my nose!" he gasped, his eyes slitted and wet with pain. "You sumbitch, you busted my nose!"

The sight of blood skidded Dan back to reality. He hadn't meant to hurt anyone; he hadn't meant to tear up this man's office. He was in a bad dream, and surely he must soon wake up.

But the bad dream took another, more wicked turn.

"You sumbitch," the guard said again, and he reached with bloody fingers to the pistol in a holster at his waist. He pulled the gun loose, snapping off the safety as it cleared the leather.

Going to shoot me, Dan thought. He saw the man's finger on the trigger. For an instant the smell of ozone came to him—a memory of danger in the silver-dripping jungle—and the flesh prickled at the back of his neck.

He lunged for the guard, seized the man's wrist, and twisted the gun aside. The guard reached up with his free hand to claw at Dan's eyes, but Dan hung on. He heard Mrs. Duvall shout, "The police are comin'!" The guard was trying to get to his feet; a punch caught Dan in the rib cage and almost toppled him, but still he held on to the guard's wrist. Another punch was coming, and Dan snapped his left hand forward with the palm out and smashed the man's bleeding nose. As the guard bellowed and fell back, Dan wrenched the pistol loose. He got his hand on the grip and fumbled to snap the safety on again.

He heard a *click* behind him.

He knew that sound.

Death had found him. It had slid from its hole here in this sweltering office, and it was about to sink its fangs.

Dan whirled around. Blanchard had opened a desk drawer and was lifting a pistol to take aim, the hammer cocked back and a finger on the trigger. Blanchard's face was terrified, and Dan knew the man meant to kill him.

It took a second.

One second.

Something as old as survival took hold of Dan. Something ancient and unthinking, and it swept Dan's sense aside in a feverish rush.

He fired without aiming. The pistol's *crack* vibrated through his hand, up his snake-tattooed forearm and into his shoulder.

"Uh," Blanchard said.

Blood spurted from a hole in his throat.

Blanchard staggered back, his yellow necktie turning scarlet. His gun went off, and Dan flinched as he heard the bullet hiss past his head and thunk into the doorjamb. Then Blanchard crashed to the floor amid the family photographs, fox-hunt prints, and leather-bound books.

Mrs. Duvall screamed.

Dan heard someone moan. It was not Blanchard, nor the guard. He looked at the pistol in his hand, then at the splatter of red that lay across Blanchard's desk. "Oh, God," Dan said as the horror of what he'd just done hit him full force. "Oh, my God . . . no . . ."

The gears of the universe seemed to shift. Everything shut down to a hazy slow-motion. Dan was aware of the guard cowering against a wall. Mrs. Duvall fled into the corridor, still shrieking. Then Dan felt himself moving around the desk toward Blanchard, and though he knew he was moving as fast as he could, it was more like a strange, disembodied drifting. Bright red arterial blood was pulsing from Blanchard's throat in rhythm with his heart. Dan dropped the pistol, got down on his knees, and pressed his hands against the wound. "No!" Dan said, as if to a disobedient child. "No!" Blanchard stared up at him, his chilly blue eyes glazed and his mouth half open. The blood kept spurting, flowing between Dan's fingers. Blanchard shuddered, his legs moving feebly, his heels plowing the carpet. He coughed once. A red glob of chewing gum rolled from his mouth, followed by rivulets of blood that streamed over his lower lip.

"No oh God no please no don't die," Dan began to beg. Something broke inside him, and the tears ran out. He was trying to stop the bleeding, trying to hold the blood back, but it was a tide that would not be turned. "Call an ambulance!" he shouted. The guard didn't move; without his gun the man's courage had crumpled like cheap tin. "Somebody call an ambulance!" Dan pleaded. "Hang on!" he told Blanchard. "Do you hear? Hang on!"

Blanchard had begun making a harsh hitching noise deep in his chest. The sound filled Dan with fresh terror. He knew what it was. He heard it before, in 'Nam: the death watch, ticking.

The police, Mrs. Duvall had said.

The police are comin'.

Blanchard's face was white and waxen, his tie and shirt soaked with gore. The blood was still pulsing, but Blanchard's eyes stared at nothing.

Murder, Dan realized. *Oh Jesus, I've murdered him.*

No ambulance could make it in time. He knew it. The bullet had done too much damage. "I'm sorry, I'm sorry," Dan said, his voice cracking. His eyes blurred up with tears. "I'm sorry, dear God I'm sorry."

The police are comin'.

The image of handcuffs and iron bars came to him. He saw his future, confined behind stone walls topped with barbed wire.

There was nothing more he could do.

Dan stood up, the room slowly spinning around him. He looked at his bloodied hands, and smelled the odor of a slaughterhouse.

He ran, past the guard and out of the office. Standing in the corridor were people who'd emerged from their own offices, but when they saw Dan's bloody shirt and his gray-tinged face they scurried out of his way. He ran past the elevator, heading for the stairwell.

At the bottom of the stairwell were two doors, one leading back into the teller's area and another with a sign that said EMERGENCY EXIT ONLY! ALARM WILL SOUND! As Dan shoved the exit door open, a high-pitched alarm went off in his ear. Searing sunlight hit him; he was facing the parking lot beside the bank. His truck was in a space twenty yards away, past the automatic teller machine and the drive-up windows. There was no sign yet of a police car. He ran to his truck, frantically unlocked the door, and slid behind the wheel. Two men, neither of them a police officer, came out of the emergency exit and stood gawking as Dan started the engine, put the truck into reverse, and backed out of the parking space. His brakes shrieked when he stomped on the pedal to keep from smashing the car parked behind him. Then he twisted the wheel and sped out of the lot, and with another scream of brakes and tires he took a left on the street. A glance in his rearview mirror showed a police car, its bubble lights spinning, pulling up to the curb in front of the building. He had no sooner focused his attention on the street ahead than a second police car flashed past him, trailing a siren's wail, in the direction of the bank.

Dan didn't know how much time he had. His apartment was five miles to the west. Beads of sweat clung to his face, blood smeared all over the steering wheel.

A sob welled up and clutched his throat.

He cried, silently.

He had always tried to live right. To be fair. To obey orders and be a good soldier no matter what slid out of this world full of snake holes.

As he drove to his apartment, fighting the awful urge to sink his foot to the floorboard, he realized what one stupid, senseless second had wrought.

I've gone south, he thought. He wiped his eyes with his snake-clad forearm, the metallic smell of blood sickening him in the hellish August heat. *Gone South, after all this time.*

And he knew, as well, that he'd just taken the first step of a journey from which there could be no return.

3

Mark of Cain

*H*URRY! DAN TOLD HIMSELF as he pulled clothes from a dresser drawer and jammed them into a duffel bag. *Movin' too slow hurry they'll be here soon any minute now . . .*

The sound of a distant siren shocked his heart. He stood still, listening, as his pulse rioted. A precious few seconds passed before he realized the sound was coming through the wall from Mr. Wycoff's apartment. The television set. Mr. Wycoff, a retired steelworker, always watched the *Starsky and Hutch* reruns that came on every day at three-thirty. Dan turned his mind away from the sound and kept packing, pain like an iron spike throbbing in his skull.

He had torn off the bloody shirt, hastily scrubbed his hands in the bathroom's sink, and struggled into a clean white T-shirt. He didn't have time to change his pants or his shoes; his nerves were shredding with each lost second. He pushed a pair of blue jeans into the duffel bag, then picked up his dark blue baseball cap from the dresser's top and put it on. A framed photograph of his son, Chad, taken ten years ago when the boy was seven, caught his attention and it too went into the bag. Dan went to the closet, reached up to the top shelf, and brought down the shoebox that held thirty-eight dollars, all his money in the world. As he was shoving the money into his pocket, the telephone rang.

The answering machine—a Radio Shack special—clicked on after three rings. Dan heard his own voice asking the caller to leave a message.

"I'm callin' about your ad in the paper," a man said. "I need my backyard fenced in, and I was wonderin'—"

Dan might have laughed if he didn't feel the rage of the law bearing down on him.

"—if you could do the job and what you'd charge. If you'd call me back sometime today I'd appreciate it. My number's . . ."

Too late. Much, much too late.

He zipped the bag shut, picked it up, and got out.

There were no sounds yet of sirens in the air. Dan threw the bag into the back of his truck, next to the toolbox, and he got behind the wheel and tore out of the parking lot. He crossed the railroad tracks, drove six blocks east, and saw the signs for Interstate 49 ahead. He swung the pickup onto the ramp that had a sign saying I-49 SOUTHBOUND. Then he steadily gave the truck more gas, and he merged with the afternoon traffic, leaving the industrial haze of Shreveport at their backs.

Killer, he thought. The image of blood spurting from Blanchard's throat and the man's waxen face was in his brain, unshakable as gospel. It had all happened so fast, he felt still in a strange, dreamlike trance. They would lock him away forever for this crime; he would die behind prison walls.

But first they had to catch him, because he sure as hell wasn't giving himself up.

He switched on his radio and turned the dial, searching Shreveport's stations for the news. There was country music, rock 'n' roll, rap, and advertisements but no bulletin yet about a shooting at the First Commercial Bank. But he knew it wouldn't take long; soon his description and the description of his truck would be all over the airwaves. Not many men bore the tattoo of a snake on their right forearms. He realized that what he'd worn as a badge of pride and courage in 'Nam now was akin to the mark of Cain.

Tears were scorching his eyes again. He blinked them away. The time of weeping was over. He had committed the most stupid, insane act of his life; he had gone south in a way he would never have thought possible. His gaze kept ticking to the rearview mirror, and he expected to see flashing lights coming after him. They weren't there yet, but they were hunting for him by now. The first place they'd go would be the apartment. They would've gotten all the information about him from the bank's computer records. How long would it take for the state troopers to get his license number and be on the lookout for a metallic-mist Chevrolet pickup truck with a killer at the wheel?

A desperate thought hit him: maybe Blanchard hadn't died.

Maybe an ambulance had gotten there in time. Maybe the paramedics had somehow been able to stop the bleeding and get Blanchard to the hospital. Then the charge wouldn't be murder, would it? In a couple of weeks Blanchard could leave the hospital and go home to his wife and children. Dan could plead temporary insanity, because that's surely what it had been. He would spend some time in jail, yes, but there'd be a light at the end of the tunnel. Maybe. May—

A horn blew, jarring him back to reality. He'd been drifting into the next lane, and a cream-colored Buick swept past him with a furious *whoosh*.

He passed the intersection of the Industrial Loop Expressway, and was moving through the outskirts of Shreveport. Subdivisions of blocky tract houses, strip malls, and apartment complexes stood near warehouses and factories with vast parking lots. The land was flat, its summer green bleached to a grayish hue by the merciless sun. Ahead of him, the long, straight highway shimmered and crows circled over small animals that had been mangled by heavy wheels.

It came to Dan that he didn't know where he was going.

He knew the direction, yes, but not the destination. Does it matter? he asked himself. All he knew is, he had to get as far from Shreveport as he could. A glance at the gas gauge showed him the tank was a little over a quarter full. The Chevy got good gas mileage for a pickup truck; that was one of the reasons he'd bought it. But how far could he get with thirty-eight dollars and some change in his pocket?

His heart jumped. A state trooper's car was approaching, heading north on the other side of the median. He watched it come nearer, all the spit drying up in his mouth. Then the car was passing him, doing a steady fifty-five. Had the trooper behind the wheel looked at him? Dan kept watching the rearview mirror, but the trooper car's brake lights didn't flare. But what if the trooper had recognized the pickup truck and radioed to another highway patrol car waiting farther south? On this interstate the troopers could be massing in a roadblock just through the next heat shimmer. He was going to have to get off I-49 and take a lesser-traveled parish road. Another four miles rolled under the tires before he saw the exit of Highway 175, heading south toward the town of Mansfield. Dan slowed his speed and eased onto the ramp, which turned into a two-lane road bordered by thick stands of pines and palmettos. As he'd figured, this route was all but deserted, just a couple of cars visible far ahead and none at his back. Still, he drove the speed limit and watched warily for the highway patrol.

Now he was going to have to decide where to go. The Texas line was about twenty miles to the west. He could be in Mexico in fifteen hours or so. If he continued on this road, he would reach the bayous and swampland on the edge of the Gulf in a little over three hours. He could get to the Gulf and head either west to Port Arthur or east to New Orleans. And what then? Go into hiding? Find a job? Make up a new identity, shave off his beard, bleach out the tattoo?

He could go to Alexandria, he thought. That city was less than a hundred miles away, just below the heart of Louisiana.

He'd lived there for nine years, when he'd been working with Fordham Construction. His ex-wife and son lived there still, in the house on Jackson Avenue.

Right. His mouth settled into a grim line. The police would have that address too, from the bank's records. Dan had faithfully made his child support payments every month. If he went to that house, the police would swarm all over him. And besides, Susan was so afraid of him anyway that she wouldn't let him in the door even if he came as a choirboy instead of a killer. He hadn't seen his ex-wife and seventeen-year-old son in over six years. It had been better that way, because his divorce was still an open wound.

He wondered what the other Snake Handlers would think of a father who had attacked his own little boy in the middle of the night. Did it matter that in those days Dan had been half crazy and suffered nightmarish flashbacks? Did it matter that when he'd put his hands around the boy's throat he'd believed he was trying to choke to death a Viet Cong sniper in the silver-puddled mud?

No, it didn't. He remembered coming out of the flashback to Susan's scream; he remembered the stark terror on Chad's tear-streaked face. Ten seconds more—just ten—and he might have killed his own son. He couldn't blame Susan for wanting to be rid of him, and so he hadn't contested the divorce.

He caught himself; the truck was drifting toward the center-line again as his attention wandered. He saw some dried blood between his fingers that he'd missed with the soap and rag, and the image of Blanchard's bleached face stabbed him.

A glance in the rearview mirror almost stopped his heart entirely. Speeding after him was a vehicle with its lights flashing. Dan hesitated between jamming the accelerator and hitting the brake, but before he could decide to do either, a cherry-red pickup truck with two grinning teenagers in the cab roared past him and the boy on the passenger side stuck a hand out with the middle finger pointed skyward.

Dan started trembling. He couldn't stop it. Sickness roiled in his stomach, a maniacal drumbeat trapped in his skull. He thought for a few seconds that he was going to pass out as dark motes spun before his eyes like flecks of ash. Around the next bend he saw a narrow dirt road going off into the woods on his right. He turned onto it and followed it fifty yards into the sheltering forest, his rear tires throwing up plumes of yellow dust.

Then he stopped the truck, cut the engine, and sat there under the pines with beads of cold sweat on his face.

His stomach lurched. As the fire rose up his throat, Dan scrambled out of the truck and was able to reach the weeds before he threw up. He retched and retched until there was nothing left, and then he sat on his knees, breathing sour steam as birds sang in the trees above him.

He pulled the tail of his T-shirt out and blotted the sweat from his cheeks and forehead. Dust hung in the air, the sunlight lying in shards amid the trees. He tried to clear his mind enough to grapple with the problem of where to go. To Texas and Mexico? To the Gulf and New Orleans? Or should he turn the truck around, return to Shreveport, and give himself up?

That was the sensible thing, wasn't it? Go back to Shreveport and try to explain to the police that he'd thought Blanchard was about to kill him, that he hadn't meant to lose his temper, that he was so very, very sorry.

Stone walls, he thought. Stone walls waiting.

At last he stood up and walked unsteadily back to his truck. He got in, started the engine, and turned on the radio. He began to move the dial through the stations; they were weaker now, diminished by distance. Seven or eight minutes passed, and then Dan came upon a woman's cool, matter-of-fact voice.

" . . . shooting at the First Commercial Bank of Shreveport just after three-thirty this afternoon . . ."

Dan turned it up.

" . . . according to police, a disturbed Vietnam veteran entered the bank with a gun and shot Emory Blanchard, the bank's loan manager. Blanchard was pronounced dead on arrival at All Saints Hospital. We'll have more details as this story develops.

In other news, the city council and the waterworks board found themselves at odds again today when . . ."

Dan stared at nothing, his mouth opening to release a soft, agonized gasp.

Dead on arrival.

It was official now. He was a murderer.

But what was that about entering the bank with a gun? "That's wrong," he said thickly. "It's wrong." The way it sounded, he'd gone to the bank intent on killing somebody. Of course they had to put the "disturbed Vietnam veteran" in there, too. Might as well make him sound like a psycho while they were at it.

But he knew what the bank was doing. What would their customers think if they knew Blanchard had been killed with a security guard's gun? Wasn't it better, then, to say that the crazy Vietnam veteran had come in packing a gun and hunting a victim? He kept searching the stations, and in another couple of minutes he found a snippet: " . . . rushed to All Saints Hospital, where he was pronounced dead on arrival. Police caution that Lambert should be considered armed and dangerous . . ."

"Bullshit!" Dan said. "I didn't go there to kill anybody!"

He saw what would happen if he gave himself up. They wouldn't listen to him. They'd put him in a hole and drop a rock on it for the rest of his life. Maybe he might live only three more years, but he wasn't planning to die in prison and be buried in a pauper's grave.

He engaged the gears. Head to the bayou country, he decided. From there he could go either to New Orleans or Port Arthur. Maybe he could find a freighter captain who needed cheap labor and didn't care to ask questions. He turned the truck around and then he drove back to Highway 175. He took a right, southbound again.

The truck's cab was a sweat box, even with both windows down. The heat was weighing on him, wearing him out. He thought about Susan and Chad. If the news was on the radio, it wouldn't be long before it hit the local TV stations. Susan might already have gotten a call from the police. He didn't particularly care what she thought of him; it was Chad's opinion that mattered. The boy was going to think his father was a cold-blooded killer, and this fact pained Dan's soul.

The question was: what could be done about it?

He heard an engine gunning behind him.

He looked in the rearview mirror.

And there was a state trooper's car right on his tail, its blue bubble lights spinning.

Dan had known true terror before, in the jungles of Vietnam and when he'd seen Blanchard's gun leveling to take aim. This instant, though, froze his blood and stiffened him up like a dime-store dummy.

The siren yowled.

He was caught.

He jerked the wheel to the right, panic sputtering through his nerves.

The trooper whipped past him and was gone around the next curve in a matter of seconds.

Before he could think to stop and turn around, Dan was into the curve and saw the trooper pulling off onto the road's shoulder. A cherry-red pickup truck was down in a ditch, and one of the teenage boys was standing on the black scrawl the tires had left when he'd lost control of the wheel. The other boy was sitting in the weeds, his head lowered and his left arm clasped against his chest. As Dan glided past the accident scene, he saw the trooper get out of the car and shake his head as if he knew the boys were lucky they weren't scattered like bloody rags amid the pines.

When the trooper's car was well behind, Dan picked up his speed again. Dark motes were still drifting in and out of his vision, the sun's glare still fierce even as the afternoon shadows lengthened. He'd had not a bite of food since breakfast, and he'd lost the meager contents of his stomach. He considered stopping at a gas station to buy a candy bar and a soft drink, but the thought of pulling off while a state trooper was so close behind him put an end to that idea. He kept going, following the sun-baked road as it twisted like the serpent on his forearm.

Mile after mile passed. The traffic was sparse, both in front and behind, but the strain of watching in either direction began to take its toll. The shooting replayed itself over and over in his mind. He thought of Blanchard's wife—widow, that is—and the two children, and what they must be going through right now. He began to fear what might be lying in wait for him around the curves. His headache returned with a vengeance, as did his tremors. The heat was sapping his last reserves of strength, and soon it became clear to him that he had to stop somewhere to rest. Another few miles passed, the highway leading between pine forest broken by an occasional dusty field, and then Dan saw a gravel road on his right. As he slowed down, prepared to turn into the woods and sleep in his truck, he saw that the road widened into a parking lot. There was a small whitewashed church standing beneath a pair of huge weeping willow trees. A little wooden sign in need of repainting said: VICTORY IN THE BLOOD BAPTIST.

It was as good a place as any. Dan pulled into the gravel lot, which was deserted, and he drove the truck around to the back of the church. When he was hidden from the road, he cut the engine and slid the key out. He pulled his wet shirt away from the backrest and lay down on the seat. He closed his eyes, but Blanchard's death leapt at him to keep him from finding sleep.

He'd been lying down for only a few minutes when someone rapped twice against the side of his truck. Dan bolted upright, blinking dazedly. Standing there beside his open window was a slim black man with a long-jawed face and a tight cap of white hair. Over the man's deep-set ebony eyes, the thick white brows had merged together. "You okay, mister?" he asked.

"Yeah." Dan nodded, still a little disoriented. "Just needed to rest."

"Heard you pull up. Looked out the winda and there you were."

"I didn't know anybody was around."

"Well," the man said, and when he smiled he showed alabaster teeth that looked as long as piano keys, "just me and God sittin' inside talkin'."

Dan started to slide the key back into the ignition. "I'd better head on."

"Now, hold on a minute, I ain't runnin' you off. You don't mind me sayin', you don't appear to be up to snuff. You travelin' far?"

"Yes."

"Seems to me that if a fella wants to rest, he oughta rest. If you'd like to come in, you're welcome."

"I'm . . . not a religious man," Dan said.

"Well, I didn't say I was gonna *preach* to you. 'Course, some would say listenin' to my sermons is a surefire way to catch up on your sleep. Name's Nathan Gwinn." He thrust a hand toward Dan, who took it.

"Dan . . ." His mind skipped tracks for a few seconds. A name came to him. "Farrow," he said.

"Pleased to meet you. Come on in, there's room to stretch out on a pew if you'd like."

Dan looked at the church. It had been years since he'd set foot in one. Some of the things he'd seen, both in Vietnam and afterward, had convinced him that if any supernatural force was the master of this world, it smelled of brimstone and devoured innocent flesh as its sacrament.

"Cooler inside," Gwinn told him. "The fans are workin' this week."

After a moment of deliberation, Dan opened the door and got out. "I'm obliged," he said, and he followed Gwinn—who wore black trousers and a plain light blue short-sleeve shirt—through the church's back door. The interior of the church was Spartan, with an unvarnished wooden floor that had felt the Sunday shoes of several generations. "I was writin' my sermon when I heard you," Gwinn said, and he motioned into a cubicle of an office whose open window overlooked the rear lot. Two chairs, a desk and lamp, a file cabinet, and a couple of peach crates full of religious books had been squeezed into the little room. On the desk was a pad of paper and a cup containing a number of ballpoint pens. "Not havin' much luck, I'm a'feared," he confided. "Sometimes you dig deep and just wind up scrapin' the bottom. But I ain't worried, somethin'll come to me. Always does. You want some water, there's a fountain this way."

Gwinn led him through a corridor lined with other small rooms, the floor creaking underfoot. A ceiling fan stirred the heat. There was a water fountain, and Dan went to work satisfying his thirst. "You a regular camel, ain't you?" Gwinn asked. "Come on in here, you can stretch yourself out." Dan followed him through another doorway, into the chapel. A dozen pews faced the preacher's podium, and the sunlight that entered was cut to an underwater haze by the pale green glass of the stained windows. Overhead, two fans muttered like elderly ladies as they turned, fighting a lost cause. Dan sat down on a pew toward the middle of the church, and he pressed his palms against his eyes to ease the pain throbbing in his skull.

"Nice tattoo," Gwinn said. "You get that around here?"

"No. Someplace else."

"Mind if I ask where you're headin' from and where you're goin'?"

"From Shreveport," Dan said. "I'm goin' to—" He paused. "I'm just goin'."

"Your home in Shreveport, is it?"

"Used to be." Dan took his hands away from his eyes. "I'm not real sure where I belong right now." A thought struck him. "I didn't see your car outside."

"Oh, I walked from my house. I just live 'bout a half-mile up the road. You hungry, Mr. Farrow?"

"I could do with somethin', yeah." Hearing that name was strange, after all this time. He didn't know why he'd chosen it; probably it was from seeing the young man who was begging work at Death Valley.

"You like crullers? I got some in my office; my wife baked 'em just this mornin'."

Dan told him that sounded fine, and Gwinn went to his office and returned with three sugar-frosted crullers in a brown paper bag. It took about four seconds for Dan to consume one of them. "Have another," Gwinn offered as he sat on the pew in front of Dan. "I believe you ain't et in a while."

A second pastry went down the hatch. Gwinn scratched his long jaw and said, "Take the other one, too. My wife sure would be tickled to see a fella enjoyin' her bakin' so much." When the third one was history, Dan licked the sugar from his fingers. Gwinn laughed, the sound like the rasp of a rusty saw blade. "Part camel, part goat," he said. "Don't you go chewin' on that bag, now."

"You can tell your wife she makes good crullers."

Gwinn reached into a trouser pocket, pulled out a silver watch, and checked the time. " 'Bout quarter to five. You can tell Lavinia yourself if you want to."

"Pardon?"

"Supper's at six. You want to eat with Lavinia and me, you're welcome." He returned the watch to his pocket. "Won't be no fancy feast, but it'll warm your belly up. I can go call her, tell her to put another plate on the table."

"Thanks, but I've gotta get back on the road after I rest some."

"Oh." Gwinn lifted his shaggy white brows. "Decide where you're goin', have you?"

Dan was silent, his hands clasped together.

"The road'll still be there, Mr. Farrow," Gwinn said quietly. "Don't you think?"

Dan looked into the preacher's eyes. "You don't know me. I could be . . . somebody you wouldn't want in your house."

"True enough. But my Lord Jesus Christ says we should feed the wayfarin' stranger." Gwinn's voice had taken on some of the singsong inflections of his calling. " 'Pears to me that's what you are. So if you want a taste of fried chicken that'll make you hear the heavenly choir, you just say the word and you got it."

Dan didn't have to think very long to make a decision. "All right. I'd be grateful."

"Just be hungry! Lavinia always makes a whoppin' supper on Thursday nights anyhow." Gwinn stood up. "Lemme go on back and call her. Why don't you rest some and I'll fetch you when I'm ready to go."

"Thank you," Dan said. "I really do appreciate this." He lay down on the pew as Gwinn walked back to his office. The pew was no mattress, but just being able to relax for a little while was glorious. He closed his eyes, the sweat cooling on his body, and he searched for a few minutes of sleep that might shield him from the image of Emory Blanchard bleeding to death.

In his office, Reverend Gwinn was on the telephone to his wife. She stoically took the news that a white stranger named Dan Farrow was joining them for supper, even though Thursday was always the night their son and daughter-in-law came to visit from Mansfield. But everything would work out fine, Lavinia told her husband, because Terrence had called a few minutes before to let her know he and Amelia wouldn't be there until after seven. There'd been a raid on a house where drugs were being sold, she told Nathan, and Terrence had some paperwork to do at the jail.

"That's our boy," Gwinn said. "Gonna get elected sheriff yet."

When he hung up, the reverend turned his attention again to the unwritten sermon. A light came on in his brain. Kindness for the wayfarin' stranger. Yessir, that would do quite nicely!

They always amazed him, the mysterious workings of God did. You never knew when an answer to a problem would come right out of the blue; or, in this case, out of a gray Chevy pickup truck.

He picked up a pen, opened a Bible for reference, and began to write an outline of his message for Sunday morning.

4

The Hand of Clint

"TWO CARDS."

"I'll take three."

"Two for me."

"One card."

"Oh, oh! I don't like the sound of that, gents. Well, dealer's gonna take three and see what we got."

The poker game in the back room of Leopold's Pool Hall, on the rough west end of Caddo Street in Shreveport, had started around two o'clock. It was now five forty-nine, according to the Regulator clock hanging on the cracked sea-green wall. Beneath a gray haze of cigarette and stogie smoke, a quintet of men regarded their cards in silence around the felt-topped table. Out where the pool tables were, balls struck together like a pistol shot, and from the aged Wurlitzer jukebox Cleveland Crochet hollered about Sugar Bee to the wail of a Cajun accordion.

The room was a hotbox. Three of the men were in shirtsleeves, the fourth in a damp T-shirt. The fifth man, however, had never removed the rather bulky jacket of his iridescent, violet-blue sharkskin suit. In respect of the heat, though, he'd loosened the knot of his necktie and unbuttoned the starched collar of his white shirt. A glass of melting ice and pale, cloudy liquid was placed near his right hand. Also within reach was a stack of chips worth three hundred and nineteen dollars. His fortunes had risen and fallen and risen again during the progress of the game, and right now he was on a definite winning jag. He was the man who'd requested one card, so sure was he that he owned a hand no one else could touch.

The dealer, a bald-headed black man named Ambrose, finally cleared his throat. "It's up to you, Royce."

"I'm in for five." Royce, a big-bellied man with a flame-colored beard and a voice like a rodent's squeak, tossed a red chip on top of the ante.

"I fold." The next man, whose name was Vincent, laid his cards facedown with an emphatic *thump* of disgust.

There was a pause. "Come on, Junior," Ambrose prodded.

"I'm thinkin'." At age twenty-eight, Junior was the youngest of the players. He had a sallow, heavy-jawed face and unruly reddish-brown hair, sweat gleaming on his cheeks and blotching his T-shirt. He stared at his cards, a cigarette clenched between his teeth. His lightless eyes ticked to the player next to him. "I believe I got you this time, Mr. Lucky."

The man in the sharkskin suit was engrossed in his own cards. His eyes were pallid blue, his face so pale the purple-tinged veins were visible at his temples. He looked to be in his mid-thirties, his body as lean as a drawn blade. His black hair was perfectly combed, the part straight to the point of obsessiveness. At the center of his hairline a streak of white showed like a touch of lightning.

"Put up or fold 'em," Ambrose said.

"See the five and raise you ten." The chips clattered down.

"Fifteen dollars," the man in the sharkskin suit said, his voice so soft it neared a whisper, "and fifteen more." He tossed the chips in with a flick of his right wrist.

"Oh, lawwwwdy!" Ambrose studied his cards with heightened interest. "Talk to me, chillen, talk to me!" He picked up his cigar stub from an ashtray and puffed on it as if trying to divine the future in smoke signals.

Nick, the pool hall's bartender, came in while Ambrose was deliberating and asked if anybody needed their drinks freshened. Junior said he wanted another Budweiser, and Vincent said he'd have a refill of iced tea. The man in the sharkskin suit downed his cloudy drink in two long swallows and said, "I'll have another of the same."

"Uh . . . you sure you don't want some sugar in that?" Nick asked.

"No sugar. Just straight lemon juice."

Nick returned to the front room. Ambrose puffed out a last question mark and put his cards facedown. "Nope. My wife's gone have my ass as it is."

Royce stayed in and raised another five spot. Junior chewed his lower lip. "Damn it, I've *gotta* stay in!" he decided. "Hell, I'll raise five to you!"

"And fifteen more," came the reply.

"Sheeeeyit!" Ambrose grinned. "We gots us a showdown here!"

"I'm out." Royce's cards went on the table.

Junior leaned back in his chair, his cards close to his chest and fresh sweat sparkling on his face. He glowered long and hard at the man beside him, whom he'd come to detest in the last two hours. "You're fuckin' bluffin'," he said. "I caught you last time you tried to bluff me, didn't I?"

"Fifteen dollars to you, Junior," Ambrose said. "What'cha gone do?"

"Don't rush me, man!" Junior had two red chips in front of him. He'd come into the game with over a hundred dollars. "You're tryin' to fox me, ain't you, Mr. Lucky?"

The man's head turned. The pale blue eyes fixed upon Junior, and the whispery voice said, "The name is Flint."

"I don't give a shit! You're tryin' to rob me, I figure I can call you whatever I please!"

"Hey, Junior!" Royce cautioned. "Watch that tongue, now!"

"Well, who the hell knows this guy, anyhow? He comes in here, gets in our game, and takes us all for a ride! How do we know he ain't a pro?"

"I paid for my seat," Flint said. "You didn't holler when you took my money."

"Maybe I'm hollerin' *now!*" Junior sneered. "Does anybody know him?" he asked the others. Nick came in with the drinks on a tray. "Hey, Nick! You ever see this here dude before?"

"Can't say I have."

"So how come he just wandered in off the street lookin' to play poker? How come he's sittin' there with all our damn money?"

Flint snapped the cards shut in his left hand, drank some of the fresh lemon juice, and rubbed the cold glass across his forehead. "Meet the raise," he said, "or go home and cry to your mommy."

Junior exhaled sworls of smoke. Crimson had risen in his cheeks. "Maybe you and me oughta go dance in the alley, what do you think about that?"

"Come on, Junior!" Ambrose said. "Play or fold!"

"Nick, loan me five dollars."

"No way!" Nick retreated toward the door. "This ain't no bank in here, man!"

"Somebody loan me five dollars," Junior said to the others. This demand was met with a silence that might have made stones weep. "Five dollars! What's wrong with you guys?"

"We don't loan money in this room," Ambrose reminded him. "Never have and never will. You know the house rules."

"I'd loan it to you if you were in a tight!"

"No you wouldn't. And I wouldn't ask. The rule is: you play with your own money."

"Well, it's sure nice to know who your friends are!" Junior wrenched the cheap wristwatch off his arm and slid it in front of Flint. "Here, damn it! That's gotta be worth fifteen or twenty bucks!"

Flint picked up the watch and examined it. Then he returned it to the table and leaned back, his cards fanned out again and resting against his chest. "Merchandise isn't money, but since you're so eager to walk out of here a loser I'll grant you the favor."

"*Favor.*" Junior almost spat the word. "Yeah, right! Come on, let's see what you've got!"

"Lay yours down first," Flint said.

"Glad to!" *Slap* went the cards on the table. "Three queens! I always was lucky with the women!" Junior grinned, one hand already reaching out to rake in the chips and his watch.

But before his hand got there, it was blocked by three aces.

"I was always smart at poker," Flint said. "And smart beats lucky any day."

Junior's grin evaporated. He stared at the trio of aces, his mouth crimping around the cigarette.

Flint scooped up the chips and put the wristwatch into his inside coat pocket. While Nick didn't loan money, he did sell poker chips. It was time, Flint knew, to cash in and be on his way. "That does it for me." He pocketed the rest of his winnings and stood up. "Thank you for the game, gentlemen."

"*Cheater.*"

"Junior!" Ambrose snapped. "Hush up!"

"*Cheater!*" Junior scraped his chair back and rose to his feet. His sweating face was gorged with blood. "You cheated me, by God!"

"Did I?" Flint's eyes were heavy-lidded. "How?"

"I don't know how! I just know you won a few too many hands today! Oh, yeah, maybe you lost some, but you never lost enough to put you too far behind, did you? Nosir! You lost just to keep us playin', so you could set me up for this shit!"

"Sit down, Junior," Vincent told him. "Some people gotta win, some gotta lose. That's why they call it gamblin'."

"Hell, can't you see it? He's a pro is what he is! He came in here off the street, got in our game, and made fools outta every damn one of us!"

"I see," Ambrose said wearily, "that it's almost six o'clock. Honey'll skin my butt if I don't get home."

"Gone skin your butt anyhow for losin' that paycheck," Royce said with a high giggle.

"Humility keeps me an honest man, my friends." Ambrose stood up and stretched. "Junior, that look on your face could scare eight lives out of a cat. Forget it now, hear? You can't win every day, or it wouldn't be no fun when you did."

Junior watched Flint, who was buttoning his jacket. Beneath Flint's arms were dark half-moons of sweat. "I say that bastard *cheated!* There's somethin' not right about him!"

Flint suddenly turned, took two strides forward, and his face and Junior's were only inches apart. "I'll ask you once more. Tell me how I cheated, sonny boy."

"You know you did! Maybe you're just slicker'n owl shit, but I know you cheated somehow!"

"Prove it," Flint said, and only Junior saw the faint smile that rippled across his thin-lipped mouth.

"You dirty sonofa—" Junior hauled back his arm to deliver a punch, but Ambrose and Royce both grabbed him and pulled him away. "Lemme go!" Junior hollered as he thrashed with impotent rage. "I'll tear him apart, I swear to God!"

"Mister," Ambrose said, "it might be best if you don't come 'round here again."

"I wasn't plannin' on it." Flint finished off his lemon juice, his face impassive. Then he turned his back on the other men and walked out to the bar to cash in his chips. His stride was as slow and deliberate as smoke drifting. While Nick was counting the money, Junior was escorted to the street by Ambrose, Vincent, and Royce. "You'll get yours, Mr. Lucky!" was Junior's parting shot before the door closed.

"He flies off the handle sometimes, but he's okay." Nick laid the crisp green winnings in Flint's pale palm. "Better not walk around with that kinda cash in this neighborhood."

"Thank you." He gave Nick a twenty. "For the advice." He started walking toward the door, his hand finding the car keys in his pocket, and over the zydeco music on the jukebox he heard the telephone ring.

"Okay, hold on a minute. Hey, your name Murtaugh?" Nick called.

Flint stopped at the door, dying sunlight flaring through the fly-specked windows. "Yes."

"It's for you."

"Murtaugh," Flint said into the phone.

"You seen the TV in the last half hour?" It was a husky, ear-hurting voice: Smoates, calling from the shop.

"No. I've been busy."

"Well, wrap up your bidness and get on over here. Ten minutes." *Click,* and Smoates was gone.

Even as six o'clock moved past and the blue shadows lengthened, the heat was suffocating. Flint could smell the lemon juice in his perspiration as he strode along the sidewalk. When Smoates said ten minutes, he meant eight. It had to be another job, of course. Flint had just brought a skin back for Smoates this morning and collected his commission—forty percent—on four thousand dollars. Smoates, who was the kind of man who had an ear on every corner and in every back room, had told him about the Thursday afternoon poker game at Leopold's, and with some time to kill before going back to his motel Flint had eased himself into what had turned out to be child's play. If he had any passion, it was for the snap of cards being shuffled, the clack of spinning roulette wheels, the soft thump of dice tumbling across sweet green felt; it was for the smells of smoky rooms where stacks of chips rose and fell, where cold sweat collected under the collar and an ace made the heartbeat quicken. Today's winnings had been small change, but a game was a game and Flint's thirst for risk had been temporarily quenched.

He reached his ride: a black 1978 Cadillac Eldorado that had seen three or four used car lots. The car had a broken right front headlight, the rear bumper was secured with burlap twine, the passenger door was crumpled in, and the southern sun had cracked and jigsawed the old black paint. The interior smelled of mildew and the chassis moaned over potholes like a funeral bell. Flint's appetite for gambling didn't always leave him a winner; the horses, greyhounds, and the casinos of Vegas took his money with a frequency that would have terrified an ordinary man. Flint Murtaugh, however, could by no stretch of the imagination be called ordinary.

He slipped his key into the door's lock. As it clicked open, he heard another noise—a metallic *snap*—very close behind him, and he realized quite suddenly that he would have to pay for his inattention.

"Easy, Mr. Lucky."

Flint felt the switchblade's tip press at his right kidney. He let the breath hiss from between his teeth. "You're makin' a real big mistake."

"Do tell. Let's walk. Turn in that alley up there."

Flint obeyed. There weren't many people on the sidewalk, and Junior kept close. "Keep walkin'," Junior said as Flint turned into the alley. Ahead, in the shadows between buildings, was a chain-link fence and beyond it a parking garage. "Stop," Junior said. "Turn around and look at me."

Flint did, his back to the fence. Junior stood between him and the street, the knife low at his side. It was a mean-looking switchblade, and Junior held it as if he had used it before. "I believe your luck's run out." Junior's eyes were still ashine with anger. "Gimme my money."

Flint smiled coldly. He unbuttoned his sharkskin jacket, and in so doing he tapped a finger twice on his belt buckle, which bore his initials in scrolled letters. He lifted his hands. "It's inside my coat. Come get it, sonny boy."

"I'll cut you, damn it! I'll give you some shit like you never had before, man!"

"Will you? Sonny boy, I'm gonna give you three pieces of wisdom. One." He raised a finger of his left hand. "Never play poker with a stranger. Two." Two fingers of his right hand went up. "Never raise against a man who asks for a single card. And three . . ."

Something moved at Flint's chest, underneath the white linen shirt.

Flint's necktie was pushed aside. Through the opening of an undone button emerged a dwarf-sized hand and a slim, hairless white arm. The hand gripped a small double-barreled derringer aimed at Junior's midsection.

"When you've got the drop on a man," Flint continued, "never, never let him face you."

Junior's mouth hung open. *"Jesus,"* he whispered. "You've . . . got . . . three . . ."

"Clint. Steady." Flint's voice was sharp; the derringer had wobbled a few inches to the right. "Drop the knife, sonny boy." But Junior was too stunned to respond. "Clint. Down. Down. Down." The arm obeyed, and now the derringer was pointed in the vicinity of Junior's knees. "You'll be a cripple in three seconds," Flint promised.

The knife clattered to the gritty pavement.

Flint frowned, sliding his two hands into his pants pockets. The third hand held the derringer steady. "I should've figured on this," Flint said, mostly to himself. "Clint. Holster."

The wiry arm retreated into his shirt. Flint felt the gun slide into the small holster under his right shoulder. The arm twitched once, a muscle spasm, and then lay pressed against Flint's chest with the fingers wedged beneath his belt buckle. "Good Clint," Flint said, and he walked quickly toward Junior, who still stood shocked and gaping. Flint withdrew his right hand, which now wore the set of brass knuckles that had been in his pocket. The blow that followed was fast and decisive, hitting Junior on the chin and snapping his head back. Junior gave a garbled cry and staggered into some garbage cans, and then Flint swung again—a graceful, almost balletic motion—and the brass knuckles crunched into the cheekbone on the left side of Junior's face.

Gasping, Junior fell to his knees. He stayed there, his head swaying from side to side and the anger washed from his eyes by the tears of pain.

"You know," Flint observed, "what you said about givin' me some shit is really funny. It really, truly is." Flint touched the knuckles of Junior's right hand with the toe of his polished black wingtip. The cheap wristwatch fell to the pavement beside Junior's fingers. "See, nobody on this earth can give me any more shit than I've already had to endure. Do you understand?"

"Ahhhhplleesh," Junior managed.

"I've been where you are," Flint said. "It made me meaner. But it made me smarter, too. Whatever doesn't kill you makes you smarter. Do you believe that?"

"Immmmaeuff," Junior said.

"Take your watch," Flint told him. "Go on. Pick it up."

Slowly, Junior's hand closed around the watch.

"There you go." The cold smile had never left Flint's face. "Now I'm gonna help your education along."

He summoned up his rage.

It was an easy thing to find. It had grinning faces in it, and harsh, jeering laughter. It had the memory of a bad night at the blackjack table, and of a loan shark's silky threats. It had Smoates's voice in it, commanding *Ten minutes.* It had a lifetime of torment and bitterness in it, and when it emerged from Flint it was explosive. The hand of Clint felt that rage and clenched into a knotty fist. Flint inhaled, lifted his foot, exhaled in a *whoosh,* and stomped Junior's fingers beneath his shoe.

The watch broke. So did two of the fingers and the thumb. Junior gave a wail that shattered into croaking, and he lay writhing on his side with his hand clasped to his chest and bits of watch crystal sticking into his palm.

Flint stepped back, sweat on his face and the blood pounding in his cheeks. It took him a few seconds to find his voice, and it came out thick and raw. "You can tell the police about this if you want to." Flint returned the brass knuckles to his pocket. "Tell 'em a freak with three arms did it, and listen to 'em laugh."

Junior continued to writhe, his attention elsewhere.

"Fare thee well," Flint said. He stepped over Junior, walked out of the alley, and got into his car. In another moment he had fired up the rough and rumbling engine and pulled away from the curb en route to the Twilight Zone Pawn Shoppe on Stoner Avenue.

As he drove, Flint felt sick to his stomach. The rage was gone, and in its place was shame. Breaking the boy's fingers had been cruel and petty; he'd lost control of himself, had let his baser nature rule him. Control was important to Flint. Without control, men fell to the level of animals. He pushed a cassette tape into the deck and listened to the cool, clean sound of Chopin's piano preludes, some of his favorite music. It made him think of his dream. In the dream, he stood on a rolling, beautiful emerald-green lawn, looking toward a white stone mansion with four chimneys and a huge stained-glass window in front.

He believed it was his home, but he didn't know where it was.

"I'm not an animal." His voice was still coarse with emotion. "I'm not."

A dwarf-sized left hand suddenly rose up before his face, swatting at his cheek with the ace of spades.

"Stop that, you bastard," Flint said, and he pushed Clint's arm back down where it belonged.

The Twilight Zone Pawn Shoppe stood between Uncle Joe's Loans and the Little Saigon Take-out Restaurant. Flint drove around back and parked next to Eddie Smoates's late-model Mercedes-Benz. The door at the rear of the pawn shop had a sign identifying it as DIXIE BAIL BONDS AND COLLECTIONS. Clint was moving around under Flint's shirt, getting hungry, so Flint reached into the backseat for a box of Ritz crackers before he got out of the car. He pressed a button on the brick wall beside the door, and a few seconds later Smoates's voice growled through an intercom mounted there: "You're late."

"I came as soon as I—"

A buzzer cut him off, announcing that the door had been electronically unlocked. Flint pushed through it into the air-conditioning. The door locked again at his back; Smoates kept a lot of valuables around, and he was a careful man. There was a small reception area with a few plastic chairs, but the office had closed for regular business an hour ago. Flint knew where he was going; this place was as familiar to him as his brother's arm. He walked past the reception desk and knocked on a door behind it.

"In!" Smoates said, and Flint entered.

As usual, Eddie Smoates sat at the center of a rat's nest of piled-up papers and file folders. The office smelled of garlic, on-ions, and grease: the prime ingredients of the Little Saigon take-out dinner that lay in Styrofoam plates and cups atop Smoates's untidy desk. The man was stuffing the rubber-lipped mouth in his moon-round face with stringy chicken. Smoates had the quick, dark eyes of a ferret, his broad scalp shaved bald and a gray goatee adorning his chin. He had massive forearms and shoulders that swelled his lime-green Polo shirt, though his belly was be-coming voluminous as well. Twenty years ago Smoates had been a professional wrestler, wearing a mask and going by the name X the Unknown. He said, "Siddahn" as he sucked pieces of garlic chicken off the bones, and Flint sat in one of the two chairs that faced the desk. Behind Smoates was a metal door that led into the pawn shop, which he also owned. On a rack of shelves pushed precariously against a wall were a half-dozen TV sets, ten VCRs, and a dozen or so stereo amps. The TV sets were on, all tuned to different channels, though their volumes were too low to be audible.

Smoates, a noisy eater, kept feasting. Grease glistened on his chin and in his goatee. Flint was repulsed by Smoates's lack of manners. He stared fixedly at his employer's prized collection of what Smoates called his "pretties." Held in a glass curio cabinet were such items as a mummified cat with two heads, a severed human hand with seven fingers floating in a jar of murky preservative, the skull of a baby with an extra eyehole in the center of its forehead, and—nature's cruelest trick, it seemed to Flint—an embalmed monkey with a third arm protruding from its neck. On a shelf above the "pretties" were eight photo albums that contained the pictures Smoates had collected of what seemed to be his driving passion next to making money and eating. Smoates was a connoisseur of freaks. As other men enjoyed vintage wine, fine paintings, or sculpture, Smoates craved grotesque oddities of flesh and bone. Flint, who lived in an apartment in the town of Monroe a hundred miles east of Shreveport, had never visited his employer's home in the six years he'd been on the Dixie payroll, but he understood from one of his fellows that Smoates kept a basement full of freak memorabilia gleaned from five decades of carnival sideshows. Whatever it was that made a man long to gaze upon the most bizarre and hideous of malformed creations, it ran dark and twisted right to the roots of Smoates's soul.

Such fascination disgusted Flint, who considered himself a well-bred gentleman. But then, Flint himself might still be an object of disgusting fascination had Smoates not visited the sideshow tent that advertised, among other attractions, Flint and Clint, the Two in One. Smoates had paid Flint to go with him to a photography studio and pose shirtless for a series of pictures, which had presumably wound up with the others in the photo albums. Flint had no desire to page through the albums; he'd seen enough freaks in the flesh to last him a lifetime.

"You win or lose?" Smoates asked, not looking up from his garlic chicken.

"I won."

"How much?"

"Around three hundred and fifty."

"That's good. I like when you win, Flint. When you're happy, I'm happy. You *are* happy, right?"

"I am," Flint said gravely.

"I like for my boys to be happy." Smoates paused, searching his plate of bones for a shred of meat. "Don't like 'em to be late, though. Ten minutes ain't fifteen. You need a new watch?"

"No." Clint's arm suddenly slid from the front of Flint's shirt and began scratching and tickling at his chin. Flint took a Ritz cracker from the box and put it into the fingers. Immediately the arm withdrew, and from beneath Flint's shirt came the sound of crunching.

Smoates pushed his plate aside, his fingers gleaming with grease. His eyes had taken on a feverish glint. "Open your shirt," he commanded. "I like to watch him eat."

As much as he detested to, Flint obeyed. Smoates was the man with the wallet, and he didn't tolerate disobedience from his "boys." Flint's fingers undid the buttons, letting Smoates have a clear view of the slim white dwarfish arm that was connected at the elbow to an area just beneath Flint's solar plexus. "Feed him," Smoates said. Flint took another cracker from the box. He felt the soft bones of his brother move within him, a slow shifting that pressed against his own organs. Clint could smell the cracker and his hand searched the air for it, but Flint guided it toward the fist-sized growth that protruded from his right side. Smoates was leaning forward, watching. The growth was as pale as the arm, was hairless and eyeless but had a set of flared nostrils, ears like tiny seashells, and a pair of thin lips. As the cracker came nearer, the lips parted with a soft, wet noise to show the small, sharp teeth and tongue that might have belonged to a kitten. The mouth accepted the cracker, the teeth crunched down, and Flint pulled his fingers back to avoid being nicked. Sometimes Clint was overeager in his feeding.

"Amazin'." Smoates wore a dreamy smile. "I swear, I don't know how your wires got crossed, but they sure did, didn't they?"

Flint rebuttoned his shirt, except for the single button at the center he usually left open. His face was impassive. "What did you want to see me about?"

"Take a look at this." Smoates picked up a remote control from his desk, pressed down with a big, greasy thumb, and one of the VCRs clicked into Play mode. Static sizzled on one of the TV screens for a few seconds, then the attractive face of a dark-haired newswoman appeared. She was speaking into a microphone, while behind her was a police car and a knot of people standing around a building's revolving door. Smoates used a second remote control to boost the volume.

" . . . this afternoon in what police are saying was the act of a desperate and disturbed man," the newswoman said. "Emory Blanchard, who was the loan manager of the First Commercial Bank, was pronounced dead on arrival at All Saints Hospital. This was the scene just a few moments ago when Clifton Lyles, the bank's president, made a public statement."

The picture changed. A grim-faced man with white hair was standing in front of the building, reporters holding a forest of microphones around him. "I want to say we don't intend to sit still for this outrage," Lyles said. "I'm announcin' right now a reward in the amount of fifteen thousand dollars for Lambert's capture." He held up a hand to ward off the shouts. "No, I'm not takin' questions. There'll be a full statement for the press later. I just hope and pray that man is caught before he kills anybody else. Thank you very much."

The newswoman came on again. "That was Clifton Lyles, president of the First Commercial Bank. As you can see behind me, there's still a lot of activity here as the police continue to—"

The videotaped image stopped. Smoates turned the volume down. "Crazy fucker went in there and shot Blanchard. Fella lost his marbles when he found out his pickup truck was bein' repossessed. You up to goin' after this skin?"

Flint had been feeding Clint during the videotape. Now he chewed on a cracker himself, leaving his brother's fingers searching through the opening of the undone button. "I always am," he answered.

"Figured so. I got a call in." Smoates had a connection in the police department who, for a fee, fed him all the information he required. "Have to move fast on this one. Tell you the truth, I don't think there's much chance of gettin' him. Every badge in the state'll be gunnin' for him. But there's nothin' else on the docket, so you might as well give it a try." He struck a kitchen match and lit a black cheroot, which he gripped between his teeth. He leaned back in his chair and spewed smoke toward the ceiling. "Give you a chance to take the new man out on a trainin' run."

"The new man? What new man?"

"The new man I'm thinkin' of hirin' on. Name's Eisley. Came in to see me this afternoon. He's got potential, but he's green. I need to see what he's made of."

"We work alone," Flint said quietly.

"Eisley's stayin' at the Ol' Plantation Motel out by the airport." Smoates fished for his notepad on the cluttered desktop. "Room Number Twenty-three," he said when he'd found it.

"We work alone," Flint repeated, a little more forcefully.

"Uh-huh. That may be, but I want you to take Eisley along this time."

Flint shifted uneasily in his chair. A small terror had begun building within him. "I don't . . . I don't allow anyone else into my car."

"Are you *jivin'* me?" Smoates scowled across the desk, and his scowl was not pretty. "I've seen that bucket of bolts. Nothin' special about it."

"I know, but . . . I'm particular about who I ride with."

"Well, Eisley ain't a nigger, if that's what bothers you."

"No, that's not it. I just . . . Clint and me . . . we'd rather work alone."

"Yeah, you already said that. But you're elected. Billy Lee's in Arkansas on a job, Dwayne's still laid up with the flu, and I ain't heard from Tiny Boy in two weeks. Figure he must've gone back to the sideshow, so we need some fresh blood 'round here. Eisley might work out just fine."

Flint choked. He lived alone—if a man whose brother was trapped inside his body in a wicked twist of genetics could ever be truly alone—and preferred it that way. Having to deal with another person at close quarters might drive him right up the wall. "What's wrong with him?"

"Who?"

"Eisley," Flint said, speaking slowly and carefully. "Somethin' must be wrong with him, or you wouldn't want to hire him on."

Smoates drew on his cheroot and tapped ashes to the floor. "I like his personality," he said at last. "Reminds me of a fella I used to think real highly of."

"But he's a freak, right? You don't hire anybody but freaks."

"Now, that ain't exactly correct. I hire——" He paused, mulling it over. "Special talents," he decided. "People who impress me, for one reason or 'nother. Take Billy Lee, for instance. He don't have to say a word, all he has to do is stand there and show his stuff, and he gets the job done. Am I right?"

Flint didn't answer. Billy Lee Klaggens was a six-foot-six-inch-tall black man who had paid his dues on the freak-show circuit under the name of Popeye. Klaggens, a fearsome visage, could stand there and stare at you and the only thing moving about him would be his eyeballs as blood pressure slowly squeezed them almost out of his skull. Faced with such a sight, the skins Klaggens hunted became as hypnotized as rabbits watching a cobra flare its hood—and then Klaggens sprayed a burst of Mace in their eyes, snapped on the handcuffs, and that was all she wrote. Klaggens had worked for Smoates for over ten years, and he had taught Flint the ropes.

"Eisley's got a special talent, if that's what you're gettin' at." A little thread of smoke leaked from the gap between his front teeth. "He's a born communicator. I think he could make the fuckin' sphinx talk. He knows how to work people. Used to be in show business."

"Didn't we all," Flint said.

"Yeah, but Eisley's got the gift of gab. You and him, you'll make a good team."

"I'll take him out on a trainin' run, but I'm *not* teamin' up with him. Or with *anybody*."

"Okay, okay." Smoates grinned, but on his face it looked more like a sneer. "Flint, you gotta loosen up, boy! You gotta get over this antisocial problem, you'll be a lot happi—" The telephone half buried beneath file folders rang, and Smoates snatched up the receiver. "Dixie Bail Bonds and Collections . . . well, you took your sweet fuckin' time, didn't you? Let's have the story." He tossed Flint the notepad and a ballpoint pen. "Daniel Lewis Lambert . . . Vietnam veteran . . . unemployed carpenter . . ." He snorted smoke through his nostrils. "Shit, man, gimme somethin' I can *use!*" He listened, the cheroot at a jaunty angle in his mouth. "Cops think he's left town. Armed and dangerous. Ex-wife and son in Alexandria. What's the address?" He relayed it to Flint, who wrote it down. "No other relatives in state? Sumbitches are gonna be waitin' for him to show up in Alexandria then, right? Hell, they gone get him 'fore I even send my boy out. But gimme the license number and a description of his truck anyhow; we might get lucky." Flint wrote that down as well. "What's Lambert look like?" was the next question, and Lambert's description went on the notepad's page. "Anythin' else? Okay, then. Yeah, yeah, you'll get your money this week. You hear that they've picked Lambert up, you gimme a call pronto. I'll be home. Yeah, same to you." He hung up. "Cops figure he might be on his way to Alexandria. They'll have the house staked out, for sure."

"Doesn't sound to me like I've got a snowball's chance in Hell of grabbin' him." Flint tore off the page and folded it. "Too many cops in the picture."

"It's worth a shot. Fifteen thousand smacks ain't hay. If you're lucky, you might catch him 'fore he gets to the house."

"I'd agree with you if I didn't have to haul freight."

Smoates drew on his cheroot and released a ragged smoke ring that floated toward the ceiling. "Flint," he said, "you been with me—what?—six years, goin' on seven? You're one of the best trackers I ever had. You're smart, you can think ahead. But you got this attitude problem, boy. You forget who pulled you out of that sideshow and who pays your bills."

"No, I don't," Flint answered crisply. "You won't let me."

Smoates was silent for a few seconds, during which he stared without blinking at Flint through a haze of smoke. "You tired of this job?" he asked. "If you are, you can quit anytime you please. Go on and find yourself some other line of work. I ain't stoppin' you."

Flint's mouth was dry. He held Smoates's haughty stare as long as he could, and then he looked away.

"You work for me, you follow my orders," Smoates continued. "You do what I say, you draw a paycheck. That make sense to you?"

"Yeah," Flint managed to say.

"Maybe you can grab Lambert, maybe you can't. I think Eisley's got potential, and I want to see what he's made of. Only way to do that is to send him out on a run with somebody, and I say that somebody is *you*. So go get him and hit the road. You're wastin' my time and money."

Flint took the box of crackers and stood up. He pushed his brother's arm down under his shirt and held it there. Now that he'd been fed, Clint would be asleep in a few minutes; unless he was called upon, all he basically did was eat and sleep. Flint's eyes found the three-armed monkey in the curio cabinet, and the same surge of anger that had made him break Junior's fingers swelled up in him and almost spilled out.

"I'll give Eisley a call and tell him you're on the way," Smoates said. "Check in with me from the motel."

I'm not an animal, Flint thought. Blood pulsed in his face. He felt Clint's bones twitch within him like the movement of someone trapped in a very bad dream.

"Standin' there ain't gonna get you nowhere," Smoates told him.

Flint turned away from the three-armed monkey and the bald-headed man behind the desk. When the door had closed at Flint's back, Smoates released a harsh little hiccup of a laugh. His belly shook. He crushed his cheroot out in the plate of grease and bones, and it perished with a bubbly hiss. His laughter gurgled and swelled.

Flint Murtaugh was on his way to meet the Pelvis.

5

A Ways to Go

THREE HOURS AFTER SHOOTING a man to death, Dan Lambert found himself sitting on a screened porch, a ceiling fan creaking overhead, with a glass of honeysuckle tea in his hand and a black woman offering him a refill from a purple pitcher.

"No ma'am, thank you," he said.

"Lemme get on back to the kitchen, then." Lavinia Gwinn put the pitcher down on the wicker table between Dan and Reverend Gwinn. "Terrence and Amelia oughta be here 'bout another half hour."

"I hope you don't mind me stayin'. I didn't know your son was comin' over when your husband invited me."

"Oh, don't you worry, we gots plenty. Always cook up a feast on Thursday nights." She left the porch, and Dan sipped his tea and listened to the cicadas droning in the green woods around the reverend's white clapboard house. The sun was sinking lower, the shadows growing between the trees. Reverend Gwinn occupied a wicker rocking chair, his fingers laced around his tea glass and his face set with the expression of a man who is calm and comfortable with life.

"You have a nice house," Dan said.

"We like it. Had a place in the city once, but it was like livin' in an alarm clock. Lavinia and me don't need much to get by on."

"I used to have a house. In Alexandria. My ex-wife and son still live there."

"Is that where you're headed, then?"

Dan took a moment to think about his answer. It seemed to him now that all along he'd known the house on Jackson Avenue was his destination. The police would be waiting for him there, of course. But he had to see Chad, had to tell his son that it had been an accident, a terrible collision of time and circumstance, and that he wasn't the cold-blooded killer the newspapers were going to make him out to be. "Yes," he said. "I believe I am."

"Good for a man to know where he's goin'. Helps you figure out where you've been."

"That's for damn sure." Dan caught himself. "Uh . . . sorry."

"Oh, I don't think the Lord minds a little rough language now and again, long as you keep His commandments."

Dan said nothing. *Thou shalt not kill,* he was thinking.

"Tell me about your son," Gwinn said. "How old is he?"

"Seventeen. His name's Chad. He's . . . a mighty good boy."

"You see a lot of him?"

"No, I don't. His mother thought it was for the best."

Gwinn grunted thoughtfully. "Boy needs a father, I'd think."

"Maybe so. But I'm not the father Chad needs."

"How's that, Mr. Farrow?"

"I messed up some things," Dan said, but he didn't care to elaborate.

A moment passed during which the smell of frying chicken drifted out onto the porch and made the hunger pangs sharpen in Dan's belly. Then Reverend Gwinn said, "Mr. Farrow, excuse me for sayin' so, but you look like a man who's seen some trouble."

"Yes sir." Dan nodded. "That's about right."

"You care to unburden it?"

Dan looked into the reverend's face. "I wish I could. I wish I could tell you everythin' I've been through, in Vietnam and after I left that damned place, but that's no excuse for what I did today." He looked away again, shamed by Gwinn's compassion.

"Whatever you did, it can be forgiven."

"Not by me. Not by the law, either." He lifted the cool glass and pressed it against his forehead for a few seconds, his eyes closed. "I wish I could go back and make everythin' right. I wish I could wake up and it'd be mornin' again, and I could have another chance." He opened his eyes. "That's not how life works though, is it?"

"No," Gwinn said. "Not *this* life, at least."

"I'm not much of a religious man. Maybe I saw too many young boys get blasted to pieces you couldn't have recognized as part of anythin' human. Maybe I heard too many cries for God that went unanswered." Dan swigged down the rest of his tea and set the glass aside. "That might sound cynical to you, Reverend, but to me it's a fact."

"Seems to me no one's life is easy," Gwinn said, a frown settling over his features. "Not the richest nor the poorest." He rocked gently back and forth, the runners creaking. "You say you've broken the law, Mr. Farrow?"

"Yes."

"Can you tell me what you've done?"

Dan took a long breath and let it go slowly. The cicadas trilled in the woods, two of them in close harmony. "I killed a man today," he answered, and he noted that Gwinn ceased his rocking. "A man at a bank in Shreveport. I didn't mean to. It just happened in a second. It was . . . like a bad dream, and I wanted to get out of it but I couldn't. Hell, I was never even a very good shot. One bullet was all it took, and he was gone. I knew it, soon as I saw where I'd hit him."

"What had this man done to you?"

Dan had the sudden realization that he was confessing to a stranger, but Gwinn's sincere tone of voice urged him on.

"Nothin', really. I mean . . . the bank was repossessin' my pickup. I snapped. Just like that. I started tearin' up his office. Then all of a sudden a guard was there, and when he pulled a gun on me I got it away from him. Blanchard—the man I shot—brought a pistol out of his desk and aimed it at me. I heard the hammer of his gun click. Then I pulled the trigger." Dan's fingers gripped the armrests, his knuckles white. "I tried to stop the bleedin', but there wasn't much I could do. I'd cut an artery in his neck. I heard on the radio that he was dead on arrival at the hospital. I figure the police are gonna catch me sooner or later, but I've got to see my son first. There are some things I need to tell him."

"Lord have mercy," Gwinn said very quietly.

"Oh, I'm not deservin' of mercy," Dan told him. "I'd just like some time, that's all."

"Time," the reverend repeated. He took the silver watch from his pocket, snapped it open, and looked at the numerals.

"If you don't want me sittin' at your table," Dan said, "I can understand."

Gwinn's watch was returned to the pocket. "My son," he said, "will be here any minute now. You didn't ask what kinda work Terrence does."

"Never thought to."

"My son is a deputy sheriff in Mansfield," Gwinn said, and those words caused the flesh to tighten at the back of Dan's neck. "Your description on the radio?"

"Yes."

"Terrence might not have heard about it. Then again, he might've." Gwinn held Dan's gaze with his dark, intense eyes. "Is what you've told me the truth, Mr. Farrow?"

"It is. Except my name's not Farrow. It's Lambert."

"Fair enough. I believe you." Gwinn stood up, leaving the chair rocking. He went into the house, calling for his wife. Dan left his chair as well, his heart beating hard. He heard the reverend say, "Yeah, Mr. Farrow's got a ways to go and he's not gonna be stayin' for dinner after all."

"Oh, that's a shame," Lavinia answered. "The chicken's all done!"

"Mr. Farrow?" There was just a trace of tension in Gwinn's voice. "You care to take some chicken for the road?"

"Yes sir," Dan said from the front door. "I sure would."

The reverend returned carrying a paper bag with some grease stains on the bottom. His wife was following along behind him. "What's your hurry, Mr. Farrow? Our boy oughta be here directly!"

"Mr. Farrow can't stay." Gwinn pushed the paper bag into Dan's hand. "He's gotta get to . . . New Orleans, didn't you say, Mr. Farrow?"

"I believe I might have," Dan said as he accepted the fried chicken.

"Well, I'm awful sorry you're not gonna be joinin' us at the table," Lavinia told him. "You gots family waitin' for you?"

"Yes, he does," Gwinn said. "Come on, Dan, I'll walk you to your truck."

"You take care on that road now," Lavinia continued, but she didn't leave the porch. "Crazy things can happen out there."

"Yes ma'am, I will. Thank you." When he and the reverend had reached the pickup and Lavinia had gone back inside, Dan asked, "Why are you helpin' me like this?"

"You wanted some time, didn't you? I'm givin' you a little bit. You better get on in there."

Dan slid into the driver's seat and started the engine. He realized that some of Blanchard's dried blood still streaked the steering wheel. "You could've waited. Just turned me in when your son got here."

"What? And scare Lavinia half to death? Take a chance on my boy gettin' hurt? Nosir. Anyhow, seems like you've had enough trouble today without me makin' more for you. But you listen to me now: the sensible thing to do is turn yourself in after you see your son. The police ain't savages; they'll give an ear to your story. All runnin's gonna do is make things worse."

"I know that."

"One more thing," Gwinn said, his hand on the window frame. "Maybe you're not a religious man, but I'll tell you somethin' true: God can take a man along many roads and through many mansions. It's not where you are that's important; it's where you're goin' that counts. Hear what I'm sayin'?"

"I think so."

"Well, you keep it to heart. Go on now, and good luck to you."

"Thanks." *I'll need it,* he thought. He put the Chevy into reverse.

"So long." Gwinn let go of the truck and stepped back. "The Lord be with you."

Dan nodded and reversed the truck along the dirt drive that led from the reverend's house to the cracked concrete of Highway 175. Gwinn stood watching him go as Dan backed onto the road and then put the truck's gears into first. The reverend lifted his hand in a farewell gesture and Dan drove away, heading southbound again but this time rested, his head clear and for the moment free of pain and a paper bag full of fried chicken on the seat beside him. He had driven perhaps a mile from Gwinn's house when a car came around the bend and passed him, going north, and he saw a young black man at the wheel and a black woman on the passenger side. Then he was around the curve himself, and he gave the truck a little more gas. *The Lord be with you,* he thought. But where had the Lord been at three o'clock this afternoon?

Dan reached into the bag and found a drumstick, and he chewed on it as he followed the curvy country road deeper into the Louisiana heartland. As the sun continued to settle in the west and the miles clicked off, Dan focused his thoughts on what lay ahead of him. If he swung east and got on the freeway again, he would reach Alexandria in about an hour. If he stayed on this slower route, it would take double that. The sun would be gone in another thirty minutes or so. The police would surely be staking out the house on Jackson Avenue, and those prowl cars had mighty strong spotlights. He couldn't even risk driving past the house. How long would it take before the police slacked off their surveillance? He might think about giving himself up after he'd talked to Chad, but he wasn't going to let the boy see him wearing handcuffs. So the question was: how was he going to get to Chad without the police jumping all over him first?

South of a small hamlet called Belmont, Dan pulled into a Texaco station, bought five dollars worth of gas, a Buffalo Rock ginger ale to wash down the excellent fried chicken, and a Louisiana roadmap. The gray-haired woman who took his money was too interested in her *Soap Opera Digest* to pay him much attention. In the steamy blue evening Dan switched on the pickup's headlights and followed Highway 175 as it connected with Highway 171 and became a little smoother. At the town of Leesville, where he found himself stopped at a traffic light right in front of the police station, he took a left onto Highway 28 East, which was a straight shot into Alexandria. He had about thirty miles to go.

Fear started clawing at him again. The dull throbbing in his head returned. Full dark had fallen, a sickle moon rising over the trees. Traffic was sparse on the road, but every set of headlights in his rearview mirror stretched Dan's nerves. The nearer he got to Alexandria, the more he doubted this mission could be accomplished. But he had to try; if he didn't at least try, he wouldn't be worth a damn.

He passed a sign that said ALEXANDRIA 18 MI.

The police are gonna be there, he told himself. They'll get me before I can walk up the front steps. Would they have the telephone tapped, too? If I called Susan, would she put Chad on the phone or would she hang up?

He decided he couldn't drive up to the house. There had to be another way. But he couldn't drive around in circles, either.

ALEXANDRIA 10 MI. the next sign said.

He didn't know what to do. He could see the glow of Alexandria's lights on the horizon. Two more miles reeled off the odometer. And then he saw a blinking sign through the trees on his right—HIDEAWAY M TOR CO RT—and he lifted his foot from the accelerator. Dan slowed down as the turnoff to the motor court approached. He had another instant of indecision, but then he turned off Highway 28 and guided the pickup along a dirt road bordered by scraggly pines and palmettos. The headlights revealed green-painted cottages tucked back amid the trees. A red wooden arrow with OFFICE on it pointed in the direction he was going. Dan saw no lights in any of the cottages, and a couple of them looked as if their roofs were an ill wind away from collapse. The grounds were weeded-up and forlorn, a swing set rusted and drooping next to an area of decaying picnic tables. Then the driveway stopped at a house painted the same shade of vomito green as the cottages, a rust-splotched station wagon parked alongside. A yellow buglight burned on the front porch, and other lights showed in the windows. The Hideaway, it appeared, was open for business.

As Dan cut the engine, he saw a figure peer through a window at him, then withdraw. He'd just gotten out when he heard a screen door's hinges skreek.

"Howdy," a man said. "How're you doin'?"

"I'm all right," Dan lied. He was facing a slim, buck-toothed gent who must've stood six-four, his dark hair cut as if a bowl had been placed on his head as a guide for the ragged scissors. "You got a vacancy?"

The man, who wore blue jeans and a black Hawaiian-print shirt with orange flowers on it, gave a snorty laugh. "Nothin' but," he said. "Come on in and we'll fix you up."

Dan followed the man up a set of creaky stairs onto the porch. He was aware of a deep, slow rumbling noise on the sultry air; frogs, he thought it must be. Sounded like hundreds of them, not very far away. Dan went into the house behind the man, who walked to a desk in the dingy little front room and brought out a Nifty notebook and a ballpoint pen. "Allrighty," the man said, offering a grin that could've popped a bottle top. "Now we're ready to do some bidness." He opened the notebook, which Dan saw was a registration log that held only a few scribbled names. "I'm Harmon DeCayne, glad you decided to stop over with us."

"Dan Farrow." They shook hands. DeCayne's palm felt oily.

"How many nights, Mr. Farrow?"

"Just one."

"Where you from?"

"Baton Rouge," he decided to say.

"Well, you're a long way from home tonight, ain't you?"

DeCayne wrote down the fake information. He seemed so excited, his hand was trembling. "We got some nice cottages, real nice and comf'table."

"That's good." Dan hoped the cottages were cooler than the house, which might've served as a steam bath. A small fan on a scarred coffee table was chattering, obviously overmatched. "How much?" He reached for his wallet.

"Uh——" DeCayne paused, his narrow brow wrinkling. "Does six dollars suit you?"

"*Seven* dollars. Paid in advance, if you please."

DeCayne jumped. The woman's voice had been a high, nasty whiplash. She had come through a corridor that led to the rear of the house, and she stood watching Dan with small, dark eyes.

"Seven dollars," she repeated. "We don't take no checks or plastic."

"My wife," DeCayne said; his grin had expired. "Hannah."

She had red hair that flowed over her thick-set shoulders in a torrent of kinky curls. Her face was about as appealing as a chunk of limestone, all sharp edges and forbidding angles. She wore a shapeless lavender-colored shift and rubber flipflops, and she stood maybe five feet tall, her body compact and wide-hipped and her legs like white tree trunks. She was holding a meat cleaver, her fingers glistening with blood.

"Seven dollars it is," Dan agreed, and he paid the man. The money went into a metal tin that was instantly locked by one of the keys on a key ring attached to DeCayne's belt. Hannah De-Cayne said, "Give him Number Four. It's cleanest."

"Yes, hon." De Cayne plucked the proper key from a wall plaque where six other keys were hanging.

"Get him a fan," she instructed her husband. He opened a closet and brought out a fan similar to the one that fought the steam currents. "A pilla, too."

"Yes, hon." He leaned into the closet again and emerged with a bare pillow. He gave Dan a nervous smile that didn't do much to hide a glint of pain in his eyes. "Nice and comf'table cottage, Number Four is."

"Does it have a phone?" Dan asked.

"Phone's right here," the woman said, and she motioned with the meat cleaver toward a telephone on a table in the corner. "Local calls cost fifty cents."

"Are Alexandria numbers long distance?"

"We ain't in Alexandria. Cost you a dollar a minute."

And she'd time him to the second, too, he figured. He couldn't call Susan with this harpy listening over his shoulder. "Is there a pay phone around anywhere?"

"One at the gas station couple of miles up the road," she said. "If it's workin'."

Dan nodded. He stared at the cleaver in the woman's fist. "Been choppin' some meat?"

"Froglegs," she said.

"Oh." He nodded again, as if this made perfect sense.

"That's what we live on," she continued, and her lower lip curled. "Ain't no money in this damn place. We sell froglegs to a restaurant in town. Come out of the pond back that way." She motioned with the cleaver again, toward the rear of the house. Dan saw jewels of blood on the blade. "What'd you say your name was?"

"Farrow. Dan Farrow."

"Uh-huh. Well, Mr. Farrow, you ever seen a cockeyed fool before?" She didn't wait for an answer. "There's one, standin' right beside you. Ever heard of a cockeyed fool buyin' a damn motel on the edge of a swamp pond? And then puttin' every damn penny into a damn fairyland?"

"Hon?" Harmon's voice was very quiet. "Please."

"Please, my ass," she hissed. "I thought we was gonna be makin' some money by now, but no, I gotta damn fool for a husband and I'm up to my elbows in froglegs!"

"I'll show you to your cottage." Harmon started for the door.

"Watch where you step!" Hannah DeCayne warned Dan. "Damn frogs are breedin' back in that pond. There's hundreds of 'em 'round here. Show our guest the fairyland while you're at it, why don'tcha?" This last statement had been hurled at her husband like a bucketful of battery acid. He ducked his shoulders and got out of the house, and Dan darted another glance at the woman's meat cleaver before he followed.

"Enjoy your stay," she said as he went through the door.

Holding the fan and the pillow, Harmon climbed into the pickup truck and Dan got behind the wheel. Harmon made a slight nasal whistling sound as he breathed, kind of like a steam kettle on a slow boil. "Number Four's up that road," he said with an upward jerk of his chin. "Turn right."

Dan did. "Woman's always on me," Harmon said bitterly. "So I messed up, so what? Ain't the first man in the world to mess up. Won't be the last neither."

"That's true," Dan agreed.

"It's that way." Harmon motioned to a weed-grown pathway meandering off into the woods.

"What is? The cottage?"

"No. The fairyland. There's your cottage up ahead."

The headlights showed a dismal-looking green-daubed dump waiting ahead, but at least the roof appeared sturdy. Also revealed by the headlights was a squattage of frogs, maybe two dozen or more, on the dirt road between Dan's truck and the cottage. Dan hit the brake, but Harmon said, "Hell, run 'em over, I don't give a damn."

Dan tried to ease through them. Some squawked and leapt for safety, but others seemed hypnotized by the lights and met their maker in a flattened condition. Dan parked in front of the cottage and followed DeCayne inside, the noise of the frogs a low, throbbing rumble.

He hadn't expected much, so he wasn't disappointed. The cottage smelled of mildew and Lysol, and the pent-up heat inside stole the breath from his lungs. DeCayne turned on the lights and plugged in the fan, which made a racketing sound as if its blades were about to come loose and fly apart. The bed's mattress had no sheet, and none was offered. Dan checked the bathroom and found two fist-size frogs croaking on the shower tiles. DeCayne scooped them up and tossed them out the back door. Then he presented the key to Dan. "Checkout time's twelve noon. 'Course, we're not expectin' a rush, so you can take your time."

"I'll be leavin' early anyway."

"Okay." He'd already put the pillowcase on the pillow and directed the fan's sullen breeze toward the bed. "You need anythin' else?"

"Not that I can think of." Dan didn't plan to sleep here; he was going to bide his time for a few hours and then call Susan from the gas station's pay phone. He walked outside with De-Cayne and got his duffel bag from the truck.

"Hannah's right about watchin' where you step," the man said. "They can make an awful mess. And if you find any more in the cottage, just pitch 'em out back." DeCayne looked toward his own house, which stood fifty yards or so away, the lights just visible through the woods. "Well, I'd better get on back. You married, Mr. Farrow?"

"Used to be."

"I knew you were a free man. Got the look of freedom about you. I swear, sometimes I'd give anythin' to be free."

"All it takes is a judge."

DeCayne grunted. "And let her steal me blind? Oh, she laughs at me and calls me a fool, but someday I'll show her. Yessir. I'll fix up the fairyland the way it oughta be and the tourists'll come from miles around. You know, I bought all that stuff for a song."

"What stuff?"

"In the fairyland. The statues and stuff. It's all in there: Cinderella's castle, Hansel and Gretel, the whale that swallowed Jonah. All they need is patchin' and paint, they'll be like new."

Dan nodded. It was obvious the man had constructed some kind of half-baked tourist attraction along that weeded-up pathway, and obvious too that the tourists had failed to arrive.

"One of these days I'll show her who's a fool and who's smart," DeCayne muttered, mostly to himself. He sighed resignedly. "Well, hope you have a good night's sleep." He began walking back to his house, frogs jumping around his shoes.

Dan carried his duffel bag into the cottage. In the bathroom he found a sliver of soap on the sink, and he removed his baseball cap and damp shirt and washed his face and hands with cool water. He was careful to get rid of the last traces of blood between his fingers and under his nails. Then he took a wet piece of toilet paper outside and cleaned the pickup's steering wheel. When he returned to the cottage, he discovered in the bedside table's drawer a six-month-old *Newsweek* magazine with Saddam Hussein's face on the cover. Beneath the magazine was the more useful discovery of a deck of cards. He sat down on the bed, leaning back against the plastic headboard, and he took off his wristwatch and laid it beside him. It was twelve minutes after nine; he'd decided that he'd go make the call at eleven o'clock.

He dealt himself a hand of solitaire, the first of many, and he tried with little success to get Blanchard's dying face out of his mind. In a couple of hours he might either see Chad or be in the back of a police car heading for jail. Was it worth the risk? He thought it was. For now, though, all he could do was wait and play out the cards before him. The wristwatch's second hand was moving, and the future would not be denied.

6

Meet the Pelvis

A s Dan had been driving away from Reverend Gwinn's house, a black 1978 Cadillac Eldorado with a broken right headlight and a crumpled passenger door turned into the parking lot of the Old Plantation Motel near Shreveport's regional airport.

In the sultry twilight gloom, the place looked as if Sherman had already passed through. Flint Murtaugh guided his car past a rusted cannon that defiantly faced the north. A tattered Confederate flag drooped on its warped pole. The motel's office was constructed to resemble a miniature plantation manor, but the rest of the place was definitely meant for the slaves. Trash floated on the brown surface of the swimming pool's water, and two men sat sharing a bottle beside an old Lincoln up on cinder blocks. Flint stopped his car before the door marked twenty-three and got out. Beneath Flint's shirt, Clint twitched in an uneasy sleep. Flint heard a man's and woman's voices tangled in argument through an open door, cursing each other purple. Beer cans and garbage littered the parched grass. Flint thought that the South wasn't what it used to be.

He knocked on the door of number twenty-three. A dog began barking from within, a high-pitched *yap yap yap yap*.

"It's all right, Mama," he heard a man say.

That voice. Familiar, wasn't it?

A latch clicked. The door opened a few inches before the chain stopped it.

Flint was looking at a slice of pudgy face and a sapphire-blue eye. An oily comma of dark brown hair hung down over the man's forehead. "Yes sir?" that deep, slightly raspy, oh-so-familiar voice asked as the dog continued to yap in the background.

"I'm Flint Murtaugh. Smoates sent me."

"Oh, yessir! Come on in!" The man took the chain off, opened the door wider, and Flint caught his breath with a startled gasp.

Standing before him, wearing a pair of black pants and a red shirt with a wide, tall collar and silver spangles on the shoulders, was a man who had died fourteen years before.

"Don't mind Mama," Elvis Presley said with a nervous grin. "She's got a bark, but she don't have no bite."

"You're . . ." No, of course it wasn't! "Who the hell are you?"

"Pelvis Eisley's the name." He offered a fleshy hand, the fingers of which were laden with gaudy fake diamond rings. Flint just looked at it, and the other man withdrew it after a few seconds as if fearful he'd caused offense. "Mama, get on back now! Give him some room! Come on in, pardon the mess!"

Flint crossed the threshold as if in a daze. Pelvis Eisley—the big-bellied, fat-jowled twin of Elvis Presley as he'd been the year of his death at Graceland—closed the door, relocked it, and scooped up a grocery sack from the nearest chair. It was filled, Flint saw, with potato chip bags, boxes of doughnuts, and other junk food. "There you go, Mr. Murtaugh, you can set yourself right here."

"This is a joke, isn't it?" Flint asked.

"Sir?"

A spring jabbed his butt, and only then did Flint realize he'd sat down in the chair. "This has got to be a—" Before he could finish, a little barking thing covered with brown-and-white splotches leapt onto his lap, its wet pug nose mashed flat and its eyes bulbous. It began yapping in his face.

"Mama!" Pelvis scolded. "You mind your manners!" He lifted the bulldog off Flint and put her down, but the animal was instantly up on Flint's lap again.

"I reckon she likes you," Pelvis said, smiling an Elvis sneer.

"I . . . hate . . . dogs," Flint replied in his chill whisper. "Get it off me. *Now.*"

"Lordy, Mama!" Pelvis picked the dog up and held her against his jiggling belly while the animal continued to bark and struggle. "Don't ever'body in this world enjoy your shenanigans, you hear? Hold still!" The dog's thrashings made Flint think of a Slinky. Its watery eyes remained fixed on him as he used his handkerchief to brush the dog hairs from the knees of his pants.

"You want somethin' to drink, Mr. Murtaugh? How 'bout some buttermilk?"

"No." The very smell of buttermilk made him deathly ill.

"Got some pickled pig's feet, if you want a bite to—"

"Eisley," Flint interrupted, "how much did that bastard pay you?"

"Sir?"

"Smoates. How much did he pay you to pull this joke on me?"

Pelvis frowned. He and the struggling dog wore the same expression. "I don't believe I know what you mean, sir."

"Okay, it was a good joke! See, I'm laughin'!" Flint stood up, his face grim. He glanced around the cramped little room and saw that Eisley's living habits were the equivalent of buttermilk and pickled pig's feet. On one wall a large poster of Elvis Presley had been thumb-tacked up; it was the dangerous, cat-sneer face of the young Elvis before Las Vegas stole the Memphis from his soul. On a table was a beggar's banquet of cheap plaster Elvis statues and busts; a cardboard replica of Graceland; a framed photograph of Elvis standing with his gloomy, hollow-eyed mother, and a dozen other Elvis knickknacks and geegaws that Flint found utterly repugnant. Another wall held a black velvet portrait of Elvis and Jesus playing guitars on the steps of what was presumably heaven. Flint felt nauseated. "How can you stand to live in all this crap?"

Pelvis looked stunned for a few seconds. Then his grin flooded back. "Oh, now you're joshin' me!" The dog got away from him and slipped to the floor, then leapt up onto the bed amid empty Oreo and Chips Ahoy cookie bags and started yapping again.

"Listen, I've got a job to do, so I'll just say fare thee well and get out." Flint started for the door.

"Mr. Smoates said you and me was gonna be partners," Pelvis said with a hurt whine. "Said you was gonna teach me ever'thin' you knew."

Flint stopped with his hand on the latch.

"Said you and me was gonna track a skin together," Pelvis went on. "Hush, Mama!"

Flint wheeled around, his face bleached to the shade of the white streak in his hair. "You mean . . . you're tellin' me . . . this is *not* a joke?"

"No sir. I mean, yes sir. Mr. Smoates called. Fella come from the office to get me, 'cause that's where the phone is. Mr. Smoates said you was on your way, and we was gonna track a skin to-gether. Uh . . . is that the same as bein' a bounty hunter?" Pelvis took the other man's shocked silence as agreement. "See, that's what I wanna be. I took a detective course by mail from one of them magazines. I was livin' in Vicksburg then. Fella who runs a detective agency in Vicksburg said he didn't have a job for me, but he told me all about Mr. Smoates. Like how Mr. Smoates was always on the lookout for—let's see, how'd he put it?—special talent, I think he said. Anyhow, I come from Vicksburg to see Mr. Smoates and we had us a talk this afternoon. He said for me to hang 'round town a few days, maybe he'd give me a tryout. So I guess this is what this is, huh?"

"You've got to be insane," Flint rasped.

Pelvis kept grinning. "Been called worse, I reckon."

Flint shook his head. The walls seemed to be closing in on him, and on all sides there was an Elvis. The dog was yapping, the noise splitting his skull. The awful stench of buttermilk wafted in the air. Something close to panic grabbed Flint around the throat. He whirled toward the door, wrenched the latch back, and leapt out of the foul, Elvisized room. As he ran along the breezeway toward the office with Clint twitching under his shirt, he heard the nightmare calling behind him: "Mr. Murtaugh, sir? You all right?"

In the office, where a Confederate flag was nailed to the wall next to an oil portrait of Robert E. Lee, Flint all but attacked the pay phone. "Hey, careful there!" the manager warned. He wore blue jeans, a Monster Truck T-shirt, and a Rebel cap. "That's motel property!"

Flint shoved a quarter into the slot and punched Smoates's home number. After four rings Smoates answered: "Yeah?"

"I'm not goin' out with that big shit sack!" Flint sputtered. "No way in Hell!"

"Ha," Smoates said.

"You tryin' to be funny, or what?"

"Take it easy, Flint. What's eatin' you?"

"You know what, damn it! That Eisley! Hell, he thinks he's *Elvis!* I'm a professional! I'm not goin' on the road with somebody who belongs in an asylum!"

"Eisley's sane as you or me. He's one of them Elvis impersonators." Smoates let out a laugh that so inflamed Flint, he almost jerked the phone off the wall. "Looks just like him, don't he?"

"Yeah, he looks like a big shit sack!"

"Hey!" Smoates's voice had taken on a chill. "I was a fan of Elvis's. Drilled my first piece of pussy with 'Jailhouse Rock' playin' on the radio, so watch your mouth!"

"I can't believe you'd even *think* about hirin' him on! He's as green as grass! Did you know he took a detective course by *mail?*"

"Uh-huh. That puts him ahead of where *you* were when I hired you. And as I recall, you were pretty green yourself. Billy Lee raised hell about havin' to take you out your first time."

"Maybe so, but I didn't look like a damn fool!"

"Flint," Smoates said, "I like the way he looks. That's why I want to give him a chance."

"Are you crazy, or am I?"

"I hire people I think can get the job done. I hired you 'cause I figured you were the kind of man who could get on a skin's track and not let loose no matter what. I figured a man with three arms was gonna have to be tough, and he was gonna have somethin' to prove, too. And I was right about that, wasn't I? Well, I've got the same feelin' about Eisley. A man who walks and talks and looks like Elvis Presley's gotta have a lot of guts, and he's already been down a damn hard road. So you ain't the one to be sittin' in judgment of him and what he can or can't do. Hear?"

"I can't stand bein' around him! He makes me so nervous I can't think straight!"

"Is that so? Well, that's just what Billy Lee said about you, as I remember. Now, cut out the bellyachin' and you and Eisley get on your way. Call me when you get to Alexandria."

Flint opened his mouth to protest again, but he realized he would be speaking to a deaf ear because Smoates had already hung up. *"Shit!"* Flint seethed as he slammed the receiver back onto its hook.

"Watch your language there!" the manager said. "I run a refined place!" Flint shot him a glance that might've felled the walls of Fort Sumter, and wisely the manager spoke no more.

At Number Twenty-three Flint had to wait for Eisley to unlock the door again. The heat hung on him like a heavy cloak, anger churning in his constricted belly. He understood the discomfort of pregnancy, only he had carried this particular child every day of his thirty-three years. Inside the room, the little bulldog barked around Flint's shoes but was smart enough not to get in range of a kick. "You okay, Mr. Murtaugh?" Eisley asked, and the dumb innocence of his Elvis-voice was the match that ignited Flint's powder keg.

He grasped Eisley's collar with both hands and slammed his bulk up against the Elvis poster. "Ouch," Pelvis said, showing a scared grin. "That kinda smarted."

"I dislike you," Flint said icily. "I dislike you, your hair, your clothes, your dead fat hillbilly, and your damn ugly dog." He heard the mutt growling and felt it plucking at his trouser leg, but his anger was focused on Eisley. "I believe I've never met anybody I dislike worse. And Clint doesn't care for you worth a shit, either." He let go of Pelvis's collar to unhook a button. "Clint! Out!" His brother's hand and arm slid free like a slim white serpent. The fingers found Pelvis's face and began to explore his features. Pelvis made a noise like a squashed frog. "You know what you are to me?" Flint asked. "Dirt. If you get under my feet, I'll step on you. Got it?"

"Lordy, lordy, lordy." Pelvis stared transfixed at Clint's roving hand.

"You have a car?"

"Sir?"

"A *car!* Do you have one?"

"Yes sir. I mean, I did. Ol' Priscilla broke down on me when I was comin' back from seeing Mr. Smoates. Had to get her towed to the shop." His eyes followed the searching fingers. "Is that . . . like . . . a magic trick or somethin'?"

Flint had hoped that if he had to take this fool with him, Eisley would at least be confined to his own car. Then, without warning, Eisley did the unthinkable thing.

"Mr. Murtaugh," he said, "that's the damnedest best trick I ever saw!" And he reached out, took Clint's hand in his own, and shook it. "Howdy there, pardner!"

Flint almost passed out from shock. He couldn't remember anyone ever touching Clint. The sensation of a stranger's hand clasped to Clint's was like a buzz saw raked up his spine.

"I swear you could go on television with a trick as good as that!" Eisley continued to pump Clint's arm, oblivious to the danger that coiled before him.

Flint gasped for breath and staggered backward, breaking contact between Eisley and his brother. Clint's arm kept bobbing up and down, the little hand still cupped. "You . . . you . . ." Words could not convey Flint's indignation. Mama had seen this new development and had skittered away from Flint's legs, bouncing up onto the bed where she rapid-fired barks at the bobbing appendage. "You . . . don't touch me!" Flint said. "Don't you ever dare touch me again!" Eisley was still grinning. This man, Flint realized, had the power to drive him stark raving insane. "Get packed," he said, his voice choked. "We're leavin' in five minutes. And that mutt's stayin' here."

"Oh . . . Mr. Murtaugh, sir." At last Eisley's face showed genuine concern. "Mama and me go everywhere together."

"Not in my car." He shoved Clint's arm back down inside his shirt, but Clint came out again and kept searching around as if he wanted to continue the hand shaking. "I'm not carryin' a damn mutt in my car!"

"Well, I can't go, then." Pelvis sat down on the bed, his expression petulant, and at once Mama was in his lap, licking his double chins. "I don't go nowhere without Mama."

"Okay, good! Forget it! I'm leavin'!"

Flint had his hand on the doorknob when Pelvis asked, in all innocence, "You want me to call Mr. Smoates and tell him it didn't work out?"

Flint stopped. He squeezed his eyes shut for a few seconds. The rage had leapt up again from where it lived and festered, and it was beating like a dark fist behind the door of his face.

"I'll call him," Pelvis said. "Ain't no use you wastin' the quarter."

Leave the hillbilly jerk, Flint thought. To hell with Smoates, too. I don't need him or his lousy job. I don't need *anybody*.

But his anger began to recede like a bayou tide, and beneath it was the twisted, busted-up truth: he could not go back to the sideshow, and without Smoates, what would he do?

Flint turned toward Pelvis. Mama sat in Pelvis's lap, warily watching Flint. "Do you even know what this job is *about?*" Flint asked. "Do you have any idea?"

"You mean bounty huntin'? Yes sir. It's like on TV, where—"

"Wrong!" Flint had come close to shouting it, and Mama stiffened her back and began a low growling. Pelvis stroked her a couple of times and she settled down again. "It's not like on TV. It's dirty and dangerous, and you're out there on your own with nobody to help you if things screw up. You can't ask the cops for help, 'cause to them you're trash. You have to walk—or crawl— through hellholes you couldn't even imagine. Most of the time all you're gonna do is spend hours sittin' in a car, waitin'. You're gonna be tryin' to get information from the kind of slimeballs who'd just as soon be cuttin' your throat to see your blood run."

"Oh, I can take care of myself," Pelvis asserted. "I ain't got a gun, but I know how to use one. That was chapter four in the manual."

"Chapter four in the manual." Flint's voice dripped sarcasm. "Uh-huh. Well, bein' a gunslinger in this business'll either get you killed or behind bars. You can't use firepower on anybody unless it's in self-defense and you've got witnesses, otherwise it's you who's goin' to prison. And let me tell you, a bounty hunter in prison would be like a T-bone steak in a dog pound."

"You mean if the fella's runnin' away from you, you can't shoot him?"

"Right. You nail somebody in the back and he dies, it's your neck in the noose. So you have to use your wits and be a good poker player."

"Sir?"

"You've got to know how to stack the deck in your favor," Flint explained. "I've got my own tricks. At close range I use a can of Mace. Know what that is?"

"Yes sir. It's that spray stuff that burns your skin."

"The kind I use can blind a man for about thirty seconds. By that time you ought to have the cuffs on him and he's on the ground, docile as a little lamb."

"Well, I'll be!" Pelvis said. "Mr. Smoates told me you were gonna be a mighty good teacher."

Flint had to endure another wave of anger; he lowered his head and waited it out. "Eisley," he said, "you know what a loan shark is?"

"Yes sir, I do."

"That's what Smoates is. He owns five or six loan companies in Louisiana and Arkansas and ninety percent of the work he'll expect you to do is collectin' money. And that's not pretty work either, I promise you, 'cause you have to shut your eyes to people's misfortunes and either scare the cash out of them or get rough, if it comes to that. The bounty-huntin' thing is just kind of a sideline. You can make some good money out of it if the reward's high enough, but it's no game. Every time you go out after a skin, you're riskin' your life. I've been shot at, swung on with knives and billy clubs, I've had a Doberman set on me, and one skin even tried to take my head off with a samurai sword. You don't get a lot of second chances in this business, Eisley. And I don't care how many mail-order detective courses you took; if you're not cold-blooded enough, you'll never survive your first skin hunt." Flint watched the other man's eyes to see if his message was getting through, but all he saw was dumb admiration. "You know anythin' about the skin we're supposed to collect?"

"No sir."

"His name's Lambert. He's a Vietnam veteran. Killed a man at a bank this afternoon. He's probably half crazy and armed to the teeth. I wouldn't care to meet him if there wasn't a chance of some big money in it. And if I were you, I'd just go call Smoates and tell him you've thought this thing over and you've decided to pass."

Pelvis nodded. From the glint in Pelvis's eye, Flint could tell that a spark had fired in the man's brain like a bolt of lightning over Lonely Street.

"Is that what you're gonna do, then?"

"Well, I just figured it out," Pelvis said. "That ain't no trick, is it? You really *do* have three arms, don't you?"

The better to strangle you with, Flint thought. "That's right."

"I never saw such a thing before! I swear, I thought it was a trick at first, but then I got to lookin' at it and I could tell it was real! What does your wife have to say about it?"

"I've never been married." Why did I tell him that? Flint asked himself. There was no reason for me to tell him about myself! "Listen to me, Eisley. You don't want to go with me after this skin. Believe me, you don't."

"Yes sir, I do," Pelvis answered firmly. "I want to learn everythin' I can. Mr. Smoates said you was the best bounty hunter there is, and I was to listen to you like you was God hisself. You say jump, I'll ask how high. And don't you worry about Mama, she don't have accidents in the car. When she wants to pee or dookie, she lets out a howl." He shook his head, awestruck. "Three arms. Now I've seen it all. Ain't we, Mama? Ain't we seen it all now?"

Flint drew a long breath and let it out. Time was wasting. "Get up," he said, and those were two of the hardest words he'd ever uttered. "Pack enough for two nights."

"Yes sir, yes sir!" Pelvis fairly jumped up from the bed. He started throwing clothes into a brown suitcase covered with Graceland, Memphis, and Las Vegas stickers. Mama had sensed Pelvis's excitement, and she began running in circles around the room. For the first time, Flint saw that Pelvis was wearing a pair of honest-to-God blue suede shoes that were run down at the heels.

"I can't believe I'm doin' this," he muttered. "I must be out of my mind."

"Don't you worry, I'll do whatever you say," Pelvis promised. Underwear, socks, and gaudy shirts were flying into the suitcase. "I'll be so quiet, you'll hardly know I'm there!"

"I'll bet."

"Whatever you say, that's my command. Uh . . . you mind if I load up some groceries? I get kinda hungry when I travel."

"Just do it in a hurry."

Pelvis stuffed another grocery sack with glazed doughnuts, peanut butter crackers, Oreos, and dog biscuits. He smiled broadly, his idol sneering at Flint over his shoulder. "We're ready!"

"One very, very important rule." Flint stepped toward Pelvis and stared at him face-to-face. "You're not to touch me. Understand? And if that dog touches me, I'm throwin' it out the window. Hear?"

"Yes sir, loud and clear." Pelvis's breath made Flint wince; it smelled of buttermilk.

Flint turned away, pushed Clint's arm under his shirt, and stalked out of the wretched room. Pelvis hefted the suitcase and the groceries, and with a stubby, wagging tail, Mama followed her king.

7

Big Ol' Frog

D AN PUSHED A QUARTER into the pay phone's slot outside an Amoco gas station on Highway 28, less than seven
miles west of Alexandria. It was twenty minutes after eleven, and
the gas station was closed. He pressed the *O* and told the operator
his name was Daniel Lewis and he wanted to make a collect call to
Susan Lambert at 1219 Jackson Avenue in Alexandria.

He waited while the number clicked through. Pain thrummed
in his skull, and when he licked his lips his tongue scraped like
sandpaper. One ring. Two. Three. Four.

They're not home, he thought. *They're gone, because Susan knew
I'd want to see—*

Five rings. Six.

"Hello?" Her voice was as tight as barbed wire.

"I have a collect call for Susan Lambert from Daniel Lewis,"
the operator said. "Will you accept the charges?"

Silence.

"Ma'am?" the operator urged.

The silence stretched. Dan heard his heartbeat pounding.
Then: "Yes, I'll accept the charges."

"Thank you," Dan said when the operator had hung up.

"The police are here. They're waitin' to see if you'll show."

"I knew they would be. Are they listenin' in?"

"Not from in here. They asked me if I thought you'd call and I said no, we hadn't talked for years. It *has* been years, you know."

"I know." He paused, listening for clicks on the line. He heard none, and he'd have to take the risk that the police had not gone through the process of tapping the wires. "How's Chad?"

"How would you think he is, to find out his father's shot a man dead?"

That one hurt. Dan said, "I don't know what you've heard, but would you like to hear my side of it?"

Again she was silent. Susan had always had a way of making silence feel like a chunk of granite pressed down on your skull. At least she hadn't hung up yet. "The bank fired Mr. Jarrett, their loan manager," he began. "They hired a new man, and he was gonna repossess my truck. He said some bad things to me, Susan. I know that's no excuse, but—"

"You're right about that," she interrupted.

"I just went crazy for a minute. I started tearin' his office up. All I could think of was that without my truck I was one more step down the hole. A guard came in and he pulled a gun on me. I got it away from him, and then all of a sudden Blanchard had a pistol, too, and I knew he was gonna shoot me. I swear I didn't mean to kill him. Everythin' was happenin' so fast, it was like fallin' off a train. No matter what the TV or radio says, I didn't go to that bank lookin' to kill somebody. Do you believe me?"

No answer.

"We've had our troubles," Dan said. His knuckles were aching, he was gripping the receiver so tightly. "I know . . . you got afraid of me, and I can't blame you. I should've gotten help a long time ago, but I was afraid to. I didn't know what was wrong with me, I thought I was losin' my mind. I had a lot to work through. Maybe you won't believe me, but I never lied to you, did I?"

"No," she replied. "You never lied to me."

"I'm not lyin' now. When I saw the gun in Blanchard's hand, I didn't have time to think. It was either him or me. After it was done, I ran because I knew I'd killed him. I swear to God that's how it happened."

"Oh, Jesus," Susan said in a pained voice. "Where are you?"

Here was the question Dan had known she would ask. Did he trust her that the police were not listening? Wouldn't she have had to sign forms or something to permit them to run a tap? They were no longer man and wife and had a troubled history, so why would the police assume she wouldn't tell them if he called? "Are you going to tell them?" he asked.

"They said if I heard from you, I was to let them know."

"Are you?"

"They told me you'd be armed and dangerous. They said you might be out of your mind, and you'd probably want money from me."

"That's a crock of bullshit. I'm not carryin' a gun, and I didn't call you for money."

"Why *did* you call me, Dan?"

"I . . . I'd like to see Chad."

"No," she said at once. "Absolutely not."

"I know you don't care much for me. I don't blame you. But please believe me, Susan. I don't want to hurt anybody. I'm not dangerous. I made a mistake. Hell, I've made a *lot* of mistakes."

"You can fix this one," she said. "You can give yourself up and plead self-defense."

"Who's gonna listen to *me?* Hell, that guard's gonna say I had the gun stashed in my clothes. The bank'll stand behind him, 'cause they sure won't admit a sick old vet could get a pistol away from—"

"Sick? What do you mean, sick?"

He hadn't wanted this thing to come up, because he needed no sympathy. "I've got leukemia," he said. "From the Agent Orange, I think. The doctors say I can last maybe two years. Three at the most."

Susan didn't respond, but he could hear her breathing.

"If the police take me, I'll die in prison," he went on. "I can't spend the last two years of my life witherin' away behind bars. I just can't."

"You . . . you damn *fool!*" she suddenly exploded. "My God! Why didn't you let me know?"

"It's not your concern."

"I could've given you some money! We could've worked somethin' out if you were in trouble! Why'd you keep sendin' the money for Chad every month?"

"Because he's my son. Because I owe you. Because I owe *him.*"

"You were always too stubborn to ask for help! That was always your problem! Why in the name of God couldn't you"—her voice cracked, a sound of emotion that astonished Dan—"couldn't you break down just a little bit and call me?"

"I'm callin' you now," Dan said. "Is it too late?"

She was silent. Dan waited. Only when he heard her sniffle and clear her throat did he realize she was weeping.

"I'll put Chad on," she said.

"Please," he said before she could leave, "can't I see him? Just for five minutes? Before I called I thought it'd be enough to hear his voice, but I need to see him, Susan. Isn't there some way?"

"No. The police told me they're gonna watch the house all night."

"Are they out front? Could I slip in the back?"

"I don't know where they are or how many. All I've got is a phone number they gave me. I figure it's to a mobile phone, and they're sittin' in a car somewhere on the street."

"The thing is," Dan said, "I'd like to see both of you. After tonight I'm hittin' the road. Maybe I can get out of the country if I'm lucky."

"Your name and picture's all over the news. How long do you think it'll be before somebody recognizes you and the law either tracks you down or *shoots* you down? You do know about the reward, don't you?"

"What reward?"

"The president of that bank's put fifteen thousand dollars on your head."

Dan couldn't hold back an edgy laugh. "Hell, all I was askin' for was a week's extension. Now they're ready to spend fifteen thousand dollars on me? No wonder the economy's screwed up."

"You think this is funny?" Susan snapped, and again her voice was thick with emotion. "It's not a damn bit funny! Your son's gonna always know his father was a killer! You think that's funny, too?"

"No, I don't. But that's why I want to see him. I want to explain things. I want to see his face, and I want him to see mine."

"There's no way, unless you want to give yourself up first."

"Listen . . . maybe there is," he said, his shoulder pressed against a wall of rough bricks. "If you're willin', I mean. It depends on you."

A few seconds passed in which Susan made no response.

"You want to hear the idea?" he urged.

"I can't make any promises."

"Just hear me out. When I hang up, dial that number and tell 'em I called."

"*What?*"

"Tell 'em they were right. I've got two or three guns and I sound like I'm out of my head. Tell 'em I said I was comin' over to see you as soon as I could get there. Then tell 'em you're afraid to stay in the house and you want to spend the night at a motel."

"That won't work. They'll know I'm lyin'."

"Why will they? They're not watchin' you, they're watchin' the house. They already believe I'm carryin' a load of guns and I'm ravin' mad, so they'll want you to get out. They'll probably clear the whole block."

"They'd follow me, Dan. No, it wouldn't work."

"It's worth a try. They might send a man to follow you to the motel and make sure you get checked in, but likely as not he won't stay around very long. The only thing is, you've got to make 'em believe you're scared to death of me."

"That used to be true," she said.

"You're not still scared of me, are you?"

"No, not anymore."

"All I'm askin' for is five minutes," Dan said. "Then I'm gone."

She paused, and Dan knew he'd said all he could. At last she sighed heavily. "I'll need some time to get a suitcase packed. You want me to call you when we get settled?"

"No, I shouldn't stay where I am and I don't have a phone in my room. Can we meet somewhere?"

"All right. How about Basile Park? At the amphitheater?"

Basile Park was about three miles from the house. "That'll do. What time?"

"An hour or so, I guess. But listen: if a policeman comes with me, or they won't let me take my own car, I won't be there. They might follow me without me knowin'. Are you willin' to chance it?"

"I am."

"All right. I'm crazy for doin' it, but all right. I'll try to make it, but if I'm not there—"

"I'll wait as long as I can," Dan said. "Thank you, Susan. You don't know how much this means to me."

"I'll try," she repeated, and then she hung up.

He returned the receiver to its cradle. His spirit felt lightened. He and Susan had gone to several outdoor concerts at Basile Park, and he knew the amphitheater there. He checked his watch to give himself an hour, then he got back into the pickup truck and drove toward the Hideaway. He thought about the fifteen thousand dollars, and he wished he'd seen that much money in a year's time. They wanted him caught fast, that was for sure.

Before he reached the turnoff to the motor court, it crossed Dan's mind that Susan might be setting him up. The police might have been listening after all, and would be waiting for him at the park. There was no way to know for certain. He and Susan had parted on bitter terms, yes, but there *had* been some good times, hadn't there? A few good memories to hold on to? He remembered some, and he hoped she did. He was Chad's father, and that was a link to Susan that could never be broken. He would have to take the risk that she wasn't planning on turning him in. If she was . . . well, he'd cross that bridge when he came to it.

He drove past the DeCaynes' house on the way to his cottage, and he was unaware that the sound of his engine awakened Hannah from a troubled sleep.

She wasn't sure what had wakened her. Harmon was snoring in the other bed, his mouth a cavern. Hannah got up from under the sweat-damp sheet, her red hair—the texture of a Brillo pad—confined by a shower cap. She recalled bits and pieces of a nightmare she'd had; the monster in it had been a warty frog with skinny human legs. Wearing only a bra and panties that barely held her jiggling mounds in check, she padded into the kitchen, opened the refrigerator's freezer, and got an ice cube to rub over her face. The kitchen still smelled of blood and frog guts, and in the freezer were dozens of froglegs wrapped in butcher's paper for delivery to the restaurant. While she was at it, Hannah opened the carton of vanilla ice cream that was in the freezer as well, and she got a spoon and took the carton with her to the front room to gorge herself until she was sleepy again. She switched on the radio, which was tuned to the local country music station. Garth Brooks was singing about Texas girls. Hannah walked to a window and pushed aside the curtain.

The lights were on in Number Four. Something about that man she didn't like, she'd decided. Of course, she didn't like too many people to begin with, but that man in Number Four gave her a creepy feeling. He looked sick, for one thing. Skinny and pale, like he might have AIDS or something. She didn't like his tattoo, either. Her first husband had been in the merchant marine, was illustrated from wrists to shoulders, and she couldn't abide anything that reminded her of that shiftless sonofabitch.

Well, he'd be gone soon enough. They'd be seven dollars richer, and every cent helped. Hannah plopped down on the sofa, her spoon strip-mining the ice cream. Reba McEntire serenaded her, and Hannah saw the bottom of the carton. The news came on, the newscaster talking about a fire last night in Pineville. The Alexandria town council was meeting to discuss pollution in the Red River. An Anandale woman had been arrested for abandoning her baby in the bus station's bathroom. A mentally disturbed Vietnam veteran had shot to death an official at a bank in Shreveport, and—

" . . . fifteen thousand dollars reward has been offered . . ."

Hannah's spoon paused in its digging.

" . . . by the First Commercial Bank for the capture of Daniel Lewis Lambert. Police consider Lambert armed and extremely dangerous. Lambert was last seen driving a gray 1989 Chevrolet pickup truck. He is forty-two years old, six-feet-one with a slim build; he wears a beard and . . ."

Hannah had a mouthful of ice cream. She stared at the radio, her eyes widening.

" . . . has the tattoo of a snake on his right forearm. Police advise extreme caution if Lambert is sighted. The number to call is . . ."

She couldn't swallow. Her throat had seized up. As she bolted to her feet, she spat the contents of her mouth onto the floor and a cry spiraled out: *"Harrrrrrmon!* Harmon, get up *this minute!"*

Harmon wasn't fast enough for her. He found himself being grabbed by both ankles and hauled out of bed. "You crazy?" he yelped. "Whatzamatter?"

"He's a killer!" Hannah's hair, which had a life of its own, had burst free from the shower cap. Her eyes were wild, her mouth rimmed with ice cream foam. "I knew somethin' was wrong with him I knew it when I seen him he killed a man in Shreveport got that tattoo on his arm fifteen thousand dollars reward hear me?"

"*Huh?*" Harmon said.

Hannah grasped him by the collar of his red-checked pajamas. "Fifteen thousand dollars!" she shrieked into his face. "By God, we're gonna get us that money! Now, stand up and put your clothes on!"

As Harmon pulled on his pants and Hannah struggled into her shapeless shift, she managed to drill the story through his thick skull. Harmon's face blanched, his fingers working his shirt buttons into the wrong holes. He started for the telephone. "I'll go call the law right n—"

A viselike hand clamped to his shoulder. "You listen to *me!*" she thundered. "You want to throw that money out the window? You think the cops won't cheat us outta every damn penny, you're dumber than a post! We're gonna catch him and take him in *ourselves!*"

"But . . . Hannah . . . he's a *killer!*"

"He ain't nothin' but a big ol' frog!" she glowered, her hands on her stocky hips. " 'Cept his legs are worth fifteen thousand dollars, and you and me are gonna take him to market! So you just shut up and do what I say! Understand?"

Harmon shut up, his thin shoulders bowed under the red-headed pressure. Hannah left the room, and Harmon heard her rummaging around in the hallway's closet. Harmon got his ring of keys from the bureau and hooked them around a belt loop, his fingers trembling. When he looked up, Hannah was holding the double-barreled shotgun that was their protection against burglars. He said, "That gun's so old, I don't know if it'll even—" She squelched him with a stare that would freeze time. Hannah also held a box of shells; there were five inside, and she loaded the shotgun and then pushed the other three shells into a pocket.

"We gotta get him out in the open," she said. "Get him outside where he can't get to his guns."

"We ought to call the law, Hannah! Jesus, I think I'm 'bout to heave!"

"Do it *later!*" she snarled. "He might be a crazy killer, but I don't know many men who can do much killin' when they've got their legs blowed off! Now, you just do what I say and we'll be rich as Midas!" She snapped the shotgun's breech shut, slid her feet into her rubber flipflops, and stalked toward the front door. "Come on, damn it!" she ordered when she realized Harmon wasn't following, and he came slinking after her as pale as death.

8

Mysterious Ways

I N NUMBER FOUR, DAN checked his watch and saw it was
time to go. He'd swallowed two aspirin and laid down for a
while, then had put on clean underwear and socks and the pair
of blue jeans from his duffel bag. Now he stood before the bathroom's dark-streaked mirror, wetting his comb and slicking his
hair back. He put on his baseball cap and studied his face with its
deep lines and jutting cheekbones.

Susan wasn't going to recognize him. He was afraid again,
the same kind of gnawing fear as when he'd walked into the bank.
More than likely, this was the last time he would ever see his son.
He hoped he could find the words he needed.

First things first: getting to Basile Park without being stopped
by the police. Dan hefted the duffel bag over his shoulder, picked
up the cottage's key, and opened the front door into the humid
night. The frogs had quieted except for a few low burps. Dan
went to hit the wall switch to turn off the ceiling's bulb when he
heard a metallic *clink* from the direction of his pickup truck, and
he realized with a jolt that someone was standing there at the
light's edge, watching him.

Dan whipped his head toward the sound. "Hey, hey!" a man said nervously. It was Harmon DeCayne, sweat sparkling on his cheeks. He lifted his hands to show the palms. "Don't do nothin' rash, now!"

"You scared the hell out of me! What're you doin' here?"

"Nothin'! I mean to say . . . I saw the lights." He kept his hands upraised. "Thought you might need somethin'."

"I'm pullin' out," Dan said, his nerves still jangling. "I was gonna stop at your house and leave the key on the porch."

"Where you headin'? It's awful late to be on the road, don't you think?"

"No, I've got places to go." He advanced on DeCayne, intending to stow his duffel bag in the rear of the truck, and the other man retreated, that clinking noise coming from the key ring that Dan saw was fixed to one of DeCayne's belt loops. Dan abruptly stopped. His radars had gone up. He smelled a snake coiled in its hole. "You all right?"

"Sure I'm all right! Why wouldn't I be all right?"

Dan watched the man's eyes; they were glassy with fear. *He knows,* Dan thought. *Somehow, he knows.* "Here's the key," he said, and he held it out.

"Okay. Sure. That's fi—"

Dan saw DeCayne's eyes dart at something behind him.

The woman, Dan realized. He had the mental image of a meat cleaver coming at him.

He set himself and whirled around, bringing the duffel bag off his shoulder in a swinging blow.

BOOM! went a gun seemingly right in his face. He felt the heat and the shock wave and suddenly the burning rags of the duffel bag were ripped from his hands and the fiery shreds of his clothes were flying out of it like luminous bats. Hannah DeCayne staggered backward holding a shotgun with smoke boiling from the breech. Dan had an instant to register that the duffel bag had absorbed a point-blank blast, and then the woman righted herself and a holler burst from her sweat-shining face. Dan saw the shotgun leveling at his midsection. He jumped away from its dark double eyes a heartbeat before a gout of fire spewed forth and he landed on his belly in the weeds. His ears were ringing, but over that tintinnabulation he heard a wet smack and the *crump* of buckshot hitting metal. He scrambled into the woods that lay alongside the cottage, his mind shocked loose of everything but the need to run like hell.

Behind Dan, Harmon DeCayne was watching his shirt turn red. The impact had lifted him up and slammed him back against the pickup truck, but he was still on his feet. He pressed his hands against his stomach, and the blood ran between his fingers. He stared, blinking rapidly, through the haze of smoke that swirled between him and his wife.

"Now you've done it," he said, and it amazed him that his voice was so calm. He couldn't feel any pain yet; from his stomach to his groin was as cold as January.

Hannah gasped with horror. She hadn't meant to fire the first time; she'd meant to lay the barrels up against the killer's skull, but his bag had hit the gun and her finger had twitched. The second time she'd been aiming to take him down before he could rush her. Harmon kept staring at her as his knees began to buckle. And then the rage overcame Hannah's shock and she bellowed, "I *told* you to get out of the way! Didn't you *hear* what I told you?"

Harmon's knees hit the ground. He swallowed thickly, the taste of blood in his mouth. "Shot me," he rasped. "You . . . damn bitch. Shot me."

"It's not *my* fault! I told you to move! You stupid ass, I told you to move!"

"Ahhhhhh," Harmon groaned as the first real pain tore at his tattered guts. Blood was pooling in the dust below him.

Hannah turned toward the woods, her face made even uglier by its rubber-lipped contortion. "You ain't gettin' away!" she yelled into the dark. She popped the shotgun open and reloaded both barrels. "You think I'm lettin' fifteen thousand dollars get away in my woods, you're crazy! You hear me, Mr. Killer?"

Dan heard her. He was lying on his stomach in the under-brush and stubbly palmettos forty feet from where the woman was standing. He'd seen Harmon fall to his knees, had seen the woman reloading her shotgun. Now he watched as Hannah walked to her husband's side.

She looked down at Harmon's damp, agonized face. "You mess up every damn thing," she said coldly, and then she lifted the shotgun and fired a shell into the pickup's left front tire. The tire exploded with a whoosh of air and the pickup lurched like a poleaxed horse. Dan almost cried out, but he clasped a hand over his mouth to prevent it.

"You ain't goin' nowhere in your truck!" Hannah shouted to-ward the woods. "You might as well come on out!"

Dan still wore his baseball cap, beads of sweat clinging to his face. All his other clothes were blown to rags, his metallic-mist Chevrolet pickup crippled, his hopes of getting to Basile Park blasted to pieces, too. The red-haired witch held the shotgun at hip level, its barrels aimed in his direction. "Come on out, Mr. Killer!" she yelled. Beside her, Harmon was still on his knees, his hands pressed to the wet mess of his midsection and his head drooping. "All right then!" she said. "I can play hide-and-seek if you want to, and first chance I get I'll blow your damn brains out!" She suddenly began stalking into the woods almost directly toward where Dan was stretched out. Panic skittered through him; there was no way he could fight a loaded shotgun. He bolted up and ran again, deeper into the thicket. His spine crawled in expectation of the blast. "I hear you!" Hannah squalled. He heard the noise of her stocky body smashing through the foliage. "Don't you run, you bastard!"

She was coming like a hell-bound freight train. Low pine branches whipped into Dan's face as he ran, thorns grabbing at his trousers. Under his feet, frogs grumped and jumped. His right shoe caught a root and he staggered, coming perilously close to falling. The underbrush was dense, and the noise he was making would've brought his Vietnam platoon leader down on his head like a fifty-pound anvil. He had neither the quick legs nor the balance of his youth. All he cared about at the moment was putting distance between himself and a shotgun shell.

And then he smelled oily stagnance and his shoes splashed into water. Mud bogged him down. It was the frog pond.

"You wanna go swimmin'?" Hannah shouted from behind him.

Dan couldn't see how large the pond was, but he knew he didn't dare try to get across it. The woman would shoot him while he was knee-deep in muck. He backed out of the water to firmer earth and set off again through weeds and brush that edged the pond. No longer could he hear the woman following him, and it leapt through his mind that she knew these woods and might be hunkered down somewhere ahead. He pushed through a tangle of vines. Up beyond the canopy of pines and willow trees he caught sight of a few stars, as distant as Basile Park seemed to be. And then he entered a stand of waist-high weeds and he walked right into the arms of the figure that stood in front of him.

In that instant he probably gained a dozen or so new gray hairs. He came close to wetting his pants. But he swung at the figure's head and pain shot through his knuckles when he connected with its jaw. The figure toppled over, and it was then that Dan realized it was a plaster mannequin.

He stood over it, wringing his bruised hand. He could make out two more mannequins nearby as if frozen in hushed conversation, their clothes weatherbeaten rags. Dark shapes lay before him, but he was able to discern what seemed to be a carousel half covered with kudzu. He had stumbled into Harmon DeCayne's fairyland.

He went on, past the rotting facade of a miniature castle. There was a broken-down Conestoga wagon and a couple of rusted car hulks. Bricks were underfoot, and Dan figured this was supposed to have been the main street of an enchanted village. Other mannequins dressed as cowboys and Indians stood about, the citizens of DeCayne's imagination. Dan moved past a huge tattered fabric shape with rotting wooden ribs that he thought might have been Jonah's whale, and suddenly he was looking at a high mesh fence topped with barbed wire that marked the edge of DeCayne's property.

I can climb the fence, he decided. The barbs'll be tough, but they'll be kinder than that damn shotgun. Once I get over, I can—

Can *what?* he asked himself. Without my truck I'm not gettin' very far.

But there was another set of wheels close by, wasn't there?

The station wagon parked next to the DeCaynes' house.

He remembered the key ring on Harmon's belt loop. Would the station wagon's key be on it? Would the car even run? It had to; how else did they get their froglegs to market? But to get the key ring he would have to double back through the woods and avoid the woman, and that was a tall and dangerous order.

He stood there for a moment, his hands grasping the fence's mesh. Beyond the fence was just more dark woods.

If he had any hope of getting to Basile Park, he would have to go back for the key ring.

Dan let go of the fence. He drew a deep breath and released it. His head was hurting again, but the ringing in his ears had ceased. He turned away from the fence and started back the way he'd come, creeping slowly and carefully, his senses questing for sound or motion.

A one-armed mannequin wearing a crown or tiara of some kind—a deformed fairy princess—stood on his right in the high weeds as he neared Jonah's whale. And suddenly Dan caught a sinuous movement from the corner of his eye, over beside a crumbling structure festooned with kudzu. He was already diving into the weeds as the shotgun boomed, and a split second later the princess's head and neck exploded in a shower of plaster. He lay on his side, breathing hard. "Got you, didn't I?" Hannah shouted. "I know I winged you that time!"

He heard the shotgun snap open and then shut again. The woman was striding toward him, her flipflops making a smacking noise on the bricks. Dan felt what seemed to be a length of pipe next to his shoulder. He reached out and touched cold fingers. It was the princess's missing arm.

He picked it up and rose to his feet. There was Hannah De-Cayne, ten feet in front of him, the shotgun aimed just to his left. He flung the plaster arm at her, saw it pinwheel around and slam into her collarbone, and she bellowed with pain and fell on her rump, the shotgun going off into the air. Then Dan tore away through the weeds with the speed of desperation, leaving the woman cursing at his back.

He found the pond again, and ran along its boggy edge. In another few minutes he pushed out of the underbrush twenty yards away from his lamed pickup truck. Harmon DeCayne was still in the same position, kneeling with his head bowed and his hands clasping his bloody middle.

Dan leaned over the man and grasped the key ring. DeCayne's eyes were closed, his breathing ghastly. Dan pulled the keys loose, and suddenly DeCayne's eyes opened and he lifted his head, blood leaking from the corner of his mouth.

"Hannah?" DeCayne gasped.

"Be still," Dan told him. "Which key starts the station wagon?"

"Don't . . . don't hurt me."

"I'm not gonna hurt you. Which key starts the—"

DeCayne's mouth stretched open. He shrieked in a voice that sliced the night: *"Hannah! He's got the keys!"*

Dan would've slugged him if the man hadn't been gutshot. He stood up as DeCayne continued to sound the alarm. In a couple of minutes the woman would be all over him. Dan ran along the road toward the DeCaynes' house. Harmon's shouting faded, but the damage was done. Reaching the station wagon, Dan opened the door on its groaning hinges and slid behind the wheel. The inside of the car smelled like the frog pond. He tried to jam a key into the ignition, but it refused. The next key balked as well. He saw a blurred movement, and by the house lights made out Han-

nah DeCayne running toward him on the road, her hair streaming behind her, her sweating face a rictus of rage. She was holding
the shotgun like a club, and Dan realized she must be out of shells
but she still could knock his brains out of his ears.

The third key would not fit.

"You ain't gettin' away!" she roared. "You ain't gettin'
away!"

Dan's fingers were slippery with sweat. He chose not the
fourth key, but the fifth.

It slid in.

He turned it and pressed his foot down on the gas pedal.

The station wagon went *ehehehehBOOM* and a gout of black
smoke flew from the exhaust. Dan jammed the gearshift into
reverse and the car obeyed like a glacier, and then Hannah
DeCayne was right there beside him and she jerked his door
open and swung at his skull with the shotgun's stock. Dan had
seen the blow coming, and he ducked down in the seat as the
shotgun slammed against the door frame. Then Hannah was
lunging into the car after him even as Dan picked up speed in
reverse, and she tried to claw at his eyes with one hand while the
other beat at him with the gun. He kicked out at her, caught
her right hip, and she staggered back. Then he swerved the
car around in a bone-jarring half circle and dust bloomed up
between him and the woman. Dan shoved the gearshift into
drive, floored the accelerator, and the car rattled forward. One
of the side windows suddenly shattered inward from another
blow of the shotgun's stock, bits of glass stinging Dan's neck.
He looked back, saw Hannah DeCayne running after him as the
station wagon picked up speed, and she cursed his mother and
tried to grab hold of the open door again. Then he was leaving
her behind and he found the headlight switch an instant before
he would've smashed into a weeping willow tree. As it was, he
jerked the wheel and scraped a dent along the passenger side.
He got the door closed, looked in the rearview mirror but could
see nothing through the swirling dust. It wouldn't have sur-

prised him, though, if Hannah DeCayne had been hanging on to the exhaust pipe with her teeth.

Then he reached Highway 28 and steered toward Alexandria and Basile Park. The woman had given him a blow on the left shoulder with the shotgun's stock, and though it hurt like hell, it wasn't broken. Better that than a cracked skull. He debated stopping at the Amoco station to call an ambulance, but he figured Hannah would run into the house first thing and do it. The station wagon's tank was a little less than three-quarters full, which was a real blessing. He had his wallet, the clothes on his back, and his baseball cap. He still had his skin on, too. He counted himself lucky.

Hannah had stopped running. There was no use in it, and her lungs were on fire. She watched the station wagon's lights move away. For a long time she stood in the dark, her hands clenching and loosening again on the empty shotgun. She heard his voice—a weak voice now—calling her: "Hannah? Hannah?"

At last she turned her back on the highway and limped—painfully, a bruise blackening on her right hip—to where Harmon was crouched on his knees.

"Hannah," he groaned, "I'm hurt bad."

She'd lost her flipflops. She looked at the bottom of her left foot, which had been cut by a shard of glass. The sight of that wound, with its angry edges, made something start ticking like a bomb in her brain.

"Call somebody," Harmon said. His eyelids were at half mast, his hands clasped together in the gory swamp of his stomach. "You . . . gotta . . ."

"Lost us fifteen thousand dollars." Hannah's voice was hollow and weary. "You mess up every damn thing."

"No . . . I didn't. It was you . . . messed up."

She shook her head. "He read you, Harmon. He knew. I told you to get out of the way, didn't I? And there went fifteen thousand dollars down the road. Oh my God, what I could've done with that mo—" She stopped speaking and stared blankly at the dust, a pulse beating at her temple.

"I'm hurtin'," Harmon said.

"Uh-huh. The thing is, they could prob'ly sew you up at the hospital."

He reached up a bloody hand for her. "Hannah . . . I need help."

"Yes, you do," she answered. "But from now on I think I'm gonna help myself." Her eyes had taken on the glitter of small, hard stones. "Too bad that killer stopped here. Too bad we found out who he was. Too bad he fought the shotgun away from you."

"What?" Harmon whispered.

"I tried to help you, but I couldn't. I ran into the woods and hid, and then I seen what he done to you."

"Have you . . . lost your mind?"

"My mama always told me the Lord moves in mysterious ways," Hannah said. "I never believed her till this very minute."

Harmon watched his wife lift the shotgun over her head like a club.

He made a soft, mewling noise.

The shotgun's stock swung down with all the woman's bitter fury behind it. There was a noise like an overripe melon being crushed. The shotgun rose up again. Sometime during the next half-dozen blows, the stock splintered and broke away. When it was done, Hannah DeCayne was bathed in sweat and gasping, and she had bitten into her lower lip. She looked down at the ruins and wondered what she had ever seen there. She wiped the shotgun's barrel off with the hem of her shift, dropped it on the ground beside the crumpled form, and then she limped into the house to make the call.

9

Time the Thief

THE RUST-SPLOTCHED STATION WAGON crept through the streets of Alexandria, past the dark and quiet houses, past the teardrop-shaped streetlamps, past sprinklers hissing on the parched brown lawns.

Dan drove slowly, alert for the police. His shoulder was stiffening, his body felt as if he'd been tumbled a few times inside a cement mixer, but he was alive and free and Basile Park was less than a mile away.

He'd seen no police cars and only a few other vehicles out at this late hour. He turned onto a street that led into the manicured park, following it past an area of picnic tables and tennis courts. A sign pointed the way to the amphitheater, beyond the public parking lot. His heart sank; the lot was empty. But maybe she hadn't been able to shake the police. Maybe a lot of things. Or maybe she'd just decided not to show up.

He decided to wait. He stopped the station wagon, cut the lights and the engine, and sat there in the dark, the song of cicadas reaching him from a nearby stand of pines.

What had happened to his pickup truck still speared him.

This whole nightmare was accountable to the truck, and it had taken that red-haired witch two seconds to destroy its usefulness. Damn, but he was going to miss it. A real workingman's truck, he recalled the salesman saying. Easy payments, good warranty, made in America.

Dan wondered what Blanchard's wife and children were feeling like about now, and he let the thoughts of his pickup truck go.

Time ticked past. After thirty minutes Dan decided to give her fifteen more. When the fifteen was gone, he stopped looking at his watch.

She wasn't coming.

Five more minutes. Five more, and then he'd accept it and leave.

He leaned back and closed his eyes, listening to the night sounds.

It took only a few heartbeats, only a few breaths, and he was back in the village again.

The name of the village was Cho Yat. It was in the lowlands, where rice paddies steamed under the August sun and the jungle hid sniper nests and snake holes. The platoon had stopped at Cho Yat while Captain Aubrey and the South Vietnamese translator hunkered down in the shade to ask the village elders about Cong activity in the sector. The elders answered reluctantly, and in riddles. It was not their war. As the other Snake Handlers waited, eight or nine children gathered around for a closer look at the foreign giants. A new man—green as grass, just in a few days before—sitting next to Dan opened his knapsack and gave one little boy a chocolate bar. "Hershey," the man said. He was from Boston, and he had a clipped Yankee accent. "Can you say that? Her-shey."

"*Hishee,*" the child answered.

"Good enough. Why don't you give some of that to your—" But the little boy was already running away, peeling the tinfoil back and jamming the chocolate into his mouth, with other children yelling in pursuit. The Bostonian—his eyes cornflower blue in a young, unlined face, his hair as yellow as the sun—had looked at Dan and shrugged. "I guess they don't go in for sharing around here."

"Nope," Dan had replied. "If I were you, I'd leave it to the captain to do the tradin'. You'll be wanting that in a few hours."

"I'll survive."

"Uh-huh. Well, if I were you, I'd do what I was told and no more. Don't offer, don't volunteer, and don't be givin' away your food."

"It was just a chocolate bar. So what?"

"You'll find out in a minute."

It was actually less than a minute before the green Bostonian was surrounded by shouting children with their hands thrust out. Some of the other villagers came over to see what they might scrounge from the bountiful knapsacks of the foreign giants. The commotion interrupted Captain Aubrey's questioning of the elders, and he came storming at the Bostonian like a monsoon cloud. It was explained to the soldier that he was not to be giving away his food or any other item in his possession, that the elders didn't want gifts because the Cong had been known to slaughter whole villages when they found canned goods, mirrors, or other trinkets. All this had been said with Captain Aubrey's face about two inches from the Bostonian's, and by the time the captain was finished speaking in his voice that could curl a chopper's rotors, the Bostonian's face had gone chalky under his fresh sunburn.

"It was just a piece of candy," the young man had said when Captain Aubrey returned to his business and the children had been scattered away. "It's no big deal."

Dan had looked at the Bostonian's sweat-damp shirt and seen his name printed there in black stencil over the pocket: *Farrow*. "Out here everythin's a big deal," Dan had told him. "Just lay low, do what you're supposed to, and don't go south, you might live for a week or two."

The platoon had left Cho Yat, moving across the flat, gleaming rice paddies toward the dark wall of jungle that lay beyond.

Their patrol had lasted four hours and discovered not so much as the print of a Goodyear-soled sandal.

It was on the way out when the point team had radioed to Captain Aubrey with the message that something was burning in Cho Yat.

Emerging from the jungle with the others, Dan had seen the dark scrawl of smoke in the ugly yellow sky. A harsh, hot wind had washed over him, and in it he'd smelled a sickly-sweet odor like pork barbecue.

He'd known what the odor was. He'd smelled it before, after a flamethrower had done its work on a snake hole. Captain Aubrey had ordered them to double-time it to the village, and Dan had done what he was told because he'd always been a good soldier, the smell of burning flesh swirling around him in the pungent air and his boots slogging through rice-paddy mud.

His eyes opened in the dark.

He peered into the rearview mirror.

Headlights were approaching along the park road.

He stopped breathing. If it was a police car . . . His fingers went to the key in the ignition switch. The headlights came closer. Dan watched them coming, sweat glistening on his face. Then the car stopped about twenty feet away and the lights went out.

His breathing resumed on a ragged note. It was a dark-colored Toyota, not a police car. Dan watched the rearview mirror for a few seconds longer, but he saw no other lights. He sat there waiting. So did the Toyota's driver. Well, he would have to make the first move. He got out and stood beside the station wagon. The driver's door of the Toyota opened, and a woman got out. The courtesy light gave Dan a brief glimpse of the young man who sat in the passenger seat.

"Dan?" If the sound of her voice had been glass, it would have cut his throat.

"It's me," he answered. His palms were wet. His nerves seemed twisted together in the pit of his stomach.

She came toward him. She stopped suddenly, when she could see his face a little better. "You've changed," she said.

"Lost some weight, I guess."

Susan had never been one to shrink from a challenge. She showed him she still had her grit. She continued to walk toward him, toward the man who had suffered midnight rages and deliriums, who had attacked their son in his bed, who had brought some of the hell of that war back with him when the last helicopter left Saigon. Susan stopped again when she was an arm's length away.

"You look good," he told her, and it was the truth. Susan had been on the thin side when they'd divorced, but now she looked fit and healthy. He figured her nerves were a lot steadier without him around. She'd cut her dark brown hair to just above her shoulders, and Dan could tell that there was a lot of gray in it. Her face was still firm-jawed and more attractive than he remembered. More confident, too. There was some pain in her eyes, which were a shade between gray and green. She wore jeans and a short-sleeved pale blue blouse. Susan was still Susan: a minimum of makeup, no flashy jewelry, nothing to announce that she was anything other than a woman who accepted no pretense. "You must be doin' all right," he said.

"I am. We both are."

He looked anxiously toward the park road. Susan said, "I didn't bring the police."

"I believe you."

"I told 'em you called, and that I was afraid to stay at the house. I wouldn't have taken so long, but they had one of their men follow me to the Holiday Inn. He sat out in the parkin' lot for about an hour. Then all of a sudden he raced off, and I thought for sure they'd caught you."

Dan figured the man had gotten a radio call. By now the police must be swarming all over the Hideaway Motor Court.

"I thought you'd be in a pickup truck," Susan said.

"I stopped at a motel outside town and the couple who own the place found out who I was. They tried to get the reward by blastin' me with a shotgun. The woman gut-shot her own husband by accident and then blew out one of the truck's tires. Only way I could get here was by takin' their car."

"Dan—" Susan's voice cracked. "Dan, what're you gonna *do?*"

"I don't know. Keep from gettin' caught, I hope. Maybe find a place where I can rest awhile and think some things through." He offered a grim smile. "This hasn't been one of my best days."

"Why didn't you *tell* me you needed money? Why didn't you tell me you were sick? I would've helped you!"

"We're not man and wife anymore. It's not your problem."

"Oh, that's just great!" Her eyes flashed with anger. "It's not my problem, so you get yourself jammed in a corner and you wind up killin' somebody! You think it's always you against the world, you never would let anybody help you! I could've given you a loan if you'd asked! Didn't you ever think about that?"

"I thought about it," he admitted. "Not very long, though."

"Bullheaded and stubborn! Where'd it get you? Tell me that!"

"Susan?" he said quietly. "It's too late for us to be fightin', don't you think?"

"The stubbornest man in this *world!*" Susan went on, but the anger was leaving her. She put a hand up against her forehead. "Oh Jesus. Oh my God. I don't . . . I can't even believe this is real."

"You ought to see it from where I'm standin'."

"The leukemia. When'd you find out?"

"In January. I figure it had to be the Agent Orange. I knew it was gonna show up in me sooner or later." He started to tell her about the knot in his brain—that, too, he felt had to do with the chemical—but he let it slide. "They ran some tests at the V.A. hospital. Doctors wanted me to stay there, but I'm not gonna lie in a bed and wait to die. At least I could work. When I had a job, I mean."

"I'm sorry," she said. "I swear to God I am."

"Well, it's the hand I got dealt. What happened at that bank was my own damn fault. I went south, Susan. Like we used to say in 'Nam. I screwed up, the second passed and there was no bringin' it back again." He frowned, staring at the pavement between them. "I don't want to spend whatever time I have left in prison. Worse yet, in a prison hospital. So I don't know where I'm goin', but I know I can't go back." He leveled his gaze at her again. "Did you tell Chad my side of it?"

She nodded.

"You took a big chance comin' out here to meet me. I know it's not easy for you, the way I used to be and all. But I couldn't just say a few words to him over the phone and leave it like that. Lettin' me see him is the kindest thing you ever could've done for me."

"He's your son, too," she said. "You've got the right."

"You mind if I sit in the car with him for a few minutes? Just the two of us?"

She motioned toward the Toyota. Dan walked past her, his heart pounding. He opened the driver's side door and looked in at the boy.

Hi, Chad, he meant to say, but he couldn't speak. At seventeen years, Chad was hardly a boy anymore. He was husky and broad-shouldered, as Dan himself used to be. He was so changed from the picture Dan had—the picture left behind at the Hideaway Motor Court—that the sight of him was like a punch to Dan's chest. Chad's face had lost its baby fat and taken on the angles and planes of manhood. His sandy-brown hair was cut short, and the sun had burnished his skin. Dan caught the scent of Aqua Velva; the young man must've shaved before they'd left the motel. Chad wore khaki trousers and a blue-and-red tie-dyed T-shirt, the muscles in his arms defined. Dan figured he did outdoor work, maybe light construction or yardkeeping. He looked fine, and Dan realized this was going to be a lot tougher than he'd thought.

"Do you recognize me?" he asked.

"Kinda," Chad said. He paused, thinking it over. "Kinda not."

Dan eased into the driver's seat, but he left the door ajar to keep the courtesy light on. "It's been a long time."

"Yes sir," Chad said.

"You workin' this summer?"

"Yes sir. Helpin' Mr. McCullough."

"What kind of work?"

"He's got a landscapin' business. Puts in swimmin' pools, too."

"That's good. You helpin' your mom around the house?"

"Yes sir. I keep the grass cut."

Dan nodded. Chad's speech was a little hesitant and there was a dullness in his eyes. Otherwise, there was no outward sign of Chad's mental disability. Their son had been born—as the counselor put it—"learning disabled." Which meant his thinking processes were always going to be labored, and tasks involving intricate detail would be difficult for him. This fact of life had added to the fuel of Dan's anger in those bad years, had made him curse God and strike out at Susan. Now, tempered by time, he thought that the Agent Orange might have afflicted Chad. The poison that had seeped into Dan had dwelled in his sperm for years, like a beast in a basement, and passed from him through Susan into their son. None of what he suspected could be proven in any court of law, but Dan thought it was true as surely as he remembered the oily feel of the dirty silver rain on his skin. Watching Chad try to put his thoughts together was like someone struggling to open a rusted lock. Most times the tumblers fell into place, but Dan remembered that when they didn't, the boy's face became an agony of frustration.

"You've really grown up," Dan said. "I swear, time's a thief."

"Sir?" Chad frowned; the abstract statement had passed him by.

Dan rubbed the bruised knuckles of his right hand. The moment had arrived. "Your mom told you what I did, didn't she?"

"Yes sir. She said the police are after you. That's why they came to the door."

"Right. You'll probably hear a lot of bad things about me. You're gonna hear people say that I'm crazy, that I walked into that bank with a gun, lookin' to kill somebody." Dan was speaking slowly and carefully, and keeping eye contact with his son. "But I wanted to tell you, face-to-face, that it's not true. I did shoot and kill a man, but it was an accident. It happened so fast it was like a bad dream. Now, that doesn't excuse what I did. There's no excuse for such a thing." He paused, not knowing what else to say. "I just wanted you to hear it from me," he added.

Chad looked away from him and worked his hands together. "Did . . . that man you killed . . . did he do somethin' bad to you?"

"I wish I could say he did, but he was just doin' his job."

"You gonna give yourself up?"

"No."

Chad's gaze came back to him. His eyes seemed more focused and intense. "Mom says you can't get away. She says they'll find you sooner or later."

"Well," Dan said, "I'm plannin' on it bein' later."

They sat in silence for a moment, neither one looking at the other. Dan had to say this next thing; he couldn't recall his father—the spit-and-polish major—ever saying it to him, which made saying it doubly difficult and doubly important. "I wasn't such a good father," he began. "I had some things inside me that wouldn't let go. They made me blind and scared. I wasn't strong enough to get help, either. When your mom told me she wanted a divorce, it was the best thing she could've done for all of us." Tears suddenly burned his eyes, and he felt a brick wedged in his throat. "But not one day goes by that I don't think about you, and wonder how you're doin'. I know I should've called, or written you a letter, but . . . I guess I didn't know what to say. Now

I do." He cleared his throat with an effort. "I just wanted you to know I love you very, very much, and I hope you don't think too badly of me."

Chad didn't respond. Dan had said everything he needed to. It was time to go. "You gonna take good care of your mom?"

"Yes sir." Chad's voice was thick.

"Okay." He put his hand on his son's shoulder, and it crossed his mind that he would never do this again. "You hang tough, hear?"

Chad said, "I've got a picture."

"A picture? Of what?"

"You." Chad reached into his back pocket and brought out his wallet. He slid from it a creased photograph. "See?"

Dan took it. The photo, which Dan recalled was snapped at a Sears studio, showed the Lambert family in 1978. Dan—burly and beardless, his face sunburned from some outdoors carpentry job but his eyes deepset and haunted—and Susan were sitting against a paper backdrop of summer mountains, the four-year-old Chad smiling between them. Chad's arms were clutched to their shoulders. Susan, who appeared frail and tired, wore a brave smile. Looking at the picture, Dan realized it was the image of a man who hadn't yet learned that the past was a more implacable enemy than any Viet Cong crouched in a snake hole. He had given his nightmares power over him, had refused to seek help because a man—a good soldier—did not admit weakness. And in the end that war he'd survived had taken everything of worth away from him.

It was the picture, he thought, of a man who'd gone south a long, long time ago.

"You have a picture of me?" Chad asked. Dan shook his head, and Chad took a folded piece of paper from the wallet. "You can have this one if you want it."

Dan unfolded the paper. It was a picture of Chad in a football uniform, the number fifty-nine across his chest. The camera had caught him in a posed lunge, his teeth gritted and his arms reaching for an off-frame opponent.

"I cut it out of last year's annual," Chad explained. "That was the day the whole team got their pictures taken. Coach Pierce said to look mean, so that's what I did."

"You did a good job of it. I wouldn't care to line up against you." He gave his son a smile. "I do want this. Thank you." He refolded the picture and put it in his own pocket, and he returned the Sears studio photograph to Chad. And now, as much as he wished it weren't so, he had to leave.

Chad knew it, too. "You ever comin' back?" he asked.

"No," Dan said. He didn't know quite how to end this. Awkwardly, he offered his hand. "So long."

Chad leaned into him and put his arms around his father's shoulders.

Dan's heart swelled. He hugged his son, and he wished for the impossible: a rolling-back of the years. He wished the dirty silver rain had never fallen on him. He wished Chad had never been contaminated, that things could've been patched up with Susan, and that he'd been strong enough to seek help for the nightmares and flashbacks. He guessed he was wishing for a miracle.

Chad said, up close to his ear, "So long, Dad."

Dan let his son go and got out of the car. His eyes were wet. He wiped them with his forearm as he walked to the station wagon, where Susan waited. He'd almost reached her when he heard a dog barking, a high-pitched *yap yap yap*.

Dan stopped in his tracks. The sound had drifted across the park, its direction hard to pinpoint. It was close enough, though, to instantly set Dan's nerves on edge. Where had it come from? Was somebody walking a dog in the park at *this* hour? Wherever it was, the dog had stopped barking. Dan glanced around, saw nothing but the dark shapes of pine trees that stood in clusters surrounding the parking lot.

"You all right?" Susan looked as if she'd aged five years in the last few minutes.

"Yeah." A tear had trickled down his cheek into his beard. "Thanks for bringin' him."

"Did you think I wouldn't?"

"I didn't know. You took a chance, that's for sure."

"Chad needed to see you as much as you needed to see him." Susan reached into her jeans pocket. "I want you to have this." Her hand emerged with some greenbacks. "I raided the cookie jar before we left the house."

"Put it away," Dan said. "I'm not a charity case."

"This isn't the time to be proud or stupid." She grabbed his hand and slapped the money into it. "I don't know how much cash you've got, but you can use another sixty dollars."

He started to protest, but thought better of it. An extra sixty dollars was, in its own way, a small miracle. "I'll call it a loan."

"Call it whatever you please. Where're you goin' from here?"

"I don't know yet. Maybe I'll head to New Orleans and sign on a freighter. I can still do a day's work."

Susan's face had taken on the grave expression Dan remembered that meant she had something important to say but she was working up to it. "Listen," she said after a moment, "you mentioned findin' a place to rest. I've been seein' a fella for the past year. He works for an oil company, and we've talked about . . . maybe gettin' more serious."

"You mean married serious?" He frowned, not exactly sure how he felt about this bolt from the blue. "Well, you picked a fine time to tell me."

"Just hear me out. He's got a cabin in a fishin' camp, down in the bayou country south of Houma. The camp's called Vermilion. Gary's in Houston, he won't be back till next week."

It took a few seconds for what Susan was saying to get through to him. Before Dan could respond, Susan went on. "Gary's taken Chad and me down there a few weekends. He checks on the oil rigs and we do some fishin'. There's no alarm system. Nothin' much there to steal. The nearest neighbor's a mile or so away."

"Bringin' Chad was enough," Dan told her. "You don't have to—"

"I *want* to," she interrupted. "The cabin's two or three miles past the bridge, up a turnoff on the left. It's on the road that's a straight shot out of Vermilion. Painted gray with a screened-in porch. Wouldn't be hard to get past the screen and break a windowpane."

"What would Gary say about that?"

"I'll explain things. There'll be food in the pantry; you wouldn't have to go out."

Dan grasped the door's handle, but he wasn't yet ready to leave. The police would be out there, hunting him in the night, and he was going to have to be very, very careful. "I could use a day or two of rest. Figure out what to do next." He hesitated. "Is this fella . . . Gary . . . is he good to you?"

"He is. He and Chad get along real well, too."

Dan grunted. It was going to take him some time to digest this news. "Chad needs a father," he said in spite of the pain it caused him. "Somebody who takes him fishin'. Stuff like that."

"I'm sorry," Susan said. "I wish I could do more for you."

"You've done enough. More than enough." He pushed the money into his pocket. "This is my problem, and I'll handle it."

"Stubborn as hell." Her voice had softened. "Always were, always will be."

He opened the station wagon's door. "Well, I guess this is good—"

A flashlight clicked on.

Its dazzling beam hit Dan's eyes and blinded him.

"Freeze, Lambert!" a man's voice ordered.

10

Line of Fire

THE SHOCK PARALYZED DAN. Susan caught her breath with a harsh gasp and spun around to face the intruder.

"Easy, easy," the man behind the flashlight cautioned. He had a whispery, genteel southern accent. "Don't do anythin' foolish, Lambert. I'm armed."

He was standing about twenty feet away. Dan expected to be hit by a second light, and then the policemen would rush in, slam him against the car, and frisk him. He lifted his hands to shield his face from the stabbing white beam. "I'm not packin' a gun."

"That's good." It was a relief to Flint Murtaugh, who had crept up from the edge of the parking lot by keeping the woman's car between himself and the fugitive. He'd been standing there for a couple of minutes in the darkness, listening to their conversation. In his left hand was the flashlight, in his right was a .45 automatic aimed just to Lambert's side. "Put your hands behind your head and lock your fingers."

It's over, Dan thought. He could run, maybe, but he wouldn't get very far. Where were the other policemen, though? Surely there wasn't just the one. He obeyed the command.

Susan was squinting into the light. She'd talked to the policemen in charge of the stakeout on her house and to the one who'd followed her to the Holiday Inn; she hadn't heard this man's voice before. "Don't hurt him," she said. "It was self-defense, he's not a cold-blooded killer."

Flint ignored her. "Lambert, walk toward me. Slowly."

Dan paused. Something was wrong; he could feel it in the silence. Where were the backup policemen? Where were the police cars, the spinning bubble lights and the crackling radios? They should've converged on him by now, if they were even here.

"Come on, move it," Flint said. "Lady, step out of the way."

Lady, Susan thought. The other policemen had addressed her as *Mrs. Lambert.* "Who are you?"

"Flint Murtaugh. Pleased to meet you. Lambert, come on."

"Wait, Dan." Susan stepped in front of him to take the full force of the light. "Show me your badge."

Flint clenched his teeth. His patience was already stretched thin from the hellish drive with Pelvis Eisley and Mama. He was in no mood for complications. Flint had never cared to know the names of all the characters Elvis Presley had played in his wretched movies. Trying to make Eisley cease jabbering about Presley was as futile as trying to make that damn mutt stop gnawing at fleas. Flint was tired and his sharkskin suit was damp with sweat, Clint was agitated by the heat and kept twitching, and it was long past time for a cold shower and a glass of lemon juice.

"I'd like to see your badge," Susan repeated, the man's hesitation fueling her doubt. *Flint Murtaugh,* he'd said. Why hadn't he said *Officer Murtaugh?*

"Listen, I'm not plannin' on a long relationship with you people, so let's cut the chatter." Flint had taken a sidestep so the light hit Lambert's face again. Susan moved to shield her ex-husband once more. "Lady, I told you to step out of the way."

"Do you have a badge, or not?"

Flint's composure was fast unraveling. He wanted Lambert to come to him because he didn't want to have to pass the woman; if she grabbed for the flashlight or the gun, things could get messy. He wished he'd circled around the other side and crept up on Lambert from behind to keep the woman from being between them. It was Eisley's fault, he decided, for screwing up his concentration. Flint had a small spray can of Mace in his inside coat pocket, and he suspected that he might have to use it. "Lady," he replied, "that man standin' there is worth fifteen thousand dollars to me. I've come from Shreveport to find him, and I've had a hard night. You really don't want to get yourself involved in this."

"He's not a policeman," Dan said to Susan. "He's a bounty hunter. You workin' for the bank?"

"Independent contract. Keep your fingers locked, now; let's don't cause anymore trouble."

"You mind if I ask how you found me?"

"Time for that when we're drivin'. Come on, real slow and easy." It had been a lucky break, actually. Flint had driven along Jackson Avenue and had seen the police surveillance teams, one at either end of the block. He'd parked two streets away and sat beside a hedge in someone's yard, watching the house to see what developed. Then the woman had pulled out of her garage, followed by another policeman in an unmarked car, and Flint had decided to tag along at a distance. At the Holiday Inn he'd been on the verge of calling it quits when her watchdog had rushed off, obviously answering a radio summons, but then the woman had emerged again and Flint had smelled an opportunity.

"Don't do it," Susan said before Dan could move. "If he doesn't work for the state of Louisiana, he doesn't have any right to take you in."

"I've got a *gun!*" Flint was about ready to snort steam. "You understand me?"

"I know a gun's not a badge. You're not gonna be shootin' an unarmed man."

"Mom?" Chad called from the car. "You need some help?"

"No! Just stay where you are!" Susan directed her attention at the bounty hunter again. She took two steps toward him.

"Susan!" Dan said. "You'd better keep—"

"*Hush.* Let somebody help you, for God's sake." She advanced another step on Flint. "You're a vulture, aren't you? Swoopin' in on whatever meat you can snatch."

"Lady, you're tryin' to make me forget my manners."

"You ready to shoot a woman, too? You and Dan could share the same cell." She moved forward two more paces, and Flint retreated one. "Dan?" Susan said calmly. "He's not takin' you anywhere. Get in your car and go."

"*No!* No, goddamn it!" Flint shouted. "Lambert, don't you move! I won't kill you, but I'll sure as hell put some hurt on you!"

"He's empty talk, Dan." Susan had decided what needed to be done, and she was getting herself into position to do it. She took one more step toward the bounty hunter. "Go on, get in the car and drive away."

Flint hollered, "No, you don't!" It was time to put Lambert on the ground. Flint jammed the automatic into his waistband and plucked the small red can of Mace from inside his coat. He popped the cap off with his thumb and put his index finger on the nozzle. The concentrated spray had a range of fifteen feet, and Flint realized he was going to have to shove the woman aside to get a clear shot at Lambert. He was so enraged he almost fired a burst into her eyes, but he'd never Maced a woman and he wasn't going to start now. He stalked toward her and was amazed when she stood her ground. "To hell with this!" he snarled, and he jabbed an elbow at her shoulder to drive her out of the line of fire.

But suddenly she was moving.

She was moving very, very fast.

She clamped a wiry hand to his right wrist, stepped into him with her own shoulder, and pivoted, her elbow thunking upward into Flint's chin and rattling his brains. His black wingtips left the pavement. His trapped wrist was turned in on itself, pain shooting up his arm. Somewhere in midair he lost both the flashlight and the Mace. As he went over the woman's hip, one word blazed in Flint's consciousness: *sucker.* Then the ground came up fast and hard and he slammed down on his back with a force that whooshed the breath from his lungs and made stars and comets pinwheel through his skull. Susan stepped back from the fallen man and scooped up the flashlight. "Way to go, Mom!" Chad yelled, leaning out of the Toyota's window.

"Damn" was all Dan could think to say. It had happened so quickly that his hands were still locked behind his head. "How did you—"

"Tae kwon do," Susan said. She wasn't even breathing hard. "I've got a brown belt."

Now Dan understood why Susan hadn't been afraid to meet him. He lowered his hands and walked to her side, where he looked down the flashlight's beam at the bounty hunter's pained and pallid face. A comma of white-streaked hair hung over Flint Murtaugh's sweat-glistening forehead, and he'd curled up on his side and was clutching his right wrist.

Dan saw the automatic and freed it from the man's waistband. "Brown belt or not, that was a damn fool thing to do. You could've gotten yourself killed." He removed the bullet clip, threw it in one direction and the gun in another.

"He had somethin' in his other hand." Susan shone the light around. "I couldn't tell what it was, but I heard him drop it." She steadied the beam on Murtaugh again. "I can't figure out where he came from. I thought I made sure nobody was follow—" She stopped speaking. Then, her voice tight: "Dan. What is *that?*"

He looked. The front of the man's white shirt was twitching, as if his heart were about to beat through his chest. Dan stared at it, transfixed, and then he reached down to touch it.

"Mr. Murtaugh! Mr. Murtaugh, you all right?"

Dan straightened up. Another man was out there in the dark. Both Dan and Susan had the eerie sensation that they recognized the voice's deep, snarly resonance, but neither one of them could place it. A dog began to yap again, and on the pavement Flint gave a muffled half-groan, half-curse.

Susan switched the light off. "You'd better hit it. Gettin' kind of crowded around here."

Dan hurried to the station wagon and Susan followed him, and so neither of them saw the slim, pale third arm push free from Flint Murtaugh's shirt and flail angrily in the air. Dan got behind the wheel, started the engine, and turned on the headlights. Susan reached in and grasped his shoulder. "Good luck," she said over the engine's rumbling.

"Thanks for everythin'."

"I did love you," she told him.

"I know you did." He put his hand over hers and squeezed it. "Take care of Chad."

"I will. And you take care of yourself."

"So long," Dan said, and he put the station wagon in reverse and backed away past the bounty hunter. Flint pulled himself up to his knees, pain stabbing through his lower back and his right wrist surely sprained. Clint's arm was thrashing around, the hand clenched in a fighting fist. Through a dreamlike haze Flint watched the fifteen-thousand-dollar skin twist the station wagon around and drive across the parking lot. Flint tried to summon up a yell, but a hoarse rasp emerged: "Eisley! He's comin' at you!"

In another moment Dan had to stomp on the brake. He feared he must be losing his mind, because right there in front of the station wagon stood a big-bellied, pompadour-haired Elvis Presley, a beat-up black Cadillac behind him blocking the road. Elvis—a credible impersonator for sure—was holding on to a squirming little bulldog. "Where's Mr. Murtaugh?" Elvis shouted in that husky Memphis drawl. "What'cha done to him?"

Dan had seen everything now. He hit the gas pedal again, taking the station wagon up over the curb onto the park's grass. The rear tires fishtailed and threw up clods of earth. Elvis scrambled out of the way, bellowing for Mr. Murtaugh.

Flint had gotten to his feet and was hobbling in the direction of the Cadillac. His left shoe hit something that clattered and rolled away: the can of Mace. "Eisley, stop him!" he hollered as he paused to retrieve the spray can, the bruised muscles of his back stiffening. "Don't let him get—awwwww, *shit!*" He'd seen the station wagon maneuvering around the Caddy, and he watched with helpless fury as it bumped over the curb again onto the road, something underneath the vehicle banging with a noise like a dropped washtub. Then the skin was picking up speed and at the park's entrance turned right with a shriek of flayed rubber onto the street.

"Mr. Murtaugh!" Pelvis cried out with relief as Flint reached him. "Thank the Lord! I thought that killer had done—"

"Shut up and get in the car!" Flint shouted. "Move your fat ass!" Flint flung himself behind the wheel, started the engine, and as he jammed down on the gas pedal Pelvis managed to heave his bulk and Mama into the passenger side. Flint got the Cadillac turned around with a neck-twisting spin in the parking lot, the single headlight's beam grazing past the woman who stood beside her car. He had an instant to see that her son had reached out for her and their hands were clasped. Then Flint, his face a perfect picture of hellacious rage, took the Cadillac roaring out of Basile Park in pursuit.

"I thought sure he'd done killed you!" Pelvis hollered over the hot wind whipping through the car. His frozen pompadour was immobile. Mama had slipped from his grasp and was wildly bounding from backseat to front and back again, her high-pitched barks like hot nails being driven into the base of Flint's skull. Clint's arm was still thrashing, angry as a stomped cobra. Pelvis shouted, "You see that fella try to run me down? If I'd've been a step slower, I'd be lookin' like a big ol' waffle 'bout now! But I foxed him, 'cause when I jigged to one side he jagged to the other and I just kept on jiggin'. You saw it, didn't you? When that fella tried to run me—"

Flint pressed his right fist against Pelvis's lips. Mama seized Flint's sleeve between her teeth, her eyes wide and wet and a guttural growl rumbling in her throat. "I swear to Jesus," Flint seethed, "if you don't shut that mouth I'm puttin' you out right here!"

"It's shut." Pelvis caught Mama and pulled her against him. Reluctantly, she let go of Flint's sleeve. Flint returned both hands to the steering wheel, the speedometer's needle trembling toward sixty. He saw the station wagon's taillights a quarter-mile ahead.

"You want me to shut up," Pelvis said with an air of wounded dignity, "all you have to do is ask me kindly. No need to jump down my throat jus' 'cause I was tellin' you how I stared Death square in the face and—"

"*Eisley.*" Tears of frustration sprang to Flint's eyes, which utterly amazed him; he couldn't remember the last time he'd shed a tear. His nerves were jangling like fire alarms, and he felt a hair away from a rubber room. The speedometer's needle was passing sixty-five, the Cadillac's aged frame starting to shudder. But they were gaining on the station wagon, and in another few seconds they'd be right up on its rear fender.

Dan had the gas pedal pressed to the floor, but he couldn't kick any more power out of the engine. The thing was making an unearthly metallic roar as if on the verge of blowing its cylinders. He saw in his rearview mirror the one-eyed Cadillac speeding up on his tail, and he braced for collision. There was a blinking caution light ahead, marking an intersection. Dan had no time to think about it; he twisted the wheel violently to the left. As the station wagon sluggishly obeyed, its worn tires skidding across the pavement, the Cadillac hit him, a grazing blow from behind, and sparks shot between their crumpled fenders. Then, as Dan fought the wheel to keep from sliding over the curb into somebody's front yard, the Cadillac zoomed past the intersection.

"Hold on!" Flint shouted, his foot jamming the brake pedal. The Eldorado was heavy, and would not slow down without screaming, smoking protest from the tires. Pelvis clung to Mama, who was trying her damnedest to jump into the backseat. Flint reversed to the intersection, the bitter smoke of burned rubber swirling through the windows, and turned left onto a winding street bordered by brick homes with manicured lawns and honest-to-God white picket fences. He sped after Lambert, but there was no sign of the station wagon's taillights. Other streets veered off on either side, and it became clear after a few seconds that Lambert had turned onto one of them.

"I'll find you, you bastard!" Flint said between clenched teeth, and he whipped the car to the right at the next street. It, too, was dark.

"He's done gone," Pelvis said.

"Shut up! Hear me? Just shut your mouth!"

"Statin' a fact," Pelvis said.

Flint took the Cadillac roaring to the next intersection and turned left. His palms were wet on the wheel, sweat clinging to his face. Clint's hand came up and stroked his chin, and Flint cuffed his brother aside. Flint took the next right, the tires squealing. He was in a mazelike residential area, the streets going in all directions. Anger throbbed like drumbeats at his temples, pain lancing his lower back. He tasted panic like cold copper in his mouth. Then he turned right onto another street and his heart kicked.

Three blocks away was a pair of red taillights.

Flint hit the accelerator so hard the Cadillac leapt forward like a scalded dog. He roared up behind Lambert's car, intending to swerve around him and cut him off. But in the next instant Flint's triumph shriveled into terror. The Cadillac's headlight revealed the car was not a rust-eaten old station wagon but a new Chevrolet Caprice. Across its fast-approaching rear end was silver lettering that spelled out ALEXANDRIA POLICE.

Flint stood on the brake pedal. A thousand cries for God, Jesus, and Mother Mary rang like crazy bells in his brain. As the Cadillac's tires left a quarter-inch of black rubber on the pavement, the prowl car's driver punched it and the Caprice shot forward to avoid the crash. The Caddy slewed to one side before it stopped, the engine rattled and died, and the police cruiser's bubble lights started spinning. It backed up, halting a couple of feet from Flint's busted bumper. A spotlight on the driver's side swiveled around and glared into Flint's face like an angry Cyclopean eye.

"Well," Pelvis drawled, "now we've done shit and stepped in it."

Over nearer the intersection with the flashing caution light, Dan started the station wagon's engine and backed out of the driveway he'd pulled into. He eased onto the street, his headlights still off. The black Cadillac had sped past about two minutes before, and Dan had expected it to come flying back at any second. As the saying went, it was time to git while the gittin' was good. He switched on his lights and at the caution signal took a left toward Interstate 49 and the route south. There were no cars ahead of him, nor any in his rearview mirror. But it was going to be a long night, and a long drive yet before he could rest. He breathed a good-bye to Alexandria, and a good riddance to the bounty hunters.

Flint, still stunned by the sudden turn of events, was watching the red and blue lights spin around. "Eisley, you're a jinx," he said hoarsely. "That's what you are. A jinx." Two policemen were getting out of the car. Flint pushed the can of Mace under his seat. Clint's arm resisted him, but he forced it inside his shirt and buttoned his coat. The two officers both had young, rawboned faces, and they didn't appear happy. Before they reached the Cadillac, Flint dug his wallet out and pressed his left arm over his chest to pin Clint down. "Keep your mouth zipped," he told Pelvis. "I'll do all the talkin'."

The policeman who walked up on Flint's side of the car had a fresh crew cut and a jaw that looked as if it could chop wood. He shone a flashlight into Flint's eyes. "You near 'bout broke our necks, you know that? Look what you did to my cap." He held up a crushed and formless thing.

"I'm awful sorry, sir." Flint's voice was a masterpiece of studied remorse. "I'm not from around here, and I'm lost. I guess I panicked, 'cause I couldn't find my way out."

"Uh-huh. You had to be goin' at least sixty. Sign back there says fifteen miles an hour. This is a residential zone."

"I didn't see the sign."

"Well, you seen the *houses*, didn't you? You seen our car in front of you. Seems to me you're either drunk, crazy, or mighty stupid." He shifted the light, and its beam fell upon Pelvis. "Lordy, Walt! Look what we've got here!"

"How you fellas doin'?" Pelvis asked, grinning. In his arms Mama had begun a low, menacing growl.

"I bet this'll be a real interestin' story," the policeman with the light said. "Let's see a driver's license. Your ID, too, Mr. Presley sir."

Flint fumbled to remove the license from his eelskin wallet and hold Clint immobile at the same time. His wrist was still hurting like hell. Eisley produced a battered wallet that had the face of Elvis on it in brightly colored Indian beads. "I never did believe he was dead, did you, Randy?" Walt said with undisguised mirth. He was taller than his partner and not quite as husky. "I always knew it was a wax body in that coffin!"

"Yeah, we might get ourselves on Gerrado Riviera for this," Randy said. "This is better'n seein' green men from Mars, ain't it? Call the tag in." Walt walked around back to write it down and then returned to the cruiser. Randy inspected the licenses under the light. "Flint Murtaugh. From Monroe, huh? What're you doin' here in the middle of the night?"

"Uh . . . well, I'm . . ." Flint's mind went blank. He tried to pull up something, anything. "I'm . . . that is to say . . ."

"Officer, sir?" Pelvis spoke up, and Flint winced. "We're tryin' to find the Holiday Inn. I believe we must've took the wrong turn."

The light settled on Pelvis's face. "The Holiday Inn's over toward the interstate. The sign's lit up; it's hard to miss."

"I reckon we did, though."

Randy spent a moment examining Pelvis's license. Clint gave a twitch under Flint's shirt, and Flint felt sweat dripping from his armpits. "Pelvis Eisley," Randy said. "That can't be your born name."

"No sir, but it's my legal name."

"What's your born name?"

"Uh . . . well, sir, I go by the name that's written down right—"

"Pelvis ain't a name, it's a bone. What name did your mama and daddy give you? Or was you hatched?"

Flint didn't care for the nasty edge in the policeman's voice. "Hey, I don't think there's any call to be—"

"Hush up. I'll come back to you, don't you worry about it. I asked for your born name, sir."

"Cecil," came the quiet reply. "Cecil Eisley."

"Cecil." Randy slurred the name, making it sound like something that had crawled out from under a swamp log. "You dress like that all the time, Cecil?"

"Yes sir," Pelvis answered in all honesty. In his lap Mama continued her low growling.

"Well, you're 'bout the damnedest sight I ever laid eyes on. You mind tellin' me what you're in costume for?"

"Listen, Officer," Flint said. He was terrified Pelvis was going to start blabbering about being a bounty hunter, or about the fact that Lambert was somewhere close by. "I was the one drivin', not him."

"Mr. Murtaugh?" Randy leaned his head nearer, and Flint had the startling thought that he'd seen the policeman's face before, when its thin-lipped mouth was twisted into a cruel grin and the garish midway lights threw shadows into the deep-set eye sockets. "When I want you to speak, I'll ask you a question. Hear me?"

His was the face of a thousand others who had come to the freak show to leer and laugh, to fondle their girlfriends in front of the stage and spit tobacco on Flint's polished shoes. Flint felt a hard nut of disgust in his throat. Clint lurched under his shirt, but luckily Flint had a firm grip and the policeman didn't see. "There's no reason to be rude," Flint said.

Randy laughed, which was probably the worst thing he could've done. It was a humorless, harsh laugh, and it made Flint want to smash it back through the man's teeth. "You want to see rude, you keep on pushin' me. You come flyin' up on my rear end and almost wreck my car, I'm not about to kiss you for it. Now you're real, real close to a night in jail, so you'd best just sit there and keep your mouth shut."

Flint stared sullenly at him, and the policeman glared back. "It's a clean tag," Walt said, returning from the cruiser's radio.

"I'm just about to get the story from Cecil," Randy told him. "Let's hear it."

"Well, sir . . ." Pelvis cleared his throat. Flint waited, his head lowered. "We're on our way to New Orleans. Goin' to a convention there, at the Hyatt Hotel. It's for Elvis interperators like me."

"Now I can retire. I've heard everythin'," Randy said, and Walt laughed.

"Yes sir." Pelvis wore his stupid smile like a badge of honor. "See, the convention kicks off tomorrow."

"If that's so, how come you're lookin' for the Holiday Inn?"

"Well . . . see, we're supposed to meet some other fellas goin' to the convention, too. We're all gonna travel together. I reckon we just missed seein' the sign, and then we got all turned around. You know how it is, bein' in a strange place not knowin' where you are and it so late and everythin'. Couldn't find no phone, and I'm tellin' you we were gettin' mighty scared 'cause these days you gotta be careful where you wind up, all them murders you see on the news every time you turn on the—"

"All right, all right." Randy gasped like a man surfacing for air. He stabbed the light into Flint's eyes again. "You an Elvis 'interperator,' too?"

"No sir, he's my manager," Pelvis said. "We're like two peas in a pod."

Flint felt queasy. Clint's arm jumped and almost got away from him.

"Walt? You got any ideas on what to do with these two? Should we take 'em in?"

"That's the thing to do, seems to me."

"Yeah." The light was still aimed at Flint's face. "Gettin' lost is no excuse for speedin' through a residential area. You could've killed somebody."

"Us, for instance," Walt said.

"Right. You need to spend a night in jail, to get your thinkin' straight."

Great, Flint thought bitterly. When they searched him down before putting him in the cell, they were going to jump out of their jackboots.

" 'Course," Randy went on, "if everybody at the station was to find out we almost got rear-ended by Elvis Presley, we'd be takin' it in the shorts for God only knows how long. So, Mr. Manager Man, you'd best be real glad he's with you, 'cause I don't like your face and if I had my druthers I'd put you smack-dab *under* the jail. Here." The policeman handed him the licenses. For a few seconds Flint was too dumbfounded to take them.

"Mr. Murtaugh, sir?" Pelvis said. "I believe he's lettin' us go."

"With a *major* warnin'," Randy added sternly. "Hold the speed down. Next time you might be goin' to a cemetery instead of a convention."

Flint summoned up his wits and took the licenses. "Thank you," he forced himself to say. "It won't happen again."

"Damn straight it won't. You follow us, we'll take you to the Holiday Inn. But I want Cecil to drive."

"Sir?"

"I want Cecil where you're sittin'," Randy said. "I don't trust you behind my car. Come on, get out and let him take the wheel."

"But . . . it's . . . *my* car," Flint sputtered.

"He's got a valid driver's license. Anyway, the Holiday Inn's not very far. Come on, do like I'm tellin' you."

"No . . . listen . . . I don't let anybody else drive my—"

Pelvis put a hand on Flint's shoulder, and Flint jumped as if he'd received an electric shock. "Mr. Murtaugh? Don't you worry, I'll be real careful."

"Move it," Randy said. "We've got other places to be."

Pelvis put Mama into the backseat and came around to the driver's side. With an effort that bordered on the superhuman, Flint got out and, holding Clint's arm firmly against his chest, eased into the passenger seat. In another moment they were following the police cruiser out of the maze of residential streets, and Pelvis smiled and said, "I never drove me a Cadillac before. You know, Elvis loved Cadillacs. Gave 'em away every chance he got. He seen some people lookin' at a Cadillac in a showroom one time, he pulled out a big wad of cash and bought it for 'em right there on the spot. Yessir." He nodded vigorously. "I believe I could get to like drivin' a Cadillac."

"Is that so?" Flint had broken out in a cold sweat, and he couldn't help but stare at Eisley's fleshy hands guiding the car. "You'd better enjoy it, then, because ten seconds after those hick cops drive off will be the last time you sit behind my steerin' wheel! Do you have a cement block for a brain? I told you to keep your mouth shut and leave the talkin' to me! Now we've gotta go back to that damn Holiday Inn when we could've been on Lambert's ass! I could've talked our way out of trouble if you hadn't opened your big mouth! Jesus Christ! All that crap about an Elvis convention in New Orleans! We're lucky they didn't call the men with the butterfly nets right then and there!"

"Oh, I went to that convention last year," Pelvis said. "At the Hyatt Hotel, just like I said. 'Bout two hundred Elvises showed up, and we had us a high old time."

"This is a nightmare." Flint pressed his fingers against his forehead to see if he was running a fever. Reality, it seemed, had become entangled with delirium. "I'm at home in my bed, and this is the chili peppers I ate on my pizza."

Pelvis wheezed out a laugh. "Nice to know you still got your sense of humor, seein' as how we lost Lambert and all."

"We haven't lost him. Not yet."

"But . . . he's gone. How're we gonna find him again?"

"You're ridin' with a *professional,* Eisley!" Flint said pointedly. "First thing you learn in this business is to keep your eyes and ears open. I got close enough to hear Lambert and his ex-wife talkin'. She was tellin' him about a cabin in a fishin' camp south of Houma. Vermilion, she said the camp was called. I heard her tell him where it is. She said to break a windowpane, and that there'd be food in the pantry. So that might be where he's headed."

"I swanee!" Pelvis gushed. "Mr. Smoates said you was gonna be a good partner!"

"Get that partners shit out of your head!" Flint snapped. "We're not partners! I'm saddled with you for this one skin hunt, and that's all! You've already screwed up big-time, when I told you to keep that mutt quiet back in the park! That damn barkin' almost shot me out of my shoes! Made me so nervous I let him get the drop on me, and that's how he got away!"

"I was meanin' to ask you about that," Pelvis said. "What happened?"

"That damn woman—" Flint paused. No, he thought; being knocked on your ass by a woman was not a thing Smoates needed to hear about. "She distracted me," he said. "Then Lambert charged in before I could use the Mace. He's a Vietnam vet, he put me down with some kind of judo throw."

"Lucky he didn't take your gun and shoot you," Pelvis said. "Him bein' such a crazy killer, I mean."

"Yeah." Flint nodded. "Lucky."

Which led him to a question: why hadn't Lambert used the gun on him when he was lying helpless on the ground? Maybe because he hadn't wanted to commit another murder in front of his ex-wife and son, Flint decided. Whatever the reason, Flint could indeed count himself fortunate to still be alive.

At the Holiday Inn—the same motel where Flint and Pelvis had sat in the parking lot watching the door to Susan Lambert's room—the two Alexandria policemen gave them a further warning about getting the broken headlight repaired, and as soon as the police cruiser had driven away, Flint took the Cadillac's wheel and banished Pelvis and Mama to the rear seat. In another five minutes Flint was back on Interstate 49, heading south again. He kept his speed below sixty-five. There was no point courting trouble from the highway patrol, and if Lambert was going to the fishing camp cabin, he'd still be there by the time Flint found the place. *If* the troopers didn't stop Lambert first, and *if* Lambert hadn't headed off in another direction. But it was a gamble worth taking, just as Flint had gambled on following Lambert's ex-wife.

The way ahead was dark. Houma was down in swamp and Cajun territory. Flint had never heard of Vermilion before, but he'd find it when they got down there. It wasn't an area Flint would've ventured into without a good reason, though. Those swamp dwellers were a rough breed, and best left alone. At least—thank God—Eisley was quiet and Flint could get his thoughts in order.

Something that sounded like a warped buzz saw started whining in the backseat.

Flint looked into the rearview mirror. Pelvis was stretched out and snoring, with Mama's head cradled on his shoulder. The bulldog added to the noise by growling in her sleep.

A thought came to Flint unbidden: *At least he's got somethin' that gives a damn about him.*

Which was more than he could say for himself.

But then, there was always Clint. Good ol' blind and mute Clint, who had ruined his life as surely as if he had been born a leper.

The way ahead was dark. Flint was determined to find Lambert now; this was a matter of honor. He wasn't afraid of anything on this earth, least of all a crazy killer too stupid to shoot a man who was down and defenseless. This was a game to be played out to the last card, winner take all. He was going to drag that skin back to Smoates and show that bastard what being a professional was all about.

Flint thought of the mansion in his dream, the white stone mansion with four chimneys and a huge stained-glass window in front. His home, he believed. The place where his mother and father lived. The rich, refined people who had seen a mass of twitching flesh growing from their baby's chest and, horrified, had given the baby up to the four winds of adoption. His home. It had to be, because he dreamed of it so often. He would find it yet, and he would find that man and woman and show them he was their son, born of refinement into a cold and dirty world. Maybe it lay to the south. Maybe it lay somewhere at the end of this road, and if he'd gone south long before this he would've found it like a hidden treasure, an answer, a shining lamp.

Maybe.

But right now the way ahead was dark.

11

Traveling by Night

F ORTY-SIX MILES SOUTH OF Alexandria, as the sultry nightwind swept in through the station wagon, Dan felt sleep pulling at him.

He was on Highway 167, which paralleled I-49 and twisted through cane-field country. It was all but deserted. Dan had seen no trooper cars since leaving Basile Park, and there'd been no headlights behind him for the last twenty minutes. Houma was still a good seventy miles away, and Vermilion maybe twelve or fifteen miles beyond that. He had to find another roadmap; his last one had been left in his pickup truck. But the fishing camp cabin would be worth the extra miles. He could hide there for a couple of days, get some decent rest, and decide where to go.

His eyelids were heavy, the drone of the tires hypnotic. He'd tried the radio, but it was lifeless. The pain in his skull was building again, and maybe this was the only thing keeping him awake. He needed a cup of coffee, but on this road the few cafes he passed looked to have been closed up since nightfall. After three more miles he came to a crossroads that had a sign pointing east to I-49. He sat there, weighing the risk of trying to find a truck stop on the interstate. It won out over the chance of nodding off at the wheel and running into a ditch.

The interstate was a dangerous place, because the troopers prowled there. At this time of the morning, though—nearing three o'clock—the truck drivers in their big, snorting rigs were masters of the four-lane. Dan passed a sign that said Lafayette— "the heart of Acadiana"—was thirty miles ahead. Five miles later he saw green neon that announced CAJUN COUNTRY TRUCK STOP 24 HOURS and he took the next exit. The truck stop was a gray cinder-block building, not much to look at, but he could see a waitress at work through the restaurant's plate-glass window. A tractor-trailer truck was parked at the diesel pumps, its tank being filled by an attendant. In front of the restaurant was a red Camaro with a Texas vanity plate that proclaimed its owner to be AN A1 STUD. Dan drove around back and parked next to two other cars, an old brown Bonneville and a dark blue Mazda, both with Louisiana plates, that probably belonged to the employees. He felt light-headed with weariness as he trudged into the restaurant, which had a long counter and stools and a row of red vinyl booths.

"How you be doin'?" the waitress asked from behind the counter in thick Cajun dialect. "Goan set you'self anywhere." She was a heavyset blond woman, maybe in her mid-forties, and she wore a red-checked apron over a white uniform. She returned to her conversation with a gray-haired gent in overalls who sat at the counter nursing a cup of coffee and a glazed doughnut.

Dan chose a booth beside the window so he had full view of the parking lot. Sitting three booths in front of him were a young man and woman. Her back was to Dan, her wavy shoulder-length hair the color of summer wheat. The young man, who Dan figured was twenty-seven or twenty-eight, wore his dark brown hair pulled back into a ponytail, and he had a sallow, long-jawed face and deepset ebony eyes that fixed Dan with a hard stare over his companion's shoulder. Dan nodded toward him, and the young man blinked sullenly and looked away.

The waitress came with a menu. Her name tag read DONNA LEE. "Just a cup of coffee," Dan told her. "As strong as you can make it."

"Hon, I can make it jump out the cup and two-step," she promised, and she left him to go back through a swinging door to the kitchen.

Dan took off his baseball cap and ran a hand over his forehead to collect the sheen that had gathered there. Fans were turning at the ceiling, their cool breezes welcome on his skin. He leaned against the backrest and closed his eyes. But he couldn't keep them shut because the death of Emory Blanchard was still repeating itself in the haunted house of his mind. He rubbed his stiff shoulder and then reached back to massage his neck. He'd escaped two tight squeezes since midnight, but if a state trooper car pulled up right then, he didn't know if he would have the energy to get up from his seat.

"You know what I think? I think the whole thing's a pile of shit!" It was the young man in the booth, talking to the woman. His voice dripped venom. "I thought you said I was gonna make some money out of this!"

"I said I'd pay you." Her voice was smoky and careful. "Keep it down, all right?"

"No, it ain't all right! I don't know why the hell I said I'd do this! It's a bunch of lies is what it is!"

"It's not lies. Don't worry, you'll get your money."

The young man looked as if he were about to spit something back at her, but his piercing gaze suddenly shifted, locking onto Dan. "Hey! What're you starin' at?"

"I'm just waitin' for a cup of coffee."

"Well look somewhere else while you do it!"

"Fine with me." Dan averted his eyes, but not before he'd noted that the young man wore a black T-shirt imprinted with yellow skulls and the legend HANOI JANES. The woman got him to quiet down a little, but he was still mouthing off about money. He kept cutting his eyes at Dan. Lookin' for trouble, Dan thought. Pissed off about something and ready to pick a fight.

The waitress brought his coffee. Donna Lee had been right; this java had legs. "Keep the pot warm, will you?" Dan suggested as he sipped the high octane. She answered, "Goan do it," and walked behind the cash register to take the gray-haired man's money. "See you next run-through," she told him, and Dan watched him walk out to his tractor-trailer rig at the diesel pumps.

"Made a fool of me is what you did!" the young man started up again. "Come all this way to find a fuckin' fairy tale!"

"Joey, come on. Calm down, all right?"

"You think I'm supposed to be *happy?* Drive all this way, and then you gimme this big load of shit and ask me to calm down?" His voice was getting louder and harsher, and suddenly he reached out across the table and seized his companion's wrist. "You played me for a fuckin' fool, didn't you?"

"Ease up there, friend!" Donna Lee cautioned from behind the counter.

"I ain't talkin' to you!" Joey snapped. "So just shut up!"

"Hey, listen here!" She strode toward their booth on her chunky legs, her cheeks reddening. "You can get your sassy tail gone, I won't cry."

"It's okay," the young woman said, and Dan saw her pug-nosed profile as she glanced to the left at Donna Lee. "We're just talkin'."

"Talks kinda rough, don't he?"

"Gimme the damn check, how 'bout it?" Joey said.

"Pleased to." Donna Lee pulled the checkpad and a pencil from a pocket of her apron and totaled up their order. "Hon, you need any help?"

"No." She'd worked her wrist free and was rubbing where his fingers had been. "Thanks anyhow."

Dan happened to catch Joey's glare again for a split second, and the young man said, "God *damn!*" and stood up from the booth. His cowboy boots clacked on the linoleum, approaching Dan. "Joey, don't!" the young woman called, but then Joey was sliding into the seat across from him.

Dan drank down the rest of his coffee, paying him no attention. Inside, he was steeling himself for the encounter. "I thought I told you to quit starin' at me," Joey said with quiet menace.

Dan lifted his gaze to meet Joey's. The young man's eyes were red-rimmed, his gaunt face strained by whatever inner demons were torturing him. A little tarnished silver skeleton hung from the lobe of his left ear. Dan had met his kind before: a walking hair-trigger, always a hot flash away from explosion. Dan said calmly, "I don't want any trouble."

"Oh, I think you're askin' for a whole truckload of it, old man."

Dan was in no shape to be fighting, but damned if he'd take this kind of disrespect. If he was going down, he was going down swinging. "I'd like to be left alone."

"I'll leave you alone. After I take you out in the parkin' lot and beat the shit outta—" Joey didn't finish his threat, because Dan's right hand shot out, grasped the silver skeleton, and tore it from his earlobe. As Joey shouted with pain, Dan caught a left handful of T-shirt and jerked the young man's chest hard against the table's edge. Dan leaned forward, their faces almost touching. "You need some manners knocked into you, boy. Now, I'd suggest that you stand up and walk out of here, get in your car, and go wherever you're goin'. If you don't want to do that, I'd be glad to separate you from your teeth."

A drop of blood was welling from Joey's ripped earlobe. He sneered and started to fire another taunt into Dan's face, which might have cost the young punk at least a broken nose.

Whack!

Something had just slammed onto the tabletop.

Dan turned his head and looked at a baseball bat that had eight or nine wicked nails stuck through it.

"Pay attention," Donna Lee said. She was speaking to Joey, who had abruptly become an excellent listener. "You goan stand up, pay your check, leave me two dollars tip, and haul ass out my sight. Mister, let him loose."

Dan did. Joey stood up, his nervous gaze on the brainbuster. Donna Lee stepped back and then followed him to the cash register. "Get you 'nother cup in a minute," she told Dan.

"Sorry. He gets like that sometimes."

It was the young woman, standing next to his booth. Dan looked up at her, said, "No harm d—" and then he stopped because of her face.

The left side of it, the side he'd seen in profile, was very pretty. Across the bridge of her pug nose was a scatter of freckles. Her mouth had the lush lips lonely men kissed in their dreams, and her blond hair was thick and beautiful. Her eyes were soft blue, the blue of a cool mountain lake.

But the right side of her face was another story, and not a kind one.

It was covered by a huge purplish-red birthmark that began up in her hair and continued all the way down onto her throat. The mark had ragged edges like the coast on a map of some strange and unexplored territory. Because the left side of her face was so achingly perfect, the right side was that much harder to look at. "Done," Dan finished, his gaze following the maroon inlets and coves. Then he met her eyes, and he recognized in them the same kind of deep, soul-anchored pain he'd seen in his own mirror.

The instant of an inner glimpse passed. She glanced at his empty coffee cup. "You'd better get somethin' to eat, mister," she said in that voice like velvet and smoke. "You don't look so hot."

"Been a rough day." Dan noted that she wore no makeup and her clothes were simple: a violet floral-patterned short-sleeve blouse and a pair of lived-in blue jeans. She carried a small chestnut-colored purse, its strap around her left shoulder. She was a slim girl, not a whole lot of meat on her bones, and she had that wiry, hardscrabble Texas look. Maybe she stood five-two, if that. Dan tried to envision her without the birthmark; lacking it, she might resemble the kind of fresh-faced girl-next-door in magazine ads. With it, though, she was traveling by night in the company of Joey the punk.

"Arden!" His money had been slapped down beside the cash register. "You comin' or not?"

"I am." She started to walk away, but Dan said, "Hey, you think he wants this?" and he offered her the silver skeleton. "Reckon he does," she answered as she took it from his palm.

"Fuck it, I'm goin'!" Joey shouted, and he stormed through the front door.

"He's got a mouth on him," Dan told the girl.

"Yeah, he does get a little profane now and again. Sorry for the trouble."

"No apology needed."

She followed Joey, taking long strides with her dusty brown boots, and Donna Lee said to her, "Honey, don't you suffer no shit, hear?" After the girl was gone, Donna Lee brought the coffeepot over to Dan and refilled his cup. "I hate a bastard think he can stomp on a woman," she confided. "Remind me of my ex-husband. Didn't have a pot to pee in the way he laid 'round all day, and he had that mean mouth, too. You travelin' far?"

"A distance," Dan said.

"Where to?"

Dan watched her set the coffeepot down on his table, a sure sign she wanted to stick around and talk. "South," he decided to say.

"Such a shame, huh?"

"What is?"

"That girl. You know. Her face. Never seen a birthmark so bad before. No tellin' what that do to a person."

Dan nodded and tasted his fresh cup.

"Listen," Donna Lee continued, "you don't mind me bein' so personal, you don't look to be feelin' well. You up to drivin'?"

"I'm all right." He felt, however, as if he had the strength of a wrung-out dishrag.

"How 'bout a piece of strawberry pie? On the house?"

He was about to say that sounded fine, when Donna Lee's eyes suddenly flicked up from him and she stared out the window. "Uh-oh. Looky there, he's at it again!"

Dan turned his head and saw Joey the punk and the girl named Arden arguing beside the red Camaro. She must've said something that made his hair-trigger flare, because he lifted his arm as if to strike her a backhanded blow and she retreated a few steps. His face was contorted with anger, and now Dan and Donna Lee could hear his shouting through the glass. "I swear to gumbo," Donna Lee said resignedly, "I knew when I stuck eye on him he was gonna be trouble. Lemme go get my slugger." She went behind the counter, where she'd stashed the nail-studded baseball bat.

Outside, Joey had stopped short of attacking the girl. Dan watched him throw open the Camaro's trunk and toss a battered brown suitcase onto the pavement. Its latches popped, the suitcase spilling clothes in a multicolored spiral. A small pink drawstring bag fell out, and Joey attacked it with relish. He charged it and gave it a vicious kick, and Arden scooped it up and backed away, holding it protectively against her chest, her mouth crimped with bitterness.

"You get on outta here!" Donna Lee yelled from the door, her slugger ready for action. Two attendants from the gas station were coming over to see what the ruckus was about, and they looked like fellows who could chew Joey up at least as well as the slugger could. "Go on, 'fore I call the law!"

"Kiss my ass, you old bitch!" Joey hollered back, but he'd seen the two men coming and he started moving faster. He banged the trunk shut and climbed into the car. "Arden, I'm quits with you! Hear me?"

"Go on, then! Here, take it and go on!" She had some money in her fist, and she flung the bills at him through the Camaro's window. The engine boomed. Joey shouted something else at her, but it was drowned by the engine's noise. Then he threw the Camaro into reverse, spun the car around in a half circle facing the way out, and laid on the horn at the same time as he hit the accelerator. The wide rear tires shrieked and smoked, and when they bit pavement they left black teethmarks. As the Camaro roared forward, the two gas station attendants had to jump for their lives. Dan watched through the window as the studmobile tore off across the parking lot and in three eyeblinks it had dwindled to the size of its red taillights. The car headed for the I-49 northbound ramp, and very soon it was lost from sight.

Dan took a drink of coffee and watched the girl.

She didn't cry, which is what he'd expected. Her expression was grim but resolute as she opened her purse and put the pink drawstring bag into it, and then she began to pick up her scattered items of clothing and return them to the suitcase. Donna Lee had a few words with the gas station boys, the nail-pierced slugger held at her side. Arden kept glancing in the direction the Camaro had gone as she retrieved her belongings. Donna Lee helped her round up the last few items, and then the girl snapped her suitcase shut and stood there with her birthmarked face aimed toward the northern dark. The two attendants returned to their building, Donna Lee came back into the restaurant and put the slugger away behind the counter, but Arden stood alone in the parking lot.

"She okay?" Dan asked.

"Say he'll be back," Donna Lee told him. "Say he got a bad temper and sometime it make him get crazy, but after a few minute he come to his sense."

"Takes all kinds, I guess."

"Yes, it do. I swear I would've brained him if I'd got close enough to swing. Knocked some that meanness out his ears." Donna Lee walked over to Dan's booth and motioned with a lift of her chin. "Look at her out there. Hell, if a man treat me that way, I swanee I wouldn't stand 'round waitin' on him. Would you?"

"No, I sure wouldn't."

Donna Lee gave him a smile of approval. "I'm gonna get you that strawberry pie, on the house. That suit you?"

"Sounds fine."

"You got it, then!"

The pie was mostly sugary meringue, but the strawberries were fresh. Dan was about halfway through it when Arden came back into the restaurant, lugging her suitcase. "Awful warm out there," she said. "Mind if I sit and wait?"

"'Course you can, hon! Sit down and rest you'self!" Donna Lee had found a stray to mother, it seemed, and she hurriedly poured a glass of iced tea and took it to Arden who chose a booth near the door. Donna Lee sat down across from her, willing to lend an ear to the girl's plight and Dan couldn't help but overhear since they were sitting just a couple of booths away. No, Joey wasn't her husband, Arden told Donna Lee. Wasn't even really her boy-friend, though they'd gone out together a few times. They lived in the same apartment complex in Fort Worth, and they'd been on their way to Lafayette. Joey played bass guitar in a band called the Hanoi Janes, and Arden had worked the sound board and lights for them on weekends. Mostly fraternity parties and such. Joey was so high-strung because he had an artistic temperament, Arden said. He threw a fit every once in a while, to let off steam, and this wasn't the first time he'd ditched her on the roadside. But he'd be back. He always came back.

Dan looked out the window. Just dark out there, and nothing else.

"Hon, I wouldn't wait for him, myself," Donna Lee said. "I'd just as soon take the bus back home."

"He'll be here. He'll get about ten miles up the road, then he'll cool off."

"Ain't no kinda man throw a girl out his car to take her chance. I'd go on home and tell that sucker to kiss my Dixie cup. You got business in Lafayette?"

"Yeah, I do."

"Family live there?"

"No," Arden said. "I'm goin' to meet somebody."

"That's where I'd go, then. I wouldn't trust no fella threw me out the car. Next time he might throw you out where there's not a soul to help you."

"Joey'll be back." Arden kept watching through the window. "Any minute now."

"Damned if I'd be waitin' here for him. Hey, friend!"

Dan turned his head.

"You goin' south, aren't you? Gotta go through Lafayette. You want to give this young lady a ride?"

"Sorry," Dan answered. "I'm not carryin' passengers."

"Thanks anyway," Arden said to Donna Lee, "but I wouldn't ride with a stranger."

"Well, I'll tell you somethin' 'bout Donna Lee Boudreax. I've worked here goin' on nine year, I've seen a lot of folk come and go, and I've got to where I can read 'em real good. I knew your friend was trouble first sight, and if I say that fella over there's a gentleman, you can write it in the book. Friend, you wouldn't harm this young lady, would you?"

"No," Dan said, "but if I was her father I sure wouldn't want her ridin' with a stranger in the middle of the night."

"See there?" Donna Lee lifted her penciled-on eyebrows. "He's a gentleman. You want to go to Lafayette, you'd be safe with him."

"I'd better stay here and wait," Arden insisted. "Joey'd really blow up if he came back and found me gone."

"Hell, girl, do he *own* you? I wouldn't give him the satisfaction of findin' me waitin'."

Dan took the last bite of his pie. It was time to get moving again, before this booth got too comfortable. He put his baseball cap back on and stood up. "How much do I owe you?"

"Not a thing, if you'll help this young lady out."

He looked out the window. Still no sign of a Camaro's headlights. "Listen, I'd like to, but I can't. I've got to get on down the road."

"Road goes south," Donna Lee said. "Both of you headin' that way. Ain't no skin off your snout, is it?"

"I think she's old enough to make up her own mind." Dan saw that Arden was still staring out at the dark highway. He felt a pang of sadness for her. If the right side of her face were as pretty as the left, she sure wouldn't have to be waiting for a punk who cursed her and left her to fend for herself. But he had enough problems without taking on another one. He put two dollars down on the table for the coffee, said "Thanks for the pie," and he started for the door.

"Speak up, hon," Donna Lee urged. "Train's pullin' out."

But Arden remained silent. Dan walked out of the restaurant into humidity that steamed the sweat from his pores before he'd even reached the station wagon. He drove over to the self-serve pumps, where he intended to top off the tank. He needed another roadmap as well, and when the gas stopped flowing he went into the office, bought a Louisiana map, and paid what he owed for the fill-up.

He was standing under the lights, searching the map south of Houma for a place called Vermilion, when he heard the sound of boots coming up behind him. He looked around and there she stood, suitcase in hand, her birthmark dark purple in the fluorescent glow.

"I don't think he's comin' back this time," she said. "You got room?"

"I thought you said you wouldn't ride with a stranger."

"Everybody's a stranger when you're a long way from home. I don't want to wait around here anymore. If you give me a ride, I'll pay you ten dollars."

"Sorry." Dan folded the map and got behind the steering wheel.

"It's a birthmark, not leprosy," Arden said with some grit in her voice. "You won't catch it."

Dan paused with his hand on the ignition. "A southbound trucker ought to be along pretty soon. You can hitch a ride with him."

"If I wait for a trucker, no tellin' what might turn up. You look too damn tired to try anythin', and even if you did, I believe I could outrun you."

He couldn't argue with her logic. Even with all that caffeine in his system, he still felt as weak as a whipped pup, his joints ached like bad teeth, and a glance into the rearview mirror had shown him a pasty-white face with what looked like dark bruises under his eyes. In truth, he was just about used up. The girl was waiting for his answer. Lafayette was about twenty-five miles. Maybe it would be good to have somebody along to keep him awake, and then he could find a place to rest until nightfall.

"Climb in," he said.

Arden hefted her suitcase into the rear seat. "Got a lot of glass back here."

"Yeah. Window was broken, I haven't had a chance to clean it out."

She took the passenger seat. Dan started the engine and followed the ramp to I-49 southbound. The truck stop fell behind, and in a couple of minutes the glow of green neon was gone. Arden looked back only once, then she stared straight ahead as if she'd decided that where she was going was more important than where she'd been.

Dan imagined that her birthmark would bleach white if she knew who she was riding with. Donna Lee would've taken the slugger to him rather than put this girl in his care. Dan kept his speed at fifty-five, the engine laboring. State troopers were lurking somewhere on the interstate; maybe waiting around the next curve, looking for a stolen station wagon with a killer worth fifteen thousand dollars behind the wheel.

He never had put much faith in prayer.

Right now, with the dark pressing all around, his strength tattering away, and his future a question mark, a silent prayer seemed to be the only shield at hand.

12

Jupiter

THE FIRST LIGHTS OF Lafayette were ahead. Dan said, "We're almost there. Where do you need to go?"

Arden had been quiet during the drive, her eyes closed and her head tilted to one side. Now she sat up straight and took her bearings. She opened her purse, unfolded a piece of paper, and strained to read by the highway lights what was written there. "Turn off on Darcy Avenue. Then you'll go two miles east and turn right on Planters Road."

"What are you lookin' for? Somebody's house?"

"The Twin Oaks nursin' home."

Dan glanced quickly at her. "A *nursin'* home? That's why you came all the way from Fort Worth?"

"That's right."

"You have a relative livin' there?"

"No, just somebody I have to see."

Must be somebody mighty important, Dan thought. Well, it wasn't his business. He took the turn onto Darcy Avenue and drove east along a wide thoroughfare lined with fast-food joints, strip malls, and restaurants with names like King Crawdaddy and

Whistlin' Willie's Cajun Hut. Everything was closed but an occasional gas station, and only a couple of other cars passed by. Dan turned right on Planters Road, which ran past apartment complexes and various small businesses. "How far is it from here?"

"Not far."

His curiosity about the nursing home was starting to get the best of him. If she hadn't come the distance from Fort Worth on account of a relative, then who was it she needed to see? He had his own problems, for sure, but the situation intrigued him. "Mind if I ask who you're goin' to visit?"

"Somebody I used to know, growin' up."

"This person know you're comin'?"

"No."

"You think quarter to four in the mornin' is a good time to visit somebody in a rest home?"

"Jupiter always liked early mornin'. If he's not up yet, I'll wait."

"Jupiter?" Dan asked.

"That's his name. Jupiter Krenshaw." Arden stared at him. "How come you've taken such an interest?"

"No special reason. I guess I just wanted to know."

"All right, I reckon that's only fair. I used to know Jupiter when I was fifteen, sixteen years old. He worked on the farm where I was livin'. Groomed the horses. He used to tell me stories. Things about his growin' up, down in the bayou. Some of 'em made-up stories, some of 'em true. I haven't seen him for ten years, but I remember those stories. I tracked down his nearest relative, and I found out Jupiter was in the nursin' home." She watched Planters Road unreel in the headlights. "There's somethin' I need to talk to him about. Somethin' that's very, very important to me."

"Must be," Dan commented. "I mean, you came a long way to see him."

She was silent for a moment, the warm wind blowing in around them. "You ever hear of somebody called the Bright Girl?"

Dan shook his head. "No, can't say I have. Who is she?"

"I think that might be it," Arden said, lifting her chin to indicate a low-slung brick building on the right. In another moment Dan could see the small, tastefully lit sign that announced it was indeed the Twin Oaks Retirement Home. The place was across from a strip mall, but it didn't look too bad; it had a lot of windows, a long porch with white wicker furniture, and two huge oak trees stood on either side of the entrance. Dan pulled up to the front, where there was a wheelchair ramp and steps carpeted with Astroturf. "Okay," he said. "This is your stop."

She didn't get out. "Can I ask a favor of you?"

"You can ask."

"How much of a hurry are you in?"

"I'm not hurryin', but I'm not dawdlin', either."

"Do you have time to wait for me? It shouldn't take too long, and I sure would appreciate a lift to a motel."

He thought about it, his hands on the wheel. A motel room was what he needed, too; he was just too tired to make it the rest of the way to Vermilion. He'd found the fishing camp on the roadmap: a speck on Highway 57 about fifteen miles south of Houma, near where the pavement ended in the huge bayou swamp of Terrebonne Parish. "I'll wait," he decided.

"Thanks." She leveled her gaze at him. "I'm gonna leave my suitcase. You won't run off soon as I walk in the door, will you?"

"No, I'll stick." And maybe catch some sleep while he waited, he thought.

"Okay." She nodded; he seemed trustworthy, and she counted herself lucky that she'd met him. "I don't even know your name."

"Dan," he said.

"I'm Arden Halliday." She offered her hand, and Dan shook it. "I appreciate you helpin' me like this. Hope I didn't take you too far out of your way."

He shrugged. "I'm headed down south of Houma anyhow." Instantly he regretted telling her that, because if she happened to find out who he was, that information would go straight to the police. He was so tired, he was forgetting a slip of the lip could lead him to prison.

"I won't be long," she promised, and she got out and walked up the steps, entering the building through a door with etched-glass panels.

It occurred to him that the smart thing to do might be to set her suitcase on the porch and hit the accelerator, but he dismissed the idea. Weariness was creeping through his bones, his eyes heavy-lidded. He was going to ask her to get behind the wheel when she was finished inside. He cut the engine and folded his arms across his chest. His eyes closed, and he listened to the soft humming of insects in the steamy night.

"Mister?"

Dan opened his eyes and sat bolt upright. A man was standing beside his window, peering in. Dan had an instant of cold terror because the man wore a cap and uniform with a badge at his breast pocket.

"Mister?" the policeman said again. "You can't park here."

"Sir?" It was all Dan could get out.

"Can't park here, right in front of the door. It's against the fire code."

Dan blinked, his vision blurred. But he could make out that the face was young enough to have acne eruptions, and on the badge was stamped TWIN OAKS SECURITY.

"You can park 'round the side there," the security guard said. "If you don't mind, I mean."

"No. No, I don't mind." He almost laughed; a lanky kid who was probably all of nineteen had just about scared his hair white. "I'll move it." He reached down to restart the engine, and at that moment Arden came out of the building and down the steps.

"Any problem?" she asked when she saw the security guard, and the kid looked at her and started to answer, but then his eyes got fixed on the birthmark and his voice failed him.

"I was about to move the car," Dan explained. "Fire code. You finished already?"

"No. Lady at the front desk says Jupiter usually wakes up around five. I told her he'd want to see me, but she won't get him up any earlier. That's about another hour."

Dan rubbed his eyes. An hour wasn't going to make much difference one way or another, he figured. "Okay. I'll park the car and try to get some sleep."

"Well, there's a waitin' area inside. Got a sofa you might stretch out on, and it's sure a lot cooler in there." Arden suddenly looked into the security guard's face. "You want to tell me what you're starin' at?"

"Uh . . . uh . . ." the kid stammered.

Arden stepped toward him, her chin uplifted in defiance. "It's called a port-wine stain," she said. "I was born wearin' it. Go on and take a good long look, just satisfy the hell out of yourself. You want to touch it?"

"No ma'am," he answered, taking a quick backward step. "I mean . . . no thank you, ma'am."

Arden continued to lock his gaze with her own, but she'd decided he meant no disrespect. Her voice was calmer when she spoke again. "I guess I wouldn't want to touch it, either, if I didn't have to." She returned her attention to Dan, who could see the anger fading from her eyes like the last embers of a wind-whipped fire. "Probably be more comfortable inside."

"Yeah, I guess so." He figured he could've slept in a cement mixer, but the sofa would be kinder to his bones. He fired up the engine, which sounded as rugged as he felt. "I'll pull around to the side and come on in." The security guard moved away and Dan parked the station wagon in a small lot next to the Twin Oaks. It was a tribulation to walk the distance back to the front door. Inside, though, the air-conditioning was a breath from heaven. A thin, middle-aged woman with a hairdo like a double-dip of vanilla ice cream sat behind a reception desk, her lips pursed as she absorbed the contents of a paperback romance. Arden was sitting nearby in a waiting area that held a number of overstuffed chairs, brass reading lamps, and a magazine rack, and there was the full-length sofa as pretty as a vision of the Promised Land.

Dan eased himself down, took off his shoes, and stretched out. Arden had a dog-eared *National Geographic* in her lap, but she looked needful of some sleep, too. The place was quiet, the corridors only dimly lit. From somewhere came the sound of a low, muffled coughing. Dan had the thought that no policeman in Louisiana would think to look for him at a Lafayette nursing home. Then his mind and body relaxed, as much as was possible, and he slept a dreamless sleep.

Voices brought him back to the land of the living.

"Ma'am? I believe Mr. Krenshaw's awake by now. Can I tell him who you are?"

"Just tell him Arden. He'll know."

"Yes ma'am." There was the sound of rubber-soled shoes squeaking on the linoleum.

Dan opened his eyes and looked out the nearest window. Violet light was showing at the horizon. Nearing six o'clock, he figured. His mouth was as dry as a dust bowl. He saw a water fountain a few steps away, and he summoned his strength and sat up, his joints as stiff as rusty hinges. The girl was still sitting in the chair, her face turned toward a corridor that went off past the reception desk. She'd opened her purse, Dan noted, and she had removed the small pink drawstring bag from it. The bag was in her lap, both her hands clutched together around it in an attitude that struck Dan as being either of protection or prayer. As he stood up to walk to the water fountain, he saw her pull the drawstring tight and push it into her purse again. Then she rose to her feet as well, because someone was coming along the corridor.

There were two people, one standing and one sitting. A brown-haired woman in a white uniform was pushing a wheelchair, her shoes squeaking with every step, and in the wheelchair sat a frail-looking black man wearing a red-checked robe and slippers with yellow-and-green argyle socks. Dan took a drink of water and watched Arden walk forward to meet the man she'd come so far to see.

Jupiter was seventy-eight years old now, his face was a cracked riverbed of wrinkles, and his white hair had dwindled to a few remaining tufts. Arden was sure she'd changed just as much, but he would have to be blind not to know her, and the stroke he'd suffered two years before had not robbed him of his eyes. They were ashine, and their excitement jumped into Arden like an electric spark. His nephew had told Arden about the stroke, which had happened just five months after the death of Jupiter's wife, and so Arden had been prepared for the palsy of his head and hands and the severe downturn of the right side of his mouth. Still, it was hard because she remembered how he used to be, and ten years could do a lot of damage. She took the few last steps to meet him, grasped one of his palsied hands as he reached up for her, and with an effort he opened his mouth to speak.

"Miz Arden," he said. His voice was like a gasp, almost painful to hear. "Done growed up."

She gave him the best smile she had. "Hello, Jupiter. How're they treatin' you?"

"Like I'm worn out. Which I *ain't*. Gone be back to work again soon as I get on my feet." He shook his head with wonder, his hand still gripping Arden's. "My, my! You have surely become a young lady! Doreen would be so proud to see you!"

"I heard what happened. I'm sorry."

"I was awful down at first. Awful down. But Doreen's the pride of the angels now, and I'm happy for her. Gone get on my feet again. Louis thinks I'm worn out can't do a thing for m'self." He snorted. "I said you gimme the money they chargin' you, I'll show you how a man can pull hisself up. I ain't through, no ma'am." Jupiter's rheumy eyes slid toward Dan. "Who is that there? I can't—" He caught his breath. "Lord have mercy! Is that . . . is that Mr. Richards?"

"That's the man who brought me—"

"Mr. *Richards!*" The old man let go of Arden and wheeled himself toward Dan before the nurse could stop him. Dan stepped back, but the wheelchair was suddenly right there in front of him and the old man's crooked mouth was split by an ecstatic grin. "You come to see me, too?"

"Uh . . . I think you've got me mixed up with some—"

"Don't you worry, now I *know* I'm gone get up out this thing! My, my, this is a happy day! Mr. Richards, you still got that horse eats oranges skin and all? I was thinkin' 'bout that horse th'other day. Name right on the tip of my tongue, right there it was but I couldn't spit it out. What was that horse's name?"

"Jupiter?" Arden said quietly, coming up behind him. She put a hand on one of his thin shoulders. "That's not Mr. Richards."

"Well, sure it is! Right here he is, flesh and bone! I may be down, but I ain't out! Mr. Richards, what was the name of that horse eats oranges skin and all?"

Dan looked into Arden's face, seeking help. It was obvious the old man had decided he was someone else, and to him the matter was settled. Arden said, "I think the horse's name was Fortune."

"Fortune! That's it!" Jupiter nodded, his eyes fixed on Dan. "You still got that ol' wicked horse?"

"I'm not who you—" But Dan paused before he went any further. There seemed to be no point in it. "Yeah," he said. "I guess I do."

"I'll teach him some manners! God may make the horse, but I'm the one takes off the rough edges, ain't that right, Miz Arden?"

"That's right," she said.

Jupiter grunted, satisfied with the answer. He turned his attention away from Dan and stared out the window. "Sun's comin' up directly. Be dry and hot. Horses need extra water today, can't work 'em too hard."

Arden motioned the nurse aside for a moment and spoke to her, and the nurse nodded agreement and withdrew to give them privacy. Dan started to move away, too, but the old man reached out with steely fingers and caught his wrist. "Louis don't think I'm worth a damn no more," he confided. "You talk to Louis?"

"No, I didn't."

"My nephew. Put me in here. I said Louis, you gimme the money they're chargin' you, I'll show you how a man can pull hisself up."

Arden drew up a chair beside the old man and sat down. Through the window the sky was becoming streaked with pink. "You always did like to watch the sun rise, didn't you?"

"Got to get an early start, you want to make somethin' of you'self. Mr. Richards knows that's gospel. Water them horses good today, yessir."

"You want me to step outside?" Dan asked the girl. But Jupiter didn't let go of him, and Arden shook her head. Dan frowned; he felt as if he'd walked on stage in the middle of a play without knowing the title or what the damn thing was about.

"I am so pleased," Jupiter said, "that you both come to see me. I think a lot 'bout them days. I dream 'bout 'em. I close my eyes and I can see everythin', just like it was. It was a golden time, that's what I believe. A golden time." He drew a long, ragged breath. "Well, I ain't done yet. I may be down, but I ain't out!"

Arden took Jupiter's other hand. "I came to see you," she said, "because I need your help."

He didn't respond for a moment, and Arden thought he hadn't heard. But then Jupiter's head turned and he stared quizzically at her. "My help?"

She nodded. "I'm goin' to find the Bright Girl."

Jupiter's mouth slowly opened, as if he were about to speak, but nothing came out.

"I remember the stories you used to tell me," Arden went on. "I never forgot 'em, all this time. Instead of fadin' away, they kept gettin' more and more real. Especially what you told me about the Bright Girl. Jupiter, I need to find her. You remember, you told me what she could do for me? You used to say she could touch my face and the mark would come off on her hands. Then she'd wash her hands with water and it'd be gone forever and ever."

The birthmark, Dan realized she was talking about. He stared at Arden, but her whole being seemed to be focused on the old man.

"Where is she?" Arden urged.

"Where she always was," Jupiter answered. "Where she always will be. Road runs out, meets the swamp. Bright Girl's in there."

"I remember you used to tell me about growin' up in La-Pierre. Is that where I need to start from?"

"LaPierre," he repeated, and he nodded. "That's right. Start from LaPierre. They know 'bout the Bright Girl there, they'll tell you."

"Beg pardon," Dan said, "but can I ask who ya'll are talkin' about?"

"The Bright Girl's a faith healer," Arden told him. "She lives in the swamp south of where Jupiter grew up."

It came clear to Dan. Arden was searching for a faith healer to take the birthmark off her face, and she'd come to see this old man to help point the way. Dan was tired and cranky, his joints hurt, and his head was throbbing; it frankly pissed him off that he'd taken a detour and risked traveling on the interstate because of such nonsense. "What is she, some kind of voodoo woman lights incense and throws bones around?"

"It's not voodoo," Arden said testily. "She's a holy woman."

"Holy, yes she is. Carries the lamp of God," Jupiter said to no one in particular.

"I had you figured for a sensible person. There's no such thing as a faith healer." A thought struck Dan like an ax between the eyes. "Is that why Joey left you? 'Cause he figured out you were chasin' a fairy tale?"

"Oh, Mr. Richards sir!" Jupiter's hand squeezed Dan's harder. "Bright Girl ain't no fair' tale! She's as real as you and me! Been livin' in that swamp long 'fore my daddy was a li'l boy, and she'll be there long after my bones done blowed away. I seen her when I was eight year old. Here come the Bright Girl down the street!" He smiled at the memory, the warm pink light of the early sun settling into the lines of his face. "Young white girl, pretty as you please. That's why she called bright. But she carries a lamp, too. Carries a lamp from God that burns inside her, and that's how she gets her healin' touch. Yessir, here come the Bright Girl down the street and a crowd of people followin' her. She on the way to Miz Wardell's house, Miz Wardell so sick with cancer she just lyin' in bed, waitin' to die. She see me standin' there and she smile under her big purple hat and I know who she is, 'cause my mama say Bright Girl was comin'. I sing out Bright Girl! Bright Girl! and she touch my hand when I reach for her. I feel that lamp she carryin' in her, that healin' lamp from God." He lifted his eyes to Dan's face. "I never felt such light before, Mr. Richards. Never felt it since. They said the Bright Girl laid her hands on Miz Wardell and up come the black bile, all that cancer flowin' out. Said it took two days and two nights, and when it was done the Bright Girl was so tired she had to be carried back to her boat. But Miz Wardell outlived two husbands and was dancin' when she was ninety. And that ain't all the Bright Girl did for people 'round LaPierre, neither. You ask 'em down there, they'll tell you 'bout all the folks she healed of cancers, tumors, and sicknesses. So nosir, all due respect, but Bright Girl ain't no fair' tale 'cause I seen her with my own livin' eyes."

"I believe you," Arden said. "I always did."

"That's the first step," he answered. "You go to LaPierre. Go south, you'll find her. She'll touch your face and make things right. You won't never see that mark no more."

"I want things made right. More than anythin' in this world, I do."

"Miz Arden," Jupiter said, "I 'member how you used to fret 'bout you'self, and how them others treated you. I 'member them names they called you, them names that made you cry. Then you'd wipe your eyes, stick your chin out again, and keep on goin'. But it seems to me you might still be cryin' on the inside." He looked earnestly up at Dan. "You gone take care of Miz Arden?"

"Listen," Dan said. "I'm not who you think I am."

"I know who you are," Jupiter replied. "You the man God sent Miz Arden."

"Come again?"

"That's right. You the man God provided to take Miz Arden to the Bright Girl. You His hands, you gone have to steer her the right direction."

Dan didn't know what to say, but he'd had enough of this. He pulled loose from the old man's spidery fingers. "I'll be waitin' outside," he growled at Arden, and he turned toward the door.

"Good-bye!" Jupiter called after him. "You heed what I say now, hear?"

Outside, the eastern horizon was the color of burnished copper. Already the air smelled of wet, agonizing heat. Dan stalked to the station wagon, got behind the wheel, and sat there while the sweat began to bloom from his pores. Again he pondered ditching her suitcase and hitting the road, but the heat chased such thoughts away; in his present condition he wouldn't get more than a few miles before he fell asleep at the wheel. He was nodding off when the girl opened the passenger door. "You look pretty bad," she said. "Want me to drive?"

"No," he said. Don't be stupid, he told himself. Weaving all over the road was a sure way to get stopped by a police car. "Wait," he said as she started to climb in. "Yeah, I think you'd better drive."

They started off, Arden retracing the way they'd come. To Dan's aching bones the pitch and sway of the station wagon's creaking frame was pure torture. "Gonna have to pull over," he said when they were back on Darcy Avenue. He made out a small motel coming up on the right; its sign proclaimed it the Rest Well Inn, which sounded mighty good to him. "Turn in there."

She did as he said, and she drove up under a green awning in front of the motel's office. A sign in the window said that all rooms were ten dollars a night, there were phones in all of them, and the cable TV was free. "You want me to check us in?"

Dan narrowed his eyes at her. "What do you mean, check *us* in? We ain't a couple."

"I meant separate rooms. I could do with some sleep, too."

"Oh. Yeah, okay. Fine with me."

She cut the engine and got out. "What's your last name?"

"Huh?"

"Your last name. They'll want it on the register."

"Farrow," he said. "From Shreveport, if they need that, too."

"Back in a couple of minutes."

Dan leaned his head back and waited. Stopping here seemed the only thing to do; he wouldn't have driven the rest of the way to Vermilion in daylight even if he'd felt able. He was fading fast. That crazy old man, he thought. Here come the Bright Girl down the street. Laid her hands on Miz Wardell. All that cancer flowin' out. I never felt such light before, Mr. Rich—

"Here's your key."

Dan got his eyes open and took the key Arden offered. The sun had gotten brighter. Arden drove them a short distance, and then somehow he was fitting the key into a door and walking into a small but clean room with beige-painted cinder-block walls. He locked the door behind him, walked right to the bed, and climbed onto it without removing his cap or shoes. If the police were to suddenly burst into the room, they would've had to pour him into handcuffs.

Pain was throbbing through his body. He had pushed himself too far. But there was still a distance to go, and he couldn't give up. Get seven or eight hours of sleep, he'd feel better. Drive after dark, down into the swampland. They know 'bout the Bright Girl there. Go south, you'll find her. You His hands, you gone have to steer her the right direction.

Crazy old man. I'm a killer, that's what I am.

Dan turned over onto his side and curled his knees up toward his chest.

You His hands.

And with that thought he slipped away into merciful and silent darkness.

13

Satan's Paradise

"Y OU KNOW, ELVIS ALMOST gave up singin' when he was a young boy. Signed on as a truck driver, and that's what he figured on bein'. Did I tell you I used to be a truck driver?"

"Yes, Eisley," Flint said wearily. "Two hours ago."

"Well, what I was meanin' is that you never know where you're goin' in this life. Elvis thought he was gonna be a truck driver, and look where he went. Same with me. Only I guess I ain't got to where I'm goin' yet."

"Um," Flint said, and he let his eyes slide shut again.

The sun was hot enough to make a shadow sweat. The Eldorado's windows were down but the air was still, not a whisper of a breeze. The car was parked on a side road under the shade of weeping willow trees, otherwise they couldn't have stayed in it as they had for almost twelve hours. Even so, Flint had been forced to take off his coat and unbutton his shirt, and Clint's arm dangled from its root just below the conjunction of Flint's rib cage, the hand clenching every so often as if in lethargic protest of the heat. The reflexes of Clint's hand had kept Mama entertained for a while, but now she lay asleep in the backseat, her pink tongue flopped out and a little puddle of drool forming on the black vinyl.

There was one cracked and potholed highway from Houma to Vermilion, no other road in or out. It had brought Flint and Pelvis along its winding spine south through the bayou country in the predawn darkness, and though they hadn't been able to see much but the occasional glimmer of an early morning fisherman's lamp upon the water, they could smell the swamp itself, a heavy, pungent odor of intermingled sweet blossoms and sickly wet decay. They had crossed a long, concrete bridge and come through the town of Vermilion, which was a shuttered cluster of ramshackle stores and clapboard houses. Three miles past the bridge, on the left, was a dirt road that led through a forest of stunted pines and needle-tipped palmettos to a gray-painted cabin with a screened-in porch. The cabin had been dark, Lambert's car nowhere around. While Pelvis and Mama had peed in the woods, Flint had walked behind the cabin and found a pier that went out over a lake, but because of the darkness he couldn't tell how large or small the lake was. A boathouse stood nearby, its doors secured by a padlock. Lambert might or might not be on his way here, Flint decided, but it was fairly certain he hadn't shown up yet. Which was for the best, because Pelvis let out a loud yelp when a palmetto pricked him in a tender spot and then Mama started rapid-firing those high-pitched yips and yaps that made Flint's skin crawl.

They'd driven back to Vermilion and Flint had used the phone booth in front of a bait-and-tackle shop. He'd called Smoates's answering service and been told by the operator on duty that the light was still green, which meant that so far as Smoates knew, Lambert hadn't been caught. Flint had found a dirt side road about fifty yards south of the turnoff to the cabin that he could back the Cadillac onto and still have a view through the woods. It was here that they'd been sitting since four o'clock, alternately keeping watch, sleeping, or eating the glazed doughnuts, Oreo cookies, Slim Jims, and other deadly snacks from Eisley's grocery sack. They had stopped at a gas station just south of Lafayette to fill up and get something to drink, and there Flint had bought a plastic jug of water while Pelvis had opened his wallet for a six-pack of canned Yoo-Hoos.

"I swear," Pelvis said between sips from the last can, "that's an amazin' thing."

Flint remained silent; he was wise to Eisley's methods of drawing him into pointless talk.

"I swear it is," Pelvis tried again. "That little fella inside you, I mean. You know, I went to a freak show one time and saw a two-headed bull, but you take the cake."

Flint pressed his lips together tightly.

"Yessir." *Slllurrrrp* went the final swallow of the Yoo-Hoo. "People'd pay to see you, they surely would. I know *I* would. I mean, if I couldn't see you for free. Make you some money that way. You ever want to give up bounty-huntin' and go into show business, I'll tell you everythin' you need to—"

"Shut—your—mouth." Flint had whispered it, and instantly he regretted it because Eisley had worn him down yet again.

Pelvis dug down into the bottom of the sack and came up with the last three Oreos. Three bites and they were history. He wiped his lips with the back of his hand. "Really, now. You ever think about show business? All jokin' aside. You could get to be famous."

Flint opened his eyes and stared into Pelvis's sweat-beaded face. "For your information," he said coldly, "I grew up in the carnival life. I had a stomach full of 'show business,' so just drop it, understand?"

"You was with the carnival? You mean a freak show, is that right?"

Flint lifted a hand to his face and pressed index finger and thumb against his temples. "Oh, Jesus, what have I done to deserve this?"

"I'm int'rested. Really I am. I never met nobody was a real live freak before."

"Don't use that word."

"What word?"

"Freak!" Flint snapped, and Mama jumped up, growling. "Don't use that word!"

"Why not? Nothin' to be 'shamed of, is it?" Pelvis looked honestly puzzled. "I reckon there's worse words, don't you think?"

"Eisley, you kill me, you know that?" Flint summoned up a tight smile, but his eyes were fierce. "I've never met anybody so . . . so *dense* before in my entire life."

"Dense," Pelvis repeated. He nodded thoughtfully. "How do you mean that, exactly?"

"Thick-skulled! Stupid! How do you think I mean it?" Flint's smile had vanished. "Hell, what's wrong with you? Have you been in solitary confinement for the last five or six years? Can't you just shut your mouth and keep it shut for *two* minutes?"

"Course I can," Pelvis said petulantly. "Anybody can do that if they want to."

"Do it, then! Two minutes of silence!"

Pelvis clamped his mouth shut and stared straight ahead. Mama yawned and settled down to sleep again. "Whose watch we usin' to time this by?" Pelvis asked.

"Mine! I'll time it on my watch! Startin' right now!"

Pelvis grunted and rummaged down in the sack, but there was nothing left but wrappers. He upturned the last Yoo-Hoo can to try to catch a drop or two on his tongue, then he crumpled the can in a fist. "Kinda silly, I think."

"There you go!" Flint rasped. "You couldn't last fifteen seconds!"

"I'm not talkin' to *you!* Can't a man speak what's on his mind? I swear, Mr. Murtaugh, you're tryin' your very best to be hard to get along with!"

"I don't want you to get along with me, Eisley!" Flint said. "I want you to sit there and zipper your mouth! You and that damn mutt have already messed things up once, you're not gonna get a chance to do it again!"

"Don't blame that on Mama and me, now! We didn't have nothin' to do with it!"

Flint gripped the steering wheel with both hands, red splotches on his cheeks. Clint's hand rose up and clutched at the air before it fell back down again. "Just be quiet and leave me alone. Can you do that?"

"Sure I can. Ain't like I'm *dense* or anythin'."

"Good." Flint closed his eyes once more and leaned his head back.

Maybe ten seconds later Pelvis said, "Mr. Murtaugh?"

Flint's eyes were red-rimmed when he turned them on Eisley, his teeth gritting behind his lips.

"Somebody's comin'," Pelvis told him.

Flint looked through the pines along the road. A vehicle— one of only the dozen or so they'd seen on the road all day—was approaching from the direction of Vermilion. In another few seconds Flint saw it wasn't a station wagon but a truck about the size of a moving van. As the truck grew nearer, Flint made out the blue lettering on its side: Briscoe Processing Co. Under that was Baton Rouge, LA. The truck rumbled past them and kept going south, took a curve, and was gone from sight.

"I don't think Lambert's comin'," Pelvis said. "Should've been here by now if he was."

"We're waitin' right here. I told you waitin' was a big part of the job, didn't I?"

"Yessir," Pelvis agreed, "but how do you know he ain't been caught already? We could sit here till crows fly back'ards, and if he's done been caught he ain't comin'."

Flint checked his wristwatch. It was eighteen minutes until four. Eisley was right; it was time to make a call to Smoates again. But Flint didn't want to drive into Vermilion to use the phone, because if Lambert was coming, it would be across that bridge and Flint didn't care to be spotted. It would be easier to take Lambert when he thought he was safe in the cabin rather than chasing him north on the highway. Flint looked in the direction the truck had gone. There had to be some trace of civilization farther south. He unfolded his Louisiana road map, one of a half-dozen state maps he always kept in the car, and found the dot of Vermilion. About four or five miles south of that was another speck called Chandalac, and then Highway 57 ended three miles or so later at a place named LaPierre. Beyond that was swampland all the way to the Gulf of Mexico.

The truck had to be going somewhere, and there had to be at least one pay phone down there, too. Flint started the engine and eased the Eldorado out of its hiding place. He ignored Pelvis's question of "Where we headed?" and turned right, the sun's glare sitting like a fireball on the long black hood.

In the brutal afternoon light they could see the type of country they'd driven through in darkness: on both sides of the road the flat, marshy land was alternately cut by winding channels of murky water and then stubbled with thick stands of palmettos and huge ancient oak trees. Around the next curve a brown snake that had to be a yard long was writhing on the hot pavement on Flint's side of the road, and he figured the truck had just crushed it a couple of minutes earlier. His spine crawled as the car passed over it, and when he glanced in the rearview mirror he saw two hulking birds that must've been vultures swoop down on the dying reptile and start tearing it to pieces with their beaks.

Flint didn't believe in omens. Nevertheless, he hoped this wasn't one.

They'd gone maybe a couple of miles when the spiny woods fell away on the right side of the road and the sun glittered off a blue channel of water that meandered out of what appeared to be primeval swamp. Just ahead was a white clapboard building with a tin roof and a sign that said VERMILION MARINA & GROCERIES, and jutting off from shore was a pier where several small boats were tied up. One larger craft—a shrimp boat, Flint thought it was because of the nets and various hoists aboard—had just arrived and its crew was tying ropes down to the pier. And there sat the Briscoe Processing Company truck as well, parked next to the clapboard building with its loading bay facing the pier. Beside the marina, near a sun-bleached sign that advertised live bait, chewing tobacco, and fresh onions, stood a phone booth.

Flint pulled the car to a stop on a surface of crushed oyster shells. He buttoned up his shirt and shrugged into his loose-fitting suit jacket. "Stay here," he instructed Pelvis as he got out. "I'll be right back." He'd taken three strides toward the phone booth when he heard the Eldorado's passenger door creak open and Pelvis was climbing out with Mama tucked under his arm. "Just go on 'bout your business," Pelvis said when Flint fired a glare at him. "I'm goin' in there and get me some vittles. You want anythin'?"

"No." *Vittles*, Flint thought. Wasn't that what Granny fixed on "The Beverly Hillbillies"? "Wait. Yeah, I do," he decided. "Get me a bottle of lemon juice, if they've got it. And don't go in there and flap your lips about Lambert, hear me? Anybody asks, you're here to do some fishin'. Understand?"

"You don't think I've got a lick of sense, do you?"

"Bingo," Flint said, and he turned his back on Pelvis and went into the phone booth. He placed a call through to Smoates's office. "It's Flint," he said when Smoates answered. "What's the situation on Lambert?"

"Hold on a minute."

Flint waited, sweat trickling down his face. It had to be over ninety degrees, even as the sun began to fall toward the west. The heat had stunned Clint, who lay motionless. The air smelled of the steamy, sickly sweet reek of the swamp, and his own bodily aroma wasn't too delicate, either. He wasn't used to being unclean; a gentleman knew the value of cleanliness, of crisp white shirts and freshly laundered underwear. These last twenty-four hours had been a little slice of hell on earth, and this swampland looked like Satan's paradise, too. From where he was standing, Flint could see four men unloading cargo from the shrimp boat. The cargo was greenish-brown and scaly, with long snouts bound shut by copper wire, four stubby legs fastened together with wire as well.

Alligators, he realized with a start. The men were unloading alligators, each three or four feet long, from the deck of the boat and then carrying them to the Briscoe Processing Company truck and heaving them into the back. The men's workclothes were wet and muddy, the boat's deck heaped with maybe twenty or more live and squirming alligators. But there was a fifth man—slimmer than the others, with shoulder-length grayish-blond hair and wearing blue jeans and a Harvard T-shirt—who stood apart from the workers and seemed to be supervising. As Flint watched, the man in the Harvard T-shirt glanced at him and the sun flared in the round lenses of his dark glasses. The glance became a lingering stare.

"Flint?" Smoates had come back on the line. "Latest word's that Lambert's still on the loose. Where are you?"

"Down south. Little hellhole called Vermilion. I want you to know I'm standin' here watchin' a bunch of geeks unload honest-to-God live alligators off a boat."

"You ought to ask 'em if they need a hand," Smoates said with a wet chuckle.

Flint chose to let the remark pass. "I came close to nailin' Lambert last night."

"You're shittin' me! He showed up at the ex-wife's house?"

"No, not there. But I found him. I think he's on his way here, too. Probably holed up somewhere and gonna be on the move again after dark." Flint saw the man in the Harvard T-shirt still staring at him; then the dude motioned one of the workers—a shirtless, shaven-headed wall of a black man who must've stood six-four and weighed close to three hundred pounds—over to him and they started talking, their backs toward the phone booth, as the others continued to unload the alligators and throw them into the truck. "Smoates," Flint said, "Eisley's drivin' me crazy. Even God couldn't get him to shut his mouth. I don't know what you saw in him, but he's all wrong for the job."

"So he talks a lot, so what? That could be a plus. He's got the ability to wear people down."

"Yeah, he's good at that, all right. But he's slow upstairs. He can't think on his feet. I'd hate to be in a tight spot and have to depend on him, I'll tell you that."

"Forget about Eisley for a minute. You ain't heard the news, huh?"

"What news?"

"Lambert's a double murderer now. He killed a fella at a motel outside Alexandria 'round midnight. Blasted him with a shotgun, and when the fella didn't die fast enough, Lambert beat him to death. Stole his station wagon. Cable TV's picked up the story, it's on every hour."

"He was in the station wagon when I found him. I would've had him, but his ex-wife helped him get away."

"Well, sounds to me like Lambert's turned into a mad dog. Man who's killed twice won't think nothin' 'bout killin' a third time, so watch your ass."

"He's in the grocery store right now," Flint said.

"Huh? Oh, yeah! Ha! See, Flint? Eisley's givin' you a sense of humor!"

"It's his lack of sense I'm worried about. I've done all right at stayin' alive so far, but that was before you shackled him on me."

"He's gotta learn the ropes somehow," Smoates said. "Just like you did." He paused for a moment, then released a heavy sigh. "Well, I reckon you're right. Lambert's an awful dangerous skin to train Eisley on. Neither one of you are any good to me in a grave, so you can call it quits and come on in if you want to."

Flint was knocked off his wheels. He thought the earth might shake and the heavens crack open. Smoates was offering him a way out of this nightmare.

"You still there, Flint?"

"Uh . . . yeah. Yeah, I'm here." His joy had been a short-lived thing. He was thinking the unthinkable; he needed his share of the reward money for his gambling debts, and if Lambert was coming to the cabin after dark, it would be foolish to give up and go back to Shreveport now. Then again, Lambert might not

even be in Louisiana anymore. It was Flint's call to make. He had
the can of Mace and his brass knuckles in the car's glove compartment, and Clint's derringer was in its small holster against
the skin under his right arm. The derringer's bullets didn't have
much stopping power, but no man—not even a mad dog Vietnam
vet—was going to do a whole lot of running or fighting with a
hole through his kneecap. "If Lambert shows up here," Flint said,
"I believe I can take him. I'll hang in until tomorrow mornin'."

"You don't have to prove anythin'. I know what you can do.
But somebody as crazy as Lambert could be awful unpredict-
able."

Flint grunted. "Smoates, if I didn't know you better, I'd think
you were concerned about me."

"You've been a damn fine investment. Eisley's gonna turn out
to be a good investment, too, once he gets the green worn off
him."

"Oh, I see. Well, just so I know where I stand." He wiped
sweat from his eyebrows with his sleeve. The long-haired man
in the Harvard T-shirt was watching the others work again, and
paying Flint no attention. "I'll stay here awhile longer. If Lambert
doesn't show by six in the mornin', I'll start back."

"Okay, play it how you want."

"I'll check in again around dark." Flint hung the phone back
on its cradle. He was drenched with sweat under his jacket and to-
tally miserable. Still, the game had to be played out. He saw that
Eisley hadn't returned to the car, and when he looked through
a window into the grocery store he saw Pelvis standing at the
cash register eating an ice cream sandwich as he talked to a fat
red-haired girl behind the counter. The girl wore an expression of
rapture on her pudgy-cheeked face, and Flint guessed it wasn't
every day she had a customer like him. Flint spotted a sign that
said REST ROOMS and there was an arrow pointing around the side
of the building. He followed it and found two doors, one marked
GENTS and the other GALS. The GENTS door had a hole where
the knob should've been. As he pushed through the door, he was

aware of the sounds of distress the trussed-up alligators were making as they were being thrown into the truck, a combination of guttural burps and higher-pitched bleats. He figured the things were going to Baton Rouge to wind up as shoes, belts, and purses. Hell of a way to make a living, that was.

Flint stood in a small bathroom that smelled strongly of Lysol, but there were other more disagreeable odors wafting about as well. One of the two urinals seemed to have moss growing in it, and the other held a dark yellow lake clogged with cigarette butts. He didn't care to take a look into the toilet stall. He chose the mossy urinal, which had a Tropical Nights condoms machine mounted on the wall above it, and he unzipped his pants and went about the task.

As he relieved himself, he thought about what Smoates had said: *Man who's killed twice won't think nothin' 'bout killin' a third time.* So why, Flint wondered, am I still alive? Lambert had just come from his second murder, and he wouldn't have had much to lose by a third, especially the execution of a bounty hunter who'd tracked him from Shreveport. Why hadn't Lambert used the gun when he'd had the chance? Maybe because he hadn't wanted his ex-wife and son to be witnesses?

It was self-defense, Flint remembered the woman saying. *He's not a cold-blooded killer.*

Lambert's turned into a mad dog, was Smoates's opinion.

Which was the truth? *I'll let the judge sort it out,* Flint thought as he stared at the aged photo of a smiling, heavily made-up blond girl on the condom machine. He looked down to shake and zip.

The edge of a straight razor was laid against the crown of Flint's penis, which suddenly and decisively dried up.

"Get the door."

The door bumped shut.

"Easy, man. Be cool, now. Don't pee on my hand. I wouldn't like it if you peed on my hand, I might get all bent outta shape and this razor might twitch." The long-haired man wearing round-lensed sunglasses and the Harvard T-shirt was standing beside Flint; he had a soft, almost feminine voice with just a hint of a refined southern accent, but he was jabbering as if he might be flying on speed. "Wouldn't want that, man, no you wouldn't. Bummer to have all that blood shootin' out your stump. Messy, messy, messy. Virgil, find his wallet."

An ebony hand the size of a roast slid into Flint's jacket and went to the inside pocket, almost grazing Clint.

"Just look straight ahead, man. Hold on to your joy stick, both hands. That's right. Car 54, where are you?"

"No badge," Virgil said in a voice like a cement mixer turning over. "Lou'zana license. Name's Flint Murtaugh. Monroe address."

"Our man Flint!" The razor remained where it was, a threat to three shriveled inches of Flint's flesh. "Do not adjust the horizontal, do not adjust the vertical. We are in control. Talk to me."

"What's this all about?" he managed to say though his throat had seized up.

"Beeeep! Wrong answer! I'm askin' the questions, *kemo sabe!* Who are you and what're you doin' here?"

"I'm here to do some fishin'."

"Oh, yeahhhhh! Fishin' he says, Virgil! What's your nose tell us?"

Flint heard the black man sniffing the air next to his face. "Don't smell like no fisherman," Virgil rumbled. "Got kinda like a cop smell, but . . ." He kept sniffing. "Somethin' real funny 'bout him."

Flint turned his head to the left and looked into the dark lenses. The Harvard man, who stood about the same height as Flint, was in his late forties or early fifties. He was lean and sun-browned, gray grizzle covering the jaw of his deeply lined and weathered face. His hair had once been sand-colored, but most of it was now nearing silver. Part of his right ear looked as if it had been either chewed off or shot off. His T-shirt with the name of that hallowed university was mottled with sweat stains, and his blue jeans appeared to be held together by crusty patches of grime. Flint concluded his brief inspection by noting that the man wore Top-Siders without socks. "I'm not a cop," he said, lifting his gaze again to the opaque lenses. "I came down to fish for the weekend, that's all."

"Wore your best suit to fish in, did you? Come all the way here from Monroe just to hook a big mudcat? If you're a fisherman, I'm Dobie Gillis."

"Ain't no fisherman." Virgil was standing on the other side of Flint, his broad bare chest smeared with 'gator mud. His nose had wide, flared nostrils and he wore purple paisley shorts and Nikes on size thirteen feet. "Fish won't bite, weather this hot. Ain't been no fisherman 'round here all week."

"This is true," the man with the razor said. "So, Flinty, what's your story?"

"Look, I don't know who you fellas are or what this is about, but all I did was come in here to use the bathroom. If you want to rob me, go ahead and take my money, but I wish you'd put the razor away."

"Maybe it's *you* who wants to rob *us*."

"What?"

"I saw you on the phone, Flinty. You reached out and touched somebody. Who was it? Couldn't have been Victor Medina, could it? You one of his spies, Flinty?"

"I don't know any Victor Medina. I had to call my office."

"What line of work you in?"

"I sell insurance," Flint answered.

"Smellin' a lie," Virgil said, sniffing.

"The nose knows. Virgil's got a mystic snout, Flinty. So let's try it again: what line of work you in?"

Flint couldn't tell these two swamp rats why he was really there; they'd want the reward for themselves. Anger welled up inside him. "I'm an astronaut," he said before he could think better of it. "What business is it of yours?"

"Ohhhhhh, an astronaut, Virgil!" The man grinned, his greenish teeth in dire need of brushing. "We've got us a celebrity here! What do you say about that?"

"Say he wants it done the hard way, Doc."

"This is true." Doc nodded, his grin evaporating. "The hard way it shall be, then."

Virgil looked into the toilet stall. Now it was his turn to grin. "Heh-heh! Somebody done forgot to flush!"

"Oh me oh me oh my!" Doc pulled the razor away from Flint's penis and closed the blade with a quick snap of his wrist, and Flint took the opportunity to zip himself up out of harm's way. "I believe this is a job for an astronaut, don't you?"

"Surely." Virgil took a step forward and gripped the nape of Flint's neck with one huge hand while the other grasped Flint's right wrist and wrenched his arm up behind his back.

"Hey, hey! Wait a minute!" Flint yelled, true fear kicking his heart and pain shooting through his arm. Clint had awakened and was thrashing under his shirt, but Virgil was manhandling Flint like a sack of straw into the toilet stall. Though Flint grabbed the stall's door with his left hand and tried to fight free, Virgil made short work of that attempt by sweeping his legs out from under him and forcing him to his knees on the gritty floor. The hair rose up on the back of Flint's neck when he saw the brown mess in the slimy bowl and what might have been fist-size crabs scuttling around down in the murk.

"Yum-yum!" Doc said. "Candygram for Mongo!"

Virgil pushed Flint's face toward the toilet bowl. The man's strength was awesome, and though Flint did his damnedest at resisting, all he could do was slow the inevitable. He couldn't get to the derringer and neither could he find the breath to command Clint to get it. His only hope was that he would pass out before his face broke the scummy, clotted surface.

"*Sir?*"

Doc turned his head toward the husky voice behind him. He gasped; Elvis Presley was standing there, framed by the hot white glare through the open doorway. Doc stood gaping and stunned as Pelvis Eisley reached up with his left hand and plucked off the sunglasses. Doc blinked, his pale green eyes overloaded with light.

" 'Scuse me," Pelvis said, and he lifted his right hand—the hand that held the red can of Mace he'd taken from the Cadillac's glove compartment—and sprayed a burst of fine mist squarely into Doc's face.

The result was immediate. Doc let out a scream that curled Pelvis's ducktail, and he staggered back, raking at his inflamed eyeballs. In the toilet stall, Flint's nose was two inches away from disaster when the scream echoed off the tiles and Virgil's hand left the back of his head. Flint jabbed an elbow backward into the man's chest, but Virgil just grunted and turned away to help Doc.

"Lord have mercy," Pelvis said when he saw the size of the black man who'd just emerged from the toilet stall. Virgil took one look at Doc, who was down on the floor clutching his face with both hands and writhing in agony, then he stared at Pelvis as if seeing an alien from another planet. The shock didn't last but three seconds, after which Virgil charged Pelvis like a mad bull.

Pelvis stood his ground and got off another spray of Mace, but Virgil saw it coming and he jerked his head to one side, throwing up a thick forearm to protect his face. The spray wet his shoulder and burned like the furies of Hell, but Virgil was still moving and he hit his target with a body block that all but knocked Pelvis out of his blue suede shoes. Pelvis slammed against the wall, his jowls and belly quaking, and Virgil chopped at his wrist and knocked the Mace out of his hand. The stomp of a Nike crushed the can flat. Virgil grabbed Pelvis by the throat and lifted him off his feet. Pelvis's eyes bulged as he started choking, his fingers scrabbling to loosen Virgil's massive hands.

Flint had staggered out of the stall. He saw Pelvis's face swelling with blood and he knew he had to do something—anything—fast. He yanked his shirt open, pulled the derringer from its holster, and cocked it. "Leave him alone!" Flint shouted, but Virgil paid no attention. There was no time for a second try. Flint stepped forward, pressed the derringer's double barrels against the back of Virgil's left knee, and squeezed the trigger. The little weapon made only a polite firecracker *pop*, but the force of the slug couldn't help but shatter the big man's kneecap. Virgil cried out and released Pelvis, and he went down on the floor, gripping at the ruins of his knee.

"Gone pass out!" Pelvis gasped. "Lordy, I can't stand up!"

"Yes you can!" Flint saw his wallet on the floor where Virgil had dropped it, and he snatched it up and then took Pelvis's weight on his shoulder. "Come on, *move!*" He kicked the door open and pulled Pelvis out with him into the scorching light. The loading of the alligators was still proceeding, which made Flint think that the other three workmen had believed Doc's scream of pain to be his own. The red-haired grocery girl had probably been too scared to come look; either that, or screams of pain were commonplace around there. But then one of two workers carrying a squirming alligator along the pier saw them and let out a holler: "Hey, Mitch! Doc and Virgil are down!" The third man was on the boat, and he reached under his muddy yellow shirt and pulled out a pistol before he came running across the gangplank.

It was definitely time to vacate the premises.

Pelvis, who could hardly stand up one second, was in the next second a fairly impressive sprinter. The man with the gun got off a shot that knocked a chunk of cinder block from the wall eight inches above Flint's head, and Flint fired the derringer's other bullet without aiming though he knew he was out of range. All the workmen threw themselves flat on the pier, the 'gator landing belly-up. Then Flint was running for the car, too, where Mama was barking frantically in the driver's seat. He almost crushed her as he flung himself behind the wheel, and Pelvis did crush the sack of Twinkies, potato chips, and cookies that occupied his own seat. Flint jammed the key in, started the engine, and roared away from the store in reverse. The man with the gun hadn't come around the corner yet. Flint put the pedal to the metal, the engine still shrieking in reverse.

And then there was the gunman, skidding around the building's edge. He planted his feet in a firing stance and took aim at the retreating car. Flint shouted, "Get down!" and Pelvis ducked his head, both arms clutching Mama. But before the man could pull the trigger, the Eldorado got behind the cover of woods and Flint's heart fell back into his chest from where it had lodged in his throat. He kept racing backward another fifty yards before he found a clear place on the weedy shoulder to turn the car around, then he gave it the gas again.

Pelvis had hesitantly lifted his head. The first faint blue bruises were coming up on his neck. "I come to the bathroom and heard 'em in there!" he croaked over the howl of wind and engine. "Looked through the hole in the door and seen 'em tryin' to rob you! I 'membered what you said 'bout the Mace blindin' a man!"

"They were crazy, that's what they were!" Flint's face glistened with sweat, his eyes darting back and forth from the rearview mirror to the road. The truck wasn't following. He cut his speed to keep from flying off the dangerous curves into the marsh. Clint was still writhing, as if he shared his brother's fury. "Goddamned swamp rats, tried to drown me!" Still the truck wasn't following, and Flint eased up on the gas some more. Pelvis kept looking back, too, his face mottled with crimson splotches. "I don't see 'em yet!"

In another moment Flint realized—or hoped—the truck wasn't coming after them at all. The dirt road where they'd been sitting watching for Lambert would soon be on the left. It was time to take a gamble. What were the odds that the truck was following as opposed to the odds that it was not? Doc probably couldn't see yet, and Virgil was going to need a stretcher. Flint put his foot on the brake as they approached the dirt road.

"What're you doin'? You ain't stoppin', are you?" Pelvis squawked.

"I'm here to get Lambert," Flint said as he backed off the highway into the shade of the weeping willows once more. "I'm not lettin' a bunch of swamp rats run me off." He got far enough down the road so as not to be seen by anyone coming from either direction, then he opened the glove compartment, brought out a box of bullets for the derringer, and reloaded its chambers. He cut the engine, and they sat there, all four of them breathing hard.

A minute passed. "That toy gun might do fine in a pinch," Pelvis said, "but I wouldn't stake my life on it." Flint didn't respond. Five minutes went by, during which Pelvis kept mumbling to himself or Mama. After fifteen minutes they heard a vehicle approaching from the south. "Oh, Lord, here they come!" Pelvis said, scrunching down in his seat.

The truck passed their hiding place at a lawful speed and kept going. They listened to it moving away, and then its sound faded.

"I'll be." Pelvis sat up, wincing as pain lanced his lower back. If he hadn't been carrying such a pad of fat around his midsection, he might be laid out on the bathroom floor right then. "What do you make of that?"

Flint shook his head. A lot of strange things had happened to him in his bounty-hunting career, but this might have been the strangest. What had all that been about? Doc and Virgil hadn't been trying to rob him; they'd wanted to know who he was, why he was there, and who he'd been talking to on the phone. "Damned if I can figure it out." He slid Clint's derringer back into its holster. "You all right?"

"Hurtin' some, but I reckon I'm okay."

Flint kept listening for a siren that would be an ambulance or police car. If the cops showed up, they could wreck everything. But he was starting to have the feeling that the swamp rats didn't care to see the police around, either. Law-abiding citizens didn't usually carry straight razors and threaten the bodily parts of strangers. And what was all that about somebody named Victor Medina, and them thinking he might be there to rob *them?*

Rob them of what? A truckload of live alligators?

It made no sense, but Flint hadn't come this distance to worry about some crazy 'gatormen. He turned his attention back to snaring Lambert. Stupid of Eisley to have lost the Mace; he should've held on to it, no matter what. Without the Mace, the job was going to be that much tougher.

"Mr. Murtaugh, sir?"

Flint looked at Pelvis, and saw that his face had turned milky white.

"Never seen a fella get shot before," Pelvis said, in obvious distress. "Never *been* shot at, neither. Got to thinkin' 'bout it, and . . . believe I'm gone have to heave."

"Well, get out and do it! Don't you mess up my car!"

"Yes sir." Pelvis opened the door, pulled himself out and staggered into the woods, and Mama leapt from the car after him.

Flint grunted with disgust. Man who couldn't take a little violence and blood sure wasn't suited to hunt skins for bounty. His own nerves had stopped jangling several minutes earlier, but he was going to see that toilet bowl in his nightmares.

Clint had settled down to rest again. Flint looked into the crumpled sack of groceries, and he was gratified to find a small green bottle. He uncapped the lemon juice and took a long, thirsty swallow. Ever since he could remember, his system had craved acid. He decided that in a few minutes he should walk up to the cabin and make sure Lambert hadn't arrived while they'd been gone.

Still there was no siren. The police and ambulance weren't coming.

Alligators, he thought. What made alligators worth protecting with a pistol?

Well, it wasn't his business. His business was finding Lambert and taking him back to Shreveport, which he was determined to do. He could hear Eisley retching out all that junk food he'd packed himself with. Flint took another drink from the green bottle, and he thought that this was a hell of a life for a gentleman.

14

The Small Skulls

D AN WAS ONE OF the first to reach the village. The sky was stained yellow by drifting smoke, the air thick with the reek of burned flesh.

He heard the wailing, like the sound of muted trumpets.

He moved forward through the haze at a slow-motion gait, his M16 clutched before him. Sweat had stiffened the folds of his uniform, his heart thudding in his chest like distant artillery. Someone was screaming up ahead: a woman's scream, hideous in its rising and falling. The ugly smoke swirled around him, its smell stealing his breath. He pushed past a couple of other grunts from his platoon, one of whom turned away and vomited on the dirt.

At the center of the village was a smoldering pile of twisted gray shapes. Dan walked nearer to it, feeling the heat tighten his face. Some of the villagers were on their knees, shrieking. He saw four or five children clinging to their mothers' legs, their faces blank with shock. Small orange flames flickered in the burned pile; nearby was a United States Marine-issue gasoline can, probably stolen from a supply dump, that had been left as a taunt.

Dan knew what had been set afire. He knew even before he saw the small skulls. Before he saw a crisped hand reaching up from the mass of bodies. Before he saw that some of them had not burned to the bone, but were swollen and malformed and pink as seared pork.

Someone clutched his arm. He looked into the wrinkled, tear-streaked face of an old Vietnamese man who was jabbering with what must have been a mixture of rage and terror. The old man thrust his hand at Dan, and in the palm lay a tiny airplane formed out of tinfoil.

He understood, then. It was from the Hershey bar's wrapper. The Cong had circled around behind them, and had found this tinfoil toy as evidence of collusion with the enemy. How many children had been executed was difficult to tell. Flesh had melted and run together in glistening pools, bones had blackened and fused, facial features had been erased. The old Vietnamese staggered away from Dan, still jabbering, and thrust his palm in an accusatory gesture at another marine. Then he went to the next and the next, his voice breaking and giving out but his hand still flying up to show them the reason for this massacre of the innocents.

Dan backed away from the burned corpses, one hand over his mouth and nose and sickness churning in his stomach. Captain Aubrey was trying to take charge, yelling for someone to shovel dirt over the flames, but his face was pallid and his voice was weak. Dan turned his eyes from the sight, and he saw the young Bostonian with cornflower-blue eyes—Farrow—standing near him, staring fixedly at the fire as the Vietnamese elder thrust the tinfoil airplane into his face. Then Dan had to get away from the smoke before it overcame him, had to get away from the smell of it, but it was everywhere, in his khakis and his hair and in his skin. He had to get away from this war and this death, from the mindless killing and the numbing horror, and as he ran into the rice paddies he was sick all over himself but the odor was still in his nostrils and he feared he would smell it for the rest of his life.

He fell down in the wet vegetation and pushed his face into the muck. When he lifted his head, he could still smell the burned meat. Smoke drifted above him, a dark pall against the sun. Something strained to break loose inside him, and he was afraid of it. If this thing collapsed, so, too, might the wall of willpower and bravado he'd been shivering behind every moment, every hour, every day of his tour on duty. He was a good soldier, he did what he was told and he'd never gone south, never. But with brown mud on his face and black despair in his soul he fought the awful urge to get up and run toward the jungle, toward where they must be watching from the lids of their snake holes, and once there he would squeeze the trigger of his M16 until his ammo was gone and then they would emerge silently from the shadows and cut him to pieces.

Never gone south. Never. But he could feel himself trembling on the edge of the abyss, and he gripped handfuls of mud to keep from falling.

The feeling slowly passed. He was all right again. No, not all right, but he would make it. Death and cruel waste were no strangers in this land. He had seen sights enough to make him wish for blindness, but he had to stand up and keep going because he was a man and a marine and he was there to get the job done. He turned over on his back and watched the smoke drifting, a dark scrawl of senseless inhumanity, a sickening cipher. The wailing in the village behind him seemed to be growing more shrill and louder, a chorus of agony, though Dan clasped his hands to his ears *louder louder* though he squeezed his eyes shut and tried to neither think nor feel *louder louder* though he prayed for God to deliver him from this place and there was no answer but the wailing louder and louder and loud—

"*Uh,*" he said.

He sat up, his face contorted.

"Jesus!" somebody said. A female voice. "You 'bout scared the stew outta me!"

Wailing. He could still hear it. He didn't know where he was, his mind was still hazed with the smoke of Vietnam. It came to him in another few seconds that he was no longer hearing the wailing from the village in his memory. A police car! he thought as panic streaked through him. He saw a window and started to get up and hobble toward it, but his joints had tightened and the pain in his skull was excruciating. He sat on the edge of what he realized was a bed, his hands pressed to his temples.

"I've been tryin' to wake you up for five minutes. You were dead to the world. Then all of a sudden you sat up so fast I thought you were goin' right through the wall."

He hardly heard her. He was listening to the siren. Whatever it was—police car, fire truck, or ambulance—it was moving rapidly away. He rubbed his temples and tried to figure out where he was. His brain seemed to be locked up, and he was searching desperately for the key.

"You all right?"

Dan looked up at the girl who stood next to him. The right side of her face was a deep violet-red. A birthmark, terrible in its domination. Arden was her name, he remembered. Arden Holiday. No. Halliday. He remembered the Cajun Country Truck Stop, a young man in a Hanoi Janes T-shirt, and a baseball bat studded with nails thunking down on the table.

"Brought you a barbecue," she said, and she offered him a grease-stained white sack. "Restaurant's right across the road."

The smell of the charred pork made his stomach lurch. He lowered his head, trying to think through the pain.

"Don't you want it? You must be hungry. Slept all day."

"Just get it away from me." His voice was a husky growl. "Please."

"Okay, okay. I thought you'd want somethin' to eat."

She left the room. His memory was coming back to him in bits and pieces, like a puzzle linking together. A pistol shot. The dying face of Emory Blanchard. Reverend Gwinn and his wife's crullers. The DeCaynes and a shotgun blast tearing the tire of his truck apart. Fifteen thousand dollars reward. Susan and Chad at Basile Park, and her telling him about the cabin in Vermilion. The bounty hunter with the flashlight, and Elvis Presley hollering for Mr. Murtaugh.

The girl, now. He'd given her a ride to Lafayette to see a man at a nursing home. Mr. Richards, the man's name was. No, no; it was Jupiter. Old man, talking about somebody called the Bright Girl. Faith healer, down in the swamp. Take that mark right off your face. You His hands, you gone have to steer her the right direction.

A motel in Lafayette. That's where he was. Slept all day, Arden had said. The sun was still high outside, though. He struggled to focus on his wristwatch's dial, and read the time as eight minutes after four. His cap. Where was his cap? He found it lying on the bed beside him. His shirt was stiff with dried sweat, but there wasn't much he could do about that. He sat there gathering the strength to stand up. He'd pushed himself yesterday to the limit of his endurance, and now he was going to have to pay the price. His headache was easing somewhat, but his bones throbbed in raw rhythm with his pulse. At last he stood up and staggered into the bathroom, where he caught a glimpse in the mirror of a white, sunken-eyed Halloween mask with a graying beard that couldn't possibly be his face. There was a shower stall, this one thankfully with no frogs hopping about, and Dan reached in and turned on the cold tap and then put his head under the stream.

"Hey!" Arden had returned. "You decent?"

He just stood there in the downpour, wishing he'd had the sense to lock her out.

"Got somethin' to show you. Just take a minute."

The sooner he could get rid of her, the better. He turned off the water, found a towel to dry his hair, and walked into the front room. Arden was sitting in a chair at a round table next to the bed, a map spread out on the tabletop. She still wore her blue jeans, but she'd changed into a fresh beige short-sleeve blouse. "Wow," she said, staring at him. "You really look beat."

He reached back and massaged the cramped muscles of his shoulders. "I thought I locked that door before I went to sleep. How'd you get in?"

"I stood out there knockin' till my knuckles were raw. You wouldn't answer your phone, either. So I got an extra key from the lady at the front desk. I told her we were travelin' together. Look here."

"We're not travelin' together," Dan said. He saw that what she'd spread out was his own Louisiana roadmap, taken from the station wagon.

"Here's LaPierre. See?" She put her finger on a dot where Highway 57 ended at the swamp. "It's about twenty-five miles south of Houma. Didn't you say you were headed that way?"

"I don't know. Did I?"

"Yes. You said you were goin' somewhere south of Houma. Not a whole lot down there, from the looks of the map. Where're you headed?"

He examined the map a little closer. LaPierre was maybe three miles past a town called Chandalac, which was four or five miles past Vermilion. South of LaPierre the map showed nothing but Terrebonne Parish swamp. "I'm not takin' you any farther. You can catch a bus from here."

"Yeah, I guess I could, but I figured since you were goin' that way you'd help me—"

"No," he interrupted. "It's not possible."

She frowned. "Not possible? Why not? You're goin' down there, aren't you?"

"Listen, you don't know me. I could be . . . somebody you wouldn't want to be travelin' with."

"What's that mean? You a bank robber or somethin'?"

Dan eased himself down on the bed again. "I'll give you a ride to the bus station. That's the best I can do."

Arden sat there chewing her bottom lip and studying the map. Then she watched him for a moment as he wedged a pillow beneath his head and closed his eyes. "Can I ask you a personal question?"

"Depends," he said.

"Somethin' wrong with you? I mean . . . are you sick? You sure don't look healthy, if you don't mind my sayin'."

Dan opened his eyes and peered up at the ceiling tiles. There was no point in trying to hide it. He said, "Yeah, I'm sick."

"I thought so. What is it? AIDS?"

"Leukemia. Brain tumor. Worn out and at the end of my rope. Take your pick."

She didn't say anything for a while. He heard her folding the map up, or trying to, but road maps once unfolded became stubborn beasts. Arden cleared her throat. "The Bright Girl's a healer. You heard Jupiter say that, didn't you?"

"I heard an old man callin' me Mr. Richards and talkin' nonsense."

"It's not nonsense!" she answered. "And you bear a resemblance to Mr. Richards. He had a beard and was about your size. I can see how Jupiter mistook you."

Dan sat up again, his neck painfully tight, and looked at her. "Listen to me. The way I figure this, you're tryin' to track down a faith healer—who I don't think even exists—to get that mark off your face. If you're goin' on the tall tales of some crazy old man, I think you're gonna be real disappointed."

"Jupiter's not crazy, and they're not tall tales. The Bright Girl's down there. Just because you don't believe it doesn't make it not true."

"And just because you *want* to believe it doesn't make it true. I don't know anything about you, or what you've been through, but seems to me you ought to be seein' a skin doctor instead of tryin' to find a faith healer."

"I've seen dermatologists and plastic surgeons." Arden said icily. "They all told me I've got the darkest port-wine stain they ever saw. They can't promise me they can get it all off, or even half of it off without scarrin' me up. I couldn't afford the cost of the operations, anyway. And you're right about not knowin' anything about me. You sure as hell don't know what it's like to wear this thing on your face every day of your life. People lookin' at you like you're a freak, or some kind of monster not fit to be out in public. When somebody's talkin' to you, they'll try to look everywhere but your face, and you can tell they're either repulsed or they're feelin' pity for you. It's a bad-luck sign, is what it is. My own father told me that when I was six years old. Then he left the house for a pack of cigarettes and kept on goin', and my mama picked up a bottle and didn't lay it down again until it killed her. From then on I was in and out of foster homes and I can tell you none of 'em were paradise." She stopped speaking, her mouth tightening into a grim line.

"When I was fifteen," Arden went on after a long pause, "I stole a car. Got caught and put on a ranch for 'troubled youth' outside San Antonio. Mr. Richards ran it. Jupiter worked at the stable, and his wife was a cook. It was a hard place, and if you stepped out of line you earned time in the sweat box. But I got my high school diploma and made it out. If I hadn't I'd probably be dead or in prison by now. I used to help Jupiter with the horses, and he told me stories about the Bright Girl. How she could touch my birthmark and take it away. He told me where he'd grown up, and how everybody down there knew about the Bright Girl." She paused again, her eyes narrowing as she viewed some distant scene inside her head. "Those stories . . . they were so real. So full of light and hope. That's what I need right now. See, things haven't been goin' so good in my life. Lost my job at the Goodyear plant, they laid off almost a whole shift. Had to sell my car. My credit cards were gettin' me in trouble, so I put the scissors to 'em. I went to apply for a job at a burger joint, and the fella took one look at my face and said the job was already filled and there wasn't anything comin' open anytime soon. Same thing happened with a couple of other jobs I went lookin' for. I'm behind two months on my rent, and the bill collectors are barkin' after me. See . . . what I need is a new start. I need to get rid of my bad luck once and for all. If I can find the Bright Girl and get this thing off my face . . . I could start all over again. That's what I need, and that's why I pulled every cent I've got out of the bank to make this trip. Do you understand?"

"Yeah, I do," Dan said. "I know things are tough, but lookin' for this Bright Girl person's not gonna help you. If there ever *was* such a woman, she's dead by now." He met Arden's blank stare. "Jupiter said the Bright Girl was livin' in the swamp long before his daddy was a little boy. Right? So Jupiter said she came to La-Pierre when *he* was a kid. He said she was a young and pretty white girl. *Young,* he said. Tell me how that can be."

"I'll tell you." Arden finished refolding the map before she continued. "It's because the Bright Girl never ages."

"Oh, I see." He nodded. "Not only is she a healer, she's found the fountain of youth."

"I didn't say anything about the fountain of youth!" Anger lightened Arden's eyes but turned the birthmark a shade darker. "I'm tellin' you what Jupiter told me! The Bright Girl doesn't ever get old, she always stays young and pretty!"

"And you believe this?"

"Yes! I do! I—I just do, that's all!"

Dan couldn't help but feel sorry for her. "Arden," he said quietly, "you ever heard of somethin' called *folklore?* Like stories about Johnny Appleseed, or Paul Bunyan, or . . . you know, people who're bigger than life. Maybe a long, long time ago there was a faith healer who lived down in that swamp, and after she died she got bigger than life, too, because people didn't want to let her go. So they made up these stories about her, and they passed 'em down to their children. That way she'd never die, and she'd always be young and pretty. See what I'm sayin'?"

"You don't know!" she snapped. "Next thing you'll be sayin' Jesus was a made-up story, too!"

"Well, it's your business if you want to go sloggin' through a swamp lookin' for a dead faith healer. I'm not gonna stop you."

"Damn right you're not!" Arden stood up, taking the map with her. "If I was as sick as you are, I'd be hopin' I could find the Bright Girl, too, not sittin' there denyin' her!"

"One thing that'll kill you real quick," he said as she neared the door, "is false hope. You get a little older, you'll understand that."

"I hope I never get that old."

"Hey," Dan said before she could leave. "You want a ride to the bus station, I'll be ready to go after dark."

Arden hesitated with her hand on the doorknob. "How come you don't want to go until dark?" She had to ask another question that had bothered her as well. "And how come you're not even carryin' a change of clothes?"

He thought fast. "Cooler after dark. I don't want my radiator boilin' over. And I've got friends where I'm goin', I wasn't plannin' on stoppin'."

"Uh-huh."

He avoided her eyes because he feared she was starting to see through him. "I'm gonna take a shower and get some food. *Not* barbecue. You ought to call the bus station and find out where it is."

"Even if I take a bus to Houma, I still have to get down to LaPierre somehow. Listen," she said, determined to try again, "I'll pay you thirty dollars to take me there. How about it?"

"No."

"How much out of your way can it be?" Desperation had tightened her voice. "I can do some of the drivin' for you. Besides, I've never been down in there before and . . . you know . . . a girl travelin' alone could get into trouble. That's why I paid Joey to drive me."

"Yeah, he sure took good care of you, all right. I hope you get where you're goin', but I'm sorry. I can't take you."

She kept staring at him. Something mighty strange was going on, she thought. There was the broken glass in the back of the station wagon, the fact that he was traveling without even a toothbrush, and was it happenstance that he hadn't awakened until a shrieking siren had gone past the motel? *I could be some-body you wouldn't want to be travelin' with,* he'd said. What did that mean?

She was making him nervous. He stood up and pulled off his T-shirt. She could see the outline of every rib under his pale skin. "You want to watch me get naked and take a shower, that's fine with me," Dan said. He began unbuckling the belt of his jeans.

"Okay, I'm leavin'," she decided when he pushed down his zipper. "My room's right next door, when you get ready." She re-treated, and Dan closed the door in her face and turned the latch.

He breathed a sigh of relief. She was starting to wonder about him, that much was clear. He knew he should never have given her a ride; she was a complication he didn't need. But right now there was nothing to be done but take his shower and try to relax, if he could. Get some food, that would make him feel a whole lot better. He started for the bathroom, but before he got there, curiosity snared him and he turned on the TV and clicked through the channels in search of a local newscast. He found CNN, but it was the financial segment. He switched the set off. Then, after a few seconds of internal debate, he turned it back on again. Surely he wouldn't have made the national news, but a local broadcast might come on at five and he'd find out if Lafayette had picked up the story. He felt as grimy as a mudflap at a tractor pull, and he went into the bathroom and cranked the shower taps to full blast.

Arden had gone to the office to return the extra key. The small-boned, grandmotherly woman behind the registration desk looked up over her eyeglasses from working a crossword puzzle in the Lafayette newspaper. "Your friend all right?"

"Yeah, he is. He was just extra tired, didn't hear me knockin'." She laid the key down on the desk. "Could you tell me how to get to the bus station from here?"

"Got a phone book, I'll look up the address." The woman reached a vein-ridged hand into a drawer for the directory. "Where you plannin' on goin'?"

"To Houma, first. Then on down south."

"Ain't much south of Houma but the bayou. You got relatives down there?"

"No, I'm on my own."

"On your *own?* What about your friend?"

"He's . . . goin' somewhere else."

"Lord, I wouldn't go down in that swamp country by myself, that's for gospel!" The woman had her finger on the bus station's address, but first she felt bound to deliver a warning. "All kinda roughnecks and heathens livin' down there, they don't answer to no law but their own. Look right here." She picked up the newspaper's front page and thrust it at Arden. "Headline up top, 'bout the ranger. See it?"

Arden did. It said *Terrebonne Ranger Still Missing,* and beneath that was a smaller line of type that said *Son of Lafayette Councilman Giradoux.* A photograph showed a husky, steely-eyed young man wearing a police uniform and a broad-brimmed hat.

"Missin' since Tuesday," the woman told Arden. "Been the big news here all week. He went down in that swamp one too many times, is what he did. Swallowed him up, you can bet on it."

"I'm sorry about that," Arden said, "but it's not gonna stop me from—" And then she did stop, because her gaze had gone to a story at the bottom of the page and a headline that read *Second Murder Attributed to Shreveport Fugitive.* A photograph was included with this story, too, and the bearded face in it made Arden's heart freeze.

It wasn't the best quality picture, but he was recognizable. It looked like a mug shot, or a poorly lit snapshot for a driver's license. He was bare headed and unsmiling, and he'd lost twenty pounds or more since the camera had caught him. Beneath the picture was his name: Daniel Lewis Lambert.

"They found his boat," the woman said.

"Huh?" Arden looked up, her insides quaking.

"Jack Giradoux's boat. They found it, but there wasn't hide nor hair of him. I know his folks. They eat breakfast every Saturday mornin' at the Shoneys down the road. They thought that boy hung the moon, and they're gonna take it awful hard."

Arden returned to reading the story. "I'd be mighty careful in that swamp country," the woman urged. "It's bad people can make a parish ranger disappear." She busied herself writing the bus station's address down on a piece of notepad paper.

Arden felt close to passing out as she realized what kind of man Dan Farrow—no, Dan *Lambert*—really was. Vietnam veteran, had the tattoo of a snake on his right forearm. Shot and killed the loan manager at a bank in Shreveport. Shot and beat to death a man at a motel outside Alexandria and stole his station wagon. "Oh my God," she whispered.

"Pardon?" The woman lifted her silver eyebrows.

Arden said, "This man. He's—"

. . . the man God sent Miz Arden.

Jupiter had said it. *You the man God provided to take Miz Arden to the Bright Girl. You His hands, you gone have to steer her the right direction.*

No, Dan Lambert was a killer. This newspaper said so. He'd killed two people, so what was to stop him from killing her if he wanted to? But he was sick, anybody could look at him and tell that. If he wanted to kill her, why hadn't he just pulled off the highway before they'd reached Lafayette?

"You say somethin'?" the woman asked.

"I . . . yeah. I mean . . . I'm not sure."

"Not sure? About what?"

Arden stared at the photograph. *The man God sent.* She'd wanted to believe that very badly. That there was some cosmic order of things, some undercurrent in motion that had brought her to this time and place. But if Jupiter had been so wrong, then what did that say about his belief in the Bright Girl?

She felt something crumbling inside her, and she feared that when it fell away she would have nothing left to hold her together.

"You still want the address?"

"What?"

"The bus station. You want me to tell you how to get there? It's not far."

The walls were closing in on her. She had to get out of there, had to find a place to think. "Can I take this?" She held the newspaper's page so the woman couldn't see Dan's picture.

"Sure, I'm through with it. Don't you want the—"

Arden was already going out the door.

"Guess not," the woman said when the door closed. She'd wanted to ask the girl if that mark on her face hurt, but she'd decided that wouldn't be proper. It was a shame; that girl would've been so pretty if she weren't disfigured. But that was life, wasn't it? You had to take the bad with the good, and make the best of it. Still, it was a terrible shame.

She turned her attention again to the crossword puzzle. The next word across was four letters, and its clue was "destiny."

15

The Truth

D AN HAD STEPPED OUT of the shower and was toweling
off when he heard someone speak his name.

He looked at the television set. His face—his driver's license
picture—was looking back at him from the screen. He thought
he'd been prepared for the shock, but he was wrong; in that instant he felt as if he'd simultaneously taken a gut punch and had
icy water poured on the back of his neck. The newscaster was
talking about the shooting of Emory Blanchard, and the camera showed scenes of policemen at the First Commercial Bank.
And then the vision truly became nightmarish, because suddenly
a distraught face framed with kinky red curls was talking into a
reporter's microphone.

"He went crazy when he found out we knew who he was,"
Hannah DeCayne was saying. "Harmon and me tried to stop
him, but he was out of his mind. Grabbed the shotgun away from
Harmon and blasted him right there in front of me, and then
he—oh, dear Lord, it was terrible—then he started beatin' my
husband in the head with the gun. I never saw anybody so wild in
my life, there wasn't a thing I could do!"

The camera showed the dismal Hideaway Motor Court in daylight, then focused on the crippled pickup truck. There was a shot of blood on the sandy ground. "DeCayne was pronounced dead early this morning at an Alexandria hospital," the newscaster said.

Dan's knees gave way. He sat down on the edge of the bed, his mouth agape.

"Police believe Lambert may be on his way to Naples, Florida, where his nearest family member lives . . ."

Christ! Dan thought. They'd brought his mother into this thing now!

" . . . but there've been reports that Lambert's been seen both in New Orleans and Baton Rouge. Repeating what we understand from Alexandria police, Lambert may be traveling under the name Farrow, and he should be considered extremely dangerous. Again, the First Commercial Bank of Shreveport has put a fifteen-thousand-dollar reward on Lambert, and the number to call with information is 555-9045." The photograph of Dan came up on the screen again. "Lambert is forty-two years old, has brown hair and brown eyes and stands—"

Dan got up and snapped the TV off. Then he had to sit down once more because his bones felt rubbery and his head was reeling. Anger started boiling up inside him. What kind of damned shit was that woman trying to shovel? No, not *trying;* she was doing a pretty good job of it, fake tears and all. Dan saw what had happened. The bitch had killed her husband, and who was going to call her a liar? He sensed the net starting to close around him. Who would believe he hadn't murdered DeCayne? Pretty soon the newscasts were going to make him out to be a bloodthirsty fiend who killed everybody in his path. With his picture on TV, the reward, the police looking for the station wagon—what chance did he have of getting to Vermilion, much less out of the country?

He clasped his hands to his face. His heart was beating hard, the pulse pounding at his temples. How much farther could he get? Even traveling with the shield of darkness he knew it was only a matter of time now before the law found him. And his time, it seemed, was fast ticking away. Should he try to keep going, or just give it up and call the police? What was the point of running anymore? There was no escaping prison; there was no escaping the disease that was chewing his life away. Gone south, gone south, he thought. Where could you run to when all roads were blocked?

He didn't know how long he sat there, his eyes squeezed shut and his head bowed, his thoughts scrambling like mice in mazes. There was a tentative knock at the door. Dan didn't say anything. The knock came again, a little louder this time.

"Go away!" he said. It had to be her. Or the police. He'd find out soon enough.

A long silence followed. Then her voice: "I . . . want to talk to you for a minute."

"Just go away and leave me alone. Please."

She was silent, and Dan thought she'd gone. But then he heard a rustling at the bottom of the door and something slid under it into the room. It was a newspaper page.

Dan had the feeling that the bad news was about to get worse. He put the towel around his waist, went to the door, and picked up the page. There at the lower right was his picture, the same photo he'd seen on television. *Second Murder Attributed to Shreveport Fugitive*, the headline read. He reached out, unlatched the door, and pulled it open.

Arden took a backward step, half of her face pale with fear, and she lifted a tire iron she'd taken from the back of the station wagon over her head. "Don't touch me," she said. "I'll knock your head in!"

They stared at each other for a few seconds, like two wary and frightened animals. At last Dan said, "Well, you've got my attention. What'd you want to talk about?"

"That's you, isn't it? You killed two people?"

"It's me," he answered. "But I didn't kill two people. Just the man in Shreveport."

"Oh, is that supposed to make me feel better?"

"Right now I don't give a damn what you feel. You're not the one goin' to prison. I guess you've already called the police?"

"Maybe I have," she said. "Maybe I haven't."

"You saw there's fifteen thousand dollars reward on me, didn't you? That ought to be enough to get your birthmark off. See? This must be your lucky day."

"Don't try to rush me," she warned. "I swear I'll hit you."

"I'm not rushin' anybody. Where am I gonna go wearin' a towel? You mind if I get dressed before the police get here?"

"I haven't called 'em. Not yet, I mean."

"Well, do what you have to do. I figure I'm through runnin'." He turned his back on her and went to his clothes, which were lying on a chair near the bathroom door.

Arden didn't enter the room. She watched him as he dropped the towel and put on his underwear and socks. His body was thin and sinewy, the vertebrae visible down his spine. His muscles looked shrunken and wasted. There was nothing physically threatening about him at all. Arden lowered the tire iron, but she didn't cross the threshold. Dan put on his T-shirt and then his jeans. He sat down in the chair to slip his shoes on. "I didn't kill the man in Alexandria," he told her. "For what it's worth, his wife did it and she's blamin' me. Yeah, I did steal their station wagon, only because the damn woman shot my pickup truck's tire out. She blasted him with a shotgun, aimin' at me, but when I left there he was still alive. She beat him to death and she's tellin' the police I did it. That's the truth."

Arden swallowed thickly, the fear still fluttering around in her throat. "The paper said you went crazy in a bank. Shot a man dead. That you're supposed to be armed and dangerous."

"They got the crazy part right. Bank was repossessin' my truck. It was the last thing I had left. I got in a fight with a guard, the loan manager pulled a pistol on me, and . . . it just happened. But I'm not armed, and I never was carryin' a gun. I guess I ought to be flattered that they think I'm so dangerous, but they're wrong." He sat back in the chair and put his hands on the armrests. "I meant it about the reward money. Ought to be you who gets it as much as anybody else. You want to go call the law, I'll be right here."

Her common sense told her to go to her room and use the phone there, but she hesitated. "How come you didn't give yourself up after you shot that man?"

"I panicked. Couldn't think straight. But I was tellin' you the truth about the leukemia. The doctors don't give me a whole lot of time, and I don't care to pass it in prison."

"So how come you're just gonna sit there and let me turn you in?"

"Somebody will, sooner or later. I thought I could get out of the country, but . . . there's no use in tryin' to run when your name and face is plastered all over TV and the newspapers. It's just hurtful to my family."

"Your *family?* You married?"

"Ex-wife. A son. I stopped to see 'em in Alexandria, that's why I was stayin' at that damn motel. I was headin' to a place called Vermilion. Cabin down there I was gonna hide in for a while, until I could decide what to do." He shook his head. "No use in it."

Arden didn't know exactly what she'd expected, but this wasn't it. After she'd digested the newspaper story, she'd gone to the station wagon to search it, looking for a gun. She'd found the tire iron in the back and in the glove compartment a couple of old receipts—for froglegs, of all things—made out to Hannah De-Cayne from the Blue Gulf Restaurant. The hell of this thing was that the fifteen thousand dollars would bail her out of her financial troubles and buy her a car, but after the bills were paid off there still wouldn't be enough left for the plastic surgery. The doctors had told her there would have to be two or more operations, and they couldn't promise what the results would be. But here was fifteen thousand dollars sitting in front of her if she wanted it.

"Go on," Dan said. "Call 'em, I don't care."

"I will. In a minute." She frowned. "If you're so sick, why aren't you in a hospital?"

"Ever set foot in a V.A. hospital? I was in one for a while. People waitin' to die, hollerin' and cryin' in their sleep. I wasn't gonna lie there and fade away. Besides, most days I could still work. I'm a carpenter. Was, I mean. Listen, are you gonna call the police, or do you want to write my life story?"

Arden didn't answer. She was thinking of what it had felt like when she was joy-riding in that car she'd stolen—speeding from nowhere to nowhere, trying to outrace reality—and the state troopers' car had roared up behind her with its siren wailing and the bubble light awhirl. She remembered the snap of cuffs on her wrists, and the sharp, dark terror that had pierced her tough fuck-you attitude. She'd had a lot to learn in those days. If it hadn't been for a few people like Mr. Richards and Jupiter and his wife, the lessons would've fallen like seeds on stony ground. Stealing a car was a lot different from committing murder, of course, and maybe Dan Lambert belonged in prison, but Arden wasn't sure she was the one to put him there.

"One thing I'd like to do for myself," Dan said while she was pondering the situation. He stood up, causing Arden's heart to start thumping again, and he went to the telephone on the table beside his bed. He dialed the operator and asked for directory assistance in Alexandria.

"Who're you callin'?" Arden's knuckles were aching, she was gripping the tire iron so hard.

"I'd like the police department," he said to the Alexandria operator when the call clicked through. "The main office at City Hall."

"What're you *doin'?*" Arden asked, incredulous. "Givin' yourself up?"

"Quiet," he told her. He waited until a voice answered. "Alexandria police, Sergeant Gil Parradine speakin'."

"Sergeant, my name is Dan Lambert. I think you people are lookin' for me."

There was no reply, just stunned—or suspicious—silence. Then: "Is this a joke?"

"No joke. Just listen. I didn't kill Harmon DeCayne. I saw his wife shoot him with that shotgun, but when I left there, he was still alive. She must've decided to beat him to death and blame it on me. See what I'm sayin'?"

"Uh . . . I'm . . . hold on just a minute, I'll connect you to—"

"*No!*" Dan snapped. "You pass the phone, I'm gone! I'm tellin' you, that woman killed her husband. You check the shotgun for fingerprints, you won't find one of mine on it. Will you do that for me?"

"I—I'll have to let you talk to Captain—"

"I'm through talkin'." Dan hung up.

"I can't believe you just did that! Don't you know they'll trace the call?"

"I just wanted to start 'em thinkin'. Maybe they'll check for prints and ask that damn woman some more questions. Anyway, they don't know it wasn't a local call. There's enough time for you to turn me in."

"Do you *want* to go to prison? Is that it?"

"No, I don't want to go to prison," Dan said. "But I don't have a whole hell of a lot of choice, do I?"

Arden had to do the next thing; she had to test both herself and him. She took a deep breath, crossed the threshold into his room, and closed the door behind her. She stood with her back against it, the tire iron ready if he jumped at her.

He raised his eyebrows. "Takin' a risk bein' in a room alone with me, aren't you?"

"I'm not sure yet. Am I?"

He showed her his palms and eased down on the edge of the bed. "Whatever's on your mind," he told her, "now's the time to tell me about it."

"All right." She took two steps toward him and stopped again, still testing both her own nerves and his intentions. "I don't want to turn you in. That's not gonna help me."

"Fifteen thousand dollars is a lot of money," he said. "You could buy yourself—"

"I want to find the Bright Girl," Arden went on. "That's why I'm here. Findin' the Bright Girl and gettin' this thing off my face is all I'm interested in. Not the money, not why you killed some man in Shreveport." Her intense blue gaze didn't waver. "I've seen her in my dreams, only I never could tell what she looked like. But I think I'm close to her now, closer than I've ever been. I can't give it up. Not even for fifteen thousand dollars."

"It would pay for an operation, wouldn't it?"

"The doctors can't say for sure they can get it off. They say tryin' to remove it could leave a scar just as bad as the birthmark. Then where would I be? Maybe worse off, if that's even possible. No, I'm not doin' it that way, not when I'm so close."

"You're not thinkin' straight," Dan said. "The doctors are your best chance. The Bright Girl . . . well, you know what I think about that story."

"I do. It doesn't matter. I want you to drive me to LaPierre."

He grunted. "Now I *know* you're out of your mind! Look who you're talkin' to. I killed a man yesterday. I've got a stolen car sittin' out in the parkin' lot. You don't know I wouldn't try to kill you if I could, and you're wantin' to travel with me another ninety miles down into the swamp. Wouldn't you say that might be pushin' your luck?"

"If you were gonna hurt me, you would've done it between here and the truck stop. I believe you about what happened at the motel. There's not a gun in the car, and you're not carryin' one. I've got a tire iron, and I still think I could outrun you."

"Maybe, but you can't outrun the police. Ever heard of aidin' and abettin' a fugitive?"

"If the police stop us," Arden said, "I'll say I didn't know who you were. No skin off your teeth to tell 'em the same thing."

Dan looked at her long and hard. He figured she'd had a tough life, and this obsession with the Bright Girl had grown stronger as things had started falling apart. He saw only disappointment ahead for her, but he was in no position to argue. She was right; it was no skin off his teeth. "You sure about this?"

"Yes, I am." The truth was that she hadn't decided he was worth trusting until he'd made the call to Alexandria. Still, she was going to hang on to the tire iron awhile longer.

He stood up and walked toward her. It flashed through her mind to retreat to the door, but she stayed where she was. She knew from experience that once you showed fear to a horse, the animal would never respect you again; she knew it was true with people, too. He reached out for her, and she lifted the tire iron to ward him off.

He stopped. "My cap," he said. "It's on the chair behind you."

"Oh." She stepped aside to let him get it.

Dan put his cap on and checked his wristwatch. Five thirty-four. Outside the window the shadows were lengthening, but it wouldn't be full dark until after seven. "I'll want to travel the back roads," he told her. "A little safer that way, but slower. Less likely to run across a state trooper. I hope. And I'm not gonna jump you, so you can put that thing down." He nodded toward the tool in her hand. When she didn't lower it, he narrowed his eyes and said, "If you don't trust me now, just think how you're gonna feel in a couple of hours when we're out in the dark and there's nobody around for miles."

Arden slowly let her arm fall.

"Okay, good. I'd hate to sneeze and get my brains knocked out. You got any deodorant?"

"Huh?"

"Deodorant," he repeated. "I need some. And toothpaste or mouthwash, if you've got either of those. Aspirin would help, too."

"In my suitcase. I'll bring it over."

"That's all right, I'll go with you," Dan said, and he saw her stiffen up again. "My room, your room, or the car, what does it matter?" he asked. "Better be certain you want to do this before we get started."

She realized she was going to have to turn her back on him sooner or later. She said, "Come on, then," and she went out the door first, her stomach doing slow flip-flops.

In Arden's bathroom Dan applied roll-on deodorant—and he'd never thought the day would come when he'd be using Secret—and then he wet a washcloth, put a glob of Crest on it, and scrubbed his teeth. Arden brought him a small first aid kit that contained a bottle of Tylenol, a tube of skin ointment, some adhesive bandages, and a bottle of eyedrops. "You must've been a Girl Scout," Dan said as she shook two aspirin onto his palm.

"Joey always said I missed my callin', that I should've been a nurse. That's because I took care of the band when they had hangovers or were too strung out to play. Somebody had to be responsible."

Dan swallowed the Tylenol tablets with a glass of water and gave her back the first aid kit. "I'll need to get some food and coffee somewhere. We'd better not stick around here too much longer."

"I'm ready."

It was six o'clock by the time the bill was paid and they were pulling away from the motel. Arden kept the tire iron on the seat near her right hand, and Dan decided not to make an issue of it. Not far from the motel Dan turned into a McDonald's and in the drive-through bought three hamburgers, a large order of fries, and a cup of coffee. They sat in the parking lot while he ate, and Dan unfolded the roadmap and saw that Highway 182 was the route to follow through the towns of New Iberia, Jeanerette, Baldwin, and on to Morgan City, where Highway 90 would take them deeper into the bayou country to Houma.

"Where're you gonna go?" Arden asked when he'd finished the second burger. "After you take me to LaPierre, I mean. You still gonna try to get out of the country?"

"I don't know. Maybe."

"Don't you have any relatives you could go to? Are your parents still alive?"

"Father's dead. My mother's alive, but she's old and I don't want to get her messed up in this. It'll be hard enough on her as it is."

"Does she know about the leukemia?"

"No. It's my problem." He speared her with a glance. "What do you care, anyway? You hardly know me."

She shrugged. "Just interested, I guess. You're the first killer I ever met."

Dan couldn't suppress a grim smile. "Well, I hope I'm the last one you meet." He offered her his french fries. "Take some."

She accepted a few and crunched them down. "You don't really have anywhere to go, do you?"

"I'll find a place."

Arden nodded vacantly and watched the sun sinking. The Bright Girl—a dream without a face—was on her mind, and if she had to travel with a wanted fugitive to reach that dream, then so be it. She wasn't afraid. Well, maybe a little afraid. But her life had never been easy, and no one had ever given her a free ticket. She had nowhere to go now but toward the Bright Girl, toward what she felt was the hope of healing and a new start.

I know who you are, she recalled Jupiter saying to the killer beside her.

You the man God sent Miz Arden.

She hoped that was true. She wanted to believe with all her heart it was.

Because if Jupiter could be so wrong about Dan Lambert, he could be wrong about the Bright Girl, too.

Dan finished his food and they started off again. Four miles south of Lafayette, they passed a state trooper who'd pulled a kid on a motorcycle over to the roadside. The trooper was occupied writing a ticket and they slid by unnoticed, but it was a few minutes before Arden stopped looking nervously back.

The light was fading. Purple shadows streamed across the road, and on either side there were woods broken by ponds of brackish water from which tree stumps protruded like shattered teeth. The road narrowed. Traffic thinned to an occasional car or pickup truck. A sign on stilts said KEEP YOUR HEART IN ACADIANA OR GET YOUR—there was the crude drawing of a mule's hind end here—OUT. Spanish moss festooned the trees like antebellum lace, and the mingled odors of wild honeysuckle and Gulf salt drifted on the humid air. As the first stars emerged from the darkening sky, heat lightning began to ripple across the southern horizon.

Dan switched on the headlights and kept an eye on the rearview mirror. The heat lightning's flashes reminded him of the battle zone, with artillery shells landing in the distance. He had the eerie sensation of traveling on a road that led back into time, back into the wet wilderness of a foreign country where the reptiles thrived and death was a silent shadow. He was afraid of what he might find—or what might find him—there, but it was the only road left for him to go. And like it or not, he had to follow it to its end.

16

Black Against Yellow

IT WAS JUST AFTER nine o'clock when the station wagon's headlight beams grazed a rust-streaked sign that said VER-MILION 5 MI., CHANDELAC 12 MI., LAPIERRE 15 MI. "Almost there," Dan said, relief blooming in him like a sweet flower. Arden didn't answer. She'd opened her purse two miles back and taken from it the pink drawstring bag, which she now held in her lap. Her fingers kneaded the bag's contents, but Arden stared straight ahead along the cone of the lights.

"What's in that thing?" Dan asked.

"Huh?"

"That bag. What's in it?"

"Nothin' special," she said.

"You're sure rubbin' it like it's somethin' special."

"It's . . . just what I carry for good luck."

"Oh, I should've figured." He nodded. "Anybody who believes in faith healers has to have a good-luck charm or two lyin' around."

"If I were you, I wouldn't be laughin'. I'd think you'd want to find the Bright Girl as much as I do."

"There's an idea. After she heals me, she can go back to Shreveport with me and raise Emory Blanchard from the dead. Then I can get right back to where I was, beggin' for work."

"Laugh if you want to. All I'm sayin' is, what would it hurt for you to go with me?"

"It would hurt," he said. "I told you what I think about false hope. If there really was a Bright Girl—which there's not—the only way she could help me is to crank back time and bring the man I killed back to life. Anyway, I said I'd take you to LaPierre, and that's what I'll do, but that's *all*."

"What're you gonna do, dump me out on the street once we get there?"

"No, I'll help you find someplace to spend the night." He hoped. The last motel they'd passed was ten miles behind them in the small town of Houma. Since the woods had closed in on either side of the road, they'd seen the scattered lights of only a few houses. They had left civilization behind, it seemed, and the bittersweet smell of the swamp thickened the air. If worse came to worst and a motel or boardinghouse couldn't be found anywhere near LaPierre, Dan had decided to offer Arden lodging at the cabin and then he'd take her on into town in the morning. But *only* if nothing else could be found; he didn't like having somebody depending on him, and the sooner she went on her way the better he'd feel about things.

They crossed a long, concrete bridge and suddenly they were passing through the hamlet of Vermilion. It wasn't much, just a few clapboard houses and closed-up stores. The only place that was lit up with activity was a little dump called Cootie's Bar, and Dan noted that the four pickup trucks parked around the place all had shotguns or rifles racked in the rear windows. This did not help Dan's hopes of finding a decent motel room for Arden. He had the feeling that a woman alone in this territory could find herself pinned to a pool table, and a man with a fifteen-thousand-dollar reward on his head would be torn clean apart. He drove on through Vermilion, luckily attracting the attention of only a couple of dogs who stopped scrapping over a bone to get out of the road.

As they drew away from town, Dan watched the odometer. Susan had said the turnoff to Gary's cabin was three miles past the bridge, on the left. It ought to be coming up any minute now. He didn't plan on stopping there yet, but he wanted to make sure he found it. And then, yes, there it was, a dirt road snaking off to the left into the woods. Good. Now at least he knew where he'd be resting his head tonight. He passed the turnoff, and neither he nor Arden saw the black Eldorado hidden close by.

Pelvis was asleep and snoring with Mama sprawled out on his chest when Flint saw headlights approaching. As darkness had fallen, Flint had pulled the car closer up the dirt road to the highway's edge, and he'd kept vigilant watch while Pelvis had drowsed, awakened to prattle about Elvis's pink Cadillac and love of his mother's coconut cakes, and then drowsed again. Flint could have counted on one hand how many cars had passed, and none of them had even slowed at the turnoff to the cabin. This one, though, did slow down, if almost imperceptibly. But it didn't turn, and now here it came on the southbound road. Still, Flint's heartbeat had quickened, and Clint felt the change and responded with a questioning twitch under his brother's sweat-soaked shirt. Flint turned the key in the ignition and switched on the single headlight as the car began to glide past their hiding place.

The beam jabbed out and caught the rust-splotched station wagon. Flint saw a blond-haired woman sitting in the passenger seat; she glanced toward the light, her eyes squinted, and Flint made out that the entire right side of her face seemed to be covered with an ugly violet bruise. He couldn't see the driver's face, but he saw a head wearing a dark blue baseball cap. Then the station wagon had gone out of the light. Flint's breath hissed between his teeth; it was the same car Lambert had driven out of Basile Park.

He started the engine. Pelvis sat up bleary-eyed and rasped, "Whazhappenin?"

"He's here. Just passed us, goin' south." Flint's voice was calm and quiet, his heart pumping hot blood but his nerves icy. "He didn't turn, but that's him all right. Hold the mutt." He put the engine into gear and eased the Eldorado onto the road, turning right to follow Lambert. The station wagon's taillights were just going around a curve. "There's a woman with him," Flint said as they gained speed. "Could be a hostage. Looks like he might've beaten her up."

"A *hostage?*" Pelvis said, horrified. His arms were clamped tightly around Mama. "My Lord, what're we gonna *do?*"

"What we came for." They rounded the curve, and there was the station wagon forty yards ahead. "Hang on," Flint said. His foot pressed down on the accelerator, a cold smile of triumph twisting his mouth. "I'm gonna run the sonofabitch off the road."

The light suddenly hitting them had startled Arden as much as it had Dan. "You think that was a trooper?" she asked, her voice shaky as they started into the curve.

"Could've been. We'll find out in a minute."

"He's pullin' out!" She had her head outside the window. "Comin' after us!"

Dan watched the rearview mirror. No siren yet, no flashing light. He kept his speed steady, the needle hanging at fifty. There was no need to panic yet. Might've been just somebody parked on a side road getting stoned. No need to panic.

"Here he comes!" Arden yelled. "Pickin' up speed!"

Dan saw the car coming around the curve, closing the distance between them. The car had only one headlight.

One headlight.

A knot the size of a lemon seemed to swell in Dan's throat.

The bounty hunters' black Cadillac had one headlight.

But no, it couldn't be! How the hell would Flint Murtaugh and the Elvis clone have known where he was going? No, it wasn't them. Of course it wasn't.

He heard the roar of their engine.

Arden pulled her head in, her eyes wide. "I think he's gonna—"

Ram us, she was about to say. But then the headlight was glaring into the rearview mirror and the Cadillac was right on their bumper and Dan tried to jerk the station wagon to one side but he was a muscle-twitch too late. The Cadillac banged into their rear with threatening authority, then abruptly backed off again. The station wagon's frame was shivering, but Dan had control of the wheel. Another curve was coming up, and he had to watch where he was going. The Cadillac leapt forward again with what sounded like an angry snort, and once more banged their rear bumper and then drew back. "He's tellin' me to pull over!" Dan said above the rush of the wind. He glanced at the speedometer and saw the needle trembling at sixty.

"Who is it? The police?"

"Uh-uh! Couple of bounty hunters are after me! Damned if I know how they found me, but—"

"Comin' fast again!" Arden shouted, gripping onto the seat back.

This time the Cadillac's driver meant business. The knock rattled their bones and almost unhinged Dan's hands from the shuddering wheel. The Cadillac didn't back away, but instead began shoving the station wagon off the road. Dan put his foot on the brake pedal and the tires shrieked in protest, but the Cadillac was too strong. The station wagon was being inexorably pushed to the roadside, and now something clattered and banged under the front axle and the smell of scorched metal came up through the floorboard. The brake pedal lost its tension and slid right to the floor, and Dan realized the brakes had just given up the ghost.

Whoever was driving, Murtaugh or the imitation Elvis, they wanted to play rough. Dan was damned if he'd let those two have him without a fight. He lifted his foot from the dead pedal and jammed it down on the accelerator, at the same time twisting the wheel violently away from the roadside. A gout of oil smoke boomed from the exhaust pipe, and the station wagon jumped forward, putting six feet between its crumpled rear bumper and the Cadillac's teeth. Dan swerved back and forth across the road, trying to cut their speed and also to keep the Cadillac from shoving them again. They passed what looked like a marina on the right and then the woods closed in once more on both sides of the pavement. A SPEED LIMIT 45 MPH sign pocked with bullet holes swept past. The Cadillac roared up on them, smacking their left rear fender before Dan could jerk the station wagon aside. Now the road began a series of tight twists and turns, and it was all Dan could do to keep them from flying off. He dared to look at the speedometer and saw that it too had gone haywire, the needle flipping wildly back and forth across the dial.

"Slow down!" Arden shouted. "You'll wreck us!"

He pulled up on the emergency brake, but there was no tension in that either. Whatever had fried underneath the car had burned out the brake system, which probably had been hanging together with spit and chicken wire anyway. "No brakes!" he answered, and then he fought the car around the next sharp curve with the Cadillac on his tail, his teeth clenched and his heart pounding. WELCOME TO CHANDELAC a sign announced, and they were through a one-block strip of darkened stores in a blast of engine noise and whirlwind of sandy grit. On the other side of Chandelac, the road straightened out and overhead huge oak trees locked branches. The Cadillac suddenly veered into the left lane and came up beside Dan, and Dan looked into the puffy face of an aged Elvis Presley, who was holding on to his bulldog with one arm and waving him to pull over with the other.

Dan shook his head. The Elvis impersonator said something to Murtaugh, probably relaying Dan's answer. Murtaugh then delivered his next response by slamming the Cadillac broadside against the station wagon. Arden had been holding back a scream, but the collision of metal knocked it loose. Dan felt the right-side tires slide off the pavement and into the weeds. He had no choice but to hit the accelerator and try to jump ahead of Murtaugh, but the bounty hunter stayed with him. Dan thought they must be going seventy miles an hour, the woods blurring past and the station wagon's engine moaning with fatigue. The road curved to the right, and suddenly there were headlights coming in the left lane. Murtaugh instantly cut his speed and drifted back behind Dan, who took the curve on smoking tires. They rocketed past an old Ford crawling north, and as soon as they were out of the curve the Cadillac was banging on Dan's back door again.

He darted a glance at Arden, saw her hunched forward with the pink drawstring bag clenched between her hands. "I told you not to travel with me, didn't I?" he yelled, and then he saw in the rearview mirror the Cadillac trying to pull alongside him. He veered to the left, cutting the bounty hunter off. Murtaugh swung the Cadillac to the right, and again Dan cut him off.

"He's not gonna let you get up there!" Pelvis shouted over the windstorm. His hair was a molded ebony still life. He saw the speedometer and blanched. "Lord God, Mr. Murtaugh! We're goin' seventy—"

"I know how fast!" Flint yelled back. The station wagon's beat-up rear fender was less than ten feet ahead. Lambert had stopped using his brakes. Either the man was crazy, or demonically desperate. Flint pressed his foot down on the accelerator and the Cadillac's battered front fender again slammed into Lambert's car. This time some serious damage was done: white sparks exploded from underneath the station wagon, a piece of metal coming loose and dragging the concrete. As Flint let the Eldorado drift back he saw Lambert's left rear tire start shredding apart. "That got him!" Flint crowed. "He'll have to pull over!"

Within seconds the tire had disintegrated into flying fragments and now the wheel rim was dragging a line of sparks. But Lambert made no move to pull off, and the man's stupid stubbornness infuriated Flint. He twisted the wheel, his knuckles white and Clint's hand seizing at the air, and he veered into the left lane and powered the Eldorado up alongside Lambert to deliver the coup de grâce.

*　　*　　*

Dan saw Murtaugh coming. The big black car was going to knock them into the next parish. His heart had been gripped by a cold fist when he'd felt the rear tire going, but actually the drag was slowing them down. Still, here came Murtaugh up along-side, and what the Cadillac was going to do to them wouldn't be pretty.

He swung the car to the left and bashed the Cadillac so hard he heard the frames of both cars groan in discordant harmony. Murtaugh returned the favor with a broadside blow, and sud-denly Dan's door tore off its rusted hinges and fell away. Both cars whammed together in the center of the road, what remained of the station wagon's left side buckling inward like a stomped beer can.

Dan's speed was falling past sixty, the engine making a harsh *lug-lug-lugging*. He smelled burned rubber and hot metal, and ahead on the road a half-dozen ravens leapt up from the roadkill on which they were feasting and scattered with enraged cries. He looked at the dashboard and saw the needle on the water tem-perature gauge vibrating at the far limit of the red line. Murtaugh hit him again, his own car being reduced to rolling wreckage and steam swirling from the Cadillac's hood, and the impact knocked the station wagon across the right lane onto the shoulder.

Dan heard Arden's breath hitch.

They hit a sign, black against yellow, that he had only an instant to read before it was crushed down.

DANGEROUS BRIDGE, 10MPH.

With a *boom* and a burst of escaping steam from the volcanic radiator the hood flew up in front of the windshield. Dan twisted the wheel to get on the pavement again, but the rear end fish-tailed out of control. Three seconds later they hit something else that cracked like a pistol shot, and abruptly Dan felt his butt rise up off the seat and he knew with sickening certainty that the sta-tion wagon had left the road. Branches and vines whipped at the top of the car, he heard Arden scream again, and his own mouth was opening to cry out when they came down, the station wagon hitting water like a fatman doing a graceless bellyflop. Dan had the sensation of his body being squeezed and then stretched by the impact, his skull banging the roof and bright comets of red light streaking behind his eyes. He heard what sounded like a wall of water crashing against the hood and windshield, and the engine sizzled and moaned before it began an iron-throated gurgling. Dazed at the quickness of what had happened, his head packed with pain and his consciousness flagging, Dan sat in the darkness still gripping the steering wheel.

His feet were submerged. Water had sloshed up through the floorboard and was flooding over the crumpled sill where the door had been. He thought the car was sinking, and the terror that swept through him cleared away some of the haze. He turned his head—his neck muscles felt sprained—and made out the girl lying sprawled on the seat. He couldn't leave her there, and though he thought he was moving as fast as he could, it seemed like a slow-motion nightmare; he got his arms around Arden and pulled her with him out of the car, stepping into knee-deep water bottomed with mud. The girl was a dead weight. Dan lost his footing and splashed down with her. Her face went under, and he turned over on his back to support her so her head was above water. She didn't struggle or sputter, but she was breathing. The taste of blood was in Dan's mouth. The darkness was closing in again, but he felt a slow current flowing around his body. It came to him that the current, as weak as it might be, must be flowing south to the Gulf, however far away that was. He knew for sure that if he passed out, both of them would drown. The bounty hunters. Where were they? Somewhere close, that was for sure. He couldn't hesitate any longer. Dan began pushing himself and Arden through the muddy water, giving them up to the current's southward drift.

17

Corridors and Walls

"THEY WENT OFF!" PELVIS had yelled. "Smack off the bridge!"

Flint had fought the Eldorado to a stop fifty yards past the wooden bridge. Steam was hissing around the hood, the radiator ready to blow. Mama was barking her head off, Clint was whipping in a frenzy, and Pelvis was yelling in Flint's ear.

"Shut up! Just shut your mouth!" Flint shouted. He put the car in reverse and started backing to the bridge. The structure, except for the broken railing the station wagon had torn through, was festooned with orange reflectors. They were still twenty yards from the bridge when the engine shuddered and died, and Flint had to guide the car off into the weeds on the right side of the road. "Get out!" he told Pelvis, and then he popped open the glove compartment, removed his set of handcuffs and their key, and put them into his suit jacket's inside pocket. He got out, Clint's arm still flailing around outside his shirt, then he shrugged into his jacket and unlocked the trunk.

"He never even slowed down, did he?" Pelvis was jabbering. "Never slowed down, went right off that bridge like he had wings!"

"Take one of these." Flint had pushed aside a pair of jumper cables and a toolbox and brought out two red cylinders that were each about twelve inches long.

Pelvis recoiled. "What is that? Dynamite?"

Flint closed the trunk, set one of the cylinders on the hood, and yanked a string attached to the end of the cylinder in his hand. There was a sputter of sparks as the friction fuse ignited, and then the cylinder grew a bright red glow that pushed back the night in a fifteen-foot radius and made Pelvis squint. "Safety flare," Flint said. "Don't look at the flame. Take the other one and pull the fuse."

Pelvis did, holding Mama in the crook of his arm. His flare cooked up a bright green illumination.

"Let's see what we've got." Flint strode toward the snapped railing, and Pelvis followed behind.

The bridge was only two feet above water. There was the station wagon, mired to the tops of its wheels and glistening with mud. Flint could see the driver's seat. Lambert wasn't in it. Flint reached into his shirt with his left hand, slid the derringer from its holster, and then switched the gun to his right hand and the flare to his left. He lifted the flare higher, searching for movement. The bridge spanned a channel that was maybe ten or twelve feet wide, with thickets of sharp-tipped palmettos and other thorny swamp growth protruding from the water on either side. He saw no dry land out there; neither did he see Lambert or the woman with the bruised face. Leaning over, he shone the flare under the bridge, but Lambert wasn't there either. "Damn it to hell," he said as he eased off the bridge into the morass. He started slogging toward the car, the flare sizzling over his head, and then he stopped and looked back when Pelvis didn't join him. "Are you waitin' for a written invitation?"

"Well . . . no sir, but . . . my shoes. I mean, they're real blue suede. I paid over a hundred dollars for 'em."

"Tough. Get in here and back me up!"

Pelvis hesitated, his face folded in a frown. He looked down at his shoes and sighed, and then he got a good grip on Mama and stepped into the swamp. He flinched as he felt the mud close over his hound dogs.

His derringer ready, Flint shone the flare into the car. Water was still filling up the floorboard. He saw something floating in there: Lambert's baseball cap. In the backseat was a suitcase, and the red glare revealed a purse on the passenger side. He said, "Clint! Take!" and pushed the derringer into his brother's hand. Then he leaned in, retrieved the purse and opened it, finding a wallet and a Texas driver's license made out to Arden Halliday with a Fort Worth address. The picture showed the face of a young woman with wavy blond hair. Her face might have been valuable on the freak-show circuit: the left side was pretty enough, but the right side was covered with a dark deformity that must've been a terrible birthmark. In the wallet were no credit cards, but it held a little over a hundred dollars and some change.

"I swear, that's some trick!" Pelvis said, staring at Clint's hand with the derringer in it. "Can he shoot that thing?"

"If I tell him to." Flint slid the license and the money into his jacket, then he returned the wallet to the purse and the purse to the car.

"He can understand you?"

"I've trained him with code words, same as trainin' a dog. Clint! Release!" Flint took the derringer as Clint's fingers loosened. He scanned the swamp while he moved the light around, making the shadows shift.

"Bet you wish he could talk sometimes."

"He'd say he's as sick of me as I am of him. Get your mind back on your business. Lambert couldn't be far away, and he's got the woman with him."

"You think we ought to—"

"Hush!" Flint snapped. "Just listen!"

Pelvis, as much as he loved to hear the voice of his idol coming from his own throat, forced himself to be quiet. Mama began to growl, but Flint gave Pelvis a hellfire-and-damnation look and Pelvis gently scratched under her chin to silence her. They listened. They could hear the swamp speaking: a drone of insects pulsing like weeping guitars; something calling in the distance with a voice like a bandsaw; little muffled grunts, trills, and chitters drifting in the oppressive heat.

And then, at last, a splash.

Flint whispered, "There he is." He moved past the car and stopped again, the water up to his knees. He offered the flare toward the darkness, shards of crimson light glinting off the channel's ripply surface. He could feel a slight current around his legs. Lambert was tired and probably hurt, and he was taking the path of least resistance.

"Hey, Lambert!" Flint shouted. It could've been his imagination, but the swamp seemed to go quiet. "Listen up!" He paused, his ears straining, but Lambert had stopped moving. "It's over! All you're doin' is diggin' yourself a deeper hole! Hear me?" There was no answer, but Flint hadn't expected one yet. "Don't make us come in there after you!"

Dan was crouched down in the water forty yards ahead of the two bounty hunters' flares. He was supporting Arden's head against his shoulder. She hadn't fully come to, but she must have been waking up because her body had involuntarily spasmed and her right hand, balled into a fist, had jerked up and then splashed down again. Dan didn't recall striking his face on the steering wheel, but his nose felt mashed and blood was trickling from both nostrils. Probably broken, he'd decided; it was all right, he'd survived worse punches. Pain drummed between his temples and his vision was clouded, and he'd almost blacked out a couple of minutes before but he thought he was past it now. He had backed up as far as he could against the right side of the channel, where gnarly vegetation grew out of the muck. Something with thorns was stabbing into his shoulder. He waited, breathing hard as he watched the two figures in their overlapping circles of red and green light.

"Show yourself, Lambert!" the one named Murtaugh called. "You don't want to hurt the woman, now, do you?"

He thought of leaving her, but her head might slip under and she'd drown before they reached her. He thought of surrendering, but it had occurred to him that at his back was a wilderness where a man could disappear. It was in his mind like a fixed star to head south with the current and keep heading south, and sooner or later he would have to reach the Gulf.

Murtaugh said, "Might as well give it up! You're not goin' anywhere!"

The cold arrogance in the man's voice sealed Dan's decision. He was damned if he'd give up to those two money-hungry bastards. He began pushing himself and Arden away from them, the bottom's soft mud sucking at his legs. Arden gave a soft moan, and then water must have gotten in her mouth because her body twitched again and her arms flailed, causing another splash, and then she started coughing and retching.

Murtaugh sloshed two strides forward and threw the flare toward the noise. Dan watched the red light spin up in a high arc, illuminating twisted branches bearded with Spanish moss, and the flare began coming down. There was no hiding from the light; as it bloomed the water red around him, Dan stood up and with the strength of desperation heaved Arden's body over his shoulder in a fireman's carry. He heard the Elvis impersonator yell, "I see him!" Dan was struggling through the mire when the flare hit the surface behind him. It kept burning for four seconds more before the chemical fire winked out. He managed only a few steps before his knees gave way and he fell again, dowsing them both, and Arden came up choking and spitting.

In her mind she'd been sixteen again, when she'd lived on the youth ranch. She'd been riding full-out on one of Jupiter's horses, and suddenly the animal had stepped into a gopher hole and staggered and she'd gone flying over his head, the treacherous earth coming up at her as fast as a slap from God. But water, not Texas dust, was in her eyes and mouth now; she didn't know where she was, though the pain in her head and body told her she'd just been thrown from horseback. A flickering green light floated in the darkness. She heard a man's voice whisper, "Easy, easy! I've got you!" and an arm hooked under her chin. She was being pulled through water. There was no strength in her to resist. She reached up to grasp hold of the arm, and she realized there was something gripped in her right fist and it was vitally important not to let go of it. Then she remembered what it was, and as that came clear, so did the memory of a black-and-yellow sign that said DANGEROUS BRIDGE, 10MPH.

Flint took the flare from Pelvis and holstered his derringer. "He won't get far. Come on." He slogged after their quarry, his shoes weighted with mud.

"Mr. Murtaugh . . . we're not followin' him in *there*, are we?"

Flint turned his face, his eyes deep-socketed and his skin a sepulchral shade. "Yes, Eisley, we are. We're gonna rag his tail all night if we have to. That's the job. You wanted an audition, now, by God, you're gonna get it."

"Yes sir, but . . . it's a *swamp*, Mr. Murtaugh. I mean . . . you saw those 'gators today, and that big whopper of a snake lyin' in the road. What're we gonna do when the light burns out?"

"It'll last half an hour. I give Lambert twenty minutes at most." He'd considered rushing Lambert, but decided it was safer to wear him down. Anyway, nobody was going to do much rushing in this mud. "I don't think he's got a gun, but he must be carryin' some kind of weapon. A knife, maybe. If we crowd him too close, he might get crazy and hurt the girl."

Pelvis's sweat-shiny face was a study of Tupelo torment. "I don't want to get anybody hurt. Maybe we ought to go find the law and let 'em take it from here."

"Eisley," Flint said gravely, "no bounty hunter worth a shit goes cryin' to the police for help. They hate *us,* and we don't need *them.* We let Lambert get away from us, there goes the fifteen thousand dollars *and* the girl's life, too, most likely. Now, come on." He started off again, and again stopped when Pelvis didn't follow. Flint nodded. "Well," he said, "I figured it. I knew you were nothin' but a windbag. You thought it'd be easy, didn't you?"

"I . . . didn't know I was gonna have to wade through a swamp full of 'gators and snakes! I've got Mama to look out for."

Flint's fuse had been sparking; now, like the flare's, it ignited his charge. "God *damn* it!" he shouted, and he sloshed back to stand face-to-jowls with Pelvis. "You got us in this mess! It was you who couldn't keep your mutt quiet back in the park! It was you who lost the Mace! It's been you who's messed up my rhythm—my *life*—ever since Smoates hung you around my neck! You're an insult to me, you understand? I'm a *professional,* I'm not a freak or a clown like you are! I don't give up and quit! Hear me?" His voice ended on a rising, stabbing note.

Pelvis didn't answer. His face was downcast. A drop of sweat fell from his chin into the quagmire that was already leaching the blue dye from his mail-order shoes. In his arms, Mama's bulbous eyes stared fixedly at Flint, a low growl rippling in her throat.

Flint's anger turned incandescent. He reached out, grabbed Mama by the scruff of her neck, and jerked her away from Pelvis. Mama's growling had increased, but her ferocity was a bluff; she began yelping as Flint reared his arm back to throw her as hard and far as he could.

Pelvis seized Flint's wrist. "Please, Mr. Murtaugh!" he begged. "Please don't hurt her!"

Flint was a heartbeat away from flinging Mama farther into the swamp, but he looked into Pelvis's eyes and saw a terror there beyond any he'd ever glimpsed. Something about Eisley's face had shattered. It was like watching an Elvis mask crumble and seeing behind it the face of a frightened, simpleminded child.

"She don't mean no harm." The voice was even different now; some of the Memphis huskiness had fallen away. "She's all I got. Please don't."

Flint hesitated, his arm still flung back. Then, just that quickly, his anger began to dissolve and he realized what a mean, petty thing he'd been on the verge of doing. He thrust the shivering dog at Pelvis and backed away, a muscle working in his jaw. Pelvis enfolded Mama in his arms. "It's all right, it's all right," he said, speaking to the dog. "He won't hurt you, it's all right."

Flint turned away and began following the channel. He felt sick to his stomach, disgusted at himself and at Eisley, too. There was no doubt about it now, the man was making him crack up. Then he heard splashing behind him, and he glanced over his shoulder and saw Eisley following. It would've been better, Flint thought, if Eisley had gone back to the car and waited. It would've been better for Eisley to leave this ugly, miserable work to somebody who was more suited to it.

Clint's hand rose up and the little fingers stroked at the stubble of beard on his brother's usually clean-scraped chin. Flint swatted Clint's hand away, but it came willfully up again to feel the hairs. He pinned the hand down against his chest with his right arm, and Clint fought him. It was a silent and internal war, sinewy muscles straining, and Flint felt Clint's head jerk as if trying to tear itself and the malformed lump of tissue and ligaments it was attached to finally and completely free. Flint staggered forward, his mouth a tight line and his eyes set on the darkness yet to be traveled through. A feeling of panic rose up, like Clint's clammy hand, and seized his throat. He would never find the clean white mansion of his birth. Never. He could pore through magazines of splendid estates and drive through the immaculate streets of wealthy enclaves in town after town, but he would never find his home. Never. He was lost, a gentleman of breeding cast out on the dirty current, fated to slog through the mud with the Pelvis Eisleys of this world breathing buttermilk breath on the back of his neck.

It seemed to Flint now, in the spell of this panic, that he'd always been searching for a way out of one swamp or another: the dismal, humiliating grind of the freak shows, his overwhelming gambling debts, this soul-killing job, and the freak-obsessed lunatic who jerked his strings. His life had been a series of swamps populated with the dregs of the earth. Grinning illiterates had taunted him, hard-eyed prostitutes had shrieked and fled when they'd discovered his secret, children had been reduced to fearful tears and later, probably, he'd crept into their nightmares. For a few dirty dollars he'd used the brass knuckles on some of Smoates's loan customers, and he couldn't say that from time to time it hadn't been a pleasure using that festering rage inside him to pummel promptness into unfortunate flesh. He had kicked men when they were down. He had broken ribs and noses and grinned inside at the sound of begging. What was one more swamp to be slogged through, with all that mud already stuck to his shoes?

He had taken a wrong turn somewhere. He had taken many wrong turns. Wasn't there some way out of this filth, back toward the road that led him to the clean white mansion? Dear God of deformities and wretchedness, wasn't there some escape?

He knew the answer, and it made him afraid.

The cards have been dealt. Play or fold, your choice. It's late in the game, very very late, and it seems you're running out of chips.

Play or fold. Your choice.

Flint stopped. He felt the blood burning his face. His mouth opened and out swelled a shout that was bitter anger and pain, wounded pride and feverish determination all bound up and twisted together. At first it was a mangled, inhuman sound that scared Pelvis into believing a wild animal was about to leap at them, and then words exploded out of it: *"Lambert! I'll follow you till you drop! Understand? Until you drop!"*

The swamp had hushed again. The sound of Flint's voice rolled away across the wilderness like muffled thunder. Pelvis stood a distance behind Flint in the green flarelight, both his arms clutching Mama close. Slowly, the insect hums and buzzes and strange chittering birdcalls weaved together and grew in volume once more, the dispassionate voice of the swamp telling Flint who was master of this domain. When Flint drew a long, ragged breath and continued wading southward with the sluggish current, Pelvis got his legs moving, too.

Flint held the flare high, his eyes darting from side to side. Sweat was trickling down his face, his clothes drenched with it. He heard splashing ahead, but how far, it was hard to say. The channel took a leftward curve, and suddenly Flint realized the water level had risen three inches above his knees. "Gettin' deeper," Pelvis said at about the same time.

"Gettin' deeper for him, too," Flint answered.

The mud gripped their shoes. Pelvis watched the surface for gliding shadows. The air was rank with the odors of wet, rotting vegetation, and breathing it left the sensation of slime accumulating at the back of the throat.

Behind them, the two edges of disturbed darkness the light had passed through first linked tendrils, grew joints, and then silently sealed together again.

Up ahead, barely twenty yards beyond the light's range, Dan was down in the water with Arden. She was fully conscious now, though her vision kept fading in and out, and she could remember everything up until when they'd hit the warning sign; her bell had been rung hard, a bloody inch-long gash just past her hairline where her head had glanced off something on the dashboard, a cut inside her mouth, and a bruised chin, courtesy of a flying knee.

Dan could see the blotch of dark wetness in her hair. He figured she might have a concussion, and she was lucky she hadn't smashed her skull. "I want you to stay right here," he whispered. "They'll take you back with 'em."

"No!" She'd spoken too loudly, and he put his finger on her mouth.

"Comin' for you, Lambert!" Murtaugh called. "Nowhere else to run!"

"*No!*" Arden whispered. "I'm all right! I can keep goin'!"

"Listen to me!" He had his face right up against hers. "I'm headin' into the swamp, just as deep as I can get! You've gone far enough with me!" He saw the flare-lit figures wading slowly and steadily nearer. In another minute the light would find them.

"I'm goin' with you," Arden said. "I'm too close to turn back."

She was out of her mind, he decided. Her eyes had taken on the shine of religious fervency, like those of the walking wounded

who flocked, desperate for a healing miracle, to television evange-
lists. She had come to the end of her rope and found herself dangling, and now all she could think to do was hold on to him. "Stay
here," he told her. "Just stay here, they'll get you out." He stood
up and began sloshing southward, the water up to the middle of
his thighs.

Arden saw the circle of green light approaching, and the
two figures at its center. Her distorted vision made them out to
be monsters. She tried to stand up, slipped, and fell again. Dan
looked briefly back at her and then continued on. Arden got
her feet planted in the mud and pushed herself up, and then she
started fighting to reach Dan with the light glinting on the frothy
water just behind her.

"He's tirin' out," Flint told Pelvis. "Hear him strugglin'?" The
splashing was over on the right, and Flint angled toward it.

Pelvis suddenly jumped and bellowed, "Oh Jesus!"

Flint whipped the flare around. "What the hell is it?"

"Somethin' swam by me!" Pelvis had almost dropped Mama
in his jig of terror. "I think it was a snake!"

Flint's gaze searched the water, his own skin starting to crawl.
The light showed something dark and about three feet long, sinu-
ously moving with the current. He watched it until it slithered
beyond the light. "Just keep goin'," he said, as much to himself
as to Pelvis, and he started wading again. The sound of splashing
had quieted, but Lambert couldn't go on much longer.

Dan looked back. Arden was still straining to catch up with
him, but she'd found her balance and her strides were careful and
deliberate. The water was almost at her waist. He started to turn
and go on, but like a flash of shock the moment took him spinning back in time.

He remembered a night patrol, and a wide, muddy stream
that cut through the jungle. He remembered the crossing, and
how almost all but the grunts guarding the rear—of which he
was one—had climbed up a slippery bank when the first white
flare had exploded over their heads. The enemy had gotten around

behind them, or had come up from hidden snake holes. "Move it, move it, move it!" somebody began yelling as the second white flare popped. The rifles started up, Dan was standing in knee-deep muck and tracers were zipping past him out of the jungle. Other grunts were running and falling, trying to scramble up the bank. Within an instant the situation became as all night combat did in that jungle: a confused, surrealistic montage of shadows fleeing from the flarelight, blurred motion, screams as bullets thunked into flesh. He couldn't move; his legs were frozen. Figures were falling, some struggling up, some thrashing in the mud. It seemed pointless to move because the others were getting cut down as they tried to climb up the bank, and if he stood still, if he stood very very still with the tracers passing on either side of him, he might make himself disappear from the face of this hellish earth.

Someone gripped his shirt and yanked him.

"*Go,*" a voice urged; it was not a shout, but it was more powerful than a shout.

Dan looked at the man. He had the gaunt, sunken-eyed face of a hard-core veteran, a man who had seen death and smelled it, who had killed after hours of silent stalking and escaped being killed by inches of miraculous grace. He had a blond beard and eyes of cornflower blue, only the eyes seemed ancient now and lifeless. They had been lifeless since that day months ago at the village.

"Go," Farrow said again. Farrow, who since that day had retreated into himself like a stony sphinx, who suffered in silence, who always volunteered with a nod for the jobs no other grunt would dare take.

And now, in this little cell of time, Dan saw something glisten and surface from Farrow's eyes that he hardly recognized.

It might have been joy.

Farrow pushed him hard toward the bank, and the push got Dan moving. Dan reached the bank and started up it, clawing at vines and over the bodies of dying men. He dared to look over his shoulder, and he saw a sight that would stay with him all his days.

Farrow was walking to the other side, and he was sprayfiring his M16 back and forth into the jungle. Dan saw the enemy's tracers start homing in on Farrow. The young man did not pause or cringe. One bullet hit him, then a second. Farrow kept moving and firing. A third bullet knocked him to his knees. He got up. Somebody was shouting at him to come back, for the love of God come back. Farrow staggered on, his M16 tearing down the foliage and scattering blackclad figures. Either the weapon choked or the clip was gone, because it ceased firing. There was a stretch of silence, broken by the cries of the wounded. The Cong had stopped shooting. Dan saw Farrow jerk the clip out and pop another one in. He took two more steps and his M16 blazed again, and then maybe four or five tracers came out of the jungle and hit him at once and he was knocked backward and splashed down into the muddy water that rolled over him like a brown shroud.

All of it had taken only a span of seconds, but it had taken years for Dan to digest what he'd seen. Even so, it still sometimes came up to lodge in his throat.

He watched Arden pulling herself toward him, as resolute in her decision as Farrow had been in his. Or as crazy, Dan thought. There had been no doubt in his mind that Farrow had gone quietly insane after that day at the village, and had been—whether he was aware of it or not—searching for a way to commit suicide. How the death of those children had weighed on Farrow was impossible to say, but it must've been a terrible burden that ultimately led him to choose a slow walk into a dozen Viet Cong rifles. If Farrow hadn't taken that walk, Dan and at least three other men might have been cut to pieces. Dan's life had been spared, and for what reason? For him to be tainted by the Agent Orange and later pull the trigger that killed an innocent man? For him now to be standing in this swamp, watching a girl with a birthmarked face struggling to reach him? Life made no sense to him; it was a maze constructed by the most haphazard of hands and he, Arden, the bounty hunters, all humanity alike, were blindly searching its corridors and banging into walls.

She was almost to him. The green flarelight was chasing her. "Give it up, Lambert!" Murtaugh shouted. "It's no use!"

Maybe it wasn't. But the girl believed it was, enough to trust a killer. Enough to fight her way into the unknown. Enough to make Dan think that if he had half of her desire, he might find his way through this wilderness to freedom.

He waded to meet her and caught her left hand. She looked at him with an expression of amazement and relief. Then Dan started pulling her with him, racing against the oncoming light.

18

The Most Dangerous Place

T HOUGH FLINT STILL COULDN'T see Lambert or the girl, he knew they must not be more than fifteen or twenty yards beyond the light's edge. He was moving as fast as he could, but the channel was hard going. The water had crept up toward his waist, and it had occurred to him that if it deepened to his chest, Clint would drown. He was dripping sweat in the hot and clammy air. In another moment he heard Pelvis's lungs wheezing like the pipes of an old church organ.

"Mr. Murtaugh!" Pelvis gasped. "I'm gonna have to . . . have to stop for a minute. Get my breath."

"Keep movin'!" Flint told him, and he didn't pause.

The wheezing only worsened. "Please . . . Mr. Murtaugh . . . I gotta stop."

"Do what you want! I'm not stoppin'!"

Pelvis fell behind, his chest heaving. Oily beads of sweat were trickling down his blood-gorged face, his heart furiously pounding. Flint glanced back and then continued on, step after careful step. Pelvis tried to follow, but after a half-dozen more strides he had to stop again. Mama had sensed his distress and was frantically licking his chin. "Mr. Murtaugh!" Pelvis called, but Flint was moving away and taking the light with him. Terror of the dark and of the things that slithered through it made Pelvis slog forward once more, the blood pulsing at his temples. He couldn't get his breath, it was as if the air itself were waterlogged. He wrenched one foot free from the mud and put it down in front of him, and he was pulling the other one up when his throat seemed to close, darkness rippled across his vision, and he fell down into the water.

Flint heard splashing and looked back. He saw the mutt, paddling to keep her head up.

Pelvis was gone.

Flint's heart jumped. "Christ!" he said, and he struggled back toward the swirling water where Pelvis had submerged. The dog was trying to reach him, her eyes wide with panic. Bubbles burst from the surface to Flint's left, followed by a flailing arm, and then Pelvis's butt broached like a flabby whale. Flint got hold of the arm, but it slipped away from him. "Stand up, stand up!" he was shouting. A dark, dripping mass came up from the water, and Flint realized it was Pelvis's hair. He grabbed it and pulled, but suddenly he found himself gripping a pompadour with no head beneath it.

A wig. That's what it was. A cheap, soaked and sopping wig.

And then something white and vulnerable-looking with a few strands of dark hair plastered across it broke the surface, and Flint dropped the wig and got his arm underneath the man's chin. Pelvis was a weight to be reckoned with. He coughed out a mouthful of water and let go a mournful groan that sounded like a freight train at midnight. "Get your feet under you!" Flint told him. "Come on, stand up!"

Still sputtering, the baldheaded Pelvis got his muddy suedes planted. "Mama!" he cried out. "Where is she?"

She wasn't far, yapping against the current. Pelvis staggered to her and scooped her up, and then he almost fell down again and he had to lean his bulk against Flint. "I'll be all right," Pelvis said between coughs. "Just gotta rest. Few minutes. Lord, I thought . . . thought my ticker was givin' out." He lifted a hand to his head, and when his fingers found nothing there but pasty flesh he looked to Flint, his face contorted with abject horror, as if he indeed might be about to suffer heart failure. "My hair! Where's my hair?" He started thrashing around again, searching for it in the froth.

"It's gone, forget it!" Flint registered that Pelvis's naked head was pointed like a bullet at the crown. On the sides and back was a fringe of short, ratty hairs. Flint spotted the wig floating away like a lump of Spanish moss, and he sloshed the few feet to it and plucked it up. "Here," he said, offering it to its master. Pelvis snatched it away from him and, holding Mama in the crook of an arm, began wringing the wig out. Flint might've laughed if he hadn't been thinking of how far Lambert was getting ahead of them. "You okay?"

Pelvis snorted and spat. He was trembling. He wiped his nose on his forearm and then carefully, reverently, replaced the wet wig back on his skull. It sat crooked and some of its wavy peaks had flattened, but Flint saw relief flood into Pelvis like a soothing drug, the man's tormented face relaxing. "Can you go on, or not?" Flint asked.

"Gimme a minute. Heart's beatin' awful hard. See, I get dizzy spells. That's why I had to quit my stage show. Is it on straight?"

"Crooked to the right."

Pelvis made the adjustment. "I passed out onstage last year. Oldie Goldie's Club in Little Rock. They took me to the hospital, thought I was about to croak." He paused to draw a few slow, deep breaths. "Wasn't the first time. Word went 'round, and I couldn't get no more jobs. Gimme a minute, I'll be fine. Can you breathe? I can't hardly breathe this air."

"You weigh too much, that's your trouble. Ought to give up all that junk you eat." Flint was staring down the channel, gauging the distance that Lambert must be putting between them.

The going had to be hard on Lambert, too, but he'd probably push himself and the girl until they both gave out. When he looked at Pelvis again, Flint thought that the wig resembled a big, spongy Brillo pad stuck to the man's head. "I'll give you three minutes, then I'm goin' on. You can either stay here or go back to the car."

Pelvis didn't care to lose the protection of Flint's light. "I can make it if you just go a step or two slower."

"I told you it wasn't gonna be easy, didn't I? Don't fall down and drown on me, now, you hear?"

"Yes sir." His misshapen wig was dripping water down his face. "I reckon this washes me up, huh? I mean, with Mr. Smoates and the job and all?"

"I'd say it does. You should've told him about this, it would've saved everybody a hell of a lot of trouble." Flint narrowed his eyes and glanced quickly at the flare. Maybe they had fifteen minutes more light. Maybe. "You're not cut out for this work, Eisley. Just like I'm not cut out to . . . to dress up like Elvis Presley and try to impersonate him."

"Not impersonate," Pelvis corrected him firmly. "I'm an interperator, not an impersonator."

"Whatever. You ought to cut out the junk food and go back to it."

"That's what the doctor told me, too. I've tried, but Lord knows it ain't easy to pass up the peanut butter cookies when you can't sleep at three in the mornin'."

"Yes, it is. You just don't buy the damn things in the first place. Haven't you ever heard of self-discipline?"

"Yes sir. It's somethin' other folks have got."

"Well, it's what you *need*. A whole lot of it, too." He checked his wristwatch, impatient to get after Lambert. But Pelvis's face was still flushed, and maybe he needed another minute. If Pelvis had a heart attack, it'd be hell dragging that bulk of a body out of the swamp. Flint had become acutely aware of the flare sizzling itself toward extinction. He watched Mama licking Pelvis's chin, her stubby tail wagging. A pang of what might have been envy hit him. "How come you carry that mutt around everywhere? It just gets in the way."

"Oh, I wouldn't leave Mama, no sir!" Pelvis paused, stroking Mama's wet back before he went on in a quieter voice. "I had another dog, kinda like Mama. Had Priss for goin' on six years. Left her at the vet one weekend when I went on the road. When I got back . . . the place was gone. Just bricks and ash and burned-up cages. Electrical fire, they said. Started late at night, nobody was there to put it out. They should've had sprinklers or somethin', but they didn't." He was silent for a moment, his hand stroking back and forth. "For a long time after that . . . I had nightmares. I could see Priss burnin' up in a cage, tryin' to get out but there wasn't no way out. And maybe she was thinkin' she'd done somethin' awful bad, that I didn't come to save her. Seems to me that would be a terrible way to die, thinkin' there was nobody who gave a damn about you." He lifted his gaze to Flint's, his eyes sunken in the green glare. "That's why I wouldn't leave Mama. No sir."

Flint turned his attention to his watch again. "You ready to move?"

"I believe I am."

Flint started off, this time at a slower pace. Pelvis drew another deep breath, *whooshed* it out, and then began slogging after Flint.

Ahead, Dan still gripped Arden's hand as they followed the channel around a curve. He glanced back; they'd outdistanced the light, and he thought the bounty hunters must've stopped for some reason. His eyes were getting used to the dark now. Up through the treetops he could see pieces of sky full of sparkling stars. The water was still deepening, the bottom's mud releasing bursts of gaseous bubbles beneath their feet. Sweat clung to Dan's face, his breath rasping, and he could hear Arden's lungs straining too in the steamy heat. Something splashed in the water on their left; it sounded heavy, and Dan prayed it was simply a large catfish that had jumped instead of a 'gator's tail steering a set of jaws toward them. He braced for the unknown, but whatever it had been it left them alone for the moment.

Looking back once again, he could see the green light flickering through the undergrowth. They were still coming. Arden looked over her shoulder, too, then concentrated on getting through the water ahead. Her vision had cleared, but where she'd banged her skull against the dashboard was raw with pain. She was wearing out with every step; she felt her strength draining away, and soon she was going to have to stop to catch her breath. She wasn't on the run; it was Dan the bounty hunters were after, but when they'd take him away they'd take the man she had come to believe was her best hope of finding the Bright Girl. From a deep place within her the voice of reason was speaking, trying to tell her that it was pointless to go any farther into this swamp, that a wanted killer had her by the hand and was leading her away from civilization, that she probably had a concussion and needed a doctor, that her brain was scrambled and she wasn't thinking straight and she was in the most dangerous place she'd ever been in her life. She heard it, but she refused to listen. In her right hand was clutched the small pink drawstring bag containing what had become her talisman over the years, and she fixed her mind on Jupiter's voice saying that this was the man God had provided to take her to the Bright Girl. She had to believe it. She had to, or all hope would come crashing down around her, and she feared that more than death.

"I see a light," Dan suddenly said.

She could see it, too. A faint glow, off to the right. Not electricity. More like the light cast from a candle or oil lamp. They kept going, the water at Dan's waist and above Arden's.

Shapes emerged from the darkness. On either side of the channel were two or three tarpaper shacks built up on wooden platforms over the water. The light was coming from a window covered with what looked like waxed paper. The other shacks were dark, either empty or their inhabitants asleep. Dan had no desire to meet the kind of people who'd choose to live in such primitive arrangements, figuring they'd shoot an intruder on sight. But he made out something else in addition to the shacks: a few of them, including the one that showed a light, had small boats—fishing skiffs—tied up to their pilings.

They needed a boat in the worst way, he decided. He put his finger to his lips to tell Arden to remain silent, and she nodded. Then he guided her past the shack where the light burned and across the channel to the next dwelling. The skiff there was secured by a chain and padlock, but a single paddle with a broken handle was lying down inside it. Dan eased the paddle out and went on to the third shack. The boat that was tied there held about six inches of trash-filled water in its hull. There were no other paddles in sight, but the leaky craft was attached to a piling only by a plastic line. In this case beggars couldn't be choosers. Dan spent a moment untying the line's slimy knot, then he pulled himself as quietly as he could over into the boat though his foot thumped against the side. He waited, holding his breath, but no one came out of the shack. He helped Arden in. She sat on the bench seat at the bow, while Dan sat in the stern and shoved them away from the platform. They glided out toward the channel's center, where the current flowed the strongest, and when they were a safe distance away from the shack, Dan slid the stubby paddle into the water and delivered the first stroke.

"Grave robbers!" a woman's voice shrilled, the sound of it startling Dan and making goose bumps rise on Arden's wet arms. "Go on and steal it, then, you donkey-dick suckers!"

Dan looked behind. A figure stood back at the first shack, where the light burned.

"Go on, then!" the woman said. "Lord's gonna fix your asses, you'll find out! I'll dance on your coffins, you maggot-eaters!" She began spitting curses that Dan hadn't heard since his days in boot camp, and some that would've curled a drill sergeant's ear hairs. Another voice growled, "Shut up, Rona!" It belonged to a man who sounded very drunk. "Shut your hole, I'm sleepin' over here!"

"I wouldn't piss on your face if it was on fire!" Rona hollered across the channel. "I'm gonna cook up a spell on you. Your balls gonna dry up like little bitty black raisins!"

"Awwwww, shut up 'fore I come over there and knock your head out your ass!" A door whacked shut.

Dan's paddling had quickened. The woman continued to curse and rave, her voice rising and falling with lunatic cadence. Then she retreated into her hovel and slammed her own door so hard Dan was surprised the place hadn't collapsed. He saw the light move away from the window and he could imagine a wizened, muttering crone in there stooped over a smoking stewpot with a goat's head in it Well, at least they had a boat though they were sitting in nasty water. The phrase *up Shit Creek* came to him, but they did have a paddle. When he glanced back again, he no longer saw the green flare's glow. Maybe the bounty hunters had given up and turned away. If so, good riddance to them. Now all he could do was guide this boat down the center of the bayou and hope it would lead them eventually out to the Gulf. From there he could find somewhere safe to leave the girl and strike out on his own again.

He didn't like being responsible for her, and worrying about that knock she'd suffered, and feeling her hand clutch his so hard his knuckles cracked. He was a lone wolf by nature, that's how things were, so just as soon as he could, he was getting rid of her. Anyway, she was crazy. Her obsession with the Bright Girl made Dan think of something he'd seen on the news once: hundreds of people had converged from across the country to camp out day after day in an Oklahoma cornfield where a farmer's wife swore the Virgin Mary had materialized. He remembered thinking how desperately those people had wanted to believe in the wisdom of a higher power, and how they'd believed that the Virgin Mary would appear again at that same place with a message for mankind. Only she'd never showed up, and the really amazing thing was that none of those hundreds of people had regretted coming there, or felt betrayed or bitter. They'd simply felt that the time wasn't right for the Virgin Mary to appear again, but they were certain that sometime and somewhere she would. Dan couldn't understand that kind of blind faith; it flew in the face of the wanton death and destruction he'd witnessed in 'Nam. He wondered if any of that multitude had ever put a bullet between the eyes of a sixteen-year-old boy and felt a rush of exultation that the boy's AK-47 had jammed. He wondered if any of them had ever smelled the odor of burning flesh, or seen flames chewing on the small skulls. If any of them had walked in his boots, had stood in the dirty silver rain and seen the sights that were seared in his mind, he doubted they would put much faith in waiting for the return of Mary, Jesus, or the Holy Ghost.

Dan paddled a few strokes and then let the boat drift. Arden faced southward, the warm breeze of motion blowing past her. The water made a soft, chuckling sound at the bow, and the bittersweet swamp was alive with the hums and clicks and clacks of insects, the occasional sharp keening of a night bird, the bass thumping of frogs and other fainter noises that were not so identifiable. The only light now came from the stars that shone through spaces in the thick canopy of branches overhead.

Dan started to look back, but he decided not to. He knew where he'd been; it was where he was going that concerned him now. The moment of Emory Blanchard's death was still a bleeding wound in his mind, and maybe for the rest of his days it would torture him, but the swamp's silken darkness gave him comfort. He felt a long way from the law and prison walls. If he could find food, fresh water, and a shelter over his head—even the sagging roof of a tarpaper shack—he thought he could live and die here, under these stars. It was a big swamp, and maybe it would accept a man who wanted to disappear. An ember of hope reawakened and began to burn inside him. Maybe it was an illusion, he thought, but it was something to nurture and cling to, just as Arden clung to her Bright Girl. His first task, though, was getting her out, then he could decide on his own destination.

The boat drifted slowly onward, embraced by the current flowing to the sea.

Pelvis held Mama with one arm and his other hand gripped the back of Flint's soggy suit jacket. The green flarelight had burned out several minutes before, and the night had closed in on them. Pelvis had been asking—begging was the more correct term—Flint to turn back when they'd heard a woman's voice hollering and cursing ahead. As they'd slogged on through the stomach-deep water, Flint's left hand slid under his shirt and supported Clint's head; their eyes had started acclimating to the dark. In another moment they could make out the shapes of the tarpaper shacks, a light moving around inside the nearest one on the right. Flint saw a boat tied up to the platform the shack stood on, and as they got closer he made out that it had a scabrous-looking outboard motor. It occurred to him that Lambert might be hiding in one of the darkened shacks, waiting for them to move past. He guided Pelvis toward the flickering light they could see through a waxed-paper window, and at the platform's edge Flint said, "Stay here" and pulled himself up on the splintery boards. He paused to remove the derringer, then he pushed Clint's arm under his shirt and buttoned up his dripping jacket. He held the derringer behind his back and knocked at the shack's flimsy door.

He heard somebody scuttling around inside, but the knock wasn't answered. "Hey, in there!" he called. "Would you open up?" He reached out, his fist balled, to knock a second time.

A latch slammed back. The door swung open on creaking hinges, and from it thrust the business end of a sawed-off shotgun that pressed hard against Flint's forehead.

"I'll open *you* up, you dog-ass lickin' sonofabitch!" the woman behind the gun snarled, and her finger clicked back the trigger.

Flint didn't move; it swept through his mind that at this range the shotgun would blast his brains into the trees on the other side of the bayou. By the smoky light from within the shack, Flint saw that the woman was at least six feet tall and built as solidly as a truck. She wore a pair of dirty overalls, a gray and sweat-stained T-shirt, and on her head was a battered dark green football helmet. Behind the helmet's protective face bar was a forbidding visage with burning, red-rimmed eyes and skin like saddle leather.

"Easy," Flint managed to say. "Take it easy, all I want to do is ask—"

"I know what you want, you scum-sucker!" she yelled. "You ain't takin' me back to that damn shithole! Ain't gettin' me in a rubber room again and stickin' my head full of pins and needles!"

Crazy as a three-legged grasshopper, he thought. His heart was galloping, and the inside of his mouth would've made the Sahara feel tropical. He stared at the woman's grimy-nailed finger on the trigger in front of his face. "Listen," he croaked. "I didn't come to take you anywhere. I just want to—"

"Satan's got a silver tongue!" she thundered. "Now I'm gonna send you back to hell, where you belong!"

Flint saw her finger twitch on the trigger. His breath froze.

"Ma'am?" There was the sound of muddy shoes squeaking on the timbers. "Can I talk to you a minute, ma'am?"

The woman's insane eyes blinked. "Who is that?" she hissed. "Who said that?"

"I did, ma'am." Pelvis walked into the range of the light, Mama cradled in his arms. "Can I have a word with you, please?"

Flint saw the woman stare past him at Eisley. Her finger was still on the trigger, the barrel pressing a ring into his forehead. He was terrified to move even an inch.

Pelvis offered up the best smile he could find. "Ain't nobody wants to hurt you, ma'am. Honest we don't."

Flint heard the woman draw a long, stunned gasp. Her eyes had widened, her thin-lipped mouth starting to tremble.

"You can put that gun down if you like," Pelvis said. "Might better, 'fore somebody gets hurt."

"Oh," the woman whispered. "Oh my Jesus!" Flint saw tears shine in her eyes. "They . . . they told me . . . you died."

"Huh?" Pelvis frowned.

"They told her you died!" Flint spoke up, understanding what the madwoman meant. "Tell her you didn't die, Elvis!"

"Shut your mouth, you Satan's asshole!" the woman ranted at him. "I'm not talkin' to you!" Her finger twitched on the trigger again.

"I do wish you'd at least uncock that gun, ma'am," Pelvis said. "It'd make an awful mess if it was to go off."

She stared at him, her tongue flicking out to wet her lips. "They told me you died!" Her voice was softer now, and there was something terribly wounded in it. "I was up there in Baton Rouge, when I was livin' with Billy and that bitch wife he had. They said you died, that you took drugs and slid off the toilet and died right there, wasn't a thing nobody could do to save you but I prayed for you I cried and I lit the candles in my room and that bitch said I wanted to burn down the house but Billy, Billy he's been a good brother he said I'm all right I ain't gonna hurt nobody."

"Oh." Pelvis caught her drift. "Oh . . . ma'am, I ain't really—"

"Yes you are!" Flint yelped. "Help me out here, Elvis!"

"You dirty sonofabitch, you!" the woman hollered into his face. "You call him *Mr. Presley!*"

Flint gritted his teeth, the sweat standing out in bright oily beads on his face. "Mr. Presley, tell this lady how I'm a friend of yours, and how hurtin' me would be the same as hurtin' you. Would you tell her that, please?"

"Well . . . that'd be a lie, wouldn't it? I mean, you made it loud and clear you think I stand about gut-high to an ant."

"That was then. This is now. I think you're the finest man I've ever met. Would you please tell her?"

Pelvis scratched Mama's chin and cocked his head to one side. A few seconds ticked past, during which a bead of sweat trickled down to the end of Flint's nose and hung there. Then Pelvis said, "Yes'm, Mr. Murtaugh's a friend of mine."

The woman removed her shotgun from Flint's forehead. Flint let his breath rattle out and staggered back a couple of steps.

"That's different, then," she said, uncocking the gun. "Different, if he's your friend. My name's Rona, you remember me?"

"Uh . . ." Pelvis glanced quickly at Flint, then back to the madwoman. "I . . . believe I . . ."

"I seen you in Biloxi." Her voice trembled with excitement. "That was in—" She paused. "I can't think when that was, my mind gets funny sometimes. I was sittin' in the third row. I wrote you a letter. You remember me?"

"Uh . . ." He saw Flint nod. "Yes'm, I believe so."

"I sent my name in to that magazine, you know that *Tiger Beat* magazine was havin' that contest for a date with you? I sent my name in, and my daddy said I was the biggest fool ever lived but I did anyway and I went to church and prayed I was gonna win. My mama went to live in heaven, that's what I wrote in my letter." She looked down at her dirty overalls. "Oh, I—I must look a fright!"

"No ma'am," Pelvis said quietly. "Rona, I mean. You look fine."

"You sure have got fat," Rona told him. "They cut your balls off in the army, didn't they? Then they made you stop singin' them good songs. They're the ones fucked up the world. Put up them satellites in outer space so they could read people's minds. Them monkey-cock suckers! Well, they ain't gettin' to me no more!" She tapped her helmet. "Best protect yourself while you can!" She let her hand drop, and she looked dazedly back and forth between Flint and Pelvis. "Am I dreamin'?" she asked.

"Rona?" Flint said. "You mind if I call you Rona?" She just stared blankly at him. "We're lookin' for somebody. A man and a woman. Did you see anybody pass by here?"

Rona turned her attention to Pelvis again. "How come they tell such lies about you? That you was takin' drugs and all? How come they said you died?"

"I . . . just got tired, I reckon," Pelvis said. Flint noted that he was standing a little taller, he'd sucked his gut in as much as possible, and he was making his voice sound more like Elvis than ever, with that rockabilly Memphis sneer in it. "I wanted to go hide someplace."

"Uh-huh, me, too." She nodded. "I didn't mean to burn that house down, but the light was so pretty. You know how pretty a light can be when it's dark all the time? Then they put me in that white car, that white car with the straps, and they took me to that place and stuck pins and needles in my head. But they let me go, and I wanted to hide, too. You want some gumbo? I got some gumbo inside. I made it yesterday."

"Rona?" Flint persisted. "A man and a woman. Have you seen them?"

"I seen them grave robbers, stealin' his boat." She motioned across the channel. "John LeDuc lived there, but he died. Stepped in a cottonmouth nest, that's what the ranger said. Them grave robbers over there, stealin' his boat. I hollered at 'em, but they didn't pay no mind."

"Uh-huh. What do you get to if you keep followin' this bayou?"

"Swamp," she said as if he were the biggest fool who ever lived. "Swamp and more swamp. 'Cept for Saint Nasty."

"Saint Nasty? What's that?"

"Where they work on them oil rigs." Rona's gaze was fixed on Pelvis. "I'm dreamin', ain't I? My mama comes and visits me sometimes, I know I'm dreamin' awake. That's what I'm doin' now, ain't that right?"

"How far's Saint Nasty from here?" Flint asked.

"Four, five miles."

"Is there a road out from there?"

"No road. Just the bayou, goes on to the Gulf."

"We need a boat," he said. "How much for yours?"

"What?"

"How much money?" He took the opportunity to slip the derringer into his pocket and withdraw the wet bills he'd taken from the girl's wallet. "Fifty dollars, will that cover the boat and motor?"

"Ain't no gas in that motor," she told him. "That ranger comes 'round and visits me, he brings me gas. His name's Jack, he's a nice young fella. Only he didn't come this week."

"How about paddles, then? Have you got any?"

"Yeah, I got a paddle." She narrowed her eyes at Flint. "I don't like your looks. I don't care if you are his friend and he's a dream I'm havin'. You got somethin' mean in you."

"Sixty dollars," Flint said. "Here's the cash, right here."

Rona gave a harsh laugh. "You're crazier'n hell. You better watch out, they'll be stickin' pins and needles in your head 'fore long."

"Sooner than you think, lady." He shot a scowl at Pelvis. "Mr. Presley, how about openin' those golden lips and helpin' me out a little bit?"

Pelvis was still thinking about two words the madwoman had uttered: *Cottonmouth nest.* "We sure do need your boat, Rona," he said with genuine conviction. "It'd be doin' us a big favor if you'd sell it to us. You can even keep the motor, we'll just take the boat and paddle."

Rona didn't reply for a moment, but Flint could see her chewing on her lower lip as she thought about the proposal. "Hell," she said at last, "you two ain't real anyhow, are you?" She shrugged. "You can buy the boat, I don't care."

"Good. Here." Flint offered sixty dollars to her, and the woman accepted the cash with an age-spotted hand and then sniffed the wet bills. "We'll need the paddle, too," he told her, and she laughed again as if this were a grand illusion and walked into her shack, the interior of which Flint could see was plastered with newspaper pages and held a cast-iron stove. Flint told Pelvis to help him get the motor unclamped from the boat's stern, and they were laying it on the platform when Rona returned—without her shotgun—bringing a paddle.

"Thank you, ma'am," Pelvis said. "We sure do 'preciate it."

"I got a question for you," Rona said as they were getting into the boat. "Who sent you here? Was it Satan, to make me think I'm losin' my mind, or God, to give me a thrill?"

Pelvis stared into her leathery face. Behind the football helmet's protective bar her deep-socketed eyes glinted with what was surely insanity but might also have been—at least for a passing moment—the memory of a teenaged girl in her finest dress, sitting in the third row of a Biloxi auditorium. He worked one of the gaudy fake diamond rings from a finger and pushed it into her palm. "Darlin'," he said, "you decide."

Sitting in the stern, Flint untied the rope that secured the boat to the platform and then pushed them off with the paddle. Pelvis took the bow seat, Mama warm and drowsy against his chest. Flint began to stroke steadily toward the center of the channel, where he got them turned southward. He felt the current grasp their hull, and in another moment they were moving at about the pace of a fast walk. When Pelvis looked back at the woman standing in front of her decrepit shack, Flint said acidly, "Made yourself another fan there, didn't you, Mr. Presley?"

Pelvis stared straight ahead into the darkness. He pulled in a long breath and slowly released it, and he answered with some grit in his voice. "You can pucker up and kiss my butt."

19

Home Sweet Hellhole

I N THE STARFIRE DARK Dan and Arden drifted past other narrower bayous that branched off from the main channel. They saw no other lights or shacks, and it was clear that their detour off the bridge had left LaPierre miles behind.

When the mosquitoes found them, there was nothing they could do but take the bites. Something bumped hard against the boat before it swam away, and after his heart had descended from his throat, Dan figured it had been an amorous alligator looking for some scaly tush. He got into a pattern of paddling for three or four minutes and then resting, and he and Arden both cupped their hands and bailed out the water that was seeping up through the hull. He said nothing about this to Arden, but he guessed the boat was a rusty nail or two from coming apart.

Most of the pain had cleared from Arden's head. Her vision had stopped tunneling in and out, but her bones still ached and her fingers found a crusty patch of dried blood in her hair and a lump so sore the lightest pressure on it almost made her sick. Her purse and suitcase were gone, her money, her belongings, her identification, everything lost. Except her life, and the drawstring bag in her right hand. But that was okay, she thought. Maybe it was how things were supposed to be. She was shedding her old skin in preparation for the Bright Girl's touch. She was casting off the past, and getting ready for the new Arden Halliday to be born.

How she would find the Bright Girl in this wilderness she didn't exactly know, but she had to believe she was close now, very close. When she'd seen the light in the shack's window back there, she'd thought for a moment they might have found the Bright Girl, but she didn't think—or she didn't want to think—that the Bright Girl would choose to live in a tarpaper hovel. Arden hadn't considered what kind of dwelling the Bright Girl might occupy, but now she envisioned something like a green mansion hidden amid the cypress trees, where sunlight streamed through the high branches like liquid gold. Or a houseboat anchored in a clear, still pool somewhere up one of these bayous. But not a dirty tarpaper shack. No, that didn't suit her image of the Bright Girl, and she refused to believe it.

She strained to see through the darkness, thinking—or wishing—that just ahead would be the glow of another lantern and a cluster of squatters' shacks, somebody to help her find her way. She glanced back at Dan as he slid the paddle into the water again. *The man God provided,* Jupiter had said. She'd never have left the motel with Dan if she hadn't been clinging to Jupiter's instincts about him. Jupiter had always been a mystic; he had the sixth sense about horses, he knew their temperaments and their secret names. If he said a docile-looking animal was getting ready to snort and kick, it was wise to move away from the hindquarters. And he knew other things, too; if he smelled rain in the midst of a Texas drought, it was time to get out the buckets. He read the sky and the wind and the pain in Arden's soul; she had come to realize during her years at the youth ranch that Jupiter Krenshaw was connected to the flowing currents of life in a way she couldn't fathom. She had trusted and believed him, and now she had to trust and believe he'd been telling her the truth about the Bright Girl, and that he'd seen something in Dan Lambert that no one else could recognize.

She had to, because there was no turning back.

They drifted on, the skiff being drawn along with the slow but steady current. They passed evidence that others had come this way: a few abandoned and crumbling shacks, a wharf jutting out over the water on rotten pilings, a wrecked and vine-draped shrimp boat whose prow was jammed between the trunks of two huge moss trees. Dan felt weariness overtaking him, and he caught himself dozing off between stretches of paddling. Arden likewise had begun to close her eyes and rest, fighting thirst but not yet ready to drink any of the water they were gliding through.

Dan let himself sleep for only a few minutes at a time, then his internal alarm went off and roused him to keep the boat from drifting into the half-submerged trees on either side. The water was probably eight or ten feet deep, he figured. Their boat was still in the slow process of sinking, but he went to work bailing with his hands and Arden helped him until their craft had lightened up again.

Dan noted that the branches overhead were beginning to unlock and draw apart. In another twenty minutes or so—a little over an hour since they'd set off in the boat—the bayou merged into a wider channel that took a long curve toward the southwest. Heat lightning shimmered in the sky, and an occasional fish jumped from the channel's ebony surface and splashed down again. Dan looked at the water in the boat and decided it wasn't wise to think too much about what might be roaming the depths, making those fish want to grow wings. He paddled a few strokes and then rested again, the muscles of his back starting to cramp.

"You want me to paddle awhile?" Arden asked.

"No, I'm all right." Resting the paddle across his knees, he let the current do the work. He scratched the welts on his forehead where a couple of mosquitoes had been feasting, and he sorely missed his baseball cap. "How about you? You hangin' in?"

"Yeah."

"Good." He listened to the quiet sound of the hull moving through the water. "I sure could use a cold six-pack. I wouldn't kick a pizza out of bed, either."

"I'll take a pitcher of iced tea with some lime in it," she said after a moment of deliberation. "And a bowl of strawberry ice cream."

Dan nodded, looking from side to side at the dense walls of foliage that lined the bayou. Yes, he decided; a man could get lost in here and never be found. "This ought to take us out to the Gulf, sooner or later," he said. "Could be daylight before we get there, though." He made out ten forty-four by the luminous hands of his watch. "Once we clear the swamp, maybe we can find a fishin' camp or somethin' along the coast. Could be we can find a road and flag a car down, get you a ride out of here."

"Get *me* a ride out? What about you?"

"Never mind about me. You took a pretty hard knock on the head, you need to see a doctor."

"I don't need a doctor. You know who I need to find."

"Don't start that again!" he warned. "Hear me? Wherever LaPierre is, we're long past it. I'm gettin' you out of here, then you can do what you please. You ought to get back to Fort Worth and count yourself lucky to be alive."

"And how am I gonna do that? I lost my purse and all my money. Even if I could find a bus station, I couldn't buy a ticket."

"I've got some money," he said. "Enough to buy you a bus ticket, if you can hitch a ride back to Houma."

"Yeah, I've sure got a lot to go back to," she answered tersely. "No job, no money, nothin'. Pretty soon I'll be out on the street. How do you think I'll do at a shelter for the homeless?"

"You'll find a job, get back on your feet."

"Uh-huh. I wish it was that easy. Don't you know what it's like out there?"

"Yeah," he drawled, "I believe I do."

She grunted and allowed herself a faint, bitter smile. "I guess so. Sorry. I must sound like a whinin' fool."

"Times are hard for everybody. Except the rich people who got us into this mess." He listened to the distant call of a night bird off to the left, a lonely sound that tugged at his heart. "I never wanted to be rich," he said. "Seems to me, that's just askin' for more problems. But I always wanted to pull my own weight. Pay my bills and take pride in my work. That's what was important to me. After I got back from 'Nam, I had some tough times, but things were workin' out. Then . . . I don't know." He caught himself from going my further. "Well, you've got your own road to travel; you don't need to walk down mine."

"I think we're both headin' in the same direction."

"No, we're not," he corrected her. "How old are you?"

"Twenty-seven."

"The difference between us is that you've got your whole life ahead of you, and I'm windin' it down. Nobody said livin' was gonna be easy or fair, that's for damn sure. I'm here to tell you it's not. But you don't give up. You're gonna get knocked down and beat up and stomped, but you don't quit. You can't."

"Maybe you can," Arden said quietly. "I'm tired of bein' knocked down, beaten up, and stomped. I keep gettin' up, and somethin' comes along to knock me down again. I'm tired of it. I wish to God there was a way to . . . just find some peace."

"Go back to Fort Worth." He slid the paddle into the water and began pushing them forward again. "Somethin's bound to open up for you. But you sure don't belong in the middle of a swamp, tryin' to find a faith healer."

"Right now I don't know where I belong. I don't think I ever have known." She was silent for a moment, her hands working around the pink drawstring bag. "What was your best time?" she asked. "I mean, the time when you thought everything was right, and you were where you were supposed to be. Do you know?"

He thought about it, and the longer he thought the harder the question became to answer. "I guess . . . maybe when I'd first joined the marines. In boot camp, on Parris Island. I had a job to do—a mission—and I was gettin' ready for it. Things were black and white. I thought my country needed me, and I thought I could make a difference."

"You sound like you were eager to fight."

"Yeah, I was." Dan paddled another stroke and then paused. "I liked bein' over there the first couple of months. At first it seemed like I was doin' somethin' important. I didn't like to kill—no man in his right mind does—but I did it because I was fightin' for my country. I thought. Then, later on, it all changed. I saw so many boys get killed, I couldn't figure out what they were dyin' for. I mean, what were we tryin' to do? The Viet Cong didn't want my country. They weren't gonna invade us. They didn't have anything we needed. What was that all about?" He shook his head. "Here it's been over twenty years, and I still don't know. It was a hell of a lot of wasted lives is what it was. Lives just thrown away."

"It must've been bad," Arden said. "I've seen a couple of movies about Vietnam, and it sure wasn't like Desert Storm, was it?"

"Nope, it sure wasn't." *Movies about Vietnam*, he thought, and he lowered his head to hide his half-smile. He'd been forgetting that Arden was all of four years old when he'd shipped to 'Nam.

"My best time was when I was livin' on the youth ranch," she said. "It was a hard place, and you did your chores and toed the line, but it was all right. The others there were like I was. All of us had been through a half-dozen foster homes, and we'd screwed up and gotten in trouble with the law. It was our last chance to get straight, I guess. I hated it at first. Tried to run away a couple of times, but I didn't get very far. Mr. Richards put me to work cleanin' out the barn. There were five horses, all of 'em old and swaybacked, but they still earned their keep. Jupiter was in charge of the stable, that's where I met him."

"You think a lot of him, don't you?"

"He was always kind to me. Some of those foster homes I was in . . . well, I think solitary confinement in prison would've been better. I had trouble, too, because of . . . you know . . . my mark. Somebody looked at me too long, I was liable to lose my temper and start throwin' plates and glasses. Which didn't make me too popular with foster parents. I wasn't used to bein' treated like I had sense." She shrugged. "I guess I had a lot to prove. But Jupiter took an interest in me. He trusted me with the horses, started lettin' me feed and groom 'em. After a while, when I'd wake up early mornin's I could hear 'em callin' for me, wantin' me to hurry up. You know, all horses have got different personalities and different voices, not a one of 'em alike. Some of 'em come right out of the stall to meet you, others are shy and hang back. And when they look at you they don't care if you're ugly or deformed. They don't judge you by a mark on your face, like people do."

"Not all people," Dan said.

"Enough to hurt," she answered. She looked up at the stars for a moment, and Dan went to work with the paddle once more. "It was a good feelin', to wake up and hear the horses callin' you," she went on. "It was the first time I ever felt needed, or that I was worth a damn. After the work was done, Jupiter and I started havin' long talks. About life, and God, and stuff I'd never cared to think much about. He never mentioned my mark; he let me get to it in my own time. It took me a while to talk about it, and how I wished more than anything in the world I could be rid of it. Then he told me about the Bright Girl."

Dan said nothing; he was listening, but on this subject it was hard not to turn a deaf ear.

"I never really expected I'd ever be lookin' for her," Arden said. "But the way Jupiter talked about her . . . she seemed like somebody I'd know, if I ever found her. She seemed so real, and so alive. I mean, I know it sounds crazy for somebody to live so long and never get old. I know the faith healers on TV are frauds tryin' to squeeze out the bucks. But Jupiter would never have lied to me." She caught Dan's gaze and held it. "If he said there's a Bright Girl, there is. And if he said she can touch my mark and take it away, she can. He would never have lied. And he was right about *you,* too. If he said you're the man God sent to help me find her, then I be—"

"Stop it!" Dan interrupted sharply. "I told you I didn't want to hear that"—*bullshit,* he almost said, but he settled on—"junk."

She started to fire back a heated reply, but she closed her mouth. She just stared at him, her eyes fixed on his.

Dan said, "You're chasin' a fairy tale. Where it's gotten you? Do you think you're better off than before you left for Worth? No, you're worse off. At least you had some money in the bank. I don't want to hear any more about the Bright Girl, or what Jupiter told you, or any of that. Understand?"

"I wish *you* understood." Her voice was calm and controlled. "If—*when*—we find her, she can heal you, too."

"Oh, Christ!" He closed his eyes in exasperation for a few seconds. When he opened them, Arden was still glowering at him. "You could argue the horns off a billy goat, you know that? There is *no* Bright Girl, and there never was! It's a made-up story!"

"That's what you say."

He saw no point in going around in circles with her. "Right, that's what I say," he muttered, and then he concentrated on putting some elbow grease into the paddling. The current seemed to have gotten a little faster, which he thought must be a good sign. He was hungry and thirsty and his headache had returned, pounding with his heartbeat. Dried blood was in his nostrils, he'd lost his much-prized baseball cap and his muscles—what remained of them, that is—were rapidly wearing out. The water was rising in the bottom of the boat again, and Dan put aside the paddle for a few minutes while he and Arden cupped their hands and bailed. Then he shook off the sleep that was closing in on him and paddled them down the center of the bayou with slow, smooth strokes. He watched Arden's head droop as she fell asleep sitting up, and then he was alone with the noises of the swamp. After a while his eyelids became leaden and he couldn't keep them open. The heat pressed on him, lulling him to sleep. He fought it as hard as he could, but at last his weariness won the battle and his chin slumped.

He jerked his head up, his eyes opening.

They had drifted toward the left of the channel and were almost in the branches. Dan steered them toward the center again, and then he heard the sound that had awakened him: a muffled thudding like the heartbeats of a giant. Ahead and to the right, electric lights glinted through the thick woods. Dan looked at his wristwatch and saw that another hour had elapsed since they'd entered the wider channel.

"What's that noise?" Arden asked, waking up almost as quickly as he had.

"Machinery," he said. "I think we're comin' to somethin'."

Around the next curve the trees had been chopped away on the right to make room for a hodgepodge of weatherbeaten clapboard structures built on platforms over the water. Electric lights cast their glary circles on a dock where an assortment of motor skiffs and two houseboats were tied up. On the dock were gas pumps and an attendant's shack, also lit up with electricity supplied from a rumbling generator. Plank walkways connected the buildings, and Dan and Arden saw two men standing in conversation next to the gas pumps and a couple of other men on the walkways. A rusty barge loaded with sections of metal pipe, coils of wire, and other industrial items was anchored past the dock at a concrete pier where a long building with corrugated aluminum walls stood, the legend WAREHOUSE #1 painted in red across the building's doorway. Beyond the warehouse loomed oil storage tanks and twelve or more spidery derricks rising up from the swamp. The giant heartbeat—the sound of pumps at work—was coming from that direction.

The entire scene—a large, mechanized oil-pumping station, Dan had realized—was almost surrealistic, emerging as it had from the dark wilderness. As he steered them toward the dock, he saw a pole that held a tired-looking American flag and next to it was a sign on stilts that announced ST. NASTASE, LA. HOME SWEET HELLHOLE. On the supporting stilts were a number of other directional arrows with such things as NEW ORLEANS 52 MI., BATON

ROUGE 76 MI., and GALVESTON 208 MI. painted on them. One of the men on the dock picked up a line and tossed it to Arden as they approached, then he hauled them in. "Hey there, how you doin'?" the man asked in a thick Cajun patois. He was a husky, florid-faced gent with a red beard and a sweat-stained bandanna wrapped around his skull.

"Tired and hungry," Dan told him as he carefully stood up and helped Arden onto the dock. "Where are we?"

"Fella wanna know where he am," the Cajun said to the other man, and both of them laughed. "Friend, you *must* be in some sad shape!"

Dan stepped onto the timbers, his spine unkinking. "I mean how far from here to the Gulf?"

"Oh, blue water 'bout tree mile." He motioned south with a crusty thumb. His gaze lingered on Arden's birthmark for a few seconds, then he diverted his attention to the waterlogged skiff. "I seen some crackass boats before, but that'un done win the prize! Where ya'll come from?"

"North," Dan said. "Anyplace to get some food here?"

"Yeah, cafe's over there." The second man, who spoke with a flat midwestern accent, nodded in the direction of the clapboard buildings. He was slimmer than his companion, wore a grease-stained brown cap with a red GSP on the front—a company logo, Dan figured—and had tattoos intertwining all over his arms. "They got gumbo and hamburgers tonight. Ain't too bad if you wash 'em down with enough beer."

A door on one of the houseboats opened, and another man emerged, buckling the belt of his blue jeans. He wore a company cap turned backward. Behind him, tape-recorded rock music rumbled through the doorway and then a woman with bleached-blond hair and a hard, sunburned face peered out. "Okay!" she said with forced cheerfulness. "All-night party, boys! Who's next?"

"I believe I am." The man with tattooed arms sauntered toward the houseboat.

"Non, mon ami." The Cajun stepped forward, seized his companion by shirt back and pants seat, and, pivoting, lifted him off his feet and flung him from the dock. With a curse and squall the unfortunate flyer hit the water and skimmed its surface like a powerboat before he went under. "I believe you *was!*" the Cajun hollered as his friend came up spitting. "Hey, Lorraine!" he greeted the bleached blonde. "You got sweets for me?"

"You know I do, Tully. Get your big ol' ass in here." She narrowed her eyes at Arden. "New chickie, huh?" She gave a throaty laugh. "You gonna need a little makeup, darlin'. Well, good luck to you." Tully lumbered into the houseboat, and Lorraine closed the door behind them.

It was time to move on. Dan ventured along one of the walkways, heading toward the buildings, and Arden followed close behind. The place made Dan think of a Wild West frontier town, except it had been built up from the muck instead of being carved from the desert. It was a carpenter's nightmare, the structures cobbled together with pressure-treated pineboards and capped by rusted tin roofs. Electrical cables snaked from building to building, carrying the juice from generators. The walkways were so close to the water that in some places reeds stuck up between the planks. There was a store whose sign announced it as R.J'S GROCERY and next to it was a little narrow structure marked ST. NASTASE POST OFFICE. A Laundromat with three washers and dryers and two pool tables was lit up and doing business. Dan noted that the men they saw gazed hungrily at Arden's body, but when they looked at her face they averted their eyes as quickly as Tully had.

St. Nastase, Dan had realized, most likely never closed down, to accommodate the crews who were off shift. Dan figured that the men here had signed on with the company for three or four months at a stretch, which meant prostitutes in houseboats could make some money plying their trade. It occurred to him that Lorraine had thought Arden was a "new chickie" because the only women who dared to go there were selling sex, and he was un-aware of it but Arden had come to the same conclusions about ten seconds ahead of him.

In another moment they heard the mingled music of a fiddle and an accordion. The smell of food caught their nostrils. Ahead was a building with a sign that said simply CAFE. The place had a pair of batwing doors, like a western saloon. The music was coming from within, accompanied now by whoops and hollers. Dan figured this could be a hell of a rowdy joint, and again he wished Arden wasn't around because he was going to have to be responsible for her safety. He said, "Stick close to me," and then Arden followed him through the batwings, her right hand clenching the pink drawstring bag.

The cafe was dimly lit, blue-hazed with cigarette smoke, and at the ceiling a fan chugged around in a futile attempt to circulate the humid, sweat-smelling air. Hanging from the ceiling as well were maybe three hundred old, dirty brown caps with red GSP logos. At rough plank tables sat twenty or more men, a few of them clapping their hands in time with the jerky, raucous music, while four of their fellows danced with ladies of the evening. The fiddler and accordionist both wore company caps, and a thick-shouldered black man got up from his table, sat down at a battered old piano, and began to beat out a rhythm that added to the merry clamor. Some of the men glanced eagerly at Arden, but they looked away when Dan put his arm around her shoulders.

He guided her toward a bar where metal beer kegs, canned soft drinks, and bottles of water were on display. Behind it, a harried-looking man with glasses, a beard, and slicked-back dark hair was drawing beer into mugs, sweat stains on his red-checked shirt and a cigar stub gripped between his teeth. "Can we get somethin' to eat?" Dan asked over the noise, and the bartender said, "Burgers a buck apiece, gumbo two bucks a bowl. Take the gumbo, the burgers taste like dog meat."

They both decided on the gumbo, which the bartender ladled from a grease-filmed pot into plastic bowls. Arden asked for a bottle of water and Dan requested a beer, and as the bartender shoved trays and plastic spoons wrapped in cellophane at them, Dan said, "I'm tryin' to get this girl out of here. Is there a road anywhere nearby?"

"A *road?*" He snorted, and the tip of his cigar glowed red. "Ain't no roads outta St. Nasty. Just water and mud. She a workin' girl?"

"No. We're passin' through."

The bartender stared at Dan, his eyes slightly magnified by the glasses, and he removed the cigar from his mouth. "Passin' through," he repeated incredulously. "Now I've heard it all. Ain't no man comes here unless he's drawin' pay from Gulf States Petro, and no woman unless she's tryin' to get a man to spend it on her. Which insane asylum did ya'll get loose from?"

"We had an accident. Went off a bridge north of LaPierre. We got a boat, and—" Dan stopped, because the bartender's eyes had gotten larger. "Look, we're just tryin' to get out. Can you help us?"

"Supply boat from Grand Isle oughta be here tomorrow afternoon. I'd say you could hitch a ride with one of these ladies, but they'll be stayin' the weekend. Today was payday, see. Fridays and Saturdays, all these sumbitches wanna do is get drunk and screw when their shifts are over." He pushed the cigar stub back into his mouth. "You come all the way from *LaPierre?* Jesus, that's a hell of a hike!"

"Hey, Burt!" a man yelled. "Let's have our beers over here!"

"Your legs ain't broke!" Burt hollered back. "Get off your ass and come get 'em, I ain't no slave!" He returned his attention to Dan. "An accident, huh? You want to call somebody? I got a radio-telephone in the back."

"I'm lookin' for a woman," Arden said suddenly. "The Bright Girl. Have you ever heard of her?"

"Nope," Burt replied. A man with a prostitute in tow came up to get his beers. "Should I have?"

"The Bright Girl's a healer. She lives in the swamp some-where, and I'm tryin' to—"

"Arden?" Dan caught hold of her elbow. "I told you to stop that, didn't I?"

She pulled loose. "I've come a long way to find her," she said to Burt, and she heard the sharp, rising edge of desperation in her voice. Burt's eyes were blank, no idea of what she was talking about at all. Arden felt panic building inside her like a dark wave. "The Bright Girl *is* here, somewhere," she said. "I'm gonna find her. I'm not leavin' here until I find her."

Burt took in the birthmark and looked at Dan. "Like I asked before, what asylum did ya'll bust out of?"

"I'm not crazy," Arden went on. "The Bright Girl's real. I know she is. Somebody here has to have heard of her."

"Sorry," Burt said. "I don't know who you're talkin' a—"

"I know that name."

Arden turned her head to the left. The prostitute who stood with the beer-swiller had spoken in a nasal drawl. She was a slight, rawboned girl wearing denim shorts and a faded orange blouse. Maybe she was in her early twenties, but her high-cheekboned, buck-toothed face had been prematurely aged by scorching sun and harsh salt wind. Lines were starting to deepen around her mouth and at the corners of her dull, chocolate-brown eyes, and her peroxided hair cut in bangs across her forehead hung lifelessly around her bony shoulders. She stared with genuine interest at Arden's birthmark as her escort paid for two beers. "Jeez," she said. "You got fucked up awful bad, didn't ya?"

"Yes." Arden's heart was pounding, and for a few seconds she felt on the verge of fainting. She grasped the edge of the bar with her free hand. "You've heard of the Bright Girl?"

"Uh-huh." The prostitute began to dig at a molar with a toothpick. "Woman who healed people. Used to hear 'bout her when I was a little girl."

"Do you know where she is?"

"Yeah," came the answer, "I do."

*   *   *

As Dan and Arden had been walking into the cafe, the man who'd just gone for an unwilling swim sat on the dock in a puddle of water, watching another boat approach. There were two men in the boat. He couldn't quite trust his eyes. The man who was paddling wore a dark suit and a white shirt, which was not quite the normal attire out here at St. Nasty. The second man—well, maybe it was time to swear off the beers, because that sonofabitch Burt must be mixing the brew with toxic waste.

When the boat bumped broadside against the dock, Flint stood up and stepped out. His mud-grimed suit jacket was buttoned up over his dirty shirt, the pale flesh of his face mottled with red mosquito bites, his eyes sunken in weary purple hollows. He stared at the battered and water-filled skiff tied up just beside them, a single broken paddle lying in it. Nobody would've traveled in that damn thing unless they'd been forced to, he reasoned. "How long have you been sittin' here?" he asked the drenched man, who was watching Pelvis clamber out of the boat with Mama.

"You gotta be *kiddin'*!" the man said, unable to take his eyes off Pelvis. "What is this, *Candid Camera?*"

"Hey, listen up!" Flint demanded, his patience at its bitter end. Clint—who was equally as tired and cranky—jerked under his shirt, and Flint put an arm across his chest to hold his brother down. "I'm lookin' for a man and a woman. Shouldn't have been too long since they got here." He nodded at the sinking boat. "Did you see who that belongs to?"

"Yeah, they're here. Sent 'em over to the cafe." He couldn't help but stare at Pelvis. "I know we're hurtin' for entertainment 'round here, but please don't tell me you're on the payroll."

"Where's the cafe? Which direction?"

"Only one direction, unless you can walk on water. Scratch that," he decided, and he motioned at Pelvis with his thumb. "Maybe he *can* walk on water."

Flint started off toward the clapboard buildings, and Pelvis followed, leaving the man on the dock wondering what the next boat might bring. Others they passed stopped to gawk at Pelvis as well, and he started drawing catcalls and laughter. "Hey!" Flint called to two men standing in the shadows next to the Laundromat/poolroom. "The cafe around here?"

One of them pointed the way, and Flint and Pelvis went on. Flint reached into his pocket and put his hand on the derringer's grip.

"Who the hell are *they?*" the man who'd pointed asked his friend.

The second man, who had a long, vulpine face and close-cropped brown hair, ran his tongue across his lower lip. He wore faded jeans and a dirty yellow shirt with the tail flagging out, and the sweat on his flesh still smelled of swamp mud and alligators. "Friends of Doc's," he said quietly. "I believe he'd like to see 'em again. Here." He slid a small packet of white powder into the other man's hand.

"Keep your money. Just do me a favor and watch those two. All right?"

"Sure, Mitch. Whatever."

"Good boy." Mitch, who still had the pistol he'd fired at Flint in his waistband, turned away and hurried to his motorboat, his mouth split by a savage grin.

20

The King Bled Crimson

"**Y**EAH," CAME THE PROSTITUTE'S answer. "I do." She continued to probe with the toothpick as Arden's nerves stretched. "Dead. Must be dead by now. She was old, lived in a church on Goat Island."

"That's bull!" Burt said. "Ain't nobody ever lived on Goat Island!"

"*Was* a church there!" the prostitute insisted. "Blew down in a hurricane, back fifteen or twenty years! The Bright Girl was a nun fell in love with a priest, so they threw her out of her convent and she come down here and built a church to repent! That's what my mama said!"

"Angie, you didn't have no mama!" Burt winked at the girl's customer. "She was hatched, wasn't she, Cal?"

"Right out of a buzzard's egg," Cal agreed, his voice slurred by one too many brews.

Angie jabbed an elbow into Cal's ribs. "You don't know nothin', fool!"

Arden tried to speak, but her throat had seized up. The word *dead* was still ringing in her head like a funeral bell. "Goat Island," she managed. "Where is it?"

"Don't do this," Dan warned, but he knew there was no stopping her.

"Way the hell out in Terrebonne Bay," Burt said. "Good ten miles from here. Got wild goats runnin' all over it, but there sure ain't never been no church out there."

"My mama wasn't no liar!" Angie snapped. "You wasn't even born 'round here, how do you know?"

"I been huntin' on Goat Island before! Walked the length and width of it! If there'd ever been a church there, I think I would've seen some ruins!"

"Miss?" Dan said to the prostitute. "You say the Bright Girl was an old woman?"

"Yeah. My mama said she seen her when she was a little girl. Came to Port Fourchon to see my mama's cousin. His name was Pearly, he was seven years old when he got burned up in a fire. Mama said the Bright Girl was crippled and walked with a white cane. I reckon that was"—she paused to calculate—"near thirty years ago."

"Uh-huh." Dan felt Arden's body tensing beside him. But he decided he had to go the next step, too. "What about Pearly? Did your mama say the Bright Girl healed him?"

"No, I recollect she said the Bright Girl took him with her in a boat."

"To where?"

"Goat Island, I reckon. She never saw Pearly no more, though. Mama said she figured he was too bad off for even the Bright Girl to heal. But that was all right, 'cause the Bright Girl made sure he wasn't scairt when he went to heaven."

"Come on, baby!" Cal grabbed Angie's thin arm and tugged at her. "Let's dance!"

"Wait! Please!" Arden's anguished voice cut to Dan's heart. "Is she buried out there? Have you seen her grave?"

"No, I ain't seen her grave. But she's dead. Got to be dead after all this time."

"But you don't know for sure, do you? You're not certain she's dead?"

The prostitute stared at Arden for a few seconds and then pulled free of Cal's hand. "I'm certain as I need to be," she said. "Ohhhhh." She nodded as things came clear to her. "Ohhhhh, I see. You was lookin' for the Bright Girl to heal your face. Is that right?"

"Yes."

"I'm sorry, then. Far as I know, she's dead. I don't know where she's buried. I can ask some of the other girls. Most of 'em were born 'round here, maybe they'd know."

"Let's *dance!*" Cal yawped. "Forget this shit!"

Both women ignored him. "I'd like to see the church," Arden said. "Can you take me?"

"No, I can't. See, I would, but I don't have my own boat. It's Lorraine's boat, and she don't take it nowhere but between here and Grand Isle."

"Hey, listen up, scarface!" Cal slurred at Arden, his voice turning nasty. "I'm rentin' this bitch by the fuckin' *hour,* understand? I don't have no time to waste—"

"Come over here a minute." Dan reached out, grasped Cal's wrist, and drew him closer, beer slopping to the floor from the mug in the man's hand. Dan's face was strained with anger, his eyes hard and shiny. "The ladies are talkin'."

"Mister, you let go of me or I'm gonna have to knock the shit outta your ears!"

"No fightin' in here!" Burt warned. "You wanna fight, get out back!"

"You're drunk, friend." Dan kept his face close to Cal's, his arm low across the man's body so the beer mug wouldn't come up and smash him in the teeth. "Don't let your mouth get you in trouble."

"It's all right," Arden said. The remark wasn't anything she hadn't heard before. "Really it is."

She suddenly caught a strong whiff of body odor and swamp mud. Someone wearing a dark suit stepped between her and Dan. She thought of vulture wings sweeping onto a dying jackrabbit.

"Lambert?" A quiet voice spoke in Dan's ear. At the same time, Dan felt the little barrel of a gun press against his ribs. "The game's over."

Dan jerked his head around and looked into the pallid face he'd seen by the flashlight's glare in Basile Park, only now it was blotched with mosquito bites. His heart jumped and fluttered like a trapped bird.

Flint said, "Take it very, very easy. Nobody needs to get hurt. Okay?"

Beyond Murtaugh, Dan saw, stood the Elvis Presley impersonator holding his squirming bulldog. The music had faltered and ended on a squawked note from the squeezebox. The Presley clone was suddenly the center of attention, and he started drawing whistles and laughter.

Flint glanced quickly at the girl and saw that what he'd thought was a massive bruise was in fact a deep violet birthmark. "You all right, Miss Halliday?"

"I'm fine. Who are—" She realized then who it must be, and that he'd looked through her purse back where they'd gone off the bridge.

"My name is Flint Murtaugh. Fella," he said to Cal, "why don't you take your beer and move along?"

"I was fixin' to whip this bastard's ass," Cal answered, unsteady on his feet.

"I'll take care of him from here on out."

"Anytime, anywhere, anyplace!" Cal sneered in Dan's face, and then he grabbed Angie's arm again and jerked her onto the dance floor with him. "Well, shit a brick!" he hollered at the musicians. "How 'bout some goddamn *playin'*?"

The fiddler started up again, then the accordionist and the piano pounder joined in. Men were still laughing and gawking at Pelvis, who was trying his best to stand there and appear oblivious to the hilarity. His wig had started to slip, its glue weakened by the swamp water, and he reached up with a quick hand and straightened it.

"What the hell is *that?*" Burt grinned around his cigar stub. He hadn't seen the derringer Flint pressed against Dan's side, which was how Flint wanted it. "Is it animal, veg'table or mineral?" He spouted smoke and looked at Flint. "I swear to God, this is turnin' out to be a circus! Where'd ya'll come from?"

"We're with this fella here," Flint answered. "Just got left behind a little ways."

"Your friend's dressed up for Halloween early, ain't he?"

"He's a big Elvis fan. Don't worry about him, he's harmless."

"Maybe so, but these sumbitches in here sure smell blood. Listen to 'em howlin'!" He moved away down the bar to draw a beer for another customer.

"Hey, Elvis!" somebody yelled. "Get up there and shake that fat ass, man!"

"Give us a song, Elvis!" another one called.

Flint didn't have time to concern himself with Eisley's situation. He knew something like this was bound to happen sooner or later. But the important thing was that Daniel Lewis Lambert was standing right in front of him, and the derringer was loaded and cocked. "Did he hurt you, Miss Halliday?"

"No."

"You were lucky, then. You know he's murdered two people, don't you?"

"I know he killed a man at a bank in Shreveport. He told me about that. But he said he didn't kill the man in Alexandria, and I believe him."

"You *believe* him?" He darted another glance at her. "I thought he took you as a hostage."

"No," Arden said, "that's not how it was at all. I came with him of my own free will."

Either she was crazy, Flint figured, or somehow Lambert had brainwashed her. But she wasn't his concern, either. He kept the gun's barrel jammed into Lambert's ribs. "Well, you ran me a good chase, I'll give you that."

Dan didn't answer. His heart had stopped pounding, and now there was ice in his blood. He was looking at a closed door about ten feet away. Maybe beyond it was a bathroom with a window, and if he could get in there and lock the door to buy himself a few seconds, he might still get away.

"Face the bar and put your hands flat on top of it."

Dan obeyed, but his attention was still fixed on the door. If he could get out a window into the swamp, then he could . . .

Could *what?* he asked himself. He was dead tired, hungry, and thirsty. His strength was gone. He doubted if he'd had the energy to trade a punch or two with Cal, much less swim through 'gator-infested water. As Flint quickly frisked him, wanting to attract as little notice as possible and helped in this regard by the loud and raucous attention being thrown at Pelvis, Dan realized that cold reality had just slapped him across the face. He had come to his senses as if awakening from a fever dream.

There was nowhere else to go. His run was over.

"You bring your pink Cadillac, Elvis?"

"Hell, get up there and sing somethin'!"

"Yeah, and it better be damn good, too!"

Pelvis had played rough rooms before, where the drunks with burning eyes would boil up out of their seats, wanting to either grab the microphone away from him or show their girlfriends that the King bled crimson. This room ranked right down there with the worst of them, and Pelvis tried to pay no mind to the jeering, but the shouts began stinging his pride.

"You ain't no Elvis, you fat shit!"

"What'cha got in your arms there, Elvis? Your girlfriend?" This was followed by a barrage of barking and laughter that drowned out the struggling musicians.

Flint saw the situation getting out of control, but any man who wanted to look and talk like a dead hillbilly had to take his licks. He kept his focus on Lambert, who—he was surprised to find—carried no weapons, not even a knife. "Empty your pockets."

"What're you gonna do?" Arden asked. "Rob him?"

"No. Lambert, you must have a way with the women. First your ex-wife stands up for you, now her. She doesn't know the real you, does she?"

Dan put his wallet on top of the bar, then a few soggy dollar bills and some change. He found the yearbook picture Chad had given him, wrinkled up by the swamp water. "How'd you find me?"

Flint flipped the wallet open and felt for hidden razor blades. "I heard your ex-wife tell you about the cabin. I've been waitin' for you all day." Flint picked up the damp picture and looked at it. "Your son?"

"Yeah."

"See, that's where you screwed up. You should never have gone to that park. If you'd steered clear of Alexandria, you wouldn't be lookin' at a double murder conviction." He slid Dan's wallet and the money into his coat, which was still buttoned to hide Clint's occasional muscle twitches under his shirt. "You can keep the picture."

Dan returned it to his pocket. "That man was alive when I left the motel. His wife killed him, and she's blamin' it on me."

"Nice try. Tell it to the police and see what they think."

"He already has," Arden spoke up. "He called the Alexandria police while we were in Lafayette. He told 'em to check the shotgun for his fingerprints."

"Uh-huh. He tell you he did that?"

"I saw him do it."

"And he was probably talkin' to a dial tone, or a recorded message, or he had his finger on the cutoff switch. Lambert, put your hands down in front of you and grip 'em together."

"You don't need to cuff me," Dan said flatly. "I'm not goin' anywhere."

"Just shut up and do it."

"I'd like to eat my gumbo and drink a beer. You want to feed me?" He turned around and stared into the bounty hunter's chilly blue eyes. Murtaugh looked as worn-out as Dan felt, his face gaunt, his dark hair with its lightning-white streak oily and uncombed. A dozen mosquito bites splotched his grizzled cheeks and chin, and he had to scratch two of them even as he kept the derringer pressed into Dan's side. "I won't run," Dan said. "I'm too tired, and there's no use in it." He read the distrust in the tight crimp of Murtaugh's thin-lipped mouth. "I give you my word. All I want to do is eat some dinner and rest."

"Yeah, I know what your word is worth." Flint started to reach into his pocket for the handcuffs, but he hesitated. Lambert had no weapon, and he did look exhausted. This time, at least, there was no woman between them who knew tae kwan do. Flint said, "I swear to God, if you try to get away, I'll put a bullet through your knee or elbow and let the lawyers sort it out. Understand?"

Dan nodded, convinced that Murtaugh would do as he promised.

"All right, then. Eat."

A skinny man in a GSP cap and greasy overalls plucked at Pelvis's arm. "Hey, you!" he said. Pelvis saw the man was missing most of his front teeth. His eyes were red and heavy-lidded, and the reek of beer and gumbo on his breath was enough to make Mama whimper. "I knew Elvis," the man wheezed. "Elvis was a fren' a mine. And you big ol' turd, you sure as hell *ain't* no Elvis!"

Pelvis felt the hot blood swelling his jowls. Hoots and laughter were flying at him like jagged spears. He walked to the blond woman with the birthmark on her face and said in an anger-tensed voice, "Excuse me, would you hold Mama?"

"What?"

"My dog," he said. "Would you hold her for just two or three minutes?" He pushed Mama into her arms.

"Eisley!" Flint snapped. "What're you doin'?"

"I've got my pride. They want a song, I'm gonna give 'em a song."

"No, you're not!" But Pelvis was already walking toward the musicians, braving the intoxicated jeers and insults. "Eisley!" Flint shouted. "Come back here!"

The musicians stopped playing their Cajun stomp as Pelvis approached, and then the whoops and hollers ricocheted off the tin roof. Burt had come back down the bar, and he yelled at Flint, "Your friend ain't gonna need a burial plot! Ain't gonna be nothin' left to bury!"

"He's a fool, is what he is!" Flint seethed, still holding the derringer low against Dan's ribs, but in the dim and smoky light Burt didn't see it. While Arden held on to the bulldog, the thoughts of what Angie had told her battering around in her mind, Dan took his first bite of gumbo and the hot spices and sausage in it almost set his tongue on fire.

"You fellas know 'Hound Dog'?" Pelvis asked the band. He got three heads to swivel. "How 'bout 'I Got a Woman'? 'Heartbreak Hotel'? 'A Big Hunk o' Love'?" There were negative reactions to all those. Pelvis felt sweat collecting around his collar. "Do you know *any* Elvis songs?"

"All we play is zydeco," the accordionist said. "You know. Like 'My Toot-Toot' and 'Diggy Liggy Lo.'"

"Oh, Lord," Pelvis breathed.

"Don't just stand there, Elvis!" a shout swelled up from the others. "You ain't dead, are you?"

Pelvis turned to face his audience. Sweat was running down under his arms, his heart starting to pound. He lifted his hands to quiet the jeering, and about half of it stopped. "I have to tell you fellas I usually accomp'ny myself on the git-tar. Anybody got a git-tar I can use?"

"This ain't fuckin' *Nashville,* you asshole!" came a reply. "Either start singin' or you're gonna go swimmin'!"

Pelvis looked over at Flint, who just shook his head with pity and averted his gaze. Then Pelvis stared out at the roughnecks, the butterflies of fear swarming in his stomach. "Start croakin', you big fat frog!" somebody else hollered. A drop of sweat rolled into Pelvis's left eye and burned it shut for a couple of seconds. Suddenly a bowl of gumbo came flying up from one of the tables and it splashed all over the front of his muddy trousers. A wave of laughter followed, then somebody began to bray like a donkey. Pelvis stared down at his mud-crusted brown suede shoes, and he thought of how those men in there didn't know the many hours he'd spent watching Elvis movies, learning the King's walk and talk and sneer; they didn't know how many nights he'd listened to Elvis records in a grubby little room, catching every phrase and nuance of that rich and glorious voice, that voice of the American soul. They didn't know how much he loved Elvis, how he worshipped at the shrine of Graceland and how his wife had called him a stupid fat loser and run off with all his money and a truck driver named Boomer. They didn't know how he had suffered for his art.

His public was calling for him. Ranting at him, to tell the truth. Pelvis squared his shoulders, tucked his chins, and turned away from the audience. He said to the piano pounder, "You mind if I sit there?" and he slid onto the chair when it was gladly vacated. Pelvis cracked his knuckles, looked at the dirty keyboard with its sad and broken ivories, and then he put his fingers down and began to play.

A strain of classical music came from the rickey-tick piano. The room was shocked silent, and no one was shocked more than Flint. But only Flint recognized the music: it was the stately opening chords of Chopin's Prelude Number Nine in E major, one of the soul-soothing pieces he listened to daily on his car's cassette player.

They let him play about ten seconds of it before they regained their senses. Then a second bowl of gumbo hit the piano and a half of a hamburger flew past Pelvis's head and a roar of dissatisfaction went up like a nuclear blast. "We don't want that damn shit!" yelled a man with a face as mean as a scarred fist. "Play us somethin' with a *tune!*"

"Hold your horses!" Pelvis shouted back. "I'm just limberin' up my fingers!" He was as ready as he would ever be. "All right, this here's called 'A Big Hunk o' Love.'" And then his hands slammed down on the keyboard and the piano made a noise like a locomotive howling through a tunnel in red-hot, demon-infested, sex-dripping, and god-forsaken Hades. His fingers skittered up and down the keys in a blur of motion, the sound's power kicking all the jeers and hollers right out the swinging doors. Pelvis threw his head back, sweat shining on his face, his mouth opened, and he started bellowing about asking his baby for a bigga bigga bigga hunka love.

Flint's mouth was open, too; his jaw had dropped in amazement. Eisley's speaking voice might mimic Elvis, but his singing voice was something altogether different; though there were husky tones of the King's rockabilly Memphis in it, there was also the guttural moan of a rusty chain saw that suddenly broke into a startling, soaring, and unearthly high—*bigga hunka hunka luv-vvvvv*—more akin to the operatic wail of Roy Orbison. Watching Eisley beat that piano to pieces like a demented Jerry Lee Lewis and hearing his voice rattle the ceiling and then rumble the floorboards again, Flint realized the truth: onstage Eisley was a lousy Elvis, but that was like saying a ruby was a lousy diamond. Though Flint hated that kind of redneck thunder, though it made the skin crawl on the back of his neck and made him long for a good set of earplugs, it was clear that Pelvis Eisley was no imitator of a dead star. The man, whether he knew it or not, was an honest-to-God original fireball.

Dan followed a spoonful of the spicy gumbo with a drink of beer, and he regarded the Presley clone flailing at the piano. *Hunka hunka big olllll' love,* the man was growling. Murtaugh's gun had pulled a few inches away from Dan's ribs. The bounty hunter's focus was riveted on his companion. It flashed through Dan's mind that if he was quick enough, he could bring the beer mug down across the side of Murtaugh's head and run for the back door.

Do it, he told himself. Hit the bastard and run while there's still time.

He took another swallow of the bitter brew and held the mug ready to strike. On his forearm the ropy muscles tensed, making the tattooed snake undulate.

21

Silent Shadow

A SECOND PASSED. THEN another.
Do it! he thought, and he stared at the place on Murtaugh's skull that would bear the blow.

A third and fourth seconds went by.

No.

It was a strong voice. The voice of reason.

No, Dan decided. I gave my word, and I've caused enough misery. There'll be no more of it.

Murtaugh's head suddenly swiveled, and the pale blue eyes fixed on him.

Dan lifted the mug to his lips and drank the rest of his beer. "Your friend's not half bad."

Flint looked at the glass mug and then his gaze returned to Dan's eyes. He had the feeling that danger had just slid past like a silent shadow. "You're not thinkin' of doin' somethin' stupid, are you?"

"Nope."

"If you don't want to wear the bracelets, you'd better not be. I want to keep this as quiet and clean as I can."

Dan had wondered why Murtaugh was doing his best to hold the gun out of sight, and why he hadn't told the bartender who he was. "You afraid somebody else'll snatch me away from you if they find out about the money?"

"People hear what I do for a livin', they don't usually welcome me with hearts and flowers."

"Listen, I didn't mean to kill Blanchard," Dan said. "He drew a gun on me. I had the guard's pistol in my hand, and I—"

"Do us both a favor," Flint interrupted. "Save it for the judge."

Pelvis finished the song with a wail and a series of chords that threatened to demolish the piano. As the last notes were dying, another thunderous noise rose up: the whooping and applause of his audience. Pelvis blinked out at them, stunned by the response. Though he used to play piano in a blues band when he was a lanky boy with a headful of wavy hair and big ideas, he was accustomed to standing behind an electric guitar, which he couldn't play very well but after all it was the King's instrument. He was used to hearing club managers telling him he needed to rein his voice in and keep it snarly because those high tenor notes didn't sound like Elvis at all, that's what the customers were paying for, and if he wanted to be a decent Elvis impersonator, he was way off the mark.

Here, though, it was obvious they were starved for entertainment and they didn't care that he wasn't twanging an electric guitar or that his voice wasn't as earthy as the King's. They started shouting for another song, some of them beating on their tables with their fists and beer mugs. "Thank you, thank you kindly!" Pelvis said. "Well, I'll do you another one, then. This here's 'It's Your Baby, You Rock It'." He launched off on another display of honky-tonkin' fireworks, and though his hands were stiff and he knew he was hitting a lot of clams, all his training was coming back to him. The fiddler picked up the chords and began sewing them together, and then the accordion player added a jumpy squeal and squawk.

"Hey!" Burt shouted at Flint over the music. "He done any records?"

"Not that I know of."

"Well, he ought to! He don't sound much like Elvis, but a fella plays a piano and sings like that, he oughta be doin' some records! Make hisself a lotta money that way!"

"Tell me," Flint said, "how do we get out of here? Back to a road, I mean?"

"Like I told him"—Burt nodded at Dan—"supply boat from Grand Isle'll be here tomorrow afternoon. That's the only way out."

"Tomorrow *afternoon?* I've got to get this man to—" He paused and tried it again. "We need to get to Shreveport as soon as we can."

"You'll have to wait for the supply boat. They'll take you to Grand Isle, but that's still a hell of a long way from Shreveport. See, there ain't no roads 'round here for miles."

"I can't stay here all night! Christ almighty! We've got to get back to—" *Civilization,* he almost said, but he decided it wouldn't be wise. "Shreveport," he finished.

"Sorry. I've got a radio-telephone in the back, if you need to let anybody know where you are."

Smoates needed to know, Flint thought. Smoates needed to hear that the skin was caught and on his way back. Smoates would be asleep right now, but he wouldn't mind being awakened to hear—

Hold it, he told himself. Just one damn minute. Why should he be in such a rush to call that freak-lovin' bastard? Right now he, Flint, was in control. He didn't have to run and call Smoates like some teenager afraid of his father's paddle. Anyway, if Smoates hadn't weighed him down with Eisley, he would have finished this thing yesterday. So to hell with him.

Flint said, "No, I don't need to call anybody. But what are we supposed to do? Stay here until the boat comes?" He didn't know if he could stand smelling his own body odor that long, and

Lambert wasn't a sweet peach either. "Isn't there someplace I can get a shower and some sleep?"

"Well, this ain't exactly a tropical resort." Burt's cigar stub had gone cold, but he still kept it gripped between his teeth. Now he took it out and looked at the ashy tip, trying to decide if it was worth another match. "You talkin' about one place for all of you? Or you want somethin' separate for the lady?"

"I'm not sleepin' in a room with them!" Arden was still dazed and heartsick by what she'd heard about the Bright Girl. In her arms the little bulldog longingly watched Pelvis. "I'd rather sit in here all night!"

"How much money you got?" Burt asked Flint, and raised his eyebrows.

"Not much."

"You got a hundred dollars?"

"Maybe."

"Okay, here's the deal," Burt said. "The big boys—the execs—keep a couple of cabins to stay in when they come visit down here. They don't want to get dirty stayin' in the barracks with the workin' crews, see. I know who can pick the locks. Fifty dollars apiece, you can have 'em for the night. They ain't much, but they've got clean cots and they're private."

"There's fifty dollars in my wallet," Dan offered. Sleep on a cot—clean or dirty, he didn't care—sounded fine to him. It occurred to him that this was the last night he'd sleep without bars next to his mattress. "I'll pay for her cabin."

"Yeah, it's a deal." Flint brought out Dan's wallet and his own and paid the money.

"Fine. Wait a minute, lemme listen to this here song." Pelvis had started a slow country-western tearjerker called "Anything That's Part of You." His audience sat in rapt, respectful silence as the broody piano chords thumped and Pelvis's voice soared up in a lament that was painful enough to wet the eyes of hardcase roughnecks and bayou trash prostitutes. "I swear," Burt said, "that fella don't need to try to be Elvis. You his manager?" He looked at Flint.

"No."

"Hell, *I'll* be his manager, then. Get out of this damn swamp and get rich, I won't never look back."

"Arden?" Dan had seen the corners of her mouth quivering, her eyes glassy with shock. It was going to be tough on her, he knew. She'd put so much blind faith into finding the Bright Girl, she'd sacrificed everything, and now it was over. "You all right?"

She didn't answer. She couldn't.

"You mind steppin' aside?" he asked Flint, and the bounty hunter saw Arden's obvious distress and moved from between them. Dan stood close to her. His heart ached for her, and he started to put his arm around her shoulders but he didn't know what comfort he could give. "I'm sorry," he said. "I wish you could've found what you wanted."

"I—I can't believe she's dead. I just can't." Her eyes suddenly glistened with tears, but just as quickly she blinked them away. The bulldog licked her chin. "I can't believe it. Jupiter wouldn't have told me wrong."

"Listen to me," Dan said firmly. "Startin' from this minute, here and now, you're gonna have to go back to reality. That means back to Fort Worth and gettin' on with your life. However bad things look, they've got to get better."

"I don't think so."

"You don't know what tomorrow's gonna bring. Or next week, or next month. You've gotta go day by day, and that's how you get through the rough spots. Believe me, I've been there."

Arden nodded, but the Bright Girl was a candle she could not bear to extinguish. It struck her how selfish she'd been, consumed by her own wishes. From the moment the man in the dark suit had set foot into this cafe, Dan had been on his way to prison. "Are *you* all right?" she asked.

"I believe I am." He offered her a faint, brave smile when inside he felt as if he'd been hit by a tractor-trailer truck. "Yeah, I'm all right. This was gonna happen sooner or later." His smile faded. "I saw my son, I said what I needed to say without bars between us. That's the important thing." He shrugged. "At least where I'm goin' I'll have a roof over my head and hot food. Won't be much worse than the V.A. hospital, I guess. Anyhow——" His voice cracked, and he had to pause to summon the strength to continue. "Like I said, you go day by day. That's how you get through the rough spots."

"Miss?" Burt put his elbows on the bar and leaned toward her. Pelvis had finished the slow, sad number and was getting up from the piano to take his bows, sweat dripping from his chins. "I know who could tell you if there was ever anybody livin' on Goat Island or not. Cajun fella they call Little Train. He was born 'round here. Sometimes he takes the execs huntin' and fishin'. Sells us fish and game for the cafe, too, so he gets all 'round the swamp. If anybody would know, it'd be him."

"Arden?" Dan's voice was quiet. "Give it up. Please."

She wanted to. She really did. But she was desperate and afraid. This would be her final chance, and she would never come this way again. Even finding the Bright Girl's grave would be an answer, though not the one she wished for. She said, "Where is he?"

"Lives on a houseboat, anchored 'bout a mile south of here. Keeps to himself, mostly." He stared at her birthmark, his gaze following its ragged edges. "I've got a motorboat, and I'm off shift at six A.M. I need to run down there to see him anyhow, put in an order for some catfish and turtle meat. If you want to go, you're welcome. And I can carry two people, if *you* want to go along." He was speaking to Dan.

Dan saw the need in Arden's eyes; it was a painful thing to witness, because he knew she stood at the very edge of sanity. He had to turn away from her, and when he heard her say "I'll go alone," it was clear to him that she'd placed one foot over the precipice.

"Okay, then. Whatever suits you. Hey, fella!" He grinned at Pelvis, who was making his way to the bar through a knot of backslappers. "You 'bout knocked hell outta that piano, didn't you?"

Pelvis said, "Thank you, ma'am" as he took Mama back into his arms, and Mama trembled with love and attacked his face with her tongue. He was breathing hard, and he felt a little dizzy, but otherwise he was okay. Sweat was pouring off him in rivers. "Can I have some water, please?"

"Comin' right up!"

"Mr. Murtaugh?" Pelvis smiled broadly. "I think they like me."

"You were all right. If you care for that kind of music. Here, wipe your face." He pulled a handful of paper napkins out of a dispenser and gave it to him. "You're not gonna pass out on me again, are you?"

"Nosir. I'm just a bit winded." Pelvis took the bottle of water Burt gave him and guzzled it, then he poured some in his hand and let Mama lap it up. "Did'ja hear the way they were hollerin'?"

"Uh-huh. Well, step down off your pedestal and listen: we can't get out of here till tomorrow afternoon. We have to wait for a supply boat from Grand Isle. How the hell we're supposed to get back to the car I don't know, but that's how things are."

"At least we got him, didn't we?" Pelvis nodded toward Dan, who'd gone back to eating his gumbo.

We, my ass, Flint was about to say, but Burt stuck his bearded face over the bar again. "You play better'n you look, if you don't mind me sayin'."

"Sir?"

"You know. The Elvis thing, with the judo moves and all. That's what I expected."

"Well, all them songs I sang were ones Elvis done," Pelvis explained. "And I do them moves in my show, but I couldn't 'cause I was sittin' at the piana. Like I said, I usually play the git-tar."

"You want my advice? I'm gonna give it to you anyway. Don't hide behind Elvis. You don't need it, a fella can pound them keys and sing like you do. Hell, you oughta go to Nashville and show 'em what you can do."

"I been there. They told me I didn't sound enough like Elvis. Told me I couldn't play git-tar as good as him, neither."

"Well, hell! Don't *try* to sound like him! Don't try to look like him, or talk like him, or nothin'! Seems to me there was just one Elvis, and he's dead. Can't be another one. If I was you, I wouldn't touch a guitar again so long as I lived. I wouldn't wear my hair like that, either, and you oughta lose fifty or sixty pounds. Get yourself lean and mean, then go see them Nashville cats. You play for them like you did here, you're gonna be makin' yourself some money! Hey, do me a favor!" Burt reached for a napkin and pulled a pen out from beside the cash register. "Here. Sign me an autograph, just so I can say I spotted you first. Sign it To My Friend Burt Dunbro."

"You . . . want *my* autograph?" Pelvis asked, his cheeks reddening with embarrassment.

"Yep. Right there. To My Friend Burt Dunbro."

He put the pen to napkin and wrote what the man asked. Then he started *Pelv*—

He stopped.

"What's wrong? Pen jammed up?"

There was just one Elvis, he was thinking, *and he's dead. Can't be another one.*

Maybe there shouldn't be.

It had been fifteen years since he'd played piano in front of an audience. And that was before he'd dressed himself up as the King, studied the records and movies and hip thrusts, bought the wig, the blue suede shoes, the regalia. It was before he'd let himself get fat on the Twinkies and peanut butter cookies and cornbread sopped in buttermilk. It was before he'd decided that who he was wasn't good enough, and that he needed something much larger to cling to and hide inside.

But what if . . . what if . . .

What if he'd given up on his own talent too early? What if he'd let it go in favor of the Elvis disguise because he wasn't sure he was worth a damn? What if . . . what if . . . ?

Oh, Lord, it would be so hard to give it up now and try to go back. It would be impossible to strike out on his own, without the King to help him. Wouldn't it?

But Elvis was dead. There couldn't be another one.

"Hold on, I'll find a pen that writes," Burt offered.

"No," Pelvis said. "This one's fine."

He was terrified.

But he got the pen moving, and with a hammering heart and a dry throat he scratched out *Pelv* and beneath it wrote *Cecil Eisley*.

It was one of the hardest things he'd ever done in his life, but when he was finished he felt something inside him start to unlock, just the slightest bit. Maybe in an hour he would regret signing his own name. Maybe tomorrow he would deny that he had. But right now—this strange and wonderful moment—he felt ten feet tall.

"Griff, come over here!" Burt called. The mean-faced man who didn't care for the classics came to the bar. Burt gave him twenty dollars and quietly told him what he wanted done. "Ya'll go on with Griff, he'll take care of you," Burt said to Flint, and to Arden he added, "Six o'clock. I'll see you here."

"Let's go, Lambert." Flint pushed the gun into Dan's side again. "Take it nice and easy."

The two cabins Griff led them to were about a hundred yards from the other structures of St. Nasty, up on a platform facing a cove of smooth black water. Griff produced a large penknife and pulled up its thin blade to slide into the first cabin's door lock. It took four seconds to open the door. "I better check for snakes," he said before he disappeared into the darkness within. Two minutes later a generator rumbled to life around back and then electric lights flickered on. "No snakes," he announced when he returned to the door. "Just a skin." He held the long gossamer thing up to show them. "Who's sleepin' in this one?"

When neither of the bounty hunters responded, Arden screwed up her courage and said, "I guess I am." She crossed the threshold. The pine-paneled interior was hot, humid, and smelled of mold. There was a broken-down plaid sofa, a couple of standing lamps that appeared to have been purchased from a garage sale sometime in 1967, and a kitchen area with a rusty stove and sink. A hallway went back to what must be the sleeping area and—hopefully—an indoor bathroom. It would do for a few hours, until six o'clock.

"Shower and toilet's between the cabins," Griff said. "Pipes are hooked to a cistern, but I wouldn't drink the water. And you'd best keep the front and back doors locked. Lots of fellas 'round here can't be trusted."

Arden closed the door and locked it, then she pulled the sofa over in front of it. She found a switch that operated a ceiling fan, and turning it on helped cool the room some.

When the lights were on in the second cabin, Griff came out grinning. "Looky here!" He raised his right arm to show Dan, Flint, and Pelvis the thick brown snake his hand had seized, the head squeezed between his fingers and the coils twined around his wrist. "Big ol' sumbitch moccasin. Found him sleepin' under a cot. Ya'll step aside." He reared his arm back and flung the reptile past them into the water. It made a heavy splash. "Okay, you can go on in."

Flint guided Dan through the door first. The place was basically the same as the first cabin, a moldy-smelling assemblage of cheap furniture, pine-paneled walls, and a floor of rough planks. Pelvis entered last, his eyes peeled for creepy-crawlies. "Thing 'bout moccasins," Griff said, "is that for every one you see, there're three or four you don't. They'll keep to themselves if you don't step on 'em, but I wouldn't let that dog go nosin' 'round, hear?"

"I hear," Pelvis answered.

"Tough luck for that girl, huh? I mean, the way her face is. Awful hard to look at, but hard *not* to look at, too."

"Thanks for lettin' us in," Flint told him. "Good night."

"Allrighty. Don't let the bedbugs bite. Nor nothin' else." Griff chuckled a little to himself, slid his hands into the pockets of his blue jeans, and started walking back in the direction they'd come.

Flint closed the door and latched it. "Here, keep this on him." He gave Pelvis the derringer, then he took the cuffs and their key from his pocket and unlocked them. "Hands behind you."

"I'm gonna have to go pee in a minute," Dan said.

"Hands in front of you," Flint corrected him. "Grip 'em together."

"I gave you my word I wasn't gonna run. You don't have to—"

"Your word's not worth fifteen thousand dollars, so shut up." Flint snapped the cuffs around Dan's wrists and put the key inside his suit jacket. Dan saw a peculiar thing happen: the front of the man's shirt suddenly twitched, as if Murtaugh had just hiccupped. He recalled that he'd seen the same thing when Murtaugh was on the ground in Basile Park, just before the Elvis clone had started hollering. He had the bizarre sensation that there was more to Murtaugh than met the eye.

"Watch him for a minute," Flint told Pelvis, and he walked back through the hallway to find out what the rest of the cabin held.

"Don't try nothin', now," Pelvis said nervously, holding a sleepy Mama and aiming the derringer at Dan's belly. "I'll shoot if I have to."

"Just take it easy." Dan could tell that the man was uncomfortable holding the gun, and though it looked like a peashooter, it could still do a lot of damage at such close range. He decided silence would only increase the man's tension before Murtaugh returned. "What's your name?"

"Ce—" No, maybe he'd be ready to let go of it someday, but not yet. "Pelvis Eisley."

"Pelvis, huh?" Dan nodded; it figured. "Excuse me for sayin' this, but you and Murtaugh don't fit. You been partners long?"

"Two days. He's teachin' me the ropes."

An amateur, Dan thought. "This is your first bounty-huntin' job?"

"That's right. My very first."

"Seems to me you'd do better playin' piano in Nashville than doin' this kind of work."

"Eisley, don't talk to him." Flint came back in. What he'd found had been two grim rooms, each with two iron-framed, bare-mattressed cots. He hadn't failed to notice that the legs of the cots were standing in water-filled coffee cans to keep insects from climbing up them. If this was the executive quarters, he would have hated to see the work crew's barracks; then again, the cabin didn't look like anyone had been there in quite some time. But all he wanted was a few hours of sleep, and he didn't need a Hilton hotel pillow. Flint took the derringer back from Eisley. "Come on, Lambert. You want to do your business, let's get it done." Through a rear window he'd seen a tin-roofed shed that he figured must be where the shower and toilet were. The generator was sending juice to an electric bulb burning over the shed's door, but stepping in was going to be an act of either raw courage or sheer desperation.

Arden had already forced herself—out of desperation—to walk into the shed. Fortunately, there was a light bulb inside as well as outside, but Arden approached the toilet with trepidation. There were no water moccasins coiled up inside, as she'd feared, but it wasn't the cleanest in the world. She did what she had to do, used a roll of tissue that could have scraped paint off metal, and got out as fast as she could.

In the room in which she'd chosen to sleep, she had put the pink drawstring bag atop a battered old pine chest of drawers. Now, under the single dirty light bulb that burned at the ceiling, she opened the bag and removed what was held within.

One after the other, she lined up five little horses side by side.

They had been bought at a dime store in Fort Worth. They weren't much, but they were everything. Five horses: two brown, one black, one gray. The paint was chipping off them, revealing the red plastic they were molded from. She knew their secret names, and they watched over her. They reminded her of a time when she'd been happy, when she could believe the future was wide-open spaces, even through the Texas dust and grit and the hard work that had to be done. They reminded her that once upon a time she had been needed.

She sat on the edge of a cot and stared at the small plastic figures, her eyes glazed and tired. She was wrecked, and she knew it. But her thoughts were still circling that flame, circling, circling. The Bright Girl. A touch from the Bright Girl, and she would be healed. Jupiter said so. Jupiter wouldn't have lied to her. No. A touch from the Bright Girl, and the mark—the ugly bad-luck mark that had tormented her all her life and caused her father to walk out the door and never come back and her mother to fall under the weight of the bottle—would be taken away. The Bright Girl wasn't dead. The Bright Girl was forever young and pretty, and she carried the lamp of God. Jupiter hadn't lied. He hadn't.

But what about Dan? He couldn't go any farther. If he was the man God had provided to take her to the Bright Girl, then why was he being wrenched away from her? She'd thought about trying somehow to get him away from the bounty hunters, but what could she do? And she'd seen it in his face, there in the cafe: he was sick and weary of running, and he could not go on. *You His hands,* she remembered Jupiter saying.

But what if Jupiter had been wrong?

Six o'clock, she thought. Six o'clock. She had to press that number into her mind so she could sleep for three or four hours and then get up in time. She had to forget about Dan, had to let him go. As much as she wanted, she couldn't help him. Now she had to help herself, and it seemed to her that the morning would be her last chance. Where she would go and what she would do if she found the Bright Girl's grave, she didn't know. She couldn't think about it, because that way led to black despair.

She lay down and stared at the ceiling. The five horses, her talisman, would watch over her during the night. She might dream of waking up, and hearing them pawing and snorting for her in the barn, saying *hurry come to us hurry we will never hurt you we will never hurt.*

At last, mercifully, her eyes closed. She listened to the rumble of the generator, the grump of frogs, and the chitterings of insects and night birds, the heavy thudding heartbeat of the oil-pumping machinery in the distance. She was afraid of what daylight might bring; she was equally afraid of knowing and of not knowing. A single tear trickled down the cheek on the deep-violet-birth-marked side of her face. Sleep came for her, and took her away.

Pelvis had gone outside to let Mama answer nature's call. While he was out there, he unzipped and added some water to the cove. After Mama was finished, he picked her up and started back inside, and that was when he saw a match flare on the plank walkway that led back over the swamp grass and rushes to the center of St. Nasty. He saw the orange-daubed face of a man as the match touched the tip of a cigarette, and then the match was flicked out into the water like a little comet.

He watched the cigarette's tip glow as the man inhaled. Then the glow vanished. Either the man was cupping the cigarette in his hand or he'd walked away, it was hard to tell in the dark. Pelvis stood there, stroking Mama for a moment, but when she let out a few exhausted yaps at something that rustled in the watery weeds under the platform, he decided it was time to get back inside. He wondered how many snakes must be watching him, and the thought made him shudder as if someone had just stepped on his grave.

22

The Sound of Scales

"I'M GOIN' TO TAKE a shower," Flint told Pelvis when he walked through the door. "I want you to sit in there and watch him, hear? Take the gun and just sit there. I'll be back in a few minutes." He'd taken Dan to the shed and found a grimy cake of soap in the cramped little shower stall. Though he had no towel, he couldn't bear his own body odor any longer. He started to turn away, but he had to ask a burning question. "Eisley, where'd you learn the Chopin piece?"

"Sir?"

"The Chopin piece. The classical music you played. Where'd you learn it?"

"Oh, that was somethin' my piana teacher taught me. Mrs. Fitch was her name. Said it was a good quick finger workout and 'cause you had to think about what you were doin' it calmed you down. I reckon it did the trick for my nerves."

"I never would've thought you could play classical music."

Pelvis shrugged. "No big thing. Them fellas pooted in their pants like everybody else. You go on and take your shower, don't worry 'bout Lambert."

Flint left the cabin, not quite sure he would ever again listen to his tape of Chopin preludes with quite the same reverence.

Pelvis went into the bedroom Flint had chosen for himself and found the killer lying on one of the cots, his right hand cuffed to the iron bed frame. Pelvis sat down on the other cot, laid Mama aside, and held the derringer aimed at Dan.

"I wish you wouldn't do that," Dan said twenty seconds later, when it was clear Eisley meant to point the gun at him until Murtaugh returned. "I'd hate for that to go off."

"Mr. Murtaugh told me to watch you."

"Can't you watch me and aim that gun somewhere else?"

"I could. I don't want to."

Dan grunted and allowed a slight smile. "You must think I'm a big bad sonofabitch, huh?"

"You killed two men. That don't make you an angel in my book."

Dan started to sit up, but he thought better of making any quick moves. "I didn't kill the man at that damn motel. His wife did it."

"His *wife?* Ha, that's a good one!"

"He was alive when I left there. His wife had already shot him in the gut with a shotgun, aimin' at me. She beat him to death after I was gone. Maybe she was mad at him because I got away."

"Uh-huh. I reckon somebody else popped up and killed that fella at the bank, too. And you just happened to be standin' there."

"No," Dan said. "That one I'll bear the blame for."

"Surprised to hear it."

Dan cupped his left hand under his head and stared up at the ceiling. A moth was going around and around up there, searching for a way out. "Blanchard had a family. It wasn't his fault things are how they are. There's no way on earth I can live with what I did, so I might as well die in prison."

Pelvis was silent for a moment. The derringer had wandered. He'd never met anybody who'd committed murder before, and he found his nervousness being replaced by curiosity. "What'd that fella do to you was so bad you had to kill him?" he asked quietly.

Dan was watching the trapped moth beating itself against the stark, bare light bulb. He was too tense to sleep yet, and the room was too hot. "I didn't go to that bank meanin' to do it," he answered. "Blanchard was takin' my pickup truck away from me. It was the last thing I had. I lost my temper, a guard came in, and we fought. Blanchard pulled a pistol on me. I had the guard's gun, and . . . I squeezed the trigger first. Didn't even aim. I knew Blanchard was finished when I saw all that blood. Then I got in my truck and ran."

Pelvis frowned. "You should've stayed there. Maybe pleaded self-defense or somethin'."

"I guess so. But all I could think about right then was gettin' away."

"How 'bout the girl? We thought you took her hostage. Is she . . . kinda off in the head?"

"No, she's just scared." Dan explained how he'd met Arden, and about her belief in the Bright Girl. "In the mornin' she wants to go find some Cajun fisherman called Little Train. He's supposed to live in a houseboat a mile or so south of here. That fella who runs the cafe's takin' her. I don't have the right to tell her not to go, and I don't think she'd listen to me, anyway." An idea struck him, and he angled his face toward Eisley. "*You* could go with her."

"*Me?*"

"Yeah. They're leavin' at six." He managed to twist his cuffed wrist around so he could see his watch. "Goin' on two-thirty. You could go with her, make sure she's all right. If the supply boat doesn't come till afternoon, you'll be back in plenty of time."

"Back from *where?*" Flint peered through the doorway, his hair still wet. He had carefully and methodically scrubbed the grime from his and his brother's flesh. It had been torment to buckle the sweat-stiff miniature shoulder holster against his skin and then put on his swamp-tainted clothes again. Under his once-white shirt Clint was sleeping, but Flint could feel the soft bones shift every so often deep in his constricted guts.

"He was askin' me to go with the girl," Pelvis said. "Burt— y'know, from the cafe—is gonna take her at six o'clock to see a Cajun fella lives a mile south. She's tryin' to find a—"

"Forget it." Flint took the derringer from him. "We're not nursemaids. I don't know what her story is, but we're leavin' here on that supply boat and she can go with us or not, it's up to her."

"Yes sir, but if it's just a mile off, I'll be back before—"

"Eisley?" Flint cut him off. "The girl's crazy. She'd have to be crazy to come down here knowin' who Lambert is. Get up off there, I've gotta lie down before I fall down."

Pelvis cradled Mama in his arms and stood up. Mama awakened and gave a cranky growl, then her bulbous eyes closed and she went limp again. Flint lay down on the cot. Springs jabbed his back through the thin mattress, but he was so tired, he could have slept on a bed of nails.

"Arden shouldn't go off in the swamp with somebody she doesn't know," Dan pressed on. "It doesn't matter what you think of her. She could still get in a lot of trouble."

"She's not our business. You are."

"Maybe that's so, but she needs help."

"Not from us."

"Not from *you*, I guess." Dan looked up at Pelvis. "How about it? Would you—"

"Hey!" Flint sat up again, his deep-sunken eyes red-rimmed and angry. "He doesn't have any say-so about this! I'm callin' the shots! Now, why don't you shut your mouth and get some sleep? Eisley, you go on, too!"

Pelvis hesitated. The electric lights, and their pools of shadow, gave him little comfort. Several times already he had imagined he'd caught a slow uncoiling from the corner of his eye. "How come Mama and me have to sleep in a room by ourselves?"

"Because there're only two cots in here, that's why. Now go on!"

"That was an awful big snake that fella found. I wonder which cot it was under."

"Well, I'll tell you what," Flint said. "You and the mutt can sleep in here. Just curl up on the floor between us, maybe that'll make you feel safer."

"No, I don't think it would."

"The lights are on. All right? Nothin's gonna crawl out and get you with the lights on."

Pelvis started to retreat to the other room. It seemed a vast distance away from the protection of Flint's derringer. He paused again, his face furrowed in thought. "Mr. Murtaugh, don't you think it'd be wrong if we knew somethin' might happen to that girl and we didn't try to help her?"

"She can take care of herself."

"We don't know that for sure. Lambert says she's from Fort Worth, and she don't have any way to get home."

"It's *not* our problem, Eisley."

"Yeah, I know that and all, but . . . seems to me we oughta have a little feelin' for her situation."

Flint glared at Pelvis with a force that seemed to scorch the air between them. "You haven't learned a thing from me, have you?"

"Sir?"

"Bounty hunters don't *feel*. You start feelin', and you start gettin' interested. When you start gettin' interested, you start lettin' your guard down. Then you wind up with a knife in your back. If the girl wants to go see some Cajun swamp rat, it's her business. She knows the supply boat's leavin' in the afternoon. If she wants to be on it, she will be." He held Pelvis's gaze a few seconds longer, then he lay back down, the derringer in his right hand. "I've met all the swamp rats I care to, in case you've forgotten the marina."

"No, I ain't forgotten."

"I'd say we were lucky to get out of that alive. While you're with me, I'm responsible for you—much as I hate it—so you're not goin' off in the swamp with some crazy girl and end up gettin' your throat cut. Now go to sleep."

Pelvis chewed on Flint's logic, his brow still creased under his lopsided wig. Dan said, "She's not crazy. She's a decent person. I wish you'd help her."

"Lambert? One more word from you, and you're gonna spend the night with both arms between your legs and a sock stuffed in your damn mouth!"

"Sorry," Pelvis told Dan. "I can't." He summoned up his courage and went into the other room, where he laid Mama down on the cot and then settled himself beside her. He lay very still, listening for and dreading the sound of scales slithering across the planked floor.

Dan's head had been aching, a slow, insistent throb, for the past two hours. The pain kicked in again, getting between him and sleep. He would have given his left nut—whatever it was worth these days—for a bottle of Tylenol. Strangely, though, it was a relief his running was over. He didn't have to be afraid anymore of what might be coming up behind him. The idea of getting out of the country, he realized now, had always been an illusion. Sooner or later he would have wound up in handcuffs. He would learn to deal with prison in the time he had left. He was just sorry Arden had gotten mixed up in this.

Dan thought Murtaugh was asleep, but suddenly the bounty hunter shifted on his cot and said, "What the hell made that girl come down here with you, anyway?"

"She believes there's a faith healer livin' in here somewhere. Called the Bright Girl. She thinks that if she finds the Bright Girl, she can get that birthmark off her face."

"A faith healer? Like Oral Roberts?"

"A little quieter, I reckon. And poorer, too. I don't believe in such things, myself."

"I don't either. It's a shakedown for the rubes." Carnival talk, he realized as soon as he'd spoken.

"Arden's desperate," Dan said. "She found out who I was, but she still wanted me to bring her down here. She doesn't have any money, no car, nothin'. Lost her job. She's convinced herself that if she finds the Bright Girl and gets that mark off, her bad luck'll be gone, too, and her whole life'll change."

"To you, desperate," Flint said. "To me, that's crazy."

"I guess people have believed stranger things."

Flint was silent. He and Dan suddenly heard a noise like a buzz saw starting up, followed by a swarm of enraged bees trapped in a tin bucket. Pelvis was snoring.

"Yeah, I knew that was comin'," Flint sighed. He shifted again, trying to get comfortable. The heat was squeezing sweat from his pores, and his body was exhausted, but his mind wasn't ready to shut down and let him sleep. "Lambert, where'd you think you were gonna run to?"

"I don't know. Anywhere but prison."

"I'm surprised you got as far as you did. You've been all over the TV and newspapers. Is that why you killed the fella at the motel? Was he about to turn you in?"

"I told you I didn't do that. His wife did."

"Come on, now. You can level with me."

"I didn't kill him, I swear to God."

"Uh-huh," Flint said with a knowing half-smile. "I've heard that from a lot of guilty bastards." He recalled what Lambert's tae kwon do–loving ex-wife had said in the park: *It was self-defense, he's not a cold-blooded killer.* Another question came to him that he had to ask. "Why didn't you shoot me? When you had my gun, and I was on the ground. Why didn't you just blow my brains out? You didn't want to kill me in front of your family, right?"

"Wrong. I didn't want to kill you, period."

"You should have. If I'd had the gun and you'd been the bounty hunter after my ass, I would've shot you. At least blown away your knees. Didn't you think of that?"

"No."

Flint turned his head to look at Dan, who had his eyes closed. Of the twenty or so felons—mostly bail jumpers and small-time criminals, with a couple of real bad boys in the bunch—Flint had tracked over his seven years in the employ of Eddie Smoates, this one was different. There was something about Lambert he couldn't decipher, and this fact greatly agitated him. If Lambert had just finished killing the man at the motel before he'd come to Basile Park—if he was a "mad dog," as Smoates had said—then he would have had nothing to lose by putting a couple of bullets through Flint's knees, which was the fastest way to keep anybody from chasing after you. And why hadn't Lambert kept the gun? Why had he been carrying no weapons at all? Why had he brought the girl with him and not planned to use her as a hostage? It just didn't make sense.

It was self-defense, he's not a cold-blooded killer.

Cold-blooded or not, Flint thought, Lambert *was* a killer. Maybe Lambert had just snapped or something. Maybe he hadn't gone into that bank wanting to kill anybody, but the fact was that Lambert was worth fifteen thousand dollars and Flint wanted his share of it. Bottom line.

He listened to Lambert's deep and steady breathing. He thought the man was asleep, but he was going to keep the gun in his hand all night. Though Lambert couldn't get out of that cuff, he might go crazy, try to drag the cot across the space between them and attack Flint. It had happened before. You never knew what set killers off, and the quiet ones were the most dangerous.

Flint closed his eyes. In the other room, Pelvis's snoring had taken on the sonic charm of a cement mixer, and now Mama gave a little *yip yip yip* in her sleep.

It was going to be pure pleasure to say good riddance to those two. He needed a fat hillbilly and a flea-bitten mutt hanging around him like he needed a fourth arm.

He thought of Pelvis's performance, which had been okay if you liked that kind of low-down caterwauling. He thought of the bartender saying *Hell, I'll be his manager, then! Get out of this damn swamp and get rich, I won't never look back.*

And then he knew he must be asleep, because he was looking at the clean white mansion of his dreams.

There it was: the beautiful rolling green lawn, the huge stained-glass window, the multiple chimneys. The sight of it thrilled his soul with majestic wonder. It was the mansion of his birth, the clean white mansion that existed somewhere in this land far from the dismal grime of his life. He began to walk across the lawn toward it, but as always he couldn't get any nearer. It always drew away from him no matter how fast or how long he walked. He could hear his shoes—his shining, polished black wingtips—pressing down the velvet blades of grass. He could feel the summer breeze on his face, and see his shadow walking ahead of him. He would have to walk faster. But again the white mansion receded, a beautiful taunt. Inside that mansion lived his mother and father, and if he could only get there, he could ask them to take him in, he could tell them he forgave them for giving him up when he was a three-armed baby with a fleshy knot on his side that had an extra mouth and set of nostrils in it. He could show them he'd grown up to be a man of taste, of manners and good breeding, and he could tell them he loved them and if they took him in he would promise—he would swear to God—that he would never cause them reason to be ashame—

BAM!

The explosion blasted Flint out of his dream. As the mansion was swept away in a heartbeat, he sat up with a jolt, his eyes bleary and the derringer held in a white-knuckled grip. His first thought was that Lambert had gone crazy and was trying to drag the cot over to flail at him with his free hand.

Dan was sitting up, too, his mind still shocked by the noise that had shattered his deep and dreamless sleep. The handcuff was cutting into his right wrist. He and Flint looked at each other, both of them dazed. Mama had started barking, and Pelvis was making a sputtering noise as he struggled back to the land of the living.

Suddenly someone came into the room.

"They're in here! Got a gun!" a man shouted.

A figure lunged at Flint. He had no time to think to fire; his arm was seized, a hard blow hit him on the shoulder, and he cried out as pain streaked down to the tips of his fingers. The derringer was ripped from his hand, and a wiry arm went around his throat. He started thrashing, but the arm squeezed his larynx and took the fight out of him. Another man entered the room—a man in a dirty yellow shirt and blue jeans—and he said, "That's the bastard shot Virgil. Hey, Doc! In here he is!"

At the mention of those names Flint felt panic clutch his heart.

Doc walked in. Sauntered, actually. He was still wearing his Harvard T-shirt, but he had on chinos with patched knees. His round-lensed sunglasses had been exchanged for glasses with clear lenses. Doc grinned, showing his greenish teeth. His long gray-blond hair was pulled back into a ponytail and secured with a rubber band. "Gomer says hey," he said. "You sweet motherfucker, you." He reached out and clamped a hand onto Flint's chin. "Now, you didn't think we were gonna let you hit and run, did you?"

Flint didn't answer; he couldn't, because his lips were crushed together.

Doc's head swiveled. Still grinning widely, he looked at Dan and his gaze found the handcuff. "Well, what's this all about now, huh? Who're *you*, friend?"

"Dan Lambert." The haze of weariness hadn't quite cleared yet; everything was still weirdly dreamlike.

"I'm Doc. Pleased to meet ya. Monty, bring ol' Elvis in here with us!"

In another few seconds Pelvis was hurled through the doorway and he slammed down to the floor on his hands and knees. Behind him entered a heavyset man with narrowly slit eyes, crewcut hair, and a bristly brown beard and mustache. The man was holding a snarling and kicking Mama by the scruff of her neck. "Look what I got me!" he announced.

"Please . . ." Pelvis's face was stricken with terror, his eyes sleep-swollen. "Please, that's my dog."

"No it ain't," Monty said petulantly. "It's *mine*."

"He ain't had a dog since last week, when he got hungry after midnight." Doc put a combat-booted foot on one of Pelvis's shoulders. "Down, boy!" he said, and he shoved Pelvis flat to the floor.

"My . . . throat," Flint gasped at the man who had an arm pressed into his larynx. "You're . . . crushin' my throat."

"Awwwwww, our man Flint can't hardly talk! Ain't that a bitch?" Doc shook his head with mock pity. "Best ease up on him."

The arm loosened.

"We wouldn't want to hurt either one of you fine fellas," Doc went on. "Not till we get a chance to boogaloo on your balls, I mean. Then we'll get down to some hurtin'."

"What's goin' on?" Dan asked. "Who are you?"

"I'm me. Who are *you?*"

"I told you. My name's—"

"No." Doc put a forefinger against Dan's mouth. "Who are you, as in why are you wearin' a handcuff?"

"Listen," Flint said, and he heard his voice tremble. "Listen, all right?"

Doc bent toward him and cupped his hands behind his ears.

"There's been a mistake," Flint said.

"Mistake, he says," Doc relayed to the others.

"Fuckin' *big* mistake!" the man in the yellow shirt said. "You shot a friend of ours. Crippled him. Ain't no good for nothin' now."

"Shhhhhh," Doc whispered. "Let the man weave his noose, Mitch."

If there was ever a time for the turth, this was it. Pinpricks of sweat glistened on Flint's face. He said, "I'm a bounty hunter. Workin' out of Shreveport. Both of us are." He nodded toward Pelvis. "The man in handcuff is a wanted killer. Fifteen-thousand-dollar bounty on his head. We followed him down here, and we're takin' him back."

"Oh, first you're an astronaut, now you're Mr. Wanted-Dead-or-Alive." Doc looked at Dan. "That the truth?"

Dan nodded.

"I can't hearrrrrr youuuuuu!"

"It's true." Dan realized this man was two bricks shy of a load, but what had really set off his alarms was the fact that he'd seen a .45 automatic pushed down into the waistband of the man's chinos at the small of his back. The big bearded bastard named Monty had a holster on his hip with a pearl-handled .38 in it, and the man who gripped Flint's throat wore an honest-to-God Ingram submachine gun on a strap around his left shoulder, the derringer he'd wrenched away from Flint now held in his right hand.

"You killed somebody?" Doc's eyebrows went up.

"Two men," Flint answered. "When we were at the marina . . . I was callin' the man I work for. In Shreveport. Lettin' him know where we were."

"Where you were," Doc said quietly, "was on our territory." Pelvis had gotten up on his hands and knees once more, his eyes turned tearfully toward the man who held Mama. "Get *down*, I said!" Doc's gaunt cheeks burned red, and he jammed Pelvis to the floor with a boot again. "You stay down until I say you can move! Where's that fuckin' spray you shot me with, now, huh? I'll ram my fist up your fat ass and jerk your guts out, hear me? *Hear me?*"

"Ye-yes sir." Pelvis's body was starting to shake.

"Where you were," Doc repeated, speaking to Flint in a voice that was eerily calm after his outburst, "was in the wrong place at the wrong time. Okay, I admit it! I messed up! Okay? I thought you might've been somebody else. But when this bastard down here hurt me, and you crippled one of my friends, you crossed the line with me. I can't let that pass." He shrugged. "It's a hormone thing."

"I thought you were tryin' to kill me!" Flint said. "What was I supposed to do?"

"You were supposed to take what we gave you, Flinty. Anyhow, if you'd told us who you really were instead of pullin' that smart-ass bullshit, you wouldn't be hip-deep in hell, now, would you?" He held his palm out and wriggled his fingers. "The key."

"What key?"

"To the cuffs. Come on, give it up."

Flint hesitated. Doc smoothly pulled the automatic from his waistband, clicked the safety off, and pressed the barrel against Flint's forehead. On the floor Pelvis gave a muffled groan. "Give it up easy," Doc said, his eyes icy behind the glasses, "or I'll take it the hard way. Your choice."

Flint reached into his pocket—"Slowwwwwwly," Doc warned—and he put the key in the man's palm. Doc took two backward steps, turned toward Dan, and slid the key into the cuff's lock. He twisted it and Dan heard the mechanism click open. "Fly free, brother," Doc said.

Dan unlatched the cuff from his wrist. Flint's face had become a blood-drained study in anguish. "Listen . . . please . . . he's worth fifteen thousand dollars."

"Not to me, he's not. Not to any of us." Doc opened the other cuff and gave them and the key to Mitch. "See, man, we've all been there. There and back, on the long and twisty road. We don't give a shit for policemen, or jails. Least of all for bounty hunters. On your feet."

The man behind Flint hauled him off the cot. Again Doc placed the automatic's barrel to his forehead. "Mitch, shake him down."

"Wearin' an empty holster under his right arm," Mitch said as he frisked Flint. "And he's got somethin' . . . *holy Jesus!*" Mitch jumped aside as if his hands had been scorched, his eyes wide with shock. "*It moved!*" He fumbled under his shirt and pulled out a blue-steel revolver.

"It moved? *What* moved?" Doc tore the front of Flint's suit jacket open.

And they all saw it: a serpentine shape twisting and writhing beneath Flint's shirt.

Doc reached toward him, meaning to rip the shirt open, but before he could do it, Clint pushed free: first the small fingers and hand, followed by the slim, milky-white and hairless arm.

Doc stood very, very still. Everyone in the room was very, very still. Dan was starting to wonder what might've been in that gumbo he'd eaten.

Clint's hand clenched at the air. Flint knew what would happen next; his shirt would be torn right off his back. To prevent that indignity, he undid the rest of the buttons and opened his shirt for them all to have a good look, his face tightening with rage because their eyes had taken on that old familiar glint of ravening fascination he'd suffered so many times before.

"God*damn!*" Doc whispered. "He's a fuckin' freak!"

"My brother Clint." Flint's voice was toneless, dead. "Born this way. Here's his head. See?" He drew his shirt wider to show them the fist-size lump of Clint's eyeless face at his side. "I used to work the carnival circuit. Alive, alive, alive," Flint said, and a dark and terrible grin split his mouth.

"Ain't never seen nothin' like that before," Monty observed. He still held Mama—who'd given up on her snarling but was still kicking to get loose—by the scruff of the neck. "Seen a girl with three tits before, but nothin' like that."

"It ain't real!" The man who'd gripped Flint's throat and taken away the derringer had backed halfway across the room. "It's a trick!"

"You touch it and find out!" Mitch snapped.

Doc pushed Clint's hand with the automatic's barrel as Flint's insides trembled. Suddenly Clint's fingers closed around the barrel, and Doc gave a quiet laugh. "Farrrr out!" He carefully worked the pistol's barrel free. "He'd like to see this, wouldn't he? He'd get a rush out of it."

"Damn straight, he would," Monty agreed. "He'd laugh his ass off."

Doc finished the job of frisking Flint, then—satisfied the bounty hunter had no other weapons—he spun the .45 around a finger and pushed it back into his waistband. "Get up, Elvis. We're goin' for a boat ride. Mitch, cuff 'em together."

"Not me! I ain't touchin' that bastard!"

"You pussy." Doc took the handcuffs and snapped Pelvis's left wrist to Flint's right. The key went into a pocket of his chinos.

"Where are you takin' 'em?" Dan asked, standing up from the cot.

"Brother Dan, you really don't want to know. Just call this a gift and let it go at that. Now, if I were in your shoes—" He glanced down at them. "I'd steal some new ones. Those are about shot, kemo sabe. But if I were you, I wouldn't stick too long 'round here. Wouldn't be prudent."

"Can I have my dog, please?" Pelvis sounded close to sobbing. "Please, can I have her back?"

"I told you, it's *my* dog now!" Monty rumbled. He held Mama up and shook her. "Have it with some bacon and eggs come daylight."

One second Pelvis was a begging sack of sad flesh; the next second he was a juggernaut, leaping forward, his teeth gritted in a snarl, his unchained hand straining for Monty's throat.

Monty jerked Mama out of Pelvis's reach and hit him, hard and fast, with a scarred fist right in the mouth. Pelvis's head snapped back, his knees giving way, and as he fell he almost dragged Flint down with him. Mitch was laughing a high-pitched giggle, Mama was snarling again, and Doc said, "Get up, Elvis!" He grabbed a handful of pompadour, pulled, and wound up with a wig dangling from his fingers. "Shit!" he laughed. "This fucker's comin' apart!"

Pelvis was down on his knees, his head bent forward, and drops of blood were dripping on the planks. His back heaved, and now it was Dan's turn to be speared with anguish. He didn't know what to do; he didn't know if there was anything he *could* do. Flint shot a glare at Dan that said *Look what you got us into* and then he bent beside Pelvis and said, "Hang on. Just hang on."

"Stand him up, bounty hunter." Doc planted the wig backward on Pelvis's naked pate. "Let's go!"

"Why don't you leave him alone? He's not right in the head, can't you see that?"

"Ain't right in the teeth, ya mean," Monty said, and he grunted a laugh.

It was all Flint could do not to go for the bastard's throat himself, but he knew it would do no good. "Come on, stand up," he said. "I'll help you." He had to struggle with Pelvis's weight, but then Pelvis was standing on his own. Flint didn't want to look at the man's face. Some of the blood had dripped onto Clint's fingers and Flint's shirt.

"Out," Doc told them, and Monty gave them a shove toward the back door he'd kicked down. Dan stood, watching them go, the wheels spinning and smoking in his brain. Doc lingered behind the others. "Either of those men you killed a cop?" he asked.

It made no sense at this precarious point to tell Doc he'd killed only one man, and that by sheer bad luck. "No."

"Next time try for a cop." Doc walked out of the cabin into the dark, whistling a happy tune.

And Dan stood alone.

23

Crossbones

A POUNDING NOISE BROUGHT Arden up from the slow current of sleep. She looked out the window. Still dark. What was that noise? Louder, more insistent than the machinery. It took her another few seconds, her head still cloudy, to realize somebody was at the front door.

"Arden! Open up! It's me!"

Dan's voice. She stood up—slowly, a struggle against stiff muscles. When she was on her feet, she had to pause as dizziness made the room spin around her. "Wait!" she called. She limped to the door, then she had to use those same stiff muscles to push the sofa aside. Finally the latch was undone and Dan came in.

His face glistened with sweat, his eyes wild. "What is it?" she asked. "I thought the bounty hunters had you—"

"They're gone. Somebody came and took 'em away."

"Took 'em *away?* Where to?"

"I don't know. Takin' 'em by boat somewhere. Four men. I haven't seen so much firepower since 'Nam."

"What?"

"The four men. I thought they were gonna shoot 'em right there, but then they saw Murtaugh's arm . . . I mean, his brother's arm."

"What are you *talkin'* about?"

He knew he was sounding as crazy as a broken shutter in a windstorm. He had to calm down, take some deep breaths. He pressed his fingertips against his temples. "Four men broke into our cabin and took 'em away. To where, I don't know, but the one who was the boss said somethin' about a boat ride. They were all packin' guns." He started to tell her about Murtaugh's little secret, but he decided she wasn't ready for that yet. "They didn't want me, but they sure as hell marched Murtaugh and Eisley out of there." He looked at his watch. Five-thirteen. "Come on, we've gotta tell somebody about this!"

"Wait a minute," she said. "Just a minute." She squeezed her eyes shut and then opened them again, trying to clear some of the cobwebs. Dan saw that sleep had lightened her eyes and that the birthmark had changed color again, like the rough skin of a chameleon, to a deep blue-tinged purple. "The bounty hunters are gone, right?"

"Right."

"Then . . . that means you're *free,* doesn't it?" She ran a hand through the unruly waves of her hair. Her fingers found the painful, blood-crusted knot where her head had been banged in the car. "They tried to break your neck, and mine, too. Why should you care about 'em?"

It was a good question. Maybe he shouldn't give a damn. Maybe he should go on as if Murtaugh and Eisley had never existed. He didn't know what he could do. Nothing, most likely. But at the very least he could tell somebody. Burt at the cafe had a radio-telephone. That was the place to go.

Dan said, "They were just doin' their job, the best they could. I've already caused two murders, I can't be quiet when I know there're gonna be two more." He turned toward the door. "I'm goin' to the cafe."

"Hold on," she said. He was right, and she was ashamed of her pettiness. The bounty hunters might have wanted to take Dan away from her before she found the Bright Girl, but the time had come to think clearly. "Give me a minute." She went into the room where she'd slept and put the five little plastic horses back into the pink drawstring bag. When she'd finished, she turned around and there Dan was, standing in the doorway. He'd seen what she kept in that bag, and he remembered her telling him about the horses she'd been responsible for at the ranch. It struck him what she'd said at the Rest Well Inn about her job with that band Joey the punk had been in, the Hanoi Janes. *Somebody had to be responsible.*

He thought he understood something more about her in that moment. It was at her core to be responsible, to feed and care for the old swaybacked and broken horses, to watch over a band of drunk hell-raisers, to offer a first-aid kit to a man she knew was a wanted killer. *Joey always said I missed my callin', that I should've been a nurse.*

The horses, he realized, must have reminded her of that time in her life when she had cared about something, and been cared for. His heart hurt, because it came clear to him how alone she must feel, and how desperate to find a place of belonging. He turned his face away.

"Don't laugh," Arden said as she drew the bag tight.

"I'm not laughin'. You ready?"

She said she was, and they left the cabin. Outside, in the stifling wet heat, the night's last stars glittered overhead, but to the east there was the faintest smudge of violet. It took Dan and Arden six or seven minutes to wend their path back across the walkways and through the sprawl of clapboard buildings to the cafe. Except for the noise of generators and the incessant pumping of machinery from the direction of the derricks, St. Nasty had quieted considerably. A few men were still in the poolroom, but the walkways were deserted. The cafe's dim lights remained lit, though, and when Dan pushed through the batwing doors, there was Burt, smoking another cigar stub as he swept the planked floor, the tables pushed back against the walls. Behind the bar a second man was scrubbing beer mugs in a metal sink full of soapy, steaming water.

"Mornin'," Burt said, but he kept to his task. "Ya'll want some breakfast, you'll need to go to the chow hall over by Barracks Number Two. Start servin' at five-thirty."

"Yeah, if you like them fake eggs and turkey-shit sausage," the man behind the bar said.

"These folks are with Cecil," Burt told his companion. "I swear, you should've heard him beatin' that—"

"Four men broke into our cabin," Dan interrupted. "Maybe twenty minutes ago. They all had guns, and they took Murtaugh and Eisley with 'em."

Burt stopped sweeping, and the other man stared at them through the steam.

"The one in charge called himself Doc. Wore his hair in a ponytail. I don't know what it was all about, but I think somebody needs to know."

Burt chewed thoughtfully on his cigar. "Can I ask you a question, mister? What the hell are ya'll mixed up in?" He held up his hand as if to ward off the answer. "Wait, forget it. Maybe I don't want to hear it."

"I thought you could call somebody on the radio-telephone. The law, I mean."

"Ha!" Burt glanced over at the other man. "The law he says, Jess! He ain't from around here, is he?"

"Must be from New York City," Jess said, and he returned to his scrubbing.

"Parish ranger used to check in on us every now and again." Burt leaned on his broom. "They found his boat over on Lake Tambour. Not a sign of him, though. They won't never find him."

"Yeah, he's gone south," Jess said.

Dan looked sharply at him. *"What?"*

"Gone south. That's Cajun talk for bein' dead."

"See—" Burt pulled the cigar from his mouth. "What'd you say your name was?"

"Dan."

"See, Dan, it's like this: you look on a map of the country, you see this swamp down here and it still looks like it's part of the United States, right? Well, the map lies. This down here is a world all to its ownself. It's got its own language, its own industries, its own . . . well, I wouldn't call 'em laws, exactly. Codes would be more like it. Yeah, codes. The first one is: you don't mess with me, I don't mess with you. Livin' and workin' down here ain't easy—"

"Tell me about it," Jess groused.

"—and so you do what you have to do to slide by. You don't stir up the water and get it all muddy. You don't throw over anybody else's boat, or spit your tabacca in their gumbo. You just live and let live. Get my drift, Dan?"

"I think so. You're sayin' you don't want to call the law."

"That's half of it. The other half is that by the time the law gets here—by boat from Grand Isle—those two fellas are gonna be dead. And that's a damn shame, too, 'cause Cecil had some talent." He pushed the cigar back into his mouth, drew on it, and returned to his sweeping.

"Isn't there somebody here who could help? Don't you have any police around here?"

"We've got what we call peacekeepers," Jess told him. "Company pays 'em extra. Five mean sonsofbitches who'll take you out behind a warehouse and whip your ass till there's nothin' left but a grease stain."

"Yeah." Burt nodded. "The peacekeepers make sure nobody robs anybody, or stuff like that. But I'll tell you, Dan, not even the peacekeepers would want to tangle with those fellas you just seen."

"You know who they were?"

"Uh-huh." He aimed a glance at Arden, who was standing behind Dan. "Still want to see Little Train?"

"Yes, I do."

"I'll be ready in a few minutes, then." He swept cigarette butts and other trash into a dustpan and dumped the debris into a garbage bag. "You decide to go along, too?" The question was directed to Dan.

He felt Arden staring at him. "Yeah," he answered. "I'll go, too."

"Ya'll don't want to eat breakfast first?"

"I'd like to go ahead as soon as we can," Arden said.

"Okay, then. Lemme see what I've got over here." Burt went behind the bar. "Some coffee left in the percolator, but I reckon it would strip the taste buds off your tongues. Oh, here you go. How about these?" He came up with two Moon Pies in their wrappers and two small bags of potato chips. "Want somethin' to drink? You paid for the cabins, I'll throw this in free."

"I'll try the coffee," Dan said, and Arden asked for a can of 7-Up. Burt brought them the Moon Pies and chips, then he went back to get the drinks. Dan still felt dazed by what he'd experienced, and he couldn't let it go. "Those men. Do you know who they are?"

"I know of 'em. Never seen 'em before, myself. Don't want to, either." Burt pushed a spigot and drew black, oily-looking coffee from a cold percolator into a brown clay cup.

"Who are they, then?"

"They're fellas you don't want to be talkin' about." Burt brought the coffee and the can of 7-Up.

"Damn straight." Jess had begun drying the beer mugs. "Plenty of ears in the walls 'round here."

Dan drank some of the coffee and wondered if a layer of swamp mud might not be at the bottom of the percolator; this stuff was even tougher than Donna Lee's high octane, but it gave him a needed kick in the brain pan. He remembered the smack of the big man's fist hitting Eisley in the mouth, a sickening sound. He remembered the drops of blood on the planks. *Nothin's gonna crawl out and get you with the lights on,* Murtaugh had told Eisley.

But Murtaugh had been wrong.

Dan found himself wondering what having an extra arm hanging from your chest and a baby-size head growing from your side would do to a man. It sure would twist you. Maybe make you mean and bitter. What kind of a life had Murtaugh led? That sight alone had been enough to knock Dan's eyes out. *He'd like to see this, wouldn't he?* Doc had said to Monty. *He'd get a rush out of it.*

Who had Doc been talking about?

He drank the coffee and ate the potato chips first, then he devoured the Moon Pie. His guts felt all knotted up. Eisley had seemed all right. A little strange, yes, but all right. Murtaugh was a professional doing a job. It was nothing personal. Fifteen thousand dollars was a lot of money. Hell, if he was a bounty hunter, he would've gone after it, too.

Dan had already caused the death of two innocent people. Now two more were going to die because of him. The torment of watching Emory Blanchard bleed to death, and knowing he was the one who'd pulled that trigger, came back to him full force. He couldn't stand the thought of Murtaugh and Eisley somewhere in the dark, destined to be either beaten or shot.

And what could he do about it?

Forget about them? Just let it go?

If he did, how in the name of God could he ever call himself a man again?

"I'm ready," Burt said. "My boat's at the dock."

The aluminum motor skiff had room for three people, a fourth would have had to straddle the Evinrude. "Throw the lines off!" Burt directed Dan as he got the engine cranked. Then Burt steered them away from the dock. They picked up speed and followed the bayou south past another warehouse and an area where several dredgers and floating cranes were tied up. The air smelled of petroleum and rust, the light turning lavender-gray as the sun began to rise. Arden sat at the front of the boat, her body bent slightly forward as if in anticipation, the warm wind blowing through her hair. Dan watched her hand kneading the drawstring bag. After a few minutes he looked back and saw the derricks of St. Nasty receding against the violet-streaked sky. Then he looked forward again, toward whatever lay ahead.

The boat growled on through the dark-brown foamy water. On either side of the bayou, half-submerged trees and vegetation boiled up in a wild variety of green fronds, lacy moss, spindly reeds, gold-veined fans, and razor-edged saw grass. Here and there flowers of startling red, yellow, or purple had opened their petals amid the tangle of thorns or rigid palmetto spikes. Burt tapped Dan's shoulder and pointed to the right, and Dan saw a four-foot-long alligator sitting on the decaying length of a fallen tree, a crumpled white heron in its jaws.

As they followed the bayou farther away from St. Nasty, the smell of crude oil and machinery was left behind as well. The sun had started throwing golden light across the water and through the thick boughs, and the cloudless sky was changing from gray to pale blue. Dan could feel the humid heat building, fresh sweat blotching his dirty T-shirt. Occasionally they passed the entrances to other, narrower channels, most of them choked up with swamp grass and duck weeds. Dan smelled sweet wild honeysuckle mingled with the earthier aroma of rotting vegetation. They rounded a bend in time to see a dozen white herons flying low across the water, then the birds disappeared amid the trees. The sunlight was strengthening, sparkling off the tea-colored surface, and the early heat promised misery by nine o'clock.

Burt turned them into a bayou that wound off to the left from the main channel. They'd gone maybe fifty yards when Arden saw a piece of board with a skull and crossbones crudely painted on it in white nailed to a treetrunk. She got Burt's attention and motioned to the sign, but he only nodded. A second skull-and-crossbones sign was nailed to a tree farther up the bayou, this one in red.

"Little Train don't care much for people!" Burt told Dan over the motor's snarl. "It's okay, though! He trusts me, we get along all right!"

The bayou's green walls closed in. Thirty feet overhead the tree branches merged, breaking the light into yellow shards. Burt reduced their speed by half and steered the curve of another bend where the mossy tree trunks were as big around as tractor tires. And there, ahead of them in a still and silent cove, was Little Train's house.

Technically it was a house*boat,* but from the looks of the vines and moss that had grown over its dark green sides, like fingers enfolding it into the wilderness, it hadn't been moved for many years. It had a screened-in porch that jutted out over the water, and up top was the hooded lid of a stovepipe chimney. Next to the houseboat was a short tin-roofed pier on which stood a half-dozen rusty oil drums, an old bathtub, a clothes wringer, and various other bits and pieces of unidentifiable machinery. On the other side of the pier was an enclosed floating structure fifty feet in length and fifteen feet high, also green-painted and its sides and roof overgrown with vines. Dan could see the crack between a pair of doors at the end of the structure and he figured another boat must be stored within.

"I'll drift up against the pier, if you'll jump out and tie us," Burt said as he switched the motor off, and Dan nodded. When they were close enough, Dan stood up, found his balance, and stepped to the pier. Burt threw him a rope secured to the skiff's stern and Dan tied it up to one of the wooden posts that supported the roof. When he grasped Arden's wrist in helping her out, Dan could feel her pulse racing. Her eyes had taken on that fervent shine again, and her birthmark had become almost blood-red.

"Hey, Little Train!" Burt shouted at the houseboat. "You got some visitors!"

There was no response. Up in the trees, birds were chirping and a fish suddenly jumped from the cove's water—a flash of silver—and splashed back again.

"Hey, Train!" Burt tried again. He stood on the pier, not daring to set foot without invitation on the Astroturfed walkway that connected it to Little Train's home. "It's Burt Dunbro! Come to talk to you!"

"Who you are I be seein', *fou*," rumbled a surly, heavily accented voice from a screened window. "Who *they* are?"

"Tell him," Burt urged quietly.

"My name's Dan Lambert." Dan could see a figure beyond the screen—the blur of a face—but nothing more. "This is Arden Halliday."

Silence. Dan had the feeling the man was studying Arden's birthmark.

Arden shared the same sensation. Her right hand had squeezed tightly around the drawstring bag, her heart slamming. "I need your help," she said.

"He'p," the man repeated. "What kinda he'p?"

"I'm . . . tryin' to find someone." Her mouth was so dry she could hardly speak. "A woman called the Bright Girl."

There was another stretch of silence for Dan and Burt, but Arden was almost deafened by her heartbeat.

Burt cleared his throat. "Ol' gal at the cafe told her this Bright Girl used to live in a church on Goat Island. Said she's in a grave out there. I said I been huntin' on Goat Island, and far as I know nobody ever lived on it."

Little Train did not speak.

"What do you say?" Burt asked. "Anybody ever lived on Goat Island?"

"*Non*," came the answer.

Arden winced.

"I told her that. Told her you'd know if anybody would. Hey, listen: I need to put in an order for a hundred pounds of cat and fifty pounds of turtle. What can you deliver by next Tuesday?"

"The Bright Girl," the man said, and hearing him say it sent a chill up Arden's spine. "For her you're lookin', ay?"

"That's right. I'm tryin' to find her, because—"

"My own two eyeballs broke, they ain't. Come from where?"

"Huh?"

"He wants to know where you're from," Burt interpreted.

"Texas. Fort Worth, I'm from," she said in unconscious emulation of Little Train's Cajun patois.

"Huuuuwheee!" he said. "That distance, you gotta believe mighty hard. Ay?"

"I do believe."

"This what you believin'," he said, "is wrong."

Arden flinched again. Her hand was white-knuckled around the bag.

"Bright Girl on Goat Island, *non*," Little Train continued. "Was a church out there, never. Who you think she may be, she ain't."

"Wait," Dan said. "Are you sayin' . . . there really *is* a Bright Girl?"

"Sayin' *oui*. Sayin' *non*, too. Not who this girl come from Texay-ass to find."

"Where is she?" Arden's throat clutched. "Please. Can you take me to her?"

There was no answer. Both she and Dan realized the blurred face was gone from the window.

A door on the screened porch skreeked open, and Little Train stood before them.

24

Elephants and Tigers

H IS GRAVELLY VOICE THROUGH the window screen had made him sound as if he might be a seven-foot-tall Goliath. Instead, Little Train stood barely five-six, only four inches taller than Arden. But maybe he had the strength of a giant, because Dan figured he carried at least a hundred and sixty pounds on his stocky, muscular frame. Little Train wore a faded khaki T-shirt over a barrel chest, and brown trousers whose cuffs had been scissored off above a well-worn pair of dark-blue laceless sneakers. His forearms appeared solid enough to pound nails. The bayou sun had burned Little Train's skin to the color of old brick, and it looked as rough. His jaw and cheeks were silvered with a three-day growth of beard, his hair a pale sandpaper dust across the brown skull. Beneath his deeply creased forehead his clear gray eyes were aimed at Arden with a power that almost knocked her back a step.

"Ya'll come on in," he offered.

Dan crossed the Astroturfed plank first, then Arden and Burt. Little Train went ahead into the houseboat, and they followed him across the porch into a room with oak-planked walls and oak beams that ran the length of the ceiling. On the floor was a threadbare red rug that instantly charged Dan's memory: it had a motif of fighting elephants and tigers, and it looked like one of a thousand the street-corner businessmen had hawked from rolling racks in Saigon. The furnishings also had an Oriental—Vietnamese? Dan wondered—influence: two intricately carved ashwood chairs; a bamboo table with a black metal tray atop it; an oil lamp with a rice-paper shade; and a woven tatami neatly rolled up in a corner. A shortwave radio and microphone stood on a second bamboo table next to a shelf of hardback and paperback books. Through another doorway was a small galley, pots and pans hanging from overhead hooks.

"My place," Little Train said. "Welcome to it."

Dan was struck by the cleanliness and order. There was the ever-present smell of the swamp, yes, but no moldy stench. In the black metal tray on the first bamboo table were three smooth white stones, some pieces of dried reeds, and a few fragile-looking bones that might have been fish, fowl, or reptile. Mounted on one wall was a variety of other objects: a huge round hornet's nest, wind-sculpted pieces of bleached driftwood, an amber-colored snakeskin, and the complete skeleton of a bird with its wings out-spread. Then he knew for sure what he'd suspected, because he saw a group of framed photographs on the wall above the short-wave set. He walked across the Saigon-special rug for a closer inspection. They were snapshots of a boat's crew, bare-chested young men wearing steel helmets and grinning or firing upraised middle fingers from their stations behind .50-caliber machine guns and what looked to be an 81-millimeter mortar. There were pictures of a muddy brown river, of the garish nightlights of Saigon, of a cute Vietnamese girl who might have been sixteen or seventeen smiling and displaying the two-fingered V of a peace sign to the camera.

Dan said, "I was a leatherneck. Third Marine. Where'd you catch it?"

"Brown water Navy," Little Train replied without hesitation. "Radarman first class, Swift PCF."

"These pictures of your boat?" The Swift PCF patrol craft crews, Dan knew, had taken hell along the constricted waterways of 'Nam and Cambodia.

"The verra one."

"Your crew make it out?"

"Jus' me and the fella sittin' at the mortar. Night of May sixteen, 1970, we run into a chain stretched 'cross the river. Them black pajamas waitin' on the bank, ay? Hit us with rockets. I went swimmin', back fulla shrap."

"You never told me you were over there in Vet'nam, Little Train!" Burt said.

He burned his gaze at the other man. "Never you ask. And *bon ami,* I tell you plenty time: call me *Train.*"

"Oh. Okay. Sure. Train it is." Burt shrugged and cast a nervous grin at Arden.

"Please," Arden said anxiously. "The Bright Girl. Do you know where she is?"

He nodded. "I do."

"Don't tell me you know where her grave is. Please tell me she's alive."

"For you, then: *oui,* alive she is."

"Oh, God." Tears sprang to her eyes. "Oh, God. You don't know how . . . you don't know how much I wanted to hear that."

"Who're you talkin' about, Train?" Burt frowned. "I never heard of any Bright Girl."

"Never you needed her," Train said.

"Can you take me to her?" Arden asked. "I've come such a long way. I don't have any money, but . . . I'll sign an IOU. I'll get the money. However much you want to take me, I swear I'll pay you. All right?"

"Your money, I don't want. Got ever'ting I need, I'm a rich man."

"You mean . . . you won't—"

"Won't take no money, *non.* Who tell you 'bout the Bright Girl way up there in Fort Worth Tex-ay-ass?"

"A friend who was born in LaPierre. He saw her when he was a little boy, and he told me all about her."

"Oh, them stories. That she's a young beautimous girl and she don't never get old or die. That she can touch you and heal any sickness, or cancer . . . or scar. Your friend tell you all that?"

"Yes."

"So you believe mighty hard, and you come all the way down here to ask her touch. 'Cause that mark, it hurt you inside?"

"Yes."

Train reached toward her face. Arden's first impulse was to pull away, but his gaze was powerful enough to hold her. His rough brown fingers gently grazed the birthmark and then drew back. "You strong-hearted?" he asked.

"I . . . think I am."

"Either am or not."

"I am," she said.

Train nodded. "Then I take you, no sweat."

Dan couldn't remain silent any longer. "Don't lie to her! There's no such person! There *can't* be! I don't care if she's supposed to be some great miracle worker, no woman can live a hundred years and still look like a young girl!"

"I say I take her to see the Bright Girl." Train's voice was calm. "I say, too, the Bright Girl ain't who she come to find."

"What?" Arden shook her head. "I'm not followin' you."

"When we get there, you see tings clear. Then we find out how strong you heart."

Dan didn't know what to say, or what kind of tricks this man was trying to pull. None of it made any sense to him. What had started to gnaw at him again was the fate of Murtaugh and Eisley. He couldn't stand the thought that his pulling the trigger in Shreveport had resulted in the death of Harmon DeCayne and now, most likely, the two bounty hunters. There would be four murders on his head, and how could he live with that and not go insane? He remembered what Burt had said about Train, back in the cafe: *He gets all 'round the swamp. If anybody would know, it'd be him.*

Dan had to ask. "There were two other men with us. We were at St. Nasty. Around five o'clock, four men with guns broke in our cabin and took 'em away. The one in charge was called Doc. Do you know—"

"Oh, shit!" Burt pressed his hands to his ears. "I don't wanna hear this! I don't wanna know nothin' about it!"

"Hush up!" Train's voice rattled the screens. "Let 'im talk!"

"I'm not stayin' around for this! No way! Ya'll have fun, I'm gettin' back up the bayou!" Burt started out but paused at the door. "Train, don't do nothin' stupid! Hear me? I'll be expectin' the cat and turtle by Tuesday. Hear?"

"Go home, *bon ami*," Train said. "And to you safe passage."

"Good luck," Burt told Dan, and he went out and crossed the gangplank. Train walked past Arden to a window and watched Burt untie his boat, climb in, and start the engine. "He's okay," Train said as Burt steered the motor skiff back up the narrow bayou the way they'd come. "Hard-workin' fella."

"He knows who Doc is, doesn't he?"

"Oh, *oui*. And so do I." He turned away from the window; his face seemed to have drawn tighter across the bones, his eyes cold. "Tell me the tale, ay?"

Dan told him, omitting the fact that he was wanted for murder and that Murtaugh and Eisley were bounty hunters. He omitted, as well, the fact of Murtaugh's freak-show background. "Doc said he was takin' 'em somewhere by boat. He had some kinda score to settle with 'em, but I'm not sure what it was."

Train leveled that hard, penetrating stare at Dan. "Friends of you, they is?"

"Not friends, exactly."

"Then who they is to you?"

"More like . . . fellow travelers."

"Where was they travelin' to?"

Dan looked at the elephants and tigers in the rug. He could feel Train watching him, and he knew there was no use in lying. Train was no fool. He sighed heavily; the only path to take was the straight one. "Flint Murtaugh and Pelvis Eisley are their names. They're bounty hunters. They tracked me down here. I met Arden in a truck stop north of Lafayette and brought her with me."

"I came because I wanted to," Arden said. "He didn't force me."

"Bounty hunters," Train repeated. "What crime you did?"

"I killed a man."

Train didn't move or speak.

"He worked at a bank in Shreveport. There was a fight. I lost my head and shot him. The bank's put fifteen thousand dollars reward on me. Murtaugh and Eisley wanted it."

"Huuuuwheeee," Train said softly.

"You can have the reward, I won't give you any trouble. Can you call the law or somebody on that shortwave set?"

"I a'ready tell you, I don't need no money. I'm rich, livin' as I do. I love this swamp, I grew up in it. I like to fish and hunt. What I don't eat, I sell. I boss myself. I get fifteen thousan' dollar in my pocket—*poof!* There go my riches. Then I want another fifteen thousan' dollar, but no more there is. No, I don't need but what I got." He frowned, the lines deepening around his eyes, and he rubbed his silvered chin. "If them bounty hunters after you, how come for you wanna he'p 'em? How come you even tellin' me this?"

"Because they don't deserve to be murdered, that's why! They haven't done anything wrong!"

"Hey, hey! Calm down. Flyin' you head off ain't gonna he'p nobody." He motioned toward the porch. "Ya'll go out there, set, and take the breeze. I'll be there direct."

"What about the shortwave?"

"Yeah, I could call the law way over to Gran' Isle. Only ting is, they ain't gonna find you . . . fella travelers," he decided to say. "Likely they dead a'ready. Now go on out and set y'self."

There wasn't much of a breeze on the porch, but it was a little cooler there than inside the boat. Dan was too jumpy to sit, though Arden settled in a wicker chair that faced the cove. "You're goin' with me, aren't you?" she asked him. "We're so close, you've got to go with me."

"I'll go. I still don't believe it, but I'll go." He stood at the screen, looking out at the water's still surface. "Damn," he said. "There's gotta be somethin' somebody can do!"

"*Oui,* you can take a swaller of this here." Train came onto the porch. He had uncapped a small metal flask, and he offered it to Dan. "Ain't 'shine," he said when Dan hesitated. "It's French brandy. Buy it in Grand Isle. Go ahead, ay?"

Dan accepted the flask and took a drink. The brandy burned its flaming trail down his throat. Train offered the flask to Arden, and when she shook her head he took a sip and sloshed it around in his mouth beforé swallowing. "Now I gonna tell you 'bout them men, so listen good. They got a place 'bout five mile southwest from here. Hid real fine. I ain't got an eye set for it, but I come up on it when I'm huntin' boar near Lake Calliou. They been there maybe t'ree month. Set up camp, brung in a prefab house, build a dock, swimmin' pool, and all whatcha like. Got a shrimp boat and two of them expenseeve cigarettes. You know, them fast speederboats. Then they put bob wire' round ever'ting." He swigged from the flask and held it out to Dan again. "I hear from an ol' Cajun boy live on Calliou Bay them men be poachin' 'gator. Season don't start till September, see. Ain't no big ting, it happen. But I start to windin' in my head, how come they to poach 'gator? Somebody owns hisse'f two of them cigarettes, he got to poach 'gator? Why's that so, ay?" He took the flask back after Dan had had a drink. "Ol' boy says he seen lights at night, boats comin' and goin' all hours. So I go over there, hide my boat, and watch through my dark vision binocs 'cause I eat up with curious. Took me two night, then I see what they up to."

"What was it?" Arden asked, pulling her thoughts away from the Bright Girl for the moment.

"Freighter in the bay, unloadin' what look like grain sacks to the shrimp boat. All the time the two cigarettes they circlin' and circlin' 'round, throwin' spotlights. And—huuuuwheee!— the men in them boats with the like of guns you never did saw! Shrimp boat brung the grain sacks back in, freighter up anchor and went." He had another swig of Napoleon's finest. "Now what kinda cargo unloaded by night and be that worth protection?"

"Drugs," Dan said.

"That's what I'm figurin'. Either the heroin or the cockaine. Maybe both. All them miles and miles of swamp coast, the law cain't hardly patrol a smidgen of it, and they boats in sorry shape. So these fellas bringin' in the dope and shippin' it north, likely takin' it up by Bayou du Large or Bayou Grand Calliou and un- loadin' at a marina. Sellin' some of it at St. Nasty, too. Burt's the one found out fella named Doc Nyland was hangin' 'round the poolhall, givin' men free samples to get 'em interested. Peace- keeper tried to do somethin' about it, he went missin'. Only ting is, I cain't figure why they poachin' the 'gators. Then—boom!— it hit me like a brick upside my head." Train capped the flask. "They worry somebody gonna steal them drugs away from 'em. Worry so much they gonna be hijack they gotta figure a way to move 'em safe. So what they gonna do, ay? They gonna put them drugs somewhere they cain't be easy stole." His mouth crooked in a wicked smile. "Like inside live 'gators."

"Inside 'em?"

"*Sans doute!* You wrap that cockaine up in metal foil good and tight, then you jam it down in them bellies with a stick! How you gonna get it out unless you got a big knife and a lotta time to be cuttin'? That'd be the goddangest mess you never did saw!"

"I'll bet," Dan agreed. "So what are they doin'? Shippin' the 'gators north to be cut open?"

"*Oui,* puttin' 'em on a truck and takin' 'em to a safe place. Even if them 'gators die of bad digestion 'fore they get where they goin', the cockaine still protected in there."

"Maybe so, but I can't understand how Murtaugh and Eisley got mixed up with a gang of drug runners. Is Doc Nyland their leader?"

Train shook his head. "I seen somebody else over there, look like he was bossin'. Fella don't wear no shirt, showin' hisse'f off. Standin' by the pool, them irons and weight bars layin' ever'where. His girlfrien', all she do is lay there sunburnin'. I'm figurin' he's the honch."

Dan looked out through the screen at the water. The sun was up strong and hot now, golden light streaming through the trees. A movement caught his attention, and he saw a moccasin undulating smoothly across the surface. He watched it until it disappeared into the shadows. It seemed to Dan that in this swamp the human reptiles were the ones to be feared most of all. He lifted his forearm and stared at his snake tattoo. Once, a long time ago, he had been a brave man. He had done without hesitation what he'd thought was the right thing. He had walked the world like a giant himself, before time and fate had beaten him down. Now he was dying and he was a killer, sick at heart.

He felt as if he were peering into a snake hole, and if he reached into it to drag the thing out, he could be bitten to death. But if he turned his back on it like a coward, he was already dead.

An image came to him, unbidden: Farrow's face and voice, there on that terrible night the snipers' bullets had hissed out of the jungle.

Go, he'd said. It had not been a shout, but it was more powerful than a shout.

Go.

Dan remembered the glint of what might have been joy in Farrow's eyes as the man—a citizen of Hell, one of the walking damned—had turned and started slogging back through the mud toward the jungle, firing his M16 to give Dan and the others precious seconds in which to save their own lives.

Farrow could not live with himself because he'd gone south. There in the village of Cho Yat, his simple mistake with the foil-wrapped chocolate bar had resulted in the death of innocents, and Farrow had decided—in the muddy stream, at that crisis of time—that he had found an escape.

Dan had once been a Snake Handler, a good soldier, a decent man. But he'd gone south, there in that Shreveport bank, and now *he* was a citizen of hell, one of the walking damned.

But he knew the right thing to do.

It was time to go.

"You braingears gettin' hot," Train said in a quiet voice.

"You have guns." It was a statement, not a question.

"Two rifles. Pistol."

"How many men?"

Train knew what he meant. "I count eight last time. Maybe more I don't see."

Dan turned to face him. "Will you take me?"

"No!" Arden stood up, her eyes wide. "Dan, no! You don't owe them anything!"

"I owe myself," he said.

"Listen to me!" She stepped close to him and grasped his arm. "You can still get away! You can find—"

"No," he interrupted gently, "I can't. Train, how about it?"

"They'll kill you!" Arden said, stricken with terror for him.

"*Oui,*" Train added. "That they'll try."

"Maybe Murtaugh and Eisley are already dead." Dan stared deeply into Arden's eyes. It was a strange thing, but now he could look at her face and not see the birthmark. "Maybe they're still alive, but they won't be for very long. If I don't go after 'em—if I don't at least try to get 'em out of there—what good am I? I don't want to die in prison. But I can't live in a prison, either. And if I don't do *somethin',* I'll carry my own prison around with me every hour of every day I've got left. I have to do this. Train?" He directed his gaze to the Cajun. "I'm not askin' you to help me, just to get me close enough. I'll need to take one of the rifles, the pistol, and some ammo. You got a holster for the pistol?"

"I do."

"Then you'll take me?"

Train paused for a moment, thinking it over. He opened the flask again and took a long swig. "You a mighty strange killer,

wantin' to get killed for somebody tryin' to slam you in prison."
He licked his lips. "Huuuuwheeee! I didn't know I was gonna get
dead today."

"I can go in alone."

"Well," Train said, "it's like this here: I knew a fella, name of
Jack Giradoux. Parish ranger, he was. He come by, we'd have a talk
and eat some cat. I don't tell him about them men 'cause I know
what he'll have to do. I figure not to rock the boat, ay?" He smiled;
it was a painful sight. The smile quickly faded. "If he don't find
'em, I figure, he don't get killed. He was a good fella. Few days
ago fisherman find Jack's boat on Lake Tambour. That's a long
way from where them men are, but I know they must've got hold
of him and then towed his boat up there. Find his body, nobody
ever will. Now I gotta ask myself, did I done wrong? When they
gonna find out I know about 'em and come for me, some night?"
He closed the flask and held it down at his side. "Lived forty-five
good year. To die in bed, *non*. Could be we get it done and get out.
Could be you my death angel, and maybe I know sooner or later
you was gonna swoop down on me. It's gonna be like puttin' you
hand in a cottonmouth nest. You ready to get bit?"

"I'm ready to do some bitin'," Dan said.

"Okay, leatherneck. Okay. With you, I reckon. Got Baby to
carry us, maybe we get real lucky."

"Baby?"

"She my girl. You meet her, direct."

"One more thing," Dan added. "I want to take Arden where
she needs to go first."

"*Non,* impossible. Them men five miles southwest, the Bright
Girl nine, ten mile southeast, down in the Casse-Tete Islands. We
take her first, we gonna be losin' too much time."

Dan looked at Arden, who was staring fixedly at the floor.
"I'll leave it up to you. I know how much this means. I never
believed it . . . but maybe I should have. Maybe I was wrong, I
don't know." Her chin came up, and her eyes found his. "What
do you say?"

"I say—" She stopped, and took a deep breath to clear her head. So many things were tangled up inside her: fear and jubilation, pain and hope. She had come so far, with so much at stake. But now she knew what the important thing was. She said, "Help them."

He gave her a faint smile; he'd known what she was going to decide. "You need to stay here. We'll be back as soon as—"

"No." It was said with finality. "If you're goin', I am, too."

"Arden, it might be rougher'n hell out there. You could get yourself killed."

"I'm goin'. Don't try to talk me out of it, because you can't."

"Clock's tickin'," Train said.

"All right, then." Dan felt the urgency pulling at him. "I'm ready."

Train went into a back room and got the weapons: a Browning automatic rifle with a four-bullet magazine, a Ruger rifle with a hunter's scope and a five-shell magazine, and in a waist holster a Smith & Wesson 9mm automatic that held an eight-bullet clip. He found extra magazines for the rifles and clips for the automatic and put them in a faded old backpack, which Arden was given charge of. Dan took the Browning and the pistol. Train got a plastic jug of filtered water from the galley, slung the Ruger's strap around his shoulder, and said, "We go."

They left the houseboat and Train led them to the vine-covered floating structure next to the pier. He slid open a door. "Here she sets."

"Jesus," Dan said, stunned by what he saw.

Sitting inside was Train's second boat. It was painted navy gray, the paint job relatively fresh except for patches of rust at the waterline. It resembled a smaller version of a commercial tug, but it was leaner and meaner, its squat pilothouse set closer to the prow. The craft was about fifty feet long, and thirteen feet high at its tallest point, a tight squeeze in the oil-smelling, musty boathouse. It had not the gentle charm of an infant, but the armor-plated threat of a brute.

Though the machine-gun mounts and the mortar had been removed and other civilian modifications made to the radar mast, Dan recognized it as a Swift-type river patrol boat, the same kind of vessel Train had crewed aboard on the deadly waterways of Vietnam.

"My baby," Train said with a sly grin. "Let the good times roll."

25

Reptilian

T HE SUN HAD RISEN on a small aluminum rowboat in the middle of a muddy pond. In that rowboat Flint and Pelvis sat facing each other, linked by the short chain between their cuffed wrists.

At seven o'clock the temperature was approaching eighty-four degrees and the air steamed with humidity. Flint's shirt and suit jacket had been stripped off him, Clint's arm drooping lethargically from the pale, sweat-sparkling chest. Beads of moisture glistened on Flint's hollow-eyed face, his head bowed. Across from him, Pelvis still wore his wig backward, his clothes sweat-drenched, his eyes swollen and forlorn. Dried blood covered the split sausage of his bottom lip, one of his lower teeth gone and another knocked crooked, tendrils of crusty blood stuck to his chin. His breathing was slow and harsh, sweat dripping from the end of his nose into a puddle between his mud-bleached suedes.

Something brushed against the boat's hull and made the craft lazily turn around its anchor chain. Flint lifted his head to watch a five-foot-long alligator drift past, its snout pushing through the foul brown water. A second alligator, this one maybe three feet in length, cruised past the first. The cat-green eyes and ridged skull of a third had surfaced less than six feet from the rowboat. Two more, each four-footers, lay motionless side by side just beyond the silent watcher. Flint had counted nine alligators at any one time, but there might be others asleep on the bottom. He couldn't tell one from the other, except for their obvious size differences, so he really didn't know how many lurked in the sludgy pond. Still, they were quiet monsters. Occasionally two or three would bump together in their back-and-forth loglike driftings and there might be an instant's outburst of thrashing anger, but then everything would calm down again but for the rocking of the boat and the thudding hearts of the men in it. Flint figured the alligators were prisoners here just as he and Pelvis were.

The pond looked to be sixty-five feet across, from one side of a half-submerged, rusty barbed-wire fence to the other. Beyond the alligator corral's heavily bolted gate was a pier where two cigarette speedboats—both of them painted dark, nonreflective green—were secured, along with the larger workboat Flint had seen unloading the reptiles at the Vermilion marina. Eight feet of the pier was built out over the corral, and at its end stood a bolted-down electric winch Flint figured was used to hoist the alligators up onto the workboat's deck. During the thirty-minute journey to this place in one of the speedboats, Monty had gleefully ripped the jacket and shirt off Flint's back and taken the derringer's holster. Then, when they'd reached their destination, Doc and the others had debated for a few minutes what to do with them until "he"—whoever "he" was—woke up. Their current situation had been dreamed up by Doc, who got Mitch to row them in the aluminum skiff through the corral's gate while Monty had followed in a second rowboat. There had been much hilarity from a group of men watching on the pier as Mitch had thrown a concrete brick anchor over the side and then got into the boat with Monty, leaving Flint and Pelvis at the end of their chain.

The party had gone on for a while—"Hey, freak! Why don't you and Elvis get out of that boat and cool yourselves off?"—but

the men had drifted away as the sun had come up. Flint understood why; the novelty had faded, and they'd known how hot it
was going to get out here. Every so often Mitch, Monty, or some
other bastard would stroll out to the pier's end to take a look
and throw a remark at them that included the words "freak" or
"motherfuckers," then they would go away again. Since Pelvis had
been smashed in the mouth, he'd not spoken a single word. Flint
realized he must be in shock. Monty had taken Mama with him,
and the last time the bearded sonofabitch had come out to check
on them, the little bulldog wasn't in his arms.

Flint could smell meat cooking.

Being burned was more like it.

The pier continued on past the boats to a bizarre sight: a
large suburban ranch house with cream-colored walls, perched on
wooden pilings over the water. the place looked as if it had been
lifted up off the mowed green lawn of the perfect American town,
helicoptered in, and set down to be the envy of the neighborhood.
There was a circular swimming pool with its own redwood deck,
one of those "above-ground" pools sold in kits; here the pool was
not above ground, but on a platform above swamp. On the pool's
deck was a rack of barbells, a weight bench, and a stationary bi-
cycle. Next to it was another large deck shaded by a blue-and-
white-striped canvas awning, and on the far side of the house the
platform supported a television satellite dish.

Other walkways went off from the main platform, connecting
the house to three other smaller wooden structures. Cables snaked
from one of them to the house and the satellite dish, so Flint reasoned it stored the power generator. Though the alligator corral,
the pier, and the swimming pool were out under the full sun, most
of the house was shaded by moss-draped trees. Around the house
and the corral and everything else the swamp still held green do-
minion. Flint could see a bayou winding into the swamp beyond
the farthermost of the three outbuildings, and there were red buoys
floating in it to mark deeper passage for the workboat's hull.

His survey of the area had also found a wooden watchtower,

about forty feet high, all but hidden amid the trees at the bayou's entrance. Up top, under a green-painted cupola, a man sat in a lawn chair reading a magazine, a rifle propped against the railing beside him. Every few minutes he would stand up and scan all directions through a pair of binoculars, then he would sit down again and return to his reading.

"We," Flint said hoarsely, "are in deep shit."

Pelvis didn't speak; he just sat there and kept sweating, his eyes unfocused.

"Eisley? Snap out of it, hear me?"

There was no answer. A little thread of saliva had spooled down over his wounded lip.

"How about sayin' somethin'?" Flint asked.

Pelvis lowered his head and stared at the boat's bottom.

Flint sniffed the air, catching the smell of burned meat. It struck him that that bastard Monty might be hungry again, and he realized Pelvis was probably thinking the same thing he was: Mama was on the breakfast grill.

"Hey, we're gonna get out of this," Flint tried again. He thought it was the most idiotic thing he'd ever said in his life. "You can't go off and leave me now, hear?"

Pelvis shook his head, and he swallowed with a little dry, clicking noise.

Flint watched another alligator gliding past, so close he could have reached out and poked it in the eye if he cared to lose a hand. Well, that'd be all right; he'd still have two. Hold on, he told himself. Hold on, now. Control yourself. It's not over yet, they haven't shoveled the dirt over you. Hold on. "I'll bet this is all a big mistake," he said. "I'll bet when that fella wakes up, he'll come see us and we'll tell him the story and he'll shoot us on out of here." His throat clenched up. "I mean, *scoot* us out of here." Eisley's silence was scaring the bejesus out of him, making him start to lose his own grip. He'd gotten so used to the man's prattling, the silence was driving him crazy. "Eisley, listen. We're not givin' up. Pelvis? Come on, talk to me."

No response.

Flint leaned forward, the sun beginning to scorch his back and sweat clinging to his eyebrows. "Cecil," he said, "I'm gonna slap the crap out of you if you don't look me in the face and say somethin'."

But it was no use. Flint closed his eyes and pressed his uncuffed hand against his forehead. At his chest Clint's arm suddenly twitched and the hand fluttered, then it fell motionless again.

"What'd you call me?"

Flint opened his eyes and looked into the other man's face.

"Did you call me Cecil?" Pelvis had lifted his head. His split lip had broken open again, a little bloody fluid oozing.

"Yeah, I guess I did." A rush of relief surged through him. "Well, thank God you're back! Now's not the time to crack up, lemme tell you! We've got to hang tough! Like I said, when that fella wakes up and we tell him what a big mistake all this is—"

"*Cecil,*" Pelvis whispered, and a wan smile played across his crusty mouth. Then it passed. His eyes were very dark. "I think . . . they're cookin' Mama," he said.

"No, they're not!" Hold on to him! Flint thought in desperation. Don't let him slide away again! "That fella was just pullin' your chain! Listen now, get your mind off that. We've got other things to think about."

"Like what? Which one of us they're gonna kill first?" He squinted up at the sun. "I don't care. We ain't gettin' out of this."

"See? That's why you never would've made a good bounty hunter. *Never.* Because you're a quitter. By God, *I'm* not a quitter!" Flint felt the blood pounding in his face. He had to calm down before he had a heatstroke. "I said I was gonna get Lambert, and I got him, didn't I?"

"Yes sir, you did. I don't think neither one of us is gonna be spendin' much of that reward money, though."

"You just watch," Flint said. "You'll find out." He was aware of his own wheels starting to slip. Control! he thought. Control was the most important thing. He had to settle himself down before the pressure of this situation broke him. He enfolded Clint's clammy hand in his own, and he could feel their common pulse. "Self-discipline is what a bounty hunter needs. I've always had it. Ever since I was a little boy. I had to have it to keep Clint from jumpin' around when I didn't want him to. Jumpin' around and makin' everybody look at me like I was a freak. Self-discipline is what you need, and a whole lot of it."

"Mr. Murtaugh?" Pelvis said in a soft and agonized voice that had very little of Elvis in it. "We're gonna die today. Would you please shut up?"

Flint's brain was smoking. He was burning up. His pallid skin cringed from the raw sunlight, and there was water, water everywhere, but not enough to cool himself in. He licked his lips and tasted sweat. An alligator nudged alongside the boat, a long, scraping noise that made the flesh of Flint's spine ripple. He needed to get his mind fixed on something else—anything else. "You'd be worth a damn," he said, "if you had a manager."

Pelvis stared at him, and slowly blinked. *"What?"*

"A manager. Like that fella said. You need a manager. Somebody to teach you self-discipline, get you off that damn junk food. Get you to stop tryin' to play Elvis and be Cecil. I heard what he said, I was standin' right there."

"Are you . . . sayin' what I *think* you're sayin'?"

"Maybe I am. Maybe I'm not." Flint reached up, his fingers trembling, and wiped the beads of sweat from his eyebrows. "I'm just sayin' you've got a little talent to beat the piano, and a good manager could help you. A good *businessman*. Somebody to make sure you got paid when you were supposed to. You wouldn't have to be a headliner, you could be in somebody else's band, or play backup on records or whatever. There's money to be made in that line of work, isn't there?"

"Are you crazy, Mr. Murtaugh?" Pelvis asked. "Or am I?"

"Hell, we *both* are!" Flint had almost shouted it. Control, he thought. Control. God, the sun was getting fierce. A pungent, acidic reek—the smell of swamp mud and 'gator droppings—was steaming up off the water. "When we get out of here—which we *will,* after we talk to whoever's in charge around here—there's gonna be tomorrow to think about. You're not cut out to be a bounty hunter . . . and I've been lookin' for a way to quit it for a long time. I'm sick of the ugliness of it, and I was never gettin' anywhere. I was just goin' around and around, like . . . like a three-armed monkey in a cage," he said. "Now, it might not work. Probably won't. But it would be a new start, wouldn't—"

"Gettin' awful hot out here, ain't it?"

The voice caused both of them to jump. Monty was walking along the pier, splotches of sweat on his shirt. He was holding a plate of food, and he was chewing on some stringy meat attached to a small bone. "Ya'll ain't gone swimmin' yet?"

Neither Flint nor Pelvis spoke. They watched the big, brown-bearded man chewing on the bone in his greasy fingers.

"Don't feel much like talkin', do you?" Monty glanced quickly up at the sun. Then he threw the bone into the water beside their boat. The splash drew the attention of the alligators, and three or four of them quickly converged on the spot like scaly torpedoes. Water swirled, a tail rose up and smacked the surface, and suddenly an underwater disagreement boiled up, two reptilian bodies thrashing and the rowboat rocking back and forth on the muddy foam of combat.

"Them boys are hungry this mornin'." Monty started sucking the meat from another bone. "They'll eat anydamnthing, y'know. Got cast-iron stomachs. Bet they'd like to get their teeth in you, freak. Bet you'd be a real taste sensation."

The alligators, finding no food on their table, had stopped squabbling. Still, they crisscrossed the pond on all sides of the boat. "Don't you men think this has gone far enough?" Flint asked. "We've learned our lesson, we're not comin' back in here anymore."

Monty chewed and laughed. "Well, that's right. 'Course, you ain't leavin', either." He flung the second bone in, and again the reptiles darted for it. "Hey, Elvis! You want some breakfast?"

Pelvis didn't answer, and Flint saw his eyes glazing over again.

"It's realllll good. Lotta meat on them bones, I was surprised. Want to try a bite or two?" He held up a hunk of white meat, and he grinned through his beard. "Woof! Woof!" he said.

Pelvis shivered. A pulse had started beating hard at his temple.

"Hang on." Flint grasped Pelvis's arm. "Steady, now."

"I think he wants the rest of it, Mr. Freak. Here you go, Elvis! Arrrruuuuuu!" And as he howled like a dog, Monty tossed the rest of the plate's meat and bones up into the air over the corral.

Before the first piece of meat or bone splashed the surface, Pelvis went crazy.

He lunged over the rowboat's side. The chain of the handcuffs connecting their wrists jerked tight, and with a shout of terror Flint was pulled into the water with him.

For the last mile and a half Train had cut the Swift's husky double-diesels to one-fourth speed—about seven knots—to keep the noise down. Now he switched off the engines and let the Swift coast along the narrow bayou. "Gettin' close," he said behind the spoked wheel in the pilothouse. Dan stood at his side, and Arden had found a benchseat to park herself on toward the stern. "She gonna run minute or two, then we doin' some wadin'."

Dan nodded. The rifles, pistol, and the ammunition back-pack had been stowed away in a locker at the rear of the pilot-house. After leaving the cove Train had brought them along a series of channels at speeds approaching twenty-eight knots, the Swift's upper limit. Before them, birds had flown and alligators had dived for safety. Train had told Dan his real name was Alain Chappelle, that he'd been born on a train between Mobile and New Orleans, but that he was raised in Grand Isle, where his father had been a charter fisherman. During his tour of duty in Vietnam his parents had moved to New Orleans, and his father had accepted a consulting job with a company that built fishing boats. Train had the swamp in his blood, he'd said. He had to live there, in all that beautiful wilderness, or he would perish. He'd known that the Swift boats—based on the design of tough little utility craft used to ferry supplies out to oil derricks in the Gulf of Mexico—were built by a contractor in the town of Berwick, which Dan and Arden had passed through forty miles north of Houma. In 1976 he'd bought the armor-plated hulk of a surplus Swift and started the three-year labor of restoring it to a worthy condition. Baby could be sweet as sugar one day and a raging foul-tempered bitch the next, he'd told Dan, but she was fast and nimble and her shallow draft was ideal for the bayous. Anyway, he loved her.

"Takin' us in there," Train said, motioning with a lift of his chin toward another channel that wound off to the left. "Gonna get tight, so tell the lady if she hear some thumps, we ain't gonna wind us up ass-deep and sinkin'."

Dan went back to relay the message. Train steered Baby into the channel with a steady hand and a sharp eye. Tree branches scraped along the sides and half-submerged reeds and swamp grass parted before the prow. Overhead the trees thickened, cutting the light to a dark green murk. The Swift was slowing down now to the speed of a man's walk, and Train came out of the pilot-house and picked up a rope with one end secured to the starboard deck and at the throwing end an iron grappling-hook. The boat shuddered, something bumping along the keel. Train threw the hook into the underbrush, pulled hard on the rope, and it went taut. In another few seconds Baby eased to a stop.

They got ready. Dan was sweating in the fierce wet heat, but he wasn't afraid. Maybe just a little. In any case, the job had to be done.

"Leave the pistol here," Train said as Dan took it from the locker. "She might be gonna need it."

"Me?" Arden stood up. "I've never fired a gun in my life!"

"Ever'ting got a number-one time." Train popped a clip into the automatic. "I'm gonna tell you 'bout this safety catch here, so you pay a mind. You get you'self a caller while we gone, only two fellas to save you neck be Mr. Smith and Mr. Wesson. Ay?"

Arden decided it would be very wise to pay close attention.

"Take t'ree reloads. We need more'n that, we gonna be haulin' butt," Train told Dan after Arden's quick lesson was done. Dan took three of the Browning's box magazines from the backpack, put one in each front pocket and the third in a back pocket. Train did the same with the Ruger's ammo, then he put on a gray-and-green camouflage-print cap. " 'Bout quarter-mile from here, them fellas be," he said as he slung the Ruger barrel-down to his right shoulder so water wouldn't foul the firing mechanism. "They got guns enough to blow the horns off Satan: rifle, shotgun, machine gun, ever' damn kinda gun. So from here on we mighty careful or we mighty dead."

While Dan strapped on the Browning rifle, also barrel-down, Train opened a jar of what looked like black grease and streaked some under his eyes. "Don't want no glare blindin' you when it come time to take a shot. You miss—*poof!* That's all she wrote." He handed the grease to Dan, who applied it in the same fashion. Then Train got his face right up in Dan's, his eyes piercing. "We get in a knock-ass firefight, am I gonna can count on you? You gonna stick it to 'em, no second thought? By the time you got second thought, you be twice dead. Ay?"

"I'll do what I have to," Dan said.

"They got a man spyin' for 'em in a tower, up where he can see the Gulf and the bayou one turn 'round. They got a big metal gate blockin' the bayou, and a bob wire fence 'round the whole place." He nodded toward the forbidding wilderness, thick with spiky palmettos, hanging vines, and cypress trees. "We gonna go through there. Ain't got no serpent-bite kit, so keep both them eyeballs lookin'."

"I will."

"If we see us two dead bodies layin' out, we comin' straight back quiet as sinners on Sunday. Then I make a radio call to Gran' Isle. Okay?"

"Yeah."

Train eased over the transom and lowered himself into the water. The swamp consumed him to the middle of his chest.

"Dan?" Arden said as he started to go over. Again her tangled emotions got in the way of her voice. "Please be careful," she managed to say.

"I was wrong to let you come. You should've stayed at Train's place."

She shook her head. "I'm where I need to be. You just worry about gettin' in and back."

Dan went into the water, his shoes sinking through three inches of mud.

"Listen up," Train told Arden. "You might gonna hear some shootin'. We don't come back half-hour after them shots, we ain't comin'. Radio's up on a shelf over the wheel. Got a fresh battery, you'll see the turn-on switch. We don't come back, you need to start callin' for he'p on the mike. Turn through them frequencies and keep callin'. That don't bring nobody, you got the water jug, the pistol, and you two legs. Ay?"

"Yes."

"Just so you know." Train turned away and started moving.

Dan paused, looking up at Arden's face. The deep-purple birthmark was no longer ugly, he thought. It was like the unique pattern of a butterfly's wings, or the color and markings of a seashell never to be exactly duplicated again in a thousand years.

"I'll be back," he said, and he followed Train through the morass.

When they'd gotten out of Arden's earshot, Train said quietly, "Them fellas kill us, they gonna find her, too, eventual. What they'll do I ain't gonna think on."

Dan didn't answer. He'd already thought of that.

"Just so you know," Train said.

They waded on, and in another moment the wilderness had closed between them and Baby.

* * *

Nasty brown water had flooded Flint's eyes and mouth, choking off his shout of terror. Pelvis was flailing beside him, insanely trying to get across the 'gator corral at the man who'd chewed Mama's flesh. Flint felt Clint's arm thrash, his brother's bones squirming violently inside his body. The thought of Clint's infant-size lungs drawing in water and drowning opened a nightmarish door on gruesome possibilities. He started fighting to get his balance as he'd never fought in his life. He got his legs under him, and his shoes found a bottom of mud and mess that could be described only as gooshy.

He stood up. His head and shoulders were out of the water. Still, Clint was trapped below. Pelvis was standing up, too, his muddy wig hanging on by its last piece of flesh-colored tape, a strangled, enraged scream shredding his throat. With a surge of power that Flint had never dreamed the man possessed, Pelvis starting dragging him through the water to reach the pier.

Monty was laughing fit to bust a gut. "It's show time, boys!" he hollered toward the house.

Flint stepped on something that exploded to life under his feet and scared the pee out of him. A scaly form whipped past them, its tail thrashing. The tail of a second alligator slapped Pelvis's shoulder, and he grunted with pain but kept on going. All around them the pond was a maelstrom of reptiles fighting for the meat and bones Monty had just thrown in. Flint saw one of them coming from the left, its snout plowing through the foam and its catslit eyes fixed on him. Even as Pelvis kept hauling him, Flint struck out with his unhindered left arm at the thing, which looked large enough to make two suitcases and a handbag. He struck the surface in front of its snout, but the splash was enough to make it wheel away, its tail whacking muddy water into the air. Then Pelvis was hit at the knees by an underwater beast and he was knocked off his feet, the alligator's barklike flesh coming up from the depths for an instant, which was long enough for the crazed Pelvis to give a bellow and pound at it with his free fist. The startled reptile skittered away with a snort, pushing a small wave before it. With his feet under him again, Pelvis dragged Flint onward.

Two of the beasts were going at it fang to fang over a chunk of meat, their noisy combat drawing the attention of four or five others. A battle royal erupted, the monsters fighting on all sides of Pelvis and Flint. But more alligators were rising up from the bottom, and others were speeding in to graze past them as if to test how dangerous this particular food might be before they committed their jaws to a bite. Pelvis was single-mindedly pulling Flint toward the pier, while Flint was doing everything he could to keep the alligators away: kicking. slapping the water with the flat of his hand, and shouting gibberish.

But now the alligators were getting bolder. Flint managed to jerk the shoe from his right foot, and he used that to hammer the surface. And suddenly a horrible, thick body with gray mollusks clinging to its hide erupted from the water beside him, a pair of jaws wide open and hissing. Flint slammed his shoe down across the alligator's skull, going for an eye, and the jaws snapped shut. The head whipped to one side and its rough scales flayed the skin off his left arm from wrist to elbow. A mollusk's shell or some growth with a sharp edge did its work as well, and suddenly there was blood in the water.

"Get 'em out! Get 'em out, goddamn it!" somebody shouted.

They had reached the pier's end, which was three feet above the pond. Pelvis, his wig gone and his contorted face brown with mud, was trying to grip the timbers and pull himself up, but not even his maddened strength could do it with Flint on the other cuff. Blood floated on the surface around Flint's arm, and he saw at least four alligators coming across the corral after them, their tails sweeping back and forth with eager delight.

26

To the Edge

T HERE WAS THE RACKET of an electric motor and a chain
rattling. "Grab it! Both of you, grab it!"

The winch's hook and chain had been lowered. Pelvis and
Flint clung to its oversize links as a beggar might grasp hundred-
dollar bills. The motor growled, and the chain began to hoist
them up.

Hands caught them, pulling them onto the pier. Below Flint's
muddy shoe and sock, three alligators slammed their snouts together. They started fighting in the blood-pink foam, and as their
bodies hit the pilings the entire pier trembled and groaned.

But now Flint and Pelvis had solid wood under their feet.
Flint could smell his blood; it was coming from a blue-edged gash
across his left forearm and dripping from his hand to the planks.
He staggered, about to pass out, and he found himself clutching
Pelvis for support. Through a haze he looked at the choppy pond
and saw two alligators battling for something between their jaws
that appeared to be a mud-caked, scruffy bird. It took him a few
seconds to realize it was Pelvis's wig. He watched with a kind of

strange fascination as the two monsters ripped it apart and then each of them submerged with a souvenier of Memphis.

His chest heaving, Pelvis stared slack-jawed at the faces of Doc, Monty, Mitch, and two other men he didn't recognize. Doc was wearing his sunglasses again.

"Crazy as hell, man!" Doc was blasting Monty. "I don't want 'em dead till he sees 'em!"

"Well, shit!" Monty fired back. "How was I supposed to know they were fool enough to jump outta the—"

Flint had felt Pelvis's body tense. He thought of a hurricane about to wreak death and destruction.

Pelvis pulled back his right fist and then drove it forward like a fleshy piston into Monty's nose. With a gunshot *pop* of breaking bones the blood spewed from Monty's nostrils all over Doc's Harvard T-shirt.

Monty staggered back, his eyes wide and amazed and the blood running into his beard as if from a faucet. One step. Two steps.

And onto the corral, right on top of the reptiles fighting below the end of the pier.

"Oh, Jesus!" Doc shouted, blood on the lenses of his sunglasses and spotting his cheeks.

"Monty!" Mitch hollered, and he ran to operate the hook and chain.

But the sense had been knocked out of Monty, and maybe that was for the best because he might have been unaware exactly of his position. One of the other men Pelvis hadn't recognized drew a pistol and started shooting at the alligators, but they had already taken hold of Monty, one with jaws crunched into his left shoulder and another gripping his right leg. The winch's chain came down, but Monty didn't reach for it. The alligators started shaking him the way Pelvis had seen Mama shake one of her teddy bears. He recalled, in his dim cell of thinking at the moment, that the stuffing had come out everywhere.

So, too, it was with Monty.

Now Mitch had pulled his pistol and was firing, too, but the taste of blood and living meat had driven the creatures to a frenzy. More of them were racing over for a share. During the shooting, amid the thrashing bodies and the gory splashing, at least two bullets went into Monty. Maybe he was dead before his bones started to rip from their sockets. Maybe.

Doc didn't want to see any more. He'd known Monty was finished when he went in there, bleeding like that and with the 'gators already so riled up. He'd seen them go after the ranger, so he'd known. He turned away, removed his dark glasses, and slowly and methodically began to wipe the blood off the lenses with a clean part of his T-shirt. His fingers were trembling. Behind him Mitch threw up into the corral.

"Bummer," Doc said, mostly to himself.

He took the handcuff key from his pocket. He unlocked the cuffs and let them fall. Pelvis blinked at him, still dazed but his fury spent. Flint grasped his injured arm and then pitched to his knees, his head hanging.

Doc reached back, drew the .45 from his waistband, cocked it, and laid the barrel between Pelvis's eyes. "You're next," he said. "Walk to the edge."

Pelvis was already brain-blasted; seeing that man eat Mama for breakfast had done him in. He knew what was waiting for him, but without Mama—without his adored companion—life wasn't worth living. He walked to the edge.

Below him was something the alligators were still tearing at. It was getting smaller and smaller. It had a beard.

Doc stood behind him and put the automatic's barrel against the back of his naked head.

"Do it!" Mitch urged. "Put him down!"

Flint tried to stand, but he could not. He was near fainting, the smell of blood and mud and 'gator filth was making him sick, the harsh, hot sun had drained him. He said, "Eisley?" but that was all he could say. He hadn't felt Clint move since they'd come out of the water, but now the arm gave a feeble jerk and Clint's little lungs heaved like a hiccup deep in the folds and passages of Flint's intestines.

Doc put his other hand up to shield his face from flying bits of bone and brain matter. His finger tightened on the trigger.

He heard a gurgling noise.

He looked around, and saw brown water trickling from the mouth on the bizarre baby head that grew from the freak's side.

Flint heard boots clumping on the pier. There was the sound of bare feet on the planks as well.

Doc saw who was coming. He said, "Takin' care of business, Gault. Shondra don't need to see this."

"What's goin' on?" Flint heard a woman's irritated voice ask. A young woman, she sounded to be. "Noise woke us the fuck up. Who was hollerin' so much?"

"Shondra, you best stay put. Monty went in."

The slide of bare feet stopped, but the boots kept walking.

"Bastard here killed him!" Mitch said. "Doc was fixin' to blow his brains out!"

"These are the two from the marina." Doc was talking to whoever wore the boots. "This one got me in the eyes with the spray. One over there shot Virgil."

The boots approached Flint. They stopped beside him, and Flint lifted his head and saw they were made of bleached beige snakeskin.

"Dig that third arm, man. Got a little baby head growin' out his ribs, too. Gen-yoo-ine freak from freak city. I ain't seen nothin' like him since I ate a bag of magic mushrooms in Yuma, spring of 'sixty-eight. Damn, those were the days!"

Shondra gave an ugly snorting sound. "I wasn't even born then."

Doc might have laughed through clenched teeth.

With an effort Flint looked up at the man in the snakeskin boots.

The individual was an exercise junkie. Or a steroid freak. Or maybe he just loved himself a whole lot. Because the muscles of his exposed chest, shoulders, and arms were massive swollen lumps that strained against the tanned flesh, the connecting veins standing out in blood-pumped relief, the visible ligaments as tight as bundles of piano wire. The man wore blue jeans with ripped-out knees, a piece of rope for a belt cinching his narrow waist, and he had a red neckerchief tied loosely around his throat. His face was a hard, chiseled slab of brown rock with a dagger-sharp chin and sunken cheeks, the facial flesh cracked with a hundred deep lines caused by what must have been years of serious sun-worship. The pure ebony of his commanding eyes, his thick black brows, and his curly black hair, the sides swirled with gray, gave him a distinctive Latin appearance. Flint guessed his age at late thirties or early forties, but it was difficult to tell since his body was young but his face was sun-wrinkled.

Standing several yards behind him was a blond girl who couldn't have been older than twenty. She was barefoot, wearing denim cutoffs and a black bra. She, too, appeared to be a slave to the sun, because she was burned a darker brown than the man. Her golden hair cascaded over her shoulders and she had icy blue eyes. Flint thought she was almost beautiful, as beautiful as any Hollywood starlet, but there was an ugly, twisted set to her collagen-plumped lips, and those eyes could burn a hole through metal.

And right now he felt like a little crumpled piece of tin.

The muscle man stared down at Flint with just a hint of interest, as if he might be viewing a particularly creepy insect, but no more than that. Shondra spoke first. "Damn, Gault! Look how *white* he is!"

Gault motioned at Doc with a twirling forefinger. Doc understood the command and lowered the automatic, then said, "Turn around!" to Pelvis.

Pelvis did, his eyes deep-socketed and his face and bald head still painted with ghastly mud.

"This is the fucker thought he was Elvis Presley," Doc said.

Gault's face remained impassive.

"You know who they are? Bounty hunters. Can you believe it? From Shreveport. They had a guy in cuffs back there at St. Nasty. Said at the marina they were callin' the man they work for. Anyway, they were takin' their prisoner in to get a reward. I set the guy loose, figured it was my good deed for the month."

Gault's eyes went to Flint and returned to Pelvis.

"I thought you'd want to see 'em, 'specially the freak. Do you want me to kill 'em now, or what?"

Gault's jaws tensed; muscles that seemed as big as lemons popped up on his face and then receded again. At last his mouth opened. His teeth were unnaturally white. "How much," he said in a voice that had no discernible accent but perfect diction, "were they planning on earning as their reward?"

"Fifteen thousand."

Gault's face settled into stone again. Then, very suddenly, he laughed without smiling. When he did smile, it was a scary thing. He laughed a little louder. "Fifteen thousand!" he said, obviously finding the figure an object of humor. "Fifteen thousand dollars, is that all?" He kept laughing, only it became a low and dangerous sound, like a knife being sharpened. He looked at Shondra and laughed, and she started laughing, then he looked at Doc and laughed and Doc started laughing. Pretty soon it was a real laff riot.

Flint, grasping his wounded forearm and blood still oozing through his fingers, said, "Mind tellin' us what the hell's so funny?"

Gault laughed on for a moment longer, then his smile was abruptly eclipsed. He said, "The pitiful amount of cash that a human being will throw his life away in pursuit of." He reached into a pocket of his jeans with his right hand. Flint heard something click like a trigger being cocked, and he steeled himself for the worst. Then Gault's hand emerged holding one of those spring-loaded wrist exercisers, which he began to squeeze over and over again. "If a man should die, he should die for riches, not petty change. Or for forbidden knowledge. That might be worth dying for. But fifteen thousand dollars? Ha." The laugh was very quiet. "I don't think so." *Click . . . click . . . click* went the springs.

"I don't know what's goin' on here. I don't *care*," Flint said. "Nobody would've gotten hurt if that goon hadn't tried to drown me in a toilet bowl."

Gault nodded thoughtfully. "Tell me," he said. "You were born the way you are, yes? You had no control over the way your chromosomes came together, or how the cells grew. You had no control over your genetics, or what quirk back in your family line caused your situation." He paused for emphasis. "No control," he repeated, as if seeing to the heart of Flint's pain. "You must know, better than anyone could, that God set up tides and winds, and sometimes they take you one way and then blow you the other, and you have no control. I think a tide took you to that marina, and a wind blew you here. What's your name again?"

"His name's Murtaugh," Doc said. "The other one's Eisley."

"I didn't ask you." Gault stared fixedly at the Harvard man. "I asked him. Didn't I?"

Doc said nothing, but he looked stung. He pushed the .45 back into his waistband with the air of a petulant child. "My shows are on. You want me, I'll be watchin' my shows." He trudged back along the pier toward the area that was shaded by the blue-and-white-striped awning. As Doc passed her, Shondra wrinkled her nose as if she smelled something bad.

Gault walked to the pier's edge, where Pelvis still stood. He looked down at what the alligators were whittling to the size of a wallet. His hand worked: *click . . . click . . . click.* Sinews were standing out in the wrist. "All the mysteries, spilled out," he said. His other hand pressed against Pelvis's chest. Pelvis flinched; the man's fingers seemed cold. "Monty always was a glutton. Now look how thin he is. You know, you could stand to lose some weight yourself."

"All right, that's enough." Flint clenched his teeth and tried to stand up. He couldn't make it the first time. He saw Gault grinning at him. Mitch stepped forward and aimed his pistol at Flint's head, but Gault said, "No, no! Let him alone!"

Flint stood up. Staggered, almost fell again. Then he had his balance. It was time to face ugly reality. "If you're gonna kill us—which I guess you are—then how about doin' it humanely?"

The clicking of the springs had ceased. "Are you begging, Mr. Murtaugh?"

"No. I'm askin'." He glanced distastefully at the corral. "A bullet in the head for both of us, how about that?"

"You mean you're not going to stall for time? Try to hold out false hope? Or tell me if I let you go you'll never, never, never speak of this to any soul on earth?"

"It's hot," Flint said. "I'm tired, and I'm about to fall down. I'm not gonna play games with you."

"Don't care to gamble that I might be in a lenient mood today?" Gault lifted his eyebrows.

Flint didn't answer. Don't bite! he told himself. He wants you to bite so he can kick you in the teeth.

"Maybe you're a New Ager?" Gault asked. "You believe in reincarnation, so your death today would be just another rung on the cosmic ladder?"

"I believe in re'carnation," Shondra said. "Gault and me were lovers in . . . you know, that old city that got swallowed up in the sea?"

"Atlantis," Gault supplied. He winked quickly at Flint. "Works every time."

Flint licked his parched lips. "How about some water for us?"

"Oh, I'm forgetting my manners. I was raised better than that. Come on, then. Time for my workout anyway. Shondra, go to the kitchen and get them a pitcher of ice water. Bring me a protein shake. Chop chop." She hurried off obediently, and then Gault motioned for them to follow and started walking toward the awning-shaded area. Flint was weak from his wound and the heat, but he took hold of Pelvis's elbow. "Hang on, all right?" Pelvis, in a state of shock, allowed Flint to guide him after the clumping snakeskin boots, and the other men, their pistols drawn, followed behind.

"Non," Train whispered as he lowered the Ruger, "can't get no clean shot off. Wouldn't he'p 'em none if I could. We gonna have to move in closer."

Dan's heart was slamming, but his mind was calm. He and Train were standing in the chest-deep water seventy yards from the fenced-in alligator corral, at the edge of where the swamp's vegetation had been hacked away. They had gotten over a barbed-wire fence in the water thirty yards behind them, and their hands were cut up some but they would heal. It had been a difficult slog from the Swift boat. Dan felt his strength ebbing fast, but he had to keep pushing himself onward. His father, the quitter, had not raised a quitter.

They'd come out of the underbrush in time to see Flint and Eisley standing on the pier with men holding guns and the muscular, shirtless "boss" Train had spotted on his last visit there. Dan had seen that both the bounty hunters were covered with mud, Eisley had lost his wig, and an aluminum rowboat floated at the center of the 'gator corral. No telling what they'd been through, but at least they were alive. How long that would be was uncertain. Flint and Eisley had just followed the muscle man toward the house, with the other men—the pistol-bearing "soldiers"—behind them.

"Fella up in that watchtower, leanin' back in his chair readin' a . . . ohhhhh, that naughty fella, him!" Train had aimed the Ruger and was looking through the 'scope. "Got a rifle to his side. Walk'em-talk'em on the floor. Pair of binocs." He took his eye away from the lens. "We gonna have to cross the open, get us around that 'gator pen."

"Right."

"Might try to circle 'round the house. Get up on the platform in back. You with me?"

"Yeah."

"Okay. We go, slow and quiet."

"Hey, Gault!" Doc called from his lounge chair in front of a large color television set on metal casters. "Look what's on Oprah today! Talkin' 'bout crack in the grade schools!"

"Chicago?" Gault didn't look at the screen. He was busy pumping iron: a thirty-pound barbell in each hand, his biceps swelling up, veins moving under the skin. A light sheen of sweat glistened on his chest and face.

"No, she's in Atlanta this week."

"The Samchuk brothers'll have that market cornered in three years." Gault kept lifting the barbells up and down with the precision of a machine. "If the Jamaicans don't kill them first."

Sitting a few feet away at a wrought-iron table with a blue glass top, a bloody towel pressed to his forearm wound, Flint had a flash of understanding. "Is that what this is about? Drugs?"

"My business," Gault said. "I supply a demand. It's no big thing."

They were on the platform under the striped awning. Pelvis was sitting across the table from Flint, his hands held to his face. In more chairs arranged around Flint and Pelvis sat Mitch and the two other men with pistols. A walkie-talkie and an Ingram machine gun sat on a white coffee table in front of a sand-colored sofa, along with copies of *House Beautiful, Vogue,* and *Soldier of Fortune* magazines. Flint had seen on closer inspection Gault's own house was not so beautiful; it was a prefab job, and the swamp's humidity had warped the walls like damp cardboard. Some of the joints were splitting apart and had been reinforced with strips of duct tape. *Click . . . click . . . click:* the sound wasn't coming from Gault's squeeze-grip, but from the remote control in Doc's hand. In the five minutes they'd been sitting here, Flint had watched Doc almost incessantly going through what must be hundreds of channels brought in by the satellite dish. Doc would pause to watch quick fragments of things like Mexican game shows, "F Troop," "The Outer Limits," professional wrestling, infomercials with a manic little Englishman running around a studio selling cleaning products, "The Flintstones," MTV videos, ranting, wild-eyed preachers, soap operas, and then the remote control would click rapidly again like the noise of a feeding locust. At the most, Doc had a seven-second attention span.

Flint eased the towel away from his wound and winced at the sight. The gash was four inches long, its ragged blue edges in need of fifty or sixty stitches. An inch and a half lower and an artery would have been nicked. Thick blood was still oozing, and he pressed the towel—which Gault had given him from a hamper beside a rack of free weights—back against the wound.

Doc said, "Hey! It's your man, Flinty! Gault, that's the killer I let go!"

Flint looked at the television set. Doc had paused at CNN to watch gas bombs dispelling a prison riot, and on the screen was either a mug shot or driver's license photo of Dan Lambert. "That's him, right?" He turned the volume up with the remote.

" . . . bizarre turn in the case of Daniel Lewis Lambert, who is being sought in the slaying of a Shreveport, Louisiana, bank loan manager and had also been wanted in connection with the death of an Alexandria motel owner. Under questioning by Alexandria police last night, the slain man's wife admitted it was actually *she* who had beaten her husband to death." A mug shot of a sullen-looking woman with wild red hair came up on the screen. "Hannah DeCayne told police—"

"*Boring!*" Doc changed the channel.

"Wait!" Flint said. "Turn it back!"

"Screw you." "Star Trek" was on now, Kirk and Spock speaking in dubbed Spanish. "Beam me up, Sccccottie!" Doc said excitedly, talking to the television set.

Flint figured the remote control in Doc's head never stopped clicking. He stared at the blue glass of the tabletop, this news another little ice pick from God in the back of his neck. If Lambert had been telling the truth about the motel owner, then was the murder at the bank an accident or an act of self-defense? If Lambert was such a mad-dog killer, why hadn't he picked up the pistol and used it at Basile Park? In spite of the situation, in spite of the fact that he knew he and Pelvis were going to die in some excruciating way after Gault finished his workout, Flint had to laugh. He was going to die because he'd gone south hunting a skin who was basically a decent man.

"Something's funny?" Gault asked, his labor ceasing for the moment.

"Yeah, it is." Flint laughed again; he felt on the verge of tears, but he laughed anyway. "I think the joke's on me, too."

"Who the *fuck* messed up the kitchen?" Shondra, looking both angry and more than a bit queasy, came through an open sliding glass door, carrying a tray with a plastic pitcher, two paper cups, and frothy brown liquid in a milk-shake glass. She set the tray down between Flint and Pelvis. "There's all kinda guts and hair in the garbage can, 'bout made me puke! Blood smeared all over the countertop, and somebody left the fryin' pan dirty! Who the hell did it?"

"Monty," Mitch said. Evidently Shondra's wrath was a thing to be feared.

"Well, what'd he fry? A fuckin' polecat?"

"Fella's dog there." Mitch pointed at Pelvis.

"*Another* one?" Shondra made a disgusted face. "What's wrong with that fool, he's gotta be eatin' dogs and 'coons and polecats?"

"Go ask him, why don't you?" Doc had torn his eyes away from the television. "I'm tryin' to watch 'Dragnet,' if you'll keep it down!"

"You're not watchin' anything, you're just burnin' out that clicker! Gault, why don't you get rid of him? He makes me so nervous, I'm like to jump outta my skin every time he opens that dumb mouth!"

"Yeah?" Doc sneered. "Well, I know the only thing that has to get stuck in your dumb mouth to shut you up! I was with Gault long before you came along, girlie pearlie, and when he throws you out, I'm gonna kick your little ass back to your white-trash trailer!"

"You . . . you . . . you *old man!*" Shondra hollered, and she picked up the milk-shake glass and reared her arm back, froth flying.

"No," Gault said quietly, pumping iron again. "Not that."

She slammed the glass down on the tray, her face a pure image of hell, picked up the plastic pitcher, and flung it at Doc, water splashing everywhere.

"Look what she did!" Doc squalled. "She's tryin' to blow the TV out, Gault!"

"And I'm not cleanin' up that damn mess, neither!" she roared at all of them. "I'm not cartin' that damn stinkin' garbage out and gettin' that mess on me!" Tears of rage and frustration burst from her eyes. "You hear? I'm not doin' it!" She turned and, sobbing, fled back into the house.

"Your Academy Award's in the mail, baby!" Doc shouted after her.

Gault stopped lifting the barbells and put them on the floor. He looked at Flint, smiled wanly, and said with a shrug of his thick shoulders, "Trouble in paradise." Then he drank half of the protein shake, blotted the sweat from his face with the red neckerchief, and said, "Brian, go take the garbage out and clean the kitchen."

"Why do I have to do it?" Brian had neatly cut light brown hair, wore steel-rimmed glasses, and a chrome-plated revolver sat in a holster at his waist. He looked about as old as a college senior, wearing a sun-faded madras shirt and khaki shorts, black Nikes on his feet.

"Because you're the new boy, and because I say so."

"Heh-heh-heh," giggled the Latino man sitting next to him; he wore a Yosemite Sam T-shirt and dirty jeans, his blue-steel Colt automatic in a black shoulder holster.

"You want to laugh, Carlos, you go laugh while you're moppin' the kitchen floor," Gault said. Carlos started to protest, but Gault gave him a deadly stare. "Move *now*."

The two men went into the house without another word.

"I wouldn't let that bitch snow me," Doc said.

"Shut up about her." Gault finished his shake. "I wish you two would bury the hatchet."

"Yeah, she'll bury a hatchet in me if I don't bury one in her first."

"Children, children." Gault shook his head, then he crossed his swollen arms and stared at the two bounty hunters. "Well," he said, "I guess we need to take care of business. What would you think if I'd offer to cut your tongues out and chop your hands off? Would you rather be dead, or not?" He looked at Clint's arm. "In your case, it would be a triple amputation. How does that sound?"

"I think I might faint with excitement," Flint said. Pelvis was mute, his eyes shiny and unfocused.

"It's the best offer I can make. See, I told you I was in a lenient mood. Doc's the one who screwed things up."

"I'll be glad to cut his tongue out and chop off his hands," Flint said.

Gault didn't smile. "Forbidden-knowledge time: we've been having trouble from a competitor. His name is Victor Medina. We were trucking some merchandise in crates when we first moved our base here. He found out the route and took it away from us. So we had to come up with alternative packaging. The stomachs of live alligators do very well."

"I came up with that idea!" Doc announced.

"When Doc saw you making your phone call," Gault went on, "he—unfortunately—lost his composure. He thought you might've been working with Medina, setting up another hijack. Doc doesn't always reason things out. He was stupid, he was wrong, and I apologize. But you put a valuable man out of action. A knee injury like that . . . well, there's no health insurance in this business. A doctor would get very suspicious, and we would have a money leak. So Virgil, like a good horse, was laid to rest and you are to blame. Now Monty is gone. I have to hire new people, run them through security, train them . . . it's a pain. So." He walked to the coffee table and picked up the Ingram machine gun. "I *will* make it quick. Stand up."

"Stand us up yourself," Flint told him.

"No problem. Doc? Mitch?"

"Shit!" Doc whined. "'The Flying Nun's just started!" But he got out of his chair, pulled his gun, and Mitch likewise stood up with a pistol in his hand. Doc hauled Flint to his feet but Mitch struggled with Pelvis and Gault had to help him.

There was fresh sweat on Gault's face. "End of the pier," he said.

27

Too Damn Hot

"THERE, WE GET UP," Train said as he waded chest-deep toward a walkway at the rear of the prefabricated ranch house. Dan followed, not mired quite so deeply as Train because of their difference in heights, but he was giving out and he envied Train's rugged strength. Train slid his rifle up on the walkway, then grabbed the timbers and heaved himself out of the water. He took Dan's Browning and gave him a hand up.

"You all right?" Train had seen the dark circles under Dan's eyes, and he knew it had been a rough trek but the other man was fading fast.

"I'll make it."

"You sick, ain't you." Train wasn't asking a question.

"Leukemia," Dan said. "I can't do it like I used to."

"Hell, who can?" They were standing about eight feet from the rear entrance, which was a solid wooden door behind a screen door. The rear of the house was featureless except for a few small windows. Back here the platform was narrow, but it widened as it continued around the house. Train looked along the walkway they stood on. Behind them was more swamp and a large green metal incinerator on a platform fifty feet from the house. "Okay," Train said. "Look like this the way we go—"

He stopped abruptly. They heard voices from beyond the doors, getting closer. Someone was coming out. Train pressed his body against the wall ten feet away on the right of the door and Dan stood an equal distance away on the left, their rifles ready. Dan's heart pounded, all the saliva dried up in his mouth.

The inner door opened. "Yeah, but I'm not stayin' in the business that long." A young man wearing wire-rimmed glasses, a madras shirt, and khaki shorts emerged, both arms around a Rubbermaid garbage can. On the side of it were streaks of what looked like blood. "I'm gonna make my cash and get out while I can." He let the outer screen door slam shut at his back and he started walking toward the incinerator, a pistol in a holster at his waist.

Train was thinking whether to rush him and club at him with the rifle's butt or push through the screen door when the young man suddenly stopped.

He was looking down at the walkway. At the water and mud on the planks where they'd pulled themselves up. Then he saw the footprints.

And that, as Dan knew Train would've said, was all she wrote.

He spun around. Sunlight flared on his glasses for an instant. His mouth was opening, and then he was dropping the garbage can to go for his gun. "Carlos!" he yelled. "There's somebody out he—"

Train shot him before the pistol could clear leather. The bullet hit him in the center of his chest and he jerked like a marionette and was propelled off the walkway into the water.

A startled Latino face appeared at the screen. The inner door slammed shut. Then: *pop pop pop* went a pistol from inside, and three bullets punched holes through wood and screen. Train started shooting through the door, burning off four more shells. As Train wrenched the magazine out and pushed another one in, Dan fired twice more through the punctured doors, and then Train rushed in and with a kick knocked them both off their hinges.

"Gault! Gault!" the man named Carlos shouted. He had overthrown a kitchen table and was crouched behind it, his pistol aimed at the intruders. Train saw the table, and then a bullet knocked wood from the doorjamb beside his head and he twisted his body and threw himself against the outside wall again. A second shot cracked, the bullet tearing through the air where Train had stood an instant before. "Gault!" Carlos was screaming it now. "They're breakin' in!"

At the sound of the first shot Gault stopped in his snakeskin boots.

He knew what it had been. No doubt.

"Rifle!" Doc said. They were all standing about midway between the awning-shaded area and the alligator corral.

Pop pop pop went a pistol.

"It's Medina!" Mitch shouted. "The bastard's found us!"

"Shut up!" Gault heard more rifle shots. Carlos was shouting his name from the house. His face like a dark and wrinkled skull, Gault turned around and put the Ingram gun's barrel to Flint's throat.

"Gault!" Carlos screamed. "They're breakin' in!"

Two seconds passed. Gault blinked, and Flint saw him deciding to save his ammo for the big boys. "Mitch, stay here with them! Doc, let's go!" They turned and ran along the pier for the house. Mitch leveled his pistol at Flint's chest, just above Clint's arm.

Another pistol bullet thunked into the doorjamb. Train had sweat on his face. Dan shoved his rifle in and fired without aiming, the slug smashing glass. Carlos got off two more rapid-fire shots and then his nerve broke. He stood up and, howling in fear, left the relative safety of his makeshift shield to run for the kitchen door. He was almost there when he slipped on a smear of dog's blood on the linoleum tiles and at the same time Train shot at him. The bullet smacked into the wall as Carlos fell. Carlos twisted around, his gun coming up. Dan pulled the Browning's trigger, blood burst from Carlos's side, and he doubled up and writhed on the floor. As Train ran into the kitchen and kicked Carlos's pistol away, Dan pulled the empty magazine from his rifle and popped in another one.

The next room held a dining table and chairs, a jaguar's skin up as a wall decoration, and a small chandelier hanging from the ceiling over the table's center. A hallway went off to the left, and another room with a pool table and three pinball machines was on the right. Train and Dan started across the dining room, and suddenly Dan caught a movement and a dark-tanned blond girl wearing cutoffs and a black bra emerged from the hallway. Her icy blue eyes were puffy and furious. She lifted her right hand, and in it was gripped an automatic pistol. She let go an unintelligible, hair-raising screech and Train was swinging his rifle at her when the automatic fired twice, booming between the walls. The first bullet shattered glass in one of the pinball machines, but the second brought a cry from Train.

Train's rifle went off, the bullet breaking a window beside the blond girl. Dan had his finger on the trigger and the gun leveled at her, but the idea of killing a woman crippled him for the fastest of seconds. Then the girl scurried back into the hallway again, her hair streaming behind her.

Everything was moving in a blur, time jerking and stretching, the smell of burnt rounds and fear like bitter almonds in the smoky air. Train's cap had fallen off, and he staggered against the wall with his left hand clutched to his right side and blood between his fingers. There was a shout: "Jesus, it's that damn guy!"

Dan saw that two men had come into the game room through another doorway. One he recognized as the long-haired man named Doc, the other was a tanned bodybuilder who had a walkie-talkie in one hand and an Ingram machine gun in the other. Before the muscle man could aim and fire, Dan sent two bullets at them but Doc had already flung himself flat to the floor and at the sight of the rifle the second man—the "boss," Dan remembered Train saying—hurtled behind the pool table.

It was getting too damn hot.

"Go back!" Dan shouted to Train, but Train had seen the Ingram gun and he was already retreating. They both scrambled through the kitchen's entryway two heartbeats before the Ingram gun chattered and the woodwork around the door exploded into flying shards and splinters.

Mitch jumped when he heard the distinctive noise of Gault's gun. He had moved Flint and Pelvis so they were between him and the house, his back to the swamp and the bounty hunters facing him. Flint had seen Gault snatch the walkie-talkie off the coffee table and yell something into it, and then the man in the watchtower—the same one, Flint realized, who'd half strangled him at St. Nasty and had taken the derringer away—had strapped his rifle around his shoulder and started descending a ladder. Now the man was just reaching the walkway between the tower and the house.

Mitch was scared to death. Beads of sweat trickled down his face, his hand with the revolver in it shaking. He kept glancing back and forth from the bounty hunters to the house, wincing at the sounds of shots.

Pelvis suddenly gasped harshly and put a hand to his chest. Mitch's pistol trained on him.

Oh my God! Flint thought. He's havin' another attack!

But Pelvis was looking at something past Mitch's shoulder, his eyes widening. He let out a bawling holler: *"Don't shoot us!"*

Even as Flint realized that was the oldest trick in the book and it could never work in a million years, the terrified Mitch swung around and fired a shot at brown water and moss-covered trees.

Pelvis slammed his fist into the side of Mitch's head and was suddenly all over the man like black on tar. Stunned, Flint just stood there, watching Pelvis beat on him with one flailing fist while the other hand trapped Mitch's gun. Then the revolver went off again, its barrel aimed downward, and Flint got his legs moving and his fists, too. He attacked Mitch with grim fury. Mitch went down on his knees, his facial features somewhat rearranged. Pelvis kept hammering at the man like someone chopping firewood. Mitch's fingers opened, and Flint took the pistol.

Footsteps on the planks. Someone running toward them.

Flint looked, his pulse racing, and there was the man from the watchtower unslinging his rifle. The man, a wiry little bastard in overalls, stopped thirty feet away and fired his rifle from the hip. Flint heard the sound of an angry hornet zip past him. Then it was Flint's turn.

The first bullet missed. The second struck the man in the left shoulder, and the third got him a few inches below the heart. The man's rifle had gotten crooked in his arms, and now his finger spasmed on the trigger and a slug smashed the windshield of one of the cigarette speedboats. Then the man went down on his back on the planks, his legs still moving as if trying to outdistance death. Flint didn't fire the last bullet in the gun. In his mouth was the sharp, acidic taste of corruption; he'd never killed a man before, and it was an awful thing.

Now, however, was not the time to fall on his knees and beg forgiveness. He saw that Pelvis's fists had made raw hamburger out of Mitch's mouth, and Flint seized his arm and said, "That's enough!"

Pelvis looked at him with a sneer curling his upper lip, but he stepped back from Mitch and the half-dead man fell forward to the pier.

They had to get out, and fast. But going through the swamp meant that Clint would surely drown. Flint wanted the derringer back. He ran to the dead man's side, knelt down, and started going through his pockets. His fingers found the derringer, and something else.

A small ring with two keys on it.

Keys? Flint thought. To what?

Flint remembered this man had been driving the cigarette boat that had brought them here. Which of the two boats had it been? The one on the right, not the one with the broken windshield. He didn't know a damn thing about driving a boat, but he was going to have to learn in a hurry. He pushed the derringer into his pocket and stood up. "Cecil!" he yelled. "Come on!"

In the kitchen, the doorway splintered to pieces and blood staining the side of Train's shirt, Dan knew what had to be done.

"Go!" he said. "I'll hold 'em off!"

"The hell with that! Runnin', I ain't!"

"You're dead if you don't. I'm dead anyway. Get out before they come around back."

An automatic fired, the bullet chewing away more of the door frame. The girl was at work again.

"Don't let them get to Arden," Dan said.

Train looked down at his bleeding side. Rib was busted, but he thought his guts were holding tight. It could've been a whole lot worse.

The Ingram gun chattered once more, slugs perforating the walls, forcing Dan and Train to crouch down. Dan leaned out, burned the other two shots in that magazine, and then popped his last four bullets into the Browning.

"Okay," Train said. He put his bloody hand on Dan's shoulder and squeezed. "Us two dinosaur, we fight the good fight, ay?"

"Yeah. Now get out."

"I'm gettin'. *Bonne chance!*" Train ran for the back door, and Dan heard him splash into the swamp.

He was in it for the long haul now. When the automatic fired again, the bullet shattered dishes stacked in a cupboard. Dan heard shots from out front, but surely Train hadn't had time yet to get around the house. Where the hell were Murtaugh and Eisley?

"Come outta there, man!" Doc shouted. "We'll tear down the wall to get you!"

Dan figured his voice was meant to hide the noise of someone—the muscle man, probably—either reloading or crawling across the floor. Dan gave Train six or seven more seconds, then he fired a wild shot through the doorway and took off for the rear. He jumped from the platform into water already chopped up by Train's departure. They'd hear the splash and be after him with a vengeance. He headed directly back into the swamp, through a tangle of vines and floating garbage spilled from the can the young man had dropped. Three steps, and on the fourth his shoe came down on the edge of a root or stump and his ankle twisted, pain knifing up his calf.

Gault had heard the second splash and had gotten up from the floor beside the pool table, ready to storm the kitchen, when there came another noise from out front. The flurry of gunshots had been enough to worry about, but now he heard the rumbling bass notes of one of the cigarette boat's engines trying to fire up. "Get back there after them!" he yelled to Doc. "Try to take one alive!" Then he sprinted for the living room and the sliding glass door that opened onto the platform.

"Can't you get it goin'?" Pelvis was sitting in the white vinyl seat beside Flint, who felt he could have used two more arms to operate the complicated instrument panel.

"Just hang on and be quiet!" The key was turned in the ignition switch, red lights were blinking on some of the gauges, and the engine growled as if it were about to catch, but then it would rattle and die. They had untied the boat's lines, and were drifting from the pier.

Pelvis held the revolver they'd taken from Mitch. He'd seen one bullet remaining in the cylinder. His knuckles were scraped and bleeding; he'd been coming out of his stupor for several minutes before he'd attacked Mitch, the immediacy of their situation having cleared his head of despair for Mama, at least for right now. As Flint struggled to decipher the correct sequence of switches and throttles, Pelvis looked back over his shoulder and his stomach lurched with terror. Gault was coming.

The muscle man had just emerged from the house. He stopped, some of the tan draining from his face at the sight of his two downed associates and the bounty hunters trying to escape in a speedboat. "The Flying Nun" was still playing on the television screen. Gault staggered, as if he were beginning to realize his swamp empire was crumbling; then he came running along the pier, a rictus of rage distorting his face and his finger on the Ingram's trigger.

"Trouble!" Pelvis shouted, and he fired the revolver's last bullet, but it was a wild shot and Gault didn't slow down. Then Gault squeezed off a short burst as he ran, the slugs marching across the pier and chewing holes across the speedboat's stern. "Down!" Flint yelled, frantically trying to start the engine. "Get down!"

Crack, crack! another weapon spoke, and suddenly Gault was gripping his right leg and he stumbled and fell to the planks.

A man neither Flint nor Pelvis had ever seen before had come out from under the pier at the speedboat's bow, and he was standing in the chest-deep water, holding a rifle with a telescopic sight. He fired a third time, but Gault had already crawled over to the far side of the pier and the bullet penetrated wood but not flesh. Then the man shouted to Flint, "I'm drivin'!" and he threw the rifle in and pulled himself over the boat's side, his eyes squeezed shut with pain and effort.

Flint didn't know who the hell he was, but if he could operate this damn boat, he was welcome. He scrambled into the back and picked up the rifle as the man got behind the wheel. "Cover us, you better!" the man yelled; he pulled a chrome lever, hit a toggle switch, and twisted the key. The boat barked oily blue smoke from its exhausts, its engine damaged by the Ingram's bullets. Flint saw Gault getting up on one knee, lifting his weapon to shoot. There was no time to aim through the scope; he started firing and kept firing, and Gault flattened himself again.

The engine boomed, making the boat shake. The rifle in Flint's hands was empty. Gault raised his head. The man behind the wheel grabbed a throttle and wrenched it upward, and suddenly the boat's engine howled and the craft leapt forward with such power Flint was thrown across the stern and almost out of the boat before he could grab hold of a seat back. The man twisted the wheel, a mare's tail of foamy brown water kicking up in their wake. A burst of Ingram bullets pocked the churning surface behind them. The boat tore away toward the bayou, passing the vacant watchtower, as both Flint and Pelvis held on for dear life. Around a bend ahead, blocking the channel, stood a partly submerged pair of gates made of metal guardrails and topped with vicious coils of concertina wire.

Train chopped the throttle back. "Somebody get on the bow!"

Pelvis went, stepping over the windshield as the boat slowed. "You see a way to get that gate open?" Train asked. "Bolt on this side, oughta be!"

"I see it!" The boat's engine was muttering and coughing as Train worked the throttle and gear lever, cutting and giving power until the bow bumped the gate. The bolt, protected by a coating of black grease, was almost down at the waterline. Pelvis lay at the prow and leaned way over; he had to struggle with the bolt for a moment, but then it slid from its latch.

Train gave the engine power, and as Pelvis crawled back over the windshield, the bow shoved the gates apart through bottom mud. He smelled leaking gasoline. The oil gauges showed critical overheating, red caution lights flashing on the instrument panel. "Hang you on!" Train shouted, and he kicked the throttle up to its limit.

Dan heard a pistol shot. Water splashed three feet from his right shoulder.

"Put the rifle down! Drop it or you get dropped!"

Dan hesitated. The next shot almost kissed his ear.

He let the rifle fall into the water.

"Hands up and behind your head! Do it! Turn around!"

Dan obeyed. Standing on the walkway that led between the house's rear entrance and the incinerator were Doc and the girl, both of them aiming their guns at him.

"I saw you on television!" Doc said. His face glistened with sweat, his hair damp with it. His sunglasses had a cracked lens. "Man, how come you want to fuck us up like this? Huh? After I turned you loose?" He was whining. "Is that how you reward a fuckin' good deed?"

"Get up here!" the girl snapped, motioning with her automatic. "Come on, you sonofabitch!"

Dan eased back through the vines, the pain of his injured ankle making him flinch. From the other side of the house there were more shots and the growl of a speedboat's engine. "Where're Murtaugh and Eisley?"

"Get your ass up here, I said!" The girl glanced at Doc. "You turned him loose?"

"Those two bounty hunters had him in handcuffs, back at St. Nasty. Takin' him to Shreveport. I let him go."

"You mean . . . it's 'cause of *you* all this happened?"

"Hey, don't gimme me any shit now, you hear? Come on, Lambert! Climb up!"

Dan tried. He was exhausted, and he couldn't make it.

"I'm not gonna tell you again," the girl warned. "You get up here or you're dead meat."

"I'm dead meat anyway," Dan answered.

"This is true," Doc said, "but you can sure lose a lot of body parts before you pass on from this vale of tears. I'd try to make it easy on myself if I were you."

Playing for time, Dan grasped the planks and tried once more. With an effort of will over muscle, he got his upper body out of the water and lay there, gasping, on the walkway.

"Shit!" the girl said angrily. "You're the damnedest fool in this *world!* How come you didn't kill him and forget about it? Your mind's gettin' senile, ain't it?"

"You'd better shut your mouth." Doc's voice was very quiet.

"Wait till this sinks in on Gault. You wait till he figures out it's your fault all this happened. Then we'll see whose ass gets kicked."

Doc sighed and looked up through the trees at the sun. "I knew this minute would come," he said. "Ever since you horned in, I did. Kinda glad it's here, really." He turned his pistol toward Shondra's head and with a twitch of his trigger finger put a bullet through the side of her skull. She gave a soft gasp, her golden hair streaked with red, and as her knees buckled she fell off the walkway into the swamp.

"I just took out the garbage," he told Dan. "Stand up."

Dan got his knees under him. Then he was able to stand, the sweat streaming off him and his head packed with pain. "Move," Doc said, motioning with the gun toward the house. "Gault!" he hollered. "I got one of 'em alive!"

They went through the destroyed kitchen, the shot-up dining room, and the bullet-pocked game room. Dan limped at gunpoint through a hallway and then entered a living room where there were a few pieces of wicker furniture, a zebra skin on the floor, and a ceiling fan turning. A sliding glass door opened onto the awning-covered platform, where the screen of a large television on wheels was showing a Pizza Hut commercial.

"Oh, Lord!" Doc said.

Gault was on the platform. He was lying propped up by an elbow on his side, a trail of blood between him and the place on the pier from where he'd crawled. The right leg of his jeans was soaked with gore, his hand pressed to a wound just above the knee. Next to him lay his Ingram gun. Sweat had pooled on the planks around his body, his face strained, his ebony eyes sunken with pain and shock.

"Don't touch me," he said when Doc started to reach down for him. "Where's Shondra?"

"He had a pistol hid! Pulled it out and shot her clean through the head! I knew you wanted him alive, that's why I didn't kill him! Gault, lemme help you up!"

"Stay away from me!" Gault shouted. "I don't need you or anybody!"

"Okay," Doc said. "Okay, that's all right. I'm here."

Gault gritted his teeth and pulled himself closer to Dan. The snakeskin boot on his right foot was smeared with crimson. "Yes," he said, his eyes aimed up at Dan with scorching hatred. "You're the man."

"How was I supposed to know he was gonna come here?" Doc squawked. "He's supposed to be a killer, killed two fuckin' men! I thought he'd be grateful!" He ran a trembling hand across his mouth. "We can start over, Gault. You know we can. It'll be like the old days, just us two against the world. We can build it all again. You know we can."

Gault was silent, staring at Dan.

Dan had seen the bodies lying on the pier. The one farther away was still twitching, the nearer one looked to be stone-cold. He saw that one of the speedboats was gone. "What happened to Murtaugh and Eisley?"

"You came here"—Gault was speaking slowly, as if trying to understand something that was beyond his comprehension—"to get two men who were taking you to prison?"

"He must be crazy!" Doc said. "They must've been takin' him to a loony prison!"

"You destroyed . . . no, no." Gault stopped. His tongue flicked out and wet his lips. "You damaged my business for that reason, and that reason alone?"

"I guess that's it," Dan said.

"Ohhhhh, are you going to suffer." Gault grinned, his eyes dead. "Ohhhhh, there will be trials and tribulations for you. Who brought you here?"

Dan said nothing.

"Doc," Gault said, and Doc doubled his fist and hit Dan in the stomach, knocking him to his knees.

Dan gasped and coughed, his consciousness fading in and out.

The next thing he knew, a bloody hand had gripped his jaw and he was face-to-face with Gault. "Who brought you here?"

Dan said nothing.

"Doc," Gault said, and Doc slammed his booted foot down across Dan's back. "I want you to hold him down," Gault ordered. Doc sat on Dan's shoulders, pinning him. Gault pressed his thumbs into Dan's eye sockets, the muscles of his forearms bunching and twisting under the flesh. "I will ask you once more. Then I'll tear your eyes from your head, and I'll make you swallow them. Who brought you here?"

Dan was too exhausted and in too much pain to even manufacture a lie. Maybe it was Train who'd gotten away in the speedboat, he hoped. Maybe Train had had time by now to put the fire to the Swift's furnace and get Arden far away from this hell. He said nothing.

"You poor, blind fool," Gault said almost gently. And then his thumbs began to push brutally into Dan's eye sockets, and Dan screamed and thrashed as Doc held him down.

Suddenly the pressure relaxed. Dan still had his eyes. "Listen!" Gault said. "What's that?"

There came the sound of rolling thunder.

Dan got his eyes open, tears running from them, and tried to blink away some of the haze. Doc stood up. The noise was getting steadily louder. "Engine," Doc said, his pistol at his side. "Comin' up the bayou, fast!"

"Get me another clip!" There was desperation in Gault's voice. "Doc, help me stand up!"

But Doc was backing away toward the television set, his face blanched as he watched the bayou's entrance. Behind him, the Flying Nun was airborne.

Gault struggled to stand, but his wounded leg—the thighbone broken—would not allow it.

With a full-throated snarl, all pistons pumping, Train's armor-plated Baby came tearing past the watchtower, veered, and headed directly at the platform.

Doc starting firing. Gault made a strangling, cursing noise. Dan grinned, and heaved himself up to his knees.

The Swift boat did not slow a single knot, even as bullets pinged off the bow's armor. It hurtled toward the platform, a muddy wake shooting up behind its stern.

Dan saw what was going to happen, and he flung himself as hard and far as he could to one side, out of the Swift's path.

In the next instant Baby rammed the platform and the planks cracked with the noise of a hundred pistols going off. The pilings trembled and broke loose, the entire house shuddering from the blow. But Train kept his fist to the throttle and Baby kept surging forward, ripping through the platform, shattering the sliding glass doors, through the living room, through the prefab walls of Gault's dream house, and bursting out through the other side. Train jammed the engine into reverse and backed the Swift out between the two halves of the house, and as he cleared the broken walls the insides began to fall out: a hemorrhage of animal-skin-covered furniture, brass lamps, faux marble tables, pinball machines, exercise equipment, chairs, and even the kitchen sink.

Dan clung to one half of the platform as it groaned and shivered, the walls of the house starting to collapse into the water. On the other half Doc saw the television set rolling away from him, its plug still connected and the screen still showing the images to which he was addicted. He dropped his pistol, his sunglasses gone and his face stricken with crazed terror. He flung both arms around the television in a desperate embrace, but then the planks beneath his feet slanted as the foundation pilings gave way. The set rolled Doc right into the water, and there was a quick *snap, crackle* and *pop* and his body stiffened, smoke ringing his head like a dark halo before he went under.

"Dan! Dan! Grab my hand!"

It was Arden's voice. She was standing at the bow's railing, reaching for him as the boat began to back away from the splintered wreckage. Dan clenched his teeth, drawing up his last reserves of strength. He jumped off the platform, missing Arden's hand but grabbing hold of the railing, his legs dangling in the water.

"Pull him up! Pull him up!" Train shouted behind the pilothouse's bullet-starred glass.

Something seized Dan's legs and wrenched at him.

The fingers of one hand were pulled from the railing. He was hanging on with five digits, his shoulder about to come out of its socket. He looked back, and there was Gault beneath him, patches of the man's skin and face scorched in a gray, scaly pattern by the electrical shock, frozen nerves drawing his lips into a death's-head rictus, one eye rolled back and showing chalky yellow.

Gault made a hissing noise, the muscles twitching in his arms.

Another arm slid down past Dan's face.

In its hand was a derringer.

The little gun went off.

A hole opened in Gault's throat. Bright red blood fountained up from a severed artery.

Other arms caught Dan and held him. Gault's head rose, his mouth open. His hands loosened and slid down Dan's legs. The muddy, churning water flooded into his mouth and filled up his eyes, then his head disappeared beneath its weight.

Dan was pulled up over the railing. He saw the faces of Murtaugh and Eisley, and then Arden was beside him and there were tears in her beautiful eyes, her birthmark the color of summer twilight. Her arms went around him, and he could feel her heartbeat pounding against his chest.

He put his arms around her, too, and hung on.

Then the darkness swelled up around him. He felt himself falling, but it was all right because he knew someone was there to catch him.

28

Avrietta's Island

D AN OPENED HIS EYES. He was lying on the deck in the shadow of the pilothouse, the engine vibrating smoothly and powerfully beneath him, the blue sky above, the sound of the hull pushing deep water aside.

A wet rag was pressed to his forehead. Arden looked down at him.

"Where are we?" he whispered, hearing his own voice as if from a great distance.

"Train says we're in Timbalier Bay. We're goin' to a place called Avrietta's Island. Here." She'd poured some of the filtered water into the cup of her hand, and she supported his head while he drank.

Someone else—a man without a shirt—knelt beside him. "Hey, ol' dinosaur you. How you doin'?"

"All right. You?"

Train's face had paled, purplish hollows under his eyes. "Been better. Hurtin' a li'l bit. See, I knew bein' ugly as ten miles of bad road's gonna pay off for me someday. That ol' bullet, he say I gettin' in and out mighty quick, this fella so ugly."

"You need to get to a hospital."

"That's where we bound." Train leaned a little closer to him. "Listen, you gonna have to start associatin' with some more regular fellas, you know what I be sayin'? I take one look at that li'l bitty hand and arm movin' 'round on that fella's chest, my mouth did the open wide. Then I look at that li'l bitty head hangin' down, and I like to bust my teeth when I step on my jaw. And that other fella—the quiet one—he look in the face like somebody I seen, but no way can I figure where."

"It'll probably come to you," Dan said. He felt his consciousness—a fragile thing—fading away again. "How'd you get 'em out? The speedboat?"

"*Oui*. Skedaddled outta there, fired up Baby and *huuuuuwheeee!* she done some low-level flyin'."

"You didn't have to come back."

"For sure I did. You rest now, we gonna get where we goin' in twenty, thirty minute." He patted Dan's shoulder and then went away. Arden stayed beside Dan and took one of his hands in hers. His eyes closed again, his senses lulled by the throbbing of the engine, the languid heat, the aroma and caress of the saltwater breeze sweeping across the deck.

They passed through clouds of glistening mist. Sea gulls wheeled lazily above the boat and then flew onward.

"There she is!" Train called, and Arden looked along the line of the bow.

They had gone by several other small islands, sandy and flat and stubbled with prickly brush. This one was different. It was green and rolling, shaded by tall stands of water oaks. There were structures of some kind on it.

As the boat got nearer, Flint stood at the starboard siderail watching the island grow. He was wearing Train's T-shirt because he felt more comfortable with Clint undercover and because the sun had blistered his back and shoulders. Train had come up with a first-aid kit from a storage compartment and Flint's arm wound was bound up with gauze bandages. He had taken off his remaining shoe and his muddied socks and tossed those items overboard like a sacrifice to the swamp. Next to him stood Pelvis, his bald pate and face pink with sunburn. Pelvis hadn't spoken more than a few words since they'd gotten aboard; it was clear to Flint that there was a whole lotta thinkin' goin' on in Pelvis's head.

Train turned the wheel and guided them around to the island's eastern side. They passed spacious green meadows. A herd of goats was running free, doing duty as living lawn mowers. There was an orchard with fruit trees, and a few small white-washed clapboard buildings that looked like utility sheds. And then they came around into a natural harbor with a pier, and there it was.

Flint heard himself gasp.

It stood on the green and rolling lawn, there on a rise that must have been the island's commanding point. It was a large, clean white mansion with multiple chimneys, a fieldstone path meandering between water oaks, and weeping willow trees from the harbor to the house. Flint's heart was racing. He gripped the rail, and tears burned his eyes.

It was. It was. Oh God, oh Jesus it was . . .

not.

He realized it in another moment, as they approached the pier. There was no stained-glass window in front. The house of his birth had four chimneys; this one had only three. And it wasn't made of white stone, either. It was clapboard, and the paint was peeling. It was an old antebellum mansion, a huge two-storied thing with columns and wide porches. The rolling emerald-green lawn was the same as in his dreams, yes. A few goats were munching the blades down. But the house . . . no.

He still had a star to follow.

"Mr. Murtaugh?" Pelvis said in a voice that was more Cecil's than Elvis's. "How come you're cryin'?"

"I'm not cryin'. My eyes are sunburned, that's all. Aren't yours?"

"No."

"Well," Flint said, and he rubbed the tears away. "Mine are."

Train had cut their speed back. The engine was rumbling quietly as they drew closer. So far they'd seen no one. Arden had left Dan to stand at the bow, the breeze blowing through her hair, her eyes ashine with hope. In her right hand was gripped the pink drawstring bag with her little plastic horses in it.

"I been wonderin'," Pelvis said. " 'Bout what you offered."

"And what was that?" Flint knew, but he'd been shrinking from the memory.

"You know. 'Bout you bein' my manager and all. I sure could use somebody to help me. I mean, I don't know how successful I could be, but—"

"Chopin you're not," Flint said.

"He's dead, ain't he? Both him and Elvis. Dead as doornails." He sighed heavily. "And Mama's dead, too. It's gonna take me awhile to get over that one. Maybe I never will, but . . . I figure maybe it's time for Pelvis to be put to rest, too."

Flint looked into the other man's face. It was amazing how much more intelligent he looked without that ridiculous wig. Dress him up in a nice suit, teach him how to talk without mangling English, teach him some refinements and manners, and maybe a human being of worth would come out of there. But then, it would be an almost impossible task, and he already had a job as a bounty hunter. "I don't know, Cecil," Flint said. "I really don't."

"Well, I was just askin'." Cecil watched the pier approach. "You gonna take Lambert back to Shreveport?"

"He's still a killer. Still worth fifteen thousand dollars."

"Yes sir, that might be true. 'Course, if you decided here pretty soon you wanted to like . . . give it a try at bein' my manager, helpin' me get on a diet and get some work and such, then you wouldn't be a bounty hunter anymore, would you?"

"No," Flint said softly. "I guess I wouldn't." A thought came to him, something the man at the cafe in St. Nasty had said, speaking about Cecil: *Hell, I'll be his manager, then. Get out of this damn swamp and get rich, I won't never look back.*

384 / Robert McCammon

Maybe he could walk away, he thought. Just walk away. From Smoates, from the ugliness, from the degradation. He still had his gambling debts and his taste for gambling that had gotten him so deep in trouble over the years. He couldn't exactly walk away from those things—those faults—but if he had a purpose and a plan, he could work them out eventually, couldn't he?

Maybe. It would be the biggest gamble of his life.

He found himself stroking his brother's arm through the T-shirt. Clint was as famished as he was. As tired, too. He was going to sleep for a week.

Get out of this damn swamp and get rich, I won't never look back.

He had never been able to get out before, he realized, because he'd never had anything to go to. What if . . . ? he wondered.

What if?

Maybe those two words were the first steps out of any swamp.

"Comin' close!" Train called. "Jump over and tie us up, fellas!"

As Flint and Cecil secured the lines to cleats, Train stepped onto the pier and walked to an old bronze bell supported on a post ten feet high. He grasped the bell's rope and began to ring it, the notes rolling up over the green lawn and through the trees toward the white house on the hill.

In just a few seconds three figures came out of the house and began to hurry down the path.

They were nuns, wearing white habits.

"Sister Caroline, I sure'nuff got some hurt people here!" Train said to the one in the lead as they reached the pier.

"Got a fella with a hurt leg, one with an arm needs lookin' at. And I *do* mean lookin' at. Believe I could use a Band-Aid or two myself, ay?"

"Oh, Train!" She was a sturdy woman with light brown eyes. "What's happened to you?"

"Gonna tell you all 'bout it later. Can you put us up?"

"We always have room. Sister Brenda, will you help Train to the house?"

"No, no, my legs ain't broke!" Train said. "Tend to that man lyin' there!"

Two of the nuns helped Arden get Dan up on his feet. Sister Caroline rang the bell a few more times, and two more nuns emerged to answer the call.

"What is this place?" Arden asked Sister Caroline as Dan was taken off the boat.

The other woman paused, staring at the birthmark. Arden moved so their eyes met. "This island is the convent of the Order of the Shining Light," Sister Caroline answered. "And that"—and she nodded at the white mansion—"is the Avrietta Colbert Hospital. May I ask your name?"

"It's Arden Halliday."

"From?"

"Fort Worth, Texas." Arden turned to Train. "I thought you told me the Bright Girl lived here!"

"The Bright . . . oh, I see." Sister Caroline nodded, glancing from Arden to Train and back again. "Well, I prefer to think we are all bright . . . uh . . . women." She gave Train a hard stare. "Does she know?"

"*Non.*"

"Know what?" Arden asked. "What's goin' on?"

"We shall see," Sister Caroline said flatly, and she turned away to direct the others.

Dan was being walked up the path supported between two nuns, one a young girl maybe twenty-three, the other a woman in her fifties. The shadows of the oak and willow trees were deliciously cool, and a quartet of goats stood watching the group of pilgrims pass.

"Just a minute," someone said, beside Dan.

The nuns stopped. Dan turned his head and found himself face-to-face with Flint Murtaugh.

Flint cleared his throat. He had his arms crossed over his chest, in case Clint made a spectacle of himself. These fine ladies would get a shock soon enough. "I want to thank you," Flint said. "You saved our lives."

"You did the same for me."

"I did what I had to."

"So did I," Dan said.

They stared at each other, and Flint narrowed his eyes and looked away, then returned his cool blue gaze to Dan. "You know what I ought to do."

"Yeah." Dan nodded. Everything was still blurry around the edges; all of this—the morning's events, Gault's stronghold, the gun battle, the Swift severing of the house in two, this green and beautiful island—seemed like bits and pieces of a strange dream. "Tell me what you're *gonna* do."

"I think—" Flint paused. He had careful considerations to make. He held a man's future in the balance: his own. "I think . . . I'm gonna get out of this damn swamp," he said. "Pardon me, Sisters." He looked up the path at the man walking alone. "Cecil, can I talk to you, please?" He left Dan's side, and Dan saw Murtaugh put his hand on Eisley's shoulder as they began to walk together.

The closer they got to the house, the more in need of repair Dan saw it was. He counted a half-dozen places where rainwater must be leaking through loose boards. A section of porch railing on the first floor was rotten and sagging, and several of the columns were cracked. The place needed repainting, too, otherwise the salt breeze and the damp heat would combine to break down the wood in a very short time. He bet the old house had termites, too, chewing at the foundation.

They needed a carpenter around here, is what they needed.

Dan tried to put weight on his injured ankle, but the pain made him sick to his stomach. He was getting dizzy again, and his head was pounding. The blurred edges of things got still more blurry. He was about to give out, and though he fought it, he knew the sickness eventually had to win.

"Sisters?" he said. "I'm sorry . . . but I'm real near passin' out."

"Train!" the older one shouted. "Help us!"

As Dan's knees buckled and the darkness rushed up at him once more, he heard Train say, "Got him, ladies." Dan felt himself being lifted over Train's shoulder in a fireman's carry before he passed out completely, and Train—weak himself but unwilling to let Dan hit the ground—took him the last thirty yards to the house.

Late afternoon had come.

Arden was freshly showered and had slept for five solid hours in a four-poster bed in the room Sister Caroline had brought her to, on the antebellum mansion's first floor. Before her shower another nun about Arden's age had brought her a lunch of celery soup, a ham salad sandwich, and iced tea. When Arden had asked the young woman if the Bright Girl lived here, the nun had given her a tentative smile and left without a word.

On the way to this room they'd passed through a long ward of beds. Most of the beds were in use. Under ceiling fans and crisp white sheets lay some of the patients of the Avrietta Colbert Hospital: a mixture of men, women, and children, white, black, and Latino. Arden had heard the rattling coughs of tuberculosis, the gasping of cancerous lungs, the slow, labored breathing of people who were dying. The nuns moved around, giving what comfort they could. Some patients were getting better, sitting up and talking; for others, though, it seemed the days were numbered. Arden heard a few Cajun accents, though certainly not all the patients were of that lineage. She was left with the impression that this might be a charity hospital for the poor, probably from the Gulf Delta area, and that the patients were there because no mainland hospital would accept them or—in the case of the elderly ones who lay dying—waste time on them.

The same young nun brought Arden a change of clothes: a green hospital gown and cotton slippers. Not long after she'd awakened there'd been a knock at the door, and when she'd opened it there stood a tall, slim man who was maybe in his mid-sixties, wearing a pair of seersucker trousers, a rumpled white short-sleeve shirt, and a dark blue tie. He'd introduced himself in a gentle Cajun accent as Dr. Felicien, and he'd sat down in an armchair and asked her how she was feeling, was she comfortable, did she have any aches or pains, things like that. Arden had said she was still tired but otherwise fine; she'd said she had come here to find the Bright Girl, and did he know who she meant?

"I most think I do," Dr. Felicien had said. "But I gonna have to beg off and leave that for later. You try to get yourself some more sleep now, heah?" He'd gone without answering any further questions.

A fan turned above her bed. Her window looked out toward the Gulf, and she could see waves rolling in. Shadows lay across the lawn. She had figured this room belonged to a doctor or someone else on the staff. When she went in the small but spotless bathroom to draw water from the faucet into a Dixie cup, she looked at her face in the mirror, studying her birthmark as she had a thousand times before.

She was very, very scared.

What if it had been a lie? All along, a lie? Maybe Jupiter hadn't been lying, but he'd just been plain wrong. Maybe he'd seen a young and pretty blond woman in LaPierre when he was a little boy, and maybe later on he'd heard the myths about a Bright Girl—a faith healer who could cheat time itself—and he'd mixed up one with the other? But if there *was* a Bright Girl, then who was she, *really?* Why had Train brought her here, and what was going on?

She lifted her hand and ran her fingers along the edges of her birthmark. What would she do, she asked herself, if this mark—this bad-luck stain that had ruined her life—had to remain on her face for the rest of her days? What if there was no magic healing touch? No ageless Bright Girl who carried a lamp from God inside her?

Closing her eyes, Arden leaned her face against the mirror. She'd felt she was so close. So very close. It was a cruel trick, this was. Nothing but a cruel, cruel trick.

Someone knocked at the door. Arden went to open it, thinking that it was probably Dr. Felicien with more questions or the young nun.

She opened the door and the face that looked at her both startled and horrified her.

It belonged to a man. He had neatly combed sandy-brown hair on the right side of his head, but on the left side there were just tufts of it. A terrible burn and the subsequent healing process had drawn the skin up into shiny parchment on that left side, his mouth twisted, the left eye sunken in folds of scar tissue. The left ear was a melted nub and the man's throat was mottled with burn scar. His nose, though scarred, had escaped the worst of the damage, and the right side of his face was almost untouched. Arden stepped back, her own face mirroring the shock she felt, but at once that feeling changed to shame. If anybody understood what it meant to look at someone shrink away from you in a display of ill manners and idiocy, it was she.

But if the man was bothered by her reaction, he didn't show it. He smiled. He was wearing dark blue pants, a blue-striped shirt, and a bow tie. "Miss Halliday?"

Arden remembered she'd told Dr. Felicien she was unmarried.

"She wants to see you," the burn-scarred man said.

"She? *Who?*"

"Oh, I'm sorry. I forget that everybody 'round here doesn't know her name. Miz Kathleen McKay. I believe she's who you've come to find."

"She's—" Arden's heart slammed. "She's the Bright Girl?"

"Some would call her that, I 'magine. If you'd like to come with me?"

"Yes! I would! Just a minute!" She crossed the room and got the little pink bag from atop a dresser.

On the way out they went through another ward toward the rear of the hospital, and in passing the man spoke to the patients, calling their names, giving some encouragement, throwing a joking remark here and there. Arden couldn't help but see how the patients—even the very, very sick ones—perked up at this man's presence. She saw their faces, and she saw that not one of them flinched or showed any degree of distaste. It dawned on her that they didn't see his scars.

Arden followed him away from the house and along another fieldstone path that led toward a grove of pecan trees. "I hear you had a time findin' us," the man said as they walked.

"Yes, I did." She figured Dr. Felicien or somebody had gotten the whole story from either Dan or Train.

"That's a good sign, I think."

"It is?"

"Surely," he said, and he smiled again. "It's not far, right through here." He led her under a canopy of interlocking tree branches, and just on the other side was a small but immaculately kept white clapboard house with a screened-in front porch. Off to one side was a flower garden, and a plot of vegetables as well. Arden felt faint as the man walked up the front steps and opened the door to the screened porch.

He must have noticed her condition, because he said, "Are you all right?"

"I'm fine. Just a little light-headed."

"Breathe deep a few times, that oughta help."

She did, standing at the threshold. And suddenly she realized who this fire-scarred man must be. "What's . . . what's your name?" she asked.

"Pearly Reese."

She had known it, but still it almost knocked her knees out from under her. She remembered the prostitute at the cafe in St. Nasty saying that the Bright Girl was an old woman who *came to Port Fourchon to see my mama's cousin. His name was Pearly, he was seven years old when he got burned up in a fire. Near thirty years ago,* she'd said. *The Bright Girl took him with her in a boat.*

"Do you know me?" Pearly asked.

"Yes I do," she said. "Your second cousin helped me get here."

"Oh." He nodded, even if he didn't quite understand. "I think that must be a good sign, too. You ready to meet her?"

"I am," Arden said.

He took her inside.

29

The Bright Girl

ONCE INSIDE THE DOOR, Pearly called, "Miz McKay? I brought her!"

"Come on back, then! I know I look a fright, but come on back anyway!"

It had been the raspy voice of an old woman, yes. Dan had been right, Arden realized as the first hard punch of reality hit her. There was no such thing as a woman who could stay young forever. But even if Jupiter had been mistaken about that part of it, the Bright Girl could still have the healing touch in her hands. She was terrified as she followed Pearly through a sitting room, a short hallway, and then into a bedroom.

And there was the Bright Girl, propped up on peach-colored pillows in bed. Sunlight spilled through lace-curtained windows across the golden pine-plank floor, and above the bed a ceiling fan politely murmured.

"*Oh,*" Arden whispered, and as tears came to her eyes her hand flew up to cover her mouth so she wouldn't say something stupid.

The Bright Girl was, indeed, an elderly woman. Maybe she was eighty-five, possibly older. If her hair had ever been blond, it was all snow now. Her face was heavily lined and age-spotted, but even so, Arden could tell that in her long-ago youth this woman had been lovely. She was wearing a white gown, and now she reached to a bedside table for a pair of wire-rimmed eyeglasses. The movement was slow, and her mouth tightened with pain. The fingers of her hand were all twisted and malformed, and she had difficulty picking the glasses up. At once Pearly was at her side, but he didn't put the glasses on her face for her. He steadied her hand so her gnarled fingers could do the work. Then she got the glasses on, and Arden saw that behind the lenses there was still fire in the Bright Girl's pale amber eyes. Like lamps, Arden thought. Like shining lamps.

"Sit." The Bright Girl lifted her other hand, the fingers just as twisted, and motioned toward a flower-print armchair that had been turned to face the bed. The elderly woman's voice trembled; either from palsy or being nervous, Arden didn't know. Arden sat down, her hands clutching the pink bag in her lap, her heart galloping.

"Lemonade," the Bright Girl said. Her breathing, too, looked painful. "Want a glass?"

"I . . . think I would."

"I can put a shot of vodka in it for you." The Bright Girl, surprisingly, had a midwestern accent.

"Uh . . . no. Just lemonade."

"Pearly, would you? And I *will* take a shot of vodka in mine."

The two women were silent. The Bright Girl stared at Arden, but Arden wasn't sure where to park her eyes. She was so glad to have found this person, so glad to finally be there, but she was feeling a crush of disappointment, too. The Bright Girl wasn't who Jupiter had said she was. The Bright Girl could not cheat time, and she wasn't a faith healer. If she had a healing touch, then why hadn't she been able to smooth the scars on Pearly's face? Tears burned Arden's eyes again; they were the bitter tears of knowing she had been wrong.

The Bright Girl—at least the time-cheating, never-aging, faith-healing part of her—was a myth. The truth was that the Bright Girl was a rather small, frail, white-haired eighty-five-year-old woman who had gnarled fingers and labored breathing.

"Don't cry," the Bright Girl said.

"I'm all right. Really." Arden wiped her eyes with the back of her hand. "I'm—" She stopped. The floodgates were about to burst. It had all been wrong. It had been a cruel, cruel trick.

"Go ahead if you want to cry. I cried my eyes out, too, that first day."

The tears had begun trickling down Arden's cheeks. She sniffled. "What do you mean . . . *you* cried, too?"

"When I came here and found out." She paused, her breathing strained. "Found out the Bright Girl couldn't just put her hands on me and take it all away."

Arden shook her head. "I'm not . . . I don't understand. Take what away?"

The old woman smiled slightly. "The pain. The Bright Girl couldn't heal me of the pain. That I had to do for myself."

"But . . . *you're* the Bright Girl, aren't you?"

"I'm *a* Bright Girl."

"Are you . . . are you a nun?"

"*Me*, a nun? Unh-unh! I raised too much hell when I was a young girl to be a nun now! The thing is, I enjoyed raising hell. Seeing my father"—again, she had to pause to regulate her breathing—"squirm when the police brought me home. We didn't get along so very well."

Pearly came in, bringing a plain plastic tray with two jelly-jar glasses of lemonade. "Take this one," he said, giving Arden a glass, "unless you want your head knocked off. Miz McKay likes the occasional libation."

"I wish you would *quit* that! Over thirty damn years," she said, speaking to Arden, "and he still calls me *Miz* McKay! Like I'm some weak little old flower that just slumps in the"—a breath, a breath—"slumps in the noonday sun! My name is *Kathleen!*"

"You know I was raised to respect my elders. Don't drink that down too fast, now."

"I'll gulp it in a second if I want to!" she snapped, but she didn't. "Let us be alone now, Pearly. We have to talk."

"Yes ma'am."

"There he goes with that southern-fried crap again! Go out and pee on the flowers or something!"

Pearly left the room. The Bright Girl gripped her glass with both hands, drew it to her wrinkled mouth, and sipped. "Ahhhh," she said. "That's better." She glanced up at the ceiling fan that turned above them. "I never could get used to this heat down here. For a time I thought I couldn't stand it, that I was going to have to get back"—a breath, then another—"to Indiana. That's where I'm from. Evansville, Indiana. You said you're from Fort Worth?"

"Yes."

"Well, that's good, then. Hot in Texas, too." She sipped her vodka-laced lemonade again. "That's some birthmark you've got there."

Arden nodded, not knowing how to respond.

"You came here to be healed, didn't you?"

"Yes."

"And now you're sitting there thinking you're the biggest. Biggest fool who ever put on panties. You came down here to be healed by a young, pretty girl who never ages. Who people say lives forever. You didn't come here to"—breathing again, her lungs making a soft hitching noise—"listen to an old woman spit and snort, did you?"

"No," Arden had to admit. "I didn't."

"I came to be healed, too. My 'condition,' as my father put it"—she nodded toward a walker by the bed—"used to be able to get around on a cane, but . . . I can hardly stand up on the walker now. I've had severe arthritis since I was a young girl. About your age, maybe younger. My father was from old money. The family's in banking. Very social dogs, they are. So when the lovely daughter can't dance on her crippled"—a pause—"crippled legs at the social events, and when the white gloves won't slip over her twisted fingers, then. Then the specialists are called. But when the specialists can't do very much, then lovely daughter becomes a pariah. Lovely daughter spends more and more time alone, growing bitter. Drinking. Screwing any boy who. Boy who'll have her. Lovely daughter has several ugly public scenes. Then one day lovely daughter is told she will have a companion, to watch her and keep her out of trouble. Being enlightened bastards, we have hired a sturdy, nonthreatening woman of color who doesn't. Doesn't know what she ought to be being paid." Kathleen McKay drank from the glass once more, her gnarled fingers locked together. "That woman of color . . . was born in Thibodoux. That's about fifty miles up Highway One from Grand Isle. We used to share a bottle of Canadian Club, and she told me wonderful stories."

Arden said, "I still don't under—"

"Oh, yes, you do!" Kathleen interrupted. "You understand it all! You just don't want to let. Let go of the illusion. I've been sitting right where you are, talking to an old, used-up, and dying woman. In this very bed. Her name was Juliet Garrick, and she was from Mobile, Alabama. She had one leg three inches shorter than the other. The one before her . . . well, I don't remember. Some wicked deformity or another, I'm sure. Are you positive you don't want a shot of vodka?"

"I'm sure," Arden said. Her heart had stopped pounding, but her nerves were still raw. "How many . . . how many Bright Girls have there been?"

"Cemetery's not far. You can go count for yourself. But I think the first two were buried at sea."

Arden still felt like crying. She felt like having a cry that would break the heart of the world. Maybe she would, later. But not right now. "Who was the first one?"

"The woman who founded the hospital. Avrietta Colbert. Her journals and belongings and things are in a museum between the chapel and where the sisters live. Interesting, gutsy lady. Strong-willed. Before the Civil War she was on a ship with her husband, sailing from South America to New Orleans. He was a rancher. Wealthy people. Anyway, not far from here a storm blew up and smashed their ship. Smashed their ship in these barrier islands. She washed up here. The legend goes that she vowed to God she would build a church and hospital for the poor on the first island that would have her. This one did, and she did. There's a photograph of her over there. She was a beautiful young blond woman. But her eyes . . . you can tell she had fire in her."

Arden sighed. She lowered her head and put a hand to her face.

"The sisters came here sometime in the forties," Kathleen went on. "They manage the place, pay the staff, make sure all that work's done." She finished her lemonade and very carefully put the glass down on the bedside table. "All of us—the Bright Girls, I mean—came from different places, for different reasons. But we all have shared one very, very important thing."

Arden lifted her head, her eyes puffy and reddened. "What's that?"

"We believed," Kathleen said. "In miracles."

"But it was a lie. It was always a lie."

"No." Kathleen shook her white-crowned head. "It was an illusion, and there's a difference. What the Bright Girl could do— what she was—became what people wanted to believe. If there is no hope, what reason is there to live? A world without miracles . . . well, that would be a world I wouldn't care to live in."

"*What* miracles?" Arden asked, a little anger creeping in. "I don't see any miracles around here!"

Kathleen leaned forward, wincing with the effort. Her cheeks and forehead had become blushed with anger, too; she was a scrapper. She said three short, clipped words: "Open. Your. Eyes."

Arden blinked, surprised by the strength in the old woman's voice.

"No, you can't get your birthmark healed here! Just like I couldn't get my arthritis healed, or Juliet Garrick couldn't get her short leg lengthened! That's junk! But what's not junk"—a breath, a breath, a breath—"not junk is the fact that I can walk through those wards. Through those wards, hobbling on my walker. I can walk through them and people who are dying sit up they sit up in their beds and they smile to see me and for"—a gasp—"for a few minutes they have an escape. They smile and laugh as if they've touched the sun. For a few precious, precious minutes. And children with cancer, and tuberculosis, and AIDS, they come out of their darkness to reach for my hand, and they hold on to me. On to me like I am *somebody,* and they don't mind my ugly fingers. They don't see that Kathleen McKay of Evansville, Indiana, is old and crippled!" Her eyes were fierce behind the glasses. "No, they hold on to the Bright Girl."

She paused, getting her breath again. "I don't lie to them," she said after a moment or two. "I don't tell them they can beat their sicknesses, if Dr. Felicien or Dr. Walcott don't say so first. But I have tried—I have *tried*—to make them understand the miracle the way I and Sister Caroline see it. That flesh is going to die, yes. It's going to leave this world, and that's the way life is. But I believe in the miracle that though flesh dies, the spirit does not. It goes on, just like the Bright Girl goes on. Though the women who wear that title wither and pass away, the Bright Girl does not. She lives on and on, tending to her patients and her hospital. Walking the wards. Holding the hands. She lives on. So don't you *dare* sit there with your eyes closed and not look at what God is offering to *you!*"

Arden's mouth slowly opened. "To . . . me?"

"Yes, you! The hospital would survive without a Bright Girl— I guess it would, I don't know—but it would be. Be terribly changed. All the Bright Girls over the many years have held this place together. And it's not been easy, I'll tell you! Storms have torn the hospital half to pieces, there've been money problems, equipment problems, troubles keeping the. The old buildings from falling apart. It's far from perfect. If there wasn't a Bright Girl to solicit contributions, or fight the oil companies who want to start drilling. Drilling right offshore here and ruin our island. Keep our patients awake all night long, where would we be?"

She closed her eyes and leaned her head back against the pillow. "I don't know. I *do* know . . . I don't want to be the last one. No. I won't be the one who breaks the chain." She sighed, and was silent with her thoughts. When she spoke again, her voice was low and quiet. "The Bright Girl can't be any damn pushover. She's got to be a fighter, and she's got to do the hard work as best she can. Most of all"—Kathleen's eyes opened—"she can't be afraid to take responsibility."

Arden sat very still, her hands gripping the drawstring bag.

"Maybe you're not the one. I don't know. Damn, I'm tired. Those sisters over there, praying and praying at the chapel. I told them. I said if she's coming, she'll be here. But maybe you're not the one."

Arden didn't know what to say. She stood up from her chair, but she didn't know where to go, either.

"If you stayed," Kathleen said, "if you did what had to be done . . . I could promise you no one here would even see that birthmark. It would be gone. They'd see only the face behind it."

Arden stood in a spill of light, caught between what was and what could be.

"Go on, then." Kathleen's voice was weary. "There's a radio at the hospital. The ferry can get here from Grand Isle in half an hour. I know the man who owns the marina. He can find a ride out for you, take you up Highway One to Golden Meadow. Catch the bus from there. Do you have money?"

"No."

"Pearly!" Kathleen called. *"Pearly!"* There was no response. "If he's not outside, he's probably walked along the path to the barn. Go over there and tell him I said to give you fifty dollars and call the marina for you."

"The barn?" Arden's heart was pounding again. "What's . . . in the barn?"

"Horses, of course! Those things have always scared the skin off me, but Pearly loves them. I told him, when one of them kicks him in the head one day, he won't spend so much time over there."

"Horses," Arden whispered, and at last she smiled.

"Yes, horses. Avrietta Colbert's husband was a rancher. They were bringing horses back from South America on their ship. Some of the horses swam here, those started the herd. We raise and sell them, to make money for the hospital." Kathleen frowned. "What's wrong?"

Arden's eyes had filled with tears. She couldn't speak, her throat had clutched up. Then she got it out: "Nothing's wrong. I think . . . I think everything's right."

She was crying now, and she was half blind. But she realized at that moment that never before had she seen so much, or so clearly.

He was sitting in a chair on the upper porch, the blue shadows of twilight gathering on the emerald lawn. A crutch leaned against the railing beside him. He was watching the sun slide toward the Gulf, and he was thinking about what had happened an hour ago.

The ferryboat had come from Grand Isle. He'd been sitting right there, watching. Two men and Sister Caroline had left the hospital, walking down the path to the pier. One of the men was bald and fat, but he walked with his shoulders back as if he'd found something to be proud of about himself. The other man, tall and slim and wearing a dark suit and a new pair of black wingtips someone on the staff had brought him yesterday from the mainland, had stopped short of getting aboard the ferry and had looked back.

Dan had stared at Flint Murtaugh, across the distance.

Nothing had remained to be said. They'd still been cautious around each other during the last three days, both of them knowing how much he was worth as a wanted fugitive. Dan figured the idea of all that money still chewed at Murtaugh, but the fact that

Dan had gone after them when he could have cut and run was worth much, much more.

Then Murtaugh had turned away and stepped onto the ferryboat. Sister Caroline had waved to them as the boat's lines were cast off. Dan had watched the boat get smaller and smaller as it carried Eisley and Murtaugh onward to the rest of their lives. He wished them well.

"Hey, ol' dinosaur, you. Mind if I plop?"

"Go ahead."

Train had walked out onto the porch. He drew a wicker chair up beside Dan and eased himself into it. He was still wearing a green hospital gown, much to his displeasure. His bullet wound—a grazed gash and a broken rib—was healing, but Dr. Walcott had insisted he stay for a while. It had been two days since Dan had seen Arden, whom he'd caught a glimpse of from the window beside his bed, walking around the grounds with Sister Caroline. Arden hadn't been at lunch in the hospital's small cafeteria, either. So something was definitely going on, and he didn't know if she'd found her Bright Girl or not. One thing was for sure: she still wore her birthmark.

"How the leg feel?"

"It's gettin' along. Dr. Felicien says I almost snapped my ankle."

"Hell, you coulda done worse, ay?"

"That's right." Dan had to laugh, though he would see Gault's mottled face in his nightmares for a long time to come.

"Yeah. You done good, leatherneck. I won't never say no more bad tings 'bout marines."

"I didn't know you ever said anything bad about marines."

"Well," Train said, "I was gettin' to it."

Dan folded his hands across his chest and watched the waves rolling in and out. When the breeze blew past, he saw some paint flake off the sun-warped railing. This was a peaceful place, and its quiet soothed his soul. There were no televisions, but there was a small library down on the first floor. He felt rested and renewed, though he couldn't help but notice there was a lot of carpentry work needed on the aging structure. "How long have you known about this place?"

"Years and years. I bring 'em cat and turtle. Who you tink carted the goats here from Goat Island?"

"Did you tell 'em about me?" he had to ask.

"Sure I did!" Train said. "I told 'em you was a fine ol' fella."

Dan turned his head and looked into Train's face.

"Ain't it true?" Train asked.

"I'm still a wanted killer. They're still lookin' for me."

"I know two men who ain't. They just got on the boat and gone."

Dan leaned forward and rested his chin on his hands. "I don't know what to do, Train. I don't know where to go."

"I could put you up for a while."

"In that houseboat? You need space just like I do. That wouldn't work."

"Maybe no." Both of them watched a freighter in the shimmering distance. It was heading south. Train said, "The steamers and workboats, they come in, unload, and load again at Port Sulphur. Ain't too very far ways from here. Some of them boats lookin' for crew. You up to workin'?"

"I think I could handle some jobs, if they weren't too tough."

"I tink you could, too. Maybe you take some time, decide for y'self. Couple a' day, I'm goin' back home. Maybe you stick 'round here week, two week, we gonna go do us some fishin', little dinosaur-talkin', ay?"

"Yeah," Dan said, and he smiled again. "That'd be great."

"I take you to a lake, fulla cat—huuuuwheeee!—big like you never did saw!"

"Dan?"

They looked to their left, toward the voice. Arden had come out on the porch. Her wavy blond hair shone in the late sunlight, and she was wearing a clean pair of khakis and a green-striped blouse. "Can I talk to you for a few minutes? Alone?"

"Oh, well, I gotta shake a tail feather anyhow." Train stood up. "I'll talk at you later, *bon ami*."

"See you, Train," Dan said, and the Cajun walked back through a slatted door into the hospital. Arden took his chair. "What've you been up to?" Dan asked her. He saw she no longer carried her pink drawstring bag. "I haven't seen you for a while."

"I've been busy," she said. "Are you okay?"

"I believe I am."

She nodded. "It's a beautiful place, don't you think? A beautiful island. Of course . . . that's not sayin' it doesn't need work." She reached out to the railing and picked off some of the cracking paint. "Look there. The wood underneath that doesn't look too good either, does it?"

"No. That whole railin' oughta be replaced. I don't know who's in charge of the maintenance around here, but they're slippin'. Well"—he shrugged—"they're all old buildin's, I guess they're doin' the best they can."

"They could do better," Arden said, looking into his eyes.

He had to bring this up. Maybe he'd regret it, but he had to. "Tell me," he said, "did you ever find out who the Bright Girl is?"

"Yes," she answered, "I sure did."

Arden began to tell him the whole story. Dan listened, and as he listened he could not help but think back to his meeting with the Reverend Gwinn, and the man giving him the gift of time and saying *God can take a man along many roads and through many mansions. It's not where you are that's important; it's where you're goin' that counts. Hear what I'm sayin'?*

Dan thought he did. At last, he thought he did.

It occurred to him, as Arden told him her intention to stay on the island, that Jupiter had been right. He had a lot to think about in the time ahead, but it seemed that he had indeed been the man God had sent to take Arden to the Bright Girl. Maybe this whole thing had been about her and this hospital from the beginning, and he and Blanchard, Eisley and Murtaugh, Train and the drug runners, and all the rest of it had been cogs in a machine designed to draw Arden to this island for the work that had to be done.

Maybe. He could never know for sure. But she had found her Bright Girl and her purpose, and it seemed also that he had found his own refuge if he wanted it.

He could never go back. He didn't want to. There was nothing behind him now. There was only tomorrow and the day after that, and he would deal with them when they came.

Dan reached out and took Arden's hand.

Out in the distance, on the shining blue Gulf, there was a sailboat moving toward the far horizon. Its white sails filled with the winds of freedom, and it ventured off for a port unknown.